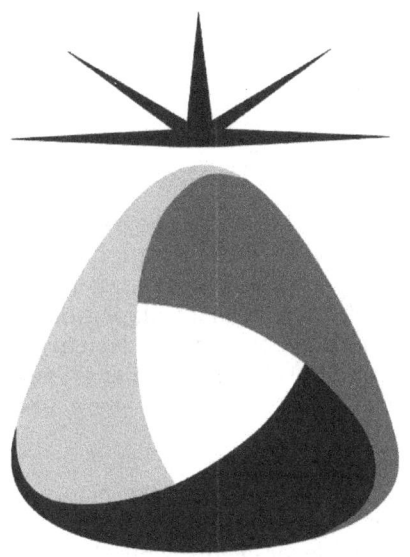

TRIANGLE:
FALSE MIRROR

D. G. SPEIRS

PERFECT IMPRESSIONS, LAKELAND, FL

Triangle logo by Rosemarie J. Ruzicka
Cover art by Ricky Gunawan
Edited by Lea-Ellen Borg

ISBN 978-0-9858115-3-2

Copyright 2012 by D. G. Speirs
Third Edition December 2016

A Perfect Impressions book
Lakeland, FL
Printed in the United States of America

To Kaitlin and Felicity-

One,
The girl who has always embodied the spirit of
"She can do anything."
In my eyes, she saves the world every day.

The other,
A young lady who fought through so much adversity,
Yet never let it get her down.
In my eyes, she is truly a special Talent
And yes, a superhero.

TRIANGLE:
FALSE MIRROR

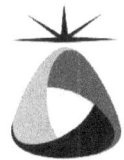

Chapter 1

The air rushed by with frightening speed as Steve Tate plummeted through it. Angled head down, arms in tight, legs together, he spotted his target and aimed for it — another parachutist fighting his rig.

As he closed in, Steve saw the skydiver struggle to pull the release on his chute. Each tug sent the parachutist into a tumble, his movements growing more panicked.

Okay, once more. Approach from behind, maneuver beside, secure harness and tandem down on my chute. The instructions hovered in his mind's eye — a simple checklist, easy enough to follow. *Piece of cake.* Steve took a deep breath, then leaned back and spread his arms and legs. The change to his aerodynamic profile added resistance and his rate of descent slowed as he came upon the target from above.

Steve leaned left and started to rotate so he would be face-to-face with his target. He slid into the target's field of vision and held his hands out in front of him, palms up, indicating for the skydiver to grab onto his harness. The guy did and flattened his body out, stopping his tumbling. He looked grateful for the moment's stability.

Steve made a quick series of hand gestures, indicating what he planned to do, and signaled to the other guy to acknowledge. He gave Steve a thumbs-up signal, indicating he understood, and Steve set to work.

First, pull this guy in and upright. Rate of descent will increase, but we'll be all right for a minute. It's just the express elevator down. Clip harnesses here, here and here. Recheck those points — 1, 2, and 3 are set and

---

1

secure. Good. Quick glance at the altimeter — passing 1,000 feet. *Ready, on three... pull!*

Steve yanked on the release for his own chute. The drogue popped open, sliding the main canopy out behind it. Two seconds later, Steve heard the snap of his fabric pulling taut as it filled with air and felt the familiar yank, like God pulling back hard on a yo-yo. The wind rush stopped, and Steve and his cargo hung there, floating downward.

Steve reached up, grabbed the steering rings in the rigging and dumped some air, angling them down and right toward the target — a large painted set of concentric red and white rings. Surrounding these were the words 'Welcome to Harvey Field – Snohomish Jump Center.' A couple of small adjustments to their spiral and they landed, just to the right of the center ring. As soon as they hit, Steve fell backward, pulling his passenger down atop him. The parachute billowed down beside them.

Steve smiled. "So... welcome to Earth."

The grizzled face looking at him scowled. "Cute. Get me unhooked, boy."

Steve sighed. "All right, Dad, relax. It was a good landing." He reached to hit the quick release on his harness. His father rolled off him and onto the ground.

"Told you I'd be able to make that rescue."

The old man grumbled noncommittally as he climbed to his feet. Steve followed suit, climbing out of his harness as he did so. *Typical,* he thought as he started to gather his chute. His father didn't say a word. He looked once at Steve, his face unreadable, and then walked over to help gather up the chute.

When Steve and his father had all the fabric bundled up, they turned and started walking down the flight line toward the low hangar and jump shop at the opposite end of the airfield. It was just before noon and the last of the morning jumpers would soon be in. After lunch, another bunch would join the cycle — *fly, plummet, land* — and then the hot air balloonists would take over the field, using the south end to prep their equipment for sunset flights over the Snohomish River Valley. High overhead, the sun was playing hide and seek among some clouds, giving rise to that unique Pacific Northwest term, the 'sun break.'

Steve kept waiting for his father to say something, but the silence just seemed to grow the farther they walked. Grey Tate didn't say anything, didn't even acknowledge his son's presence; he just continued walking, ramrod stiff in his military flight suit. Steve glanced at his father again and shook his head.

C'mon, Dad, you're not gonna do this again? Steve glanced down at his jump outfit — compression leggings and shirt and lightweight running shoes. *Yeah, I know, you're not thrilled with my jump gear — but I like wearing my running gear up there. And who made you the fashion police, anyway? Besides, what does it matter? I made the catch — exactly as we'd discussed. You made it down safe — never even touched your emergency chute. No one got hurt. Not even a second of pucker factor up there. No, this one's a win and you—*

"Keep up, son. You're falling behind."

Steve had fallen out of step with his father and was now a half-dozen yards behind him. He broke into a light jog and caught up. "Sorry, Dad."

Grey grunted once in acknowledgment and kept walking. Steve fell into step beside him, the elation he'd felt at landing draining away.

But I made the rescue, Dad! You've got to give me this one.

They reached their destination — a low, two-story orange wood and aluminum hanger that looked like it had been shiny and new when Lindbergh crossed the Atlantic but never since. Above the tall rolling doors was a brushed aluminum sign that said 'Tate Aerospace.' It was completely out of place in this small-town airport. Grey reached for a small service door, opened it and stepped inside.

The inside of the hanger was an eclectic mixture of old and new. The building structure looked like it was from the turn of the 20th century, with oak beams, windows tinted by years of windblown dust and belt-driven ceiling fans turning overhead. But the repair equipment and tools were modern, the workspaces and hangar floor meticulously clean. This was a serious working environment. The back third of the shop had a lower set of rooms housing a machine shop and parts storage. Above them were the main offices.

Rollie Johannsen, the shop's longtime chief mechanic and technician, waited for them in his customary outfit — grease-stained gray coveralls, Hawaiian shirt and faded Mariners ball cap. Rollie was a beach ball of a man — 5'10", 300 pounds, white hair, and a matching beard. His eyes twinkled merrily behind a pair of wire-rim glasses. If the whole aviation mechanic thing failed, Steve figured Rollie had a real future in toys at the North Pole.

Rollie held out his hand to congratulate Steve. "Nicely done, kid. Pretty as a picture. I have ground shots if you want."

"Thanks, Rollie. Can you upload the footage, too?" Steve detached the small HD camera from his helmet and handed it to him.

"Sure thing. Lay out your chute on the left workbench and let's get to cleaning and repacking. Grey, let's use the center bench for yours."

Steve nodded and carried his chute to the bench indicated, while his father dropped his pack on the center one. As Steve started to roll out his chute, Grey watched him with a discerning eye. Your next jump was only as good as the work done here — miss something, and you were unlikely to win the argument with the ground on appeal.

The atmosphere in the hangar was subdued. Jumpers are usually a friendly, confident lot, prone to joking, but Grey was all business, and his attitude set the tone in the shop. There was little conversation, just laying the canopy out, making sure the lines weren't tangled or frayed, and the hard-points on the harness were secure and functioning properly. Grey nodded, more satisfied than pleased, and leaving his pack behind untouched, headed up the stairs to his office.

Steve and Rollie watched him, a puzzled expression on their faces. As the door closed, Steve turned to the chief mechanic. "Rollie, what gives? He's in a particularly foul mood."

Rollie walked over to his personal workbench and terminal, plugged in the camera and started to download the footage. "Well, it's really not my place to say, Rusty. You know that. I'm just the hired help."

Steven sighed, rolling his eyes. "First, Rollie, you're no more the hired help than I am. You've known dad longer than mom, for Pete's sake. So cut the 'I don't know nuthin,' mistuh' routine; I ain't buying it. And second, how many times do I have to tell you, quit calling me that. You know I hate that nickname."

Rollie just grinned and pointed his right thumb up at a faded picture on the shelf above his computer terminal. Taken on a perfect summer's day at a baseball game years ago, it showed a bunch of people out in the center field bleachers, looking back toward home plate; you could see the words 'Welcome to Safeco Field' just visible behind them. There was Steve's dad, and Rollie, minus 100 pounds and a lot less beard, and a 9-year-old Steve in a Mariners hat and baseball glove. Behind him was an elegant woman, tall and winnowy, red hair in a ponytail, looking so happy. She had her hands on Steve's shoulders as if anchoring him safely to the ground.

Steve heard Rollie's voice as he studied the picture for the millionth time. "She thought it was a good nickname. Who am I to argue?"

Steve smiled, for a moment nine years old again. "All right, Rollie." He pointed at another person in the picture; a 9-year-old girl in black hair and pigtails, a frown on her face, looking at Steve with her tongue sticking out. "But just for you. Please, don't use it anymore around the Thornbush there, okay?"

They were interrupted by the sound of Grey Tate's voice echoing around the hangar via the PA system. "Steve, if you're finished goofing off down there, get up to my office now."

Rollie looked up at Steve quizzically. "Seriously, Steve. Any idea what's eating him?"

"Beats me. I mean, he was so hot on this rescue jump, to have me show him that I could handle it. It's all he could talk about me doing since I got back from Nice last month. But since we've landed, he's been a wall. I mean, come on, it went well. You saw that." Steve hesitated a moment, then looked back at Rollie. "Umm...it did go well, right?"

Rollie held up both hands in surrender. "From here, it looked textbook. But I wasn't up there. Maybe he saw something else we both missed. He's always had a talent for that." Rollie handed Steve back the camera. "The footage won't lie. It's on the server for analysis."

"Thanks, Rollie." He started across the hangar floor toward the office, then paused and turned back. "Oh, and would you mind finishing repacking both those chutes for me?"

"That's what I live for — cleaning up after you." He gave Steve a mocking salute. Grinning, Steve returned a slight bow from the waist, Japanese style.

Rollie watched him stride across the hangar floor for a moment, and then looked skyward, muttering, "Oh, he is definitely your son, Rose. Most definitely your son."

Steve took the wooden steps up to the office two at a time. At the top, he knocked on the door.

"Come in."

Steve opened the door and closed it behind him. It was like stepping into another time machine — this one set to circa mid-1960s. The walls were lined with oak paneling and covered with pictures of various aircraft, all with Grey Tate standing in front of them — planes he'd flown in the service, as a freelance pilot for hire, or for fun. If you knew the right order, you could see Grey aging gracefully, his hair changing from a sandy blond to the current shock of pure white, still close-cropped in a military cut.

In the center, two desks faced each other. Grey had done this a few years back when there had been other plans for the business. Grey's desk had papers, a computer and monitor, a model of a modern plane, and a phone. The newer desk had become Steve's four years ago, but other than a nameplate and a framed photograph, there was nothing to indicate it was ever used — no files, no papers, not even a pen. There was a piece of duct tape on the nameplate. Steve's name was written in Sharpie over the intended recipient's as if to remind his father he wasn't supposed to be here. The space definitely belonged to Grey.

Steve flopped down in his chair and waited for his father to say something, anything. After a few moments, it became apparent this still wasn't happening. He leaned back in the chair and put his feet up on the desk, then glanced over at Grey.

"So, you've decided to go all stealth on me? Rig for silent running and all that?"

Grey never glanced up from his computer. "Rig for silent running is Navy. I was Air Force."

"And I was neither. But, hey, the mummy speaks." Steve sat up and leaned forward, resting his chin on one hand. "Come on, Dad, lighten up. It was a good jump. And I passed the test."

Grey stopped typing, his fingers hovering over the keyboard. "Test?"

"The 'Grey Tate's son actually accomplishes something' test. You said it yourself — you weren't sure if I'd ever grow up enough to succeed at anything." Steve stood up and walked over to the window overlooking the hangar floor. "I'd say a mid-air rescue counts, don't you?"

One eyebrow rose as Grey's voice became drily sarcastic. "You complete one rescue jump and declare victory. Really."

Steve shrugged as he turned back. "Sure. Who else do you know who could pull that off?"

Grey leaned back in his chair and looked up at the ceiling. "Off the top of my head? At least three dozen people." He leaned forward and swiveled around to look directly at Steve. "Only they've also got their jump instructor certificates. And their own jump schools. And their business degrees. And the rest of their lives in place.

How much of that do you have, son?"

Steve started to protest, but Grey cut him off. "You know the answer — none. You can jump, but not instruct. You aren't a pilot. You aren't qualified to use a wrench, let alone fix a plane. In short, you have a really weak definition of success. One lucky jump is not going to change that."

Steve sputtered, "Lucky? Lucky! Come on, Dad! How old am I? How many jumps have I made in the past five years?"

"Look, we both know you can jump. You do have skills." Grey paused. "Of course, there is your...other... Talent."

Steve narrowed his eyes. "Dad, unless you plan this to be a really short conversation, you're going to drop that subject. Now."

"Why? Because of when it showed up? Now you're just being stubborn."

Steve walked over to his desk and picked up the framed photograph — a family portrait of Grey, Steve, his mother Rose, and his twin sister, Marie. A whole family, complete, frozen in another time, another world...

Five Years Earlier
July 20, 5:29 p.m. PDT

The smoke alarm blared in the kitchen as Steve ran in. White smoke wafted upward from the oven door. *Oh, man, Mom is going to kill me!*

Steve rushed over, silenced the alarm and hit the switches to turn on both the overhead and stovetop vents. He turned off the oven, put on a pair of oven mitts, and carefully opened the oven door. An acrid white cloud boiled out toward him. He waved his hands to dissipate it, and slowly the source of the alarm became apparent — a meteorite that had once been a meatloaf sat in the middle of the oven.

"Smooth move, Rusty. Mom's going to kill you."

Steve turned his head and saw his sixteen-year-old twin sister, Marie, leaning against the kitchen doorway.

Like him, Marie was tall and redheaded. She was wearing a basketball uniform. *Uh-oh*, Steve thought. *If she just got back from the gym, that means Mom —*

"Ronald Steven Tate, what have you done?"

Three names. Not good.

Steve turned around slowly, holding the pan with the charred remains of dinner in his oven mitts. Rose Tate looked at it and sighed.

"What happened this time?"

"I'm sorry. I was working on some tensor calculus problems for my freshman summer classes at Caltech and I... I..."

"Yes?"

He shuffled his foot sheepishly. "I must not have heard the oven timer go off." He looked up over at his mother and grinned weakly. "Sorry?"

"Rusty, how many times have I told you, when food is cooking, you need to stay in the kitchen? I swear you're just like your father sometimes. You get your teeth into a problem, and you don't let go."

Marie snorted. "Yeah, like how to get in Rose Johannsen's pants."

Steve blushed. "Gee, thanks, sis."

"Marie, that's enough out of you. Go get changed. Since your brother decided to turn our dinner into an experiment on carbonization of animal flesh, pizza night comes early this week. I'll call your father and have him meet us at Giorgio's."

Marie let out a whoop and headed upstairs to change, while Steve dumped the dead husk of dinner into the trash. Putting the pan into the sink, he turned and hugged his mom. "Thanks for not blowing up at me."

"Oh, you're not off the hook, young man. Trust me, you'll pay for this. I just haven't thought of a good way yet."

She kissed him on the cheek and turned away, reaching for her cell phone to call his father. Steve gulped. He knew how creative his Mom's punishments could be.

On the ride to Giorgio's, Steve's mind was somewhere else. Both he and Marie had graduated three weeks ago from Issaquah High School. *It's going to be weird, going to school and being away from Marie. I mean, she's a pain in the butt at times, but she's always been there. But she's headed into the aerospace engineering program at UW next month. Huh. I wonder if Dad's golden girl ever thought of doing anything other than follow him into the family business. But I've seen what being an engineer does to your family — no, thank you!*

Now Pasadena and Caltech — different story entirely. Mom and Dad might not understand how much I need to get away...but to be in a place like the physics department there, where I can just think about theorems and calculations and formulas...heaven!

I hope Rose understands. And maybe if I drop a few hints about Caltech and JPL partnering to build the next generation Mars Rover there, she'll consider applying for the computer engineering and robotics programs there—

He was interrupted from his musing by a sharp punch to his arm. "Hey!"

Marie grinned at him. "Stop thinking about your girlfriend, lover boy. We're here." She pointed out the window at the restaurant.

The three got out and started across the parking lot when Steve's cell phone chimed. He glanced at the caller ID. *Rose.* "Mom, I've got to take this call. I'll be right in."

"Okay, honey."

"Say hi for me, Rusty." Marie blew him a kiss.

Steve grinned at his sister and opened the phone. "Hi, Rose, what's up?"

"Not much, RST. Are you available tonight?"

"I'm not sure yet."

"Not sure yet? What does that mean?"

"It means, I burned dinner, and now we're out at Giorgio's, and I'm still waiting for the other shoe to drop. You know how creative my Mom can get when it comes to punishment—"

The flashes and gunshots from inside Giorgio's startled Steve. He'd seen violence on TV, of course, and every kid his age played first-person shooters on their

PlayStation. But he'd never been this close to a real gunshot before. He froze for a second.

"Steve, what was that?" Rose's voice brought him out of his shock.

"Rose, call 911, tell them shots have been fired at Giorgio's! I gotta go." He put the phone in his pocket and started running toward the restaurant. As he did, a woman came running out — tall, thin, blonde, wearing an overcoat. She bumped into Steve and kept running toward a car. Steve glanced at her, puzzled for a moment, then ran to the door and opened it.

His world stopped. On the floor, in spreading pools of blood were his sister and mother. They'd both been shot — his mother in the chest, his sister...

Marie has a bullet hole in her forehead. Steve swallowed hard, his world spinning. Both his mother and sister stared at the ceiling, their eyes dark and glassy, the sparks gone from them.

Steve wanted to scream, but something inside him grabbed and clamped down on it. He turned and ran out the door, searching for the woman. As he reached the curb, she started to speed by in a black SUV.

And then, suddenly, without warning, the world *stopped in place.*

Steve heard his heartbeat slow down, and the car seemed to freeze in front of him. The woman was achingly close — no more than 6 feet from him.

Suddenly, the data appeared in front of him. *6 feet, 4 inches.*

Wait. How do I know that?

Around him, other data appeared, cascading at him rapidly about the car, the environment. It was unlike anything Steve had ever seen before. It was like being trapped inside a computer program.

How do I know she's traveling 48 miles per hour to the southwest? And that the only way I could intercept her would be to increase my running speed to 28 miles per hour — faster than the record speed of an Olympic sprinter? And only if I change my vector to the left by 72 degrees?

What the hell is happening to me?

Steve tried to move and found he couldn't. He was frozen in place. All he could do was observe. But at that moment, he committed the woman's face to memory. Somehow, a grid that outlined all her features appeared in his mind's eye, just like the most advanced facial recognition programs he'd seen in documentaries. The killer's the face was seared into it — the angular lines of her nose and cheeks, the small white crescent-shaped scar just above her right eyebrow, the smirking curl upward of her mouth on one side...

As suddenly as the world stopped, it sped up again, and the car zoomed past him. Steve staggered for a moment as he tried to chase it before he tried to will time to stop again so he could get the license plate.

Nothing happened.

Behind him, a gray sedan turned into a vacant parking space. Grey Tate stepped out, unaware that his life was about to be shattered. Steve looked at his father, and the tears started down his face. Sirens wailed in the distance, getting closer, as he walked up and began to tell him the news.

Present Day
March 16, 12:03 p.m. PDT

Steve opened his eyes, back in the present, back in the world he never wanted.

"No, Dad. If this...if this Talent is the universe's way of balancing the books for taking Mom and Marie, then it's a crappy bargain. And I want no part of it."

Grey watched his son staring at the picture and sighed. "All right. If you choose not to use it to your advantage, I can't do anything to change your mind. Leave it off the table. But since that day, you've been running away from it. What are you doing with the other gifts, the other skills you already had — your intellect, your education, your looks? Nothing."

Steve looked up sharply. "Not nothing. It's not like I've been just sitting around for five years—"

"Really? Yes, you graduated high school early, before..."

"Just say it, Dad. Before Mom and Marie were murdered."

Grey nodded. "Yes. But since then, you've dropped out of college — not once, but four times—"

"Technically, it was only three times. The fourth time, they asked me to leave."

"Ah, what a subtle difference. So, fine, if academic pursuits aren't your thing, you could have instead pursued ways to assist others – a career in service. But instead, you're off by yourself, going from town to town, doing this free-running stuff. It's risk-taking, stuntman stuff, with competitions where no one actually wins."

"You don't understand, Dad—"

"You're right, I don't. I haven't for some time. If you applied yourself in a single direction, with your intelligence, you could accomplish anything. You could have been a pilot in the military service or work for an airline. If you'd wanted to, given your head start, you could even have been my junior partner here. But are you?"

Steve carefully put down the photo and picked up the nameplate. He traced over the duct tape, feeling the five engraved letters hidden below it. "Yeah, well, that was never really your plan, Dad. I was just your fallback position."

Grey crossed to his son and took the nameplate from him. "You cannot keep using your Mom and your sister as your excuse to hide from doing anything."

Steve's laugh was bitter. "Me, hiding? I think your pot's just as black as my kettle, Dad." Steve walked over to the window looking over the airfield. "After all, you sold off most of the company after that day. All hail the mighty Tate Aerospace — the most pretentiously named general aviation repair shop and jump school in the world."

Grey's closed his eyes for a moment, looking weary. "I had my reasons, son."

"And so do I, Dad. Look, we've been over this. I'm looking for what feels right — and so far, nothing does."

Grey's voice showed his frustration. "Steve, you're twenty-one years old. You need to stop wasting everyone's time. You need to start accomplishing... something. Pick a direction, start it and finish it. Yes, finish it!" Steve began to protest, but Grey cut him off. "You've been living a dilettante's life, Steve — going away for a few months, doing whatever you please, then coming home and expecting me to greet you like the prodigal son each time. That changes today." Grey opened his left desk drawer, reached in to pull out a manila envelope and tossed it onto Steve's desk.

"A friend of mine from my Air Force days and his daughter own a jump school in South Florida. They need someone on staff, temporarily, for a few months. I volunteered you."

"You volunteered me?" Steve asked incredulously as he walked over and picked up the envelope.

"Yes, I did. I figured you'd enjoy the cruise better."

"Cruise?" Steve arched an eyebrow. He opened the envelope and pulled out a brochure for Celebration Cruise Lines.

"It's a 3-month gig, helping tourists parasail off the Lido deck or something like that. My buddy had the contract, but a little mishap left him with a broken leg, and he needs a replacement. His daughter would have filled in, but she's four months pregnant, so going to sea is out of the question. I told them you'd be happy to help out."

Steve glanced through the documents — fly to Fort Lauderdale, a one-week parasail course, and then three months on the *Celebration Goddess*. He looked back at his father.

"Let me get this straight. I'm a screw-up that can't accomplish anything, and as punishment, you're sending me to work on a cruise ship? This is where I'm supposed to say 'Oh, please don't throw me in the briar patch,' right? Seriously, Dad, what's the catch?"

Grey sighed. "Look, son, I don't think you're a screw-up — at least, not most of the time. You have skills. You assimilate data as fast, or faster than most people I know. Your ability to adapt is amazing. And whether you admit it or not, your... Talent is a skill, a tool you can use if the need arises. You just have to decide where to apply it. But you lack focus — a long-term strategy. I figure this will maybe give you some exposure to something you could see a future in. Not just on the ship – but in the ports as well. Just keep your eyes and ears open, okay? And, trust me, you'll be working. It won't be a vacation." He turned back to his computer and checked the time.

"Your plane leaves Sea-Tac tonight. Go home and pack. A town car will pick you up in three hours. I'll arrange for your place to be taken care of, the same as when you were on your trips to Europe. And I'll see you back here in just over three months."

Steve looked at his father, then at his tickets, and shrugged. "Fine. I'll do it. But don't think this changes anything." Steve walked to the door. As he reached it, he turned and looked back at his father.

"I'm sorry I'm not Marie, Dad. But I'm never going to be her. And the sooner you understand that the sooner you are going to let me find my own way."

Grey just looked at his computer screen and didn't acknowledge his son. Steve shook his head again. "Whatever, Dad. Stay safe." He closed the door and started down the stairs.

Grey watched the security feed on the monitor as Steve exited the hangar and made his way to his car. As he pulled out of the parking lot, Grey unlocked his right desk drawer. Inside was a black box. It looked like it was made of wood polished to a high glossy shine, and atop it was a white symbol shaped like a three-cornered Möbius strip. When Grey placed his hand atop it, the symbol glowed and then the box clicked and slid open. He removed a cell phone from inside. The moment Grey touched the device, it recognized him biometrically and initiated the call. Grey closed his eye and waited. Moments later, a cultured voice spoke to him across the connection.

"You have news, Grey?"

"He's on his way. Are you sure about this?"

"Of course he's ready, Grey. You've trained him well."

"I never should have had to."

"I agree, but that wasn't our choice or doing. And your son is key to our future now."

"He won't fall for her, you know. I've seen her profile; she's not his type."

"Have faith, Grey. We'll see to that."

"Perhaps. You'll keep me informed?"

"One of my best will be shadowing him from the moment he arrives. And nothing is scheduled to happen for a while."

"Right. Well, keep me informed. And I'll have the other intel for you tomorrow."

"I know you will, Grey. I've been able to count on you for years."

"Yeah, well, let's just hope it runs in the family."

Chapter 2

"Swimmers, take your mark."

Amy leaned over the starting block, her breathing slowing as she waited for the starter. Toes curled at the edge, hands and head down, her mind cleared of every distraction. She looked at her target three feet ahead in the water. The momentary wave of panic that she always felt came and went, as she harmonized her mind and body together in athletic focus.

The starter's horn and strobe went off, and Amy launched herself toward the water, knifing into it with barely a splash. She immediately started a dolphin kick, her body rhythmically arching as her feet and legs whipped her forward. Thirty feet down the lane, she breached the surface and continued swimming, her arms reaching one past the other.

"The 500-yard free is a different race — half-sprint, half-marathon," her coach had told her years ago. "Pacing is the key — find a rhythm and clock it like a metronome." Amy heard those words in her mind as she started to play the music in her head. This was a timing trick — the steady rhythm of the song clocked at twenty-six strokes per length, then the flip; 50 yards up, 50 back. Five round trips. Three strokes, breathe, three strokes, breathe. These different rhythms in this race combining like a great jazz combo.

Amy didn't so much see her opponent in the next lane as sense her. Carina Summers from Wesleyan College had bested her twice this season, the last by just a touch. Amy was determined to change that today. She kept pace through the first three laps, neither swimmer pulling

17

ahead. On the seventh turn, Amy's plant for her turn was a touch weak, and she came off her turn a half-length behind Carina.

Dang it! Amy thought as she felt the wake turbulence from Summers. She lengthened her own stroke and slowly pulled forward, cutting down the size of the deficit. When the bell rang out at the next turn, signaling the final lap, Amy had cut Carina's lead in half.

Now or never, Amy thought, and she dug a little deeper, speeding up her strokes. The wake turbulence from Carina dissipated as she pulled even with her and as they hit the far wall, it was anyone's race. The two swimmers matched each other down the course, stroke for stroke, almost synchronized, fighting to pull ahead; first Amy, then Carina, back and forth, passing the ten-meter mark and then a final stretch and touch.

Amy quickly popped her head up out of the water and looked up at the results board.

Rogers, A.   4:42.21
Summers, C.   4:42.22

Amy pumped her fist into the air in triumph, then reached over and hugged Carina.

"Good race."

Carina smiled a little ruefully. "Yeah, well... I think we need a rematch. See you at next season's Invitational." She broke the hug and swam away toward her coach.

Amy reached up and pulled herself out of the pool, then made her way over to the team bench. Her coach watched a replay of the race on a small video monitor, checking some timing data, while the team's assistant coach, a tall, thin African-American graduate student named Jason Avant, looked up at Amy and smiled.

Amy smiled back at him. "I did it!"

Jason nodded, a reserved smile on his lips. "Of course, you did. Never any doubt. But go do your warm down now; 1,000 yards, comfortable pace, ten minutes. Then come back, and we'll discuss your split times."

"Split times? Really?"

Coach Carrick chimed in. "Yes, really. Just because it's the end of the season, doesn't mean you can't start planning for the opening of the next one — it *is* only four months away. Now go warm down."

"But—"

"No buts. Go warm down. Now." Coach pointed at the warm-up pool. Jason shrugged and tilted his head toward it. Amy sighed, dropped her towel on the bench and started walking. As she passed by, Jason gave her a playful pat on the butt. Surprised, Amy yelped and turned to see him looking up at the scoreboard showing the lineup for the next race. *Oh, just you wait, Mr. Avant,* she thought as she headed down the pool deck.

Her thoughts drifted as she swam natural, relaxed strokes. *Coach is right; it's never too early to start planning for next year — especially if I want to transition to the triathlon. Carrick is not going to be thrilled about that. Ugh, don't worry about that for now. You just won your league final. You're leaving on vacation — think about that. The Caribbean cruise, the sands of Paradise Island, the chance to find out if Jason is the right guy to trust with your secret...*

Amy was so distracted that she didn't see the wall of the pool until it was almost too late. She approached it much too fast and threw up an arm to brace against the impact.

There was a slight shudder as a set of concentric waves rippled from the point she touched the wall. Around the pool area, a sudden gust of wind rustled the meet sheets at the various team tables.

Amy discretely looked around, saw that no one seemed to have noticed anything, and swam rapidly to the opposite end of the pool. She quickly exited and headed for the locker room.

That evening, maintenance workers placed a work order to repair damage to the warm-up pool. It appeared that someone had struck the sidewall with a sledgehammer, denting and cracking the concrete and rebar underneath. Security officials at the aquatic center could not determine how the vandal had snuck in or why they had only damaged this one small area of the pool.

When Amelia Jane Rogers finished high school and started looking at colleges, several schools recruited her. She had lettered in three sports (gymnastics, volleyball, and swimming), carried a 3.8 GPA and was considered a quiet, friendly person who was admired by her fellow students and teachers. But Amy elected to stay away from large schools, much to their disappointment. She had her reasons, but she chose not to share them with anyone. When she found American Southern University, though, she fell in love.

ASU was a small private college situated on a lake in central Florida. A comfortable place for someone like Amy to blend in. That sort of casual anonymity was something she valued very much.

The campus itself was a design experiment from the 1940s by Frank Lloyd Wright — all angles and light and air, making it feel at once organic and timeless, and breathtakingly beautiful. Amy loved walking the grounds; it gave her such a sense of peace.

The transition to college had gone much more smoothly than she had thought it would. Part of that was her skill as an athlete, the other, her natural charm. Her grandmother had grown up a real Southern Belle, and all those lessons she drilled into Amy about politeness and listening paid dividends. She found most people would prefer to talk about themselves, given a chance, so she just sat back and let them; soon enough, they'd just move along and let her be.

She also lucked out when it came to a roommate. Rose Johannsen was from the opposite side of the world, as far as Amy was concerned — Seattle was too far away for anyone to have ever heard of her. Rose was a computer science/math geek, who lived for Starbucks and the online world. She was also something of a ghost — three months into each school year, she somehow found another exotic new boyfriend to move in with. This year's model was

Raoul, a foreign student from Paraguay — and admittedly hot. Amy usually had the room all to herself.

Amy had chosen journalism as a major; if anyone knew the whole truth about her, they would have found it an appropriately ironic choice. But journalism was just a cover. She was an athlete, pure and simple. She lived to swim, to run, to fly; everything else just facilitated that. She figured she might use her degree to have a career reporting on sports after she was done participating in them. Yet, even as she was still participating, she was shunning the spotlight on her personal life.

It all came down to her talent, and how she chose to use it.

7:23 p.m. EDT

Surprisingly, Rose was at her computer in the dorm room when Amy arrived that evening from the meet. As Amy tossed her bag onto the bed, she ruffled her roommate's short jet-black hair.

Rose winced. "Hey! I worked hard to get that the way I like it!"

"And I just improved it a little. Gave it just those right touches of early morning bed head that will make Raoul want to know what he's missing out on." Amy grinned as she unpacked her dirty clothes from the meet weekend and dumped them unceremoniously into the hamper at the end of the bed. *Do I need any of that stuff?* She considered for a moment and then smiled. *Nah. It can wait 'til I'm back.*

Rose glanced at her in the small mirror attached to the corner of her computer as she finished the coding problem on her screen. "So, all set for the cruise?"

"Yep! Seven days of sun, sand, relaxation — and no laps."

Rose smiled at her screen. "Oh, and don't forget Jason."

Amy grinned and imitated her roommate's voice. "Oh, don't worry, I haven't." She sat down on the bed.

"When the week is over, he's going to know I'm more than just another swimmer, Rose."

Rose grinned as she continued working on her computer. "I think he already knows that, Amy. You've been dating him for what, two months now?"

"That's not what I mean, Caffeine Girl, and you know it."

Rose's grin became wider. "Oh! Well, then, if you want, I have some stuff you can borrow to wear at night—"

"Rose! No, not that either. I mean...well. You know. It's time he knew."

Rose suddenly stopped typing. The absence of the sound of the keyboard clicks became very noticeable. *Very* noticeable.

Amy looked at Rose as her roomie bit her lower lip. "So, what is it now?"

Rose turned slowly in her chair and looked down at the floor for a moment, then up at Amy, pushing her black horned-rimmed glasses up on her nose. "Well, it's just... I mean..." Rose took a deep breath. "Look, Amy, I'm sure you've heard the whole 'Spiderman' argument thingy a hundred times by now. Great power, great responsibility, blah de blah blah. Well, every time you share your story, you know, about what you can...well, you also share that responsibility with someone, too. And maybe they aren't ready for it." Rose looked right at Amy, her blue eyes intense. "Are you sure Jason is, you know, ready for that sort of news?"

Amy walked over and knelt next to her friend. "Rose, I know that burden got thrust on you when you didn't ask. You've kept my secret for the better part of two years now, and you've helped keep me safe by covering for me a dozen times—"

"Seventeen, to be exact."

Amy stuck out her tongue at her roommate and then smiled again. "So, who's counting? The point is, I think Jason already suspects anyway. He's all but accusing me of slacking — like he can tell there's something more to me than, well, meets the eye. But Jason's not reacting to it like others have. He's not getting scared and backing away, or worse, looking at me with that hunger in his eyes, wanting to see more. I think he just wants me to do my best... for me."

Rose looked at her sympathetically. "Amy, just remember that wanting what's best for you and loving you are not the same thing. Just... be careful, okay?"

Amy smiled and leaned over to hug her friend. "*Moi*, careful? This is me here we're talking about. I can always take care of myself." She launched from her kneeling crouch into a forward flip, twisting in mid-air and landing in front of the bathroom door in a fighting stance, fists ready, eyes blazing, and a big smile on her face. She straightened up, winked at Rose and closed the bathroom door behind her.

Rose just shook her head and muttered to herself. "Yeah, right. I've heard that before. And had to pick up the pieces."

Chapter 3

May 22, 6:05 a.m. EDT

Pre-dawn hours on the *Celebration Goddess* were an excellent time for the crew to catch up and recover from the previous night's festivities, which typically lasted well past midnight. Most passengers were asleep or barely starting to stir, looking for a few more minutes of rest before another exhausting day of being a tourist.

The forward railing on the Promenade Deck was deserted when Steve arrived. Since he'd come aboard, he had tried to make it up here every day to greet the sunrise. He'd read about the 'green bubble' that sometimes appeared just before sunrise, and each day hoped for the right weather conditions to see it. So far, no luck, but as a consolation prize, Mother Nature had instead rewarded Steve with sunrises actually worthy of the term *breathtaking*, the interplay of clouds and light creating spectacular scenes. His mother had once described skies like these as 'God's finger paintings.'

Being here each morning brought him a sense of peace before the day's chaos. The cruise wasn't anything like he'd expected; parasailing instruction had turned out to be just a small part of his duties. But Steve learned he had a knack for this, and discovered he liked helping people. Still, just like everything else, it still felt somehow unfulfilling to him.

But I'm not leaving, Mom, he told the clouds on the horizon. *I'm going to stick out the contract if only to shove it back in Dad's face how wrong he is about—*

"Wow."

The voice startled Steve. He hadn't heard anyone approaching. Trying not to look rattled, he glanced sideways at the owner of the voice. *Hmmm. Not bad. Blonde, about 5'6", nice curves, muscle tone — must be an athlete of sorts. White sundress, barefoot. Accent — Georgia, maybe? Have to hear more for sure. Looks about my age, early 20's. And no rings of any sort. Interesting...*

Steve turned toward the woman and in a quiet voice said, "Good morning. Yeah, it certainly is wow."

The woman nodded, not taking her eyes off the horizon. "I never get tired of seeing that."

"You mean the sunrise?"

"Yes. It's so wonderful, like God's pressing the reset button on the world. A reminder of how everything starts beautifully." She finally glanced over at Steve, and he could see her making a quick mental assessment of him. Small subconscious changes in her body language told him she'd dismissed him as a potential threat.

"I'm Amy."

"Nice to meet you. I'm Steve Tate."

"I think I've seen you on board. You're with the ship's crew, correct?"

"Guilty as charged. Recreation Services — I work for the cruise director, finding ways to keep people entertained."

Amy's face broke into a mischievous smile. "That explains the where. Although I think I'd argue whether a karaoke contest qualifies as entertaining."

Steve was warming up to this young lady. "Oh, you'd be surprised. Some of them are pretty good. And the rest... well..." Steve glanced around to see if they'd be overheard, then leaned over to her and whispered in a conspiratorial manner. "What most of the others don't know is that we secretly record their voices to use as the ship's horn in case the regular one is ever damaged."

Amy giggled at that. As she did, the sun peaked over the horizon, and the first rays of sunshine splashed onto the ship. At that moment, Amy became illuminated by the sunlight. Steve looked at her, sun sparkling off her hair, her skin, her dress, that perfect golden light of early morning. "Now that is breathtaking, indeed."

Amy realized he was staring and her body posture subtly changed again into an alert stance. "Well, I think I'd better be going. My boyfriend will be waking up soon."

Steve heard the extra inflection on the word 'boyfriend.' *Of course, she's involved. No one that beautiful stays alone.* "It was a pleasure meeting you, Amy."

She started to leave, then hesitated and turned back. "Would you happen to know when we'll reach Nassau?"

"Big day planned? No worries." He pointed off the foredeck of the ship toward the horizon. Amy's eyes followed his.

"I don't see anything."

Steve gestured for Amy to come to the railing. When she reached it, he stood behind her and positioned her hand toward a small smudge of black on the horizon.

"That's Nassau?"

Smiling, he said, "Actually, New Providence Island, but Nassau is just inside the barrier islands. So, as we sailors like to say, 'Land—"

Amy turned toward him suddenly, their faces only inches apart. A moment passed between them. Then another. And one more.

Quietly, Steve finished, "—ho'."

Amy lingered, her eyes locked with Steve's. Suddenly, she stepped back. He watched as the confusion on her face was replaced with a flush of embarrassment. "I, ah. I have to be going. Thank you for showing me." She turned and rushed around the starboard side of the Promenade Deck and out of sight.

"Anytime, Amy." Steve took a deep breath in, held it, and then let it out slowly. *Cute girl. No, something more than that. Can't quite put my finger on it.* He sighed. *Too bad she's already out of play. Oh, well.* He shrugged and headed for the private door for crewmembers only.

Once inside, he walked down the central corridor, found the crew ladders — *shipboard, they're ladders, not stairs,* he remembered — and started down them. Since he'd come aboard, he'd adapted to the steeper angle used by these ladders, and had learned from more seasoned crewmates the trick to sliding down between decks. You grab both side rails and use them as tracks, then you step forward and use gravity to drop you — almost a controlled, guided jump. He quickly descended four decks and moved aft down the corridor to the Recreation Services office. He opened the door and stepped into the compartment.

Cruise ships save all their fancy amenities for paying passengers. This space was utilitarian — white steel bulkheads, fluorescent lighting, bookshelves and a pair of desks welded in place. Steve walked over, grabbed a cup of coffee from the coffee maker, and then flopped into the vacant chair next to the closest desk. Working at it was Regina Folkes, the ship's Australian cruise director. She looked up from a piece of paper with a grid on it and smiled at Steve. "Ah, good morning! Just who I'm looking for."

Seeing the look on her face, he was suddenly wary. "I was about to say good morning back, but on second thought, I'm not so sure."

Regina smiled a bit wider. "Why, Steven, whatever makes you say that?"

"Probably the fact that you're looking at me the way my cat used to after he finished catching and eating a bird. What's up?"

Regina chuckled. "Guilty as charged. I'm sorry to do this, but I need to change your assignment for today. Osgood came down with some sort of flu, and the ship's doctor ordered him to stay in his rack until tomorrow."

"Oh? That's a shame. Tad likes Nassau. He showed me around my last time here."

"He did? That's perfect — you're already familiar. I need you to take over his excursion."

Steve nodded. "All right. What is it?"

She handed him the itinerary sheet for the excursion. "A bus and walking tour of Downtown Nassau. You hit the highlights — Fort Fincastle, the Queen's Staircase, drive and narrate down Bay Street to Fort

Charlotte, and finally a drop off at the Straw Market. Four hours, max."

He scanned down the sheet, his mind already organizing the facts about the destinations. He stopped halfway down. "Regina, it says here I'm supposed to demonstrate costumes and dances at the Junkanoo Museum." He looked back up at her, suspicious. "Really?"

She tried to look innocent but was failing miserably. "Look, Steven, you have a real knack for cruise ship recreation. Whether it's a DJ at the teen dance party, running the karaoke contest, handling the small children's activities, the wine tasting event — all the passengers rave about you." She lifted up a stack of recommendation notes and letters as if to illustrate the point. "We never get this many notes about a rec services staff member. *Ever.*"

Steve looked down. "I just try to help people, Regina. They pay for a good time. But this isn't my life. When my contract is over, I'm gone."

She nodded. "I can respect that. But for today, I need a tour guide. I know it's your first time, but I think you can handle this, no problem." She paused for a second, glanced about, and then leaned in toward him. "Of course, if you think you'd find it a challenge, I could come along as a backup and help."

Steve looked at her for a moment and realization dawned on him. *She wants to spend time with me off the ship.* He considered it for a moment. *Yeah, I could go for that.* "Deal. The excursion meets on the pier at 10 a.m., so I'll be there at 9:30. But dress in civilian clothes. Otherwise, people will think you're evaluating me or something."

Regina nodded. "Fair enough, Steven. I'll just be another tourist, enjoying the sights."

Something about the way she said that, along with her look, akin to a cat enjoying a rather tasty mouse, gave Steve a bit of a pause. He got up and headed for the door. As he reached it, he turned back. "Maybe after the tour finishes, you and I could explore Nassau some more on our own."

Regina smiled, the cat-like expression growing even more satisfied. "I believe I'd like that very much, Steven." She turned back to her paperwork.

Steve exited the office, feeling very much like a mouse being toyed with. *I need an hour of alone time in my quarters — hopefully, long enough to become a leading expert on Junkanoo.*

9:55 a.m. EDT

Amy and Jason walked down the gangplank and onto the dock. Around them, the other cruise passengers were spilling out from the ship as the sun beat down. Even for late April, the sun was intense and the air thick and humid. Amy was glad for the large sun hat she wore.

"Jason, did you bring bottled water for us?"

He pointed to his backpack. "Two bottles and some granola bars if you get hungry. I figured we might also grab some fruit from a vendor as well."

"And after the tour, we'll head over to the Atlantis for some time on the beach."

"Yep. I have my suit, too. Um, where's yours?"

Amy smiled as she hung onto his arm. "I'm wearing it underneath my clothes — for now. But no promises about that later."

Jason blushed, which made Amy smile. Yeah, the first few days of the trip had been a bit awkward, but after last night...

Amy smiled again at the thought of that kiss, and the caress...

And the aftermath...

Amy was lost in her musing, so she missed the first part of what Jason was saying. "–sort that out another time. Oh, there's the tour guide."

They sped up their pace and joined the semi-circle of people gathered around the tour guide, a young man from the ship. Amy looked and thought he seemed familiar. When he turned around, she was surprised to see the same man she'd talked to on the Promenade Deck at sunrise.

Amy really hadn't looked at the guy that carefully before — other than to assess his threat level on the perv scale — but she was glad she was giving — *what was his name? Steve, that's right* — giving Steve a second glance. He looked to be a little over 6 feet tall, muscular but not bulky, and definitely toned. *Green eyes and short, curly red hair — interesting combination there. I know some girls back at ASU who would pay good money to get hair like that.* Even more interesting was his attitude. He had an easy-going smile and a look in his eye that told you he saw the humor in almost everything around him. His playfulness was infectious.

Their eyes met for a moment — the briefest glance, a flash of recognition, and then something strange — for a split second, it was as if she was frozen in place while he studied everything about her. His glance shifted to Jason, and Amy was left to puzzle over what just happened.

Steve had a clipboard with the paperwork for the excursion. "Ah, you must be Jason, and you're Amy, right?" Jason nodded, and Steve winked at her as he checked off their names. Amy glanced around at the other passengers that made up the group. Everyone was in typical cruise ship tourist clothing — khaki pants or shorts, camp or Hawaiian print shirts for the older men, T-shirts for the younger folks and light sundresses for all the women.

"All right, folks. We have about a fifteen-minute walk to where we'll meet the first transport, so let's move out. Try to stick close by. Our first stop is Rawson Square, across from Parliament House." Steve turned and held up a blue flag in the air as the group headed toward the east end of the cruise pier and turned inland

Tied up to the east side of the pier was a 110-foot luxury yacht. On its back deck, a tall blonde woman in her early 40s was sunning herself. She had an exquisite figure and was wearing a striking black bikini that made her golden tan appear even more lustrous. As the group started to pass by, the woman sat up to watch them. Amy was struck by her expression. Calculating, a slightly cruel turn of her mouth, almost as if she were a tigress watching her prey.

Then Amy saw the woman's gaze shift toward her. Her body language changed as if she became more alert. Then she lowered her sunglasses and Amy caught sight of the woman's gray eyes. The two made eye contact; the moment was like an electric shock. It was as if a circuit had somehow been completed between them. Those gray eyes seemed to grow, becoming larger, as everything else in the world started to fade away. She began to slow, still locked in the other woman's gaze.

Jason noticed her lagging behind and turned back to her, touching her shoulder. "Amy, is everything all right?"

Amy felt the connection between her and this woman break with Jason's touch, and her willpower snapped instantly back in place. She stumbled for a second, looking confused. *What the heck was that?*

Jason helped steady her, a concerned look on his face. He glanced around for a moment, then looked back at her and asked again, "Are you sure you're feeling all right? If not, we can cancel if you'd like, and just lie around on the beach. Or head back to the ship, if you'd prefer."

She took a moment. "No, it's all right. I just tripped. Besides, I know how you're really into this history stuff, and I want to see you enjoying yourself, too."

"All right, then let's catch up." He grabbed Amy's hand, and the two started walking again to catch up with the rest of the group.

Amy glanced back at the woman. *She stole my will to do anything. How did she do that?* Amy turned to Jason as they continued walking. *And he acts like nothing weird happened. But whatever was happening stopped when he touched me.* Amy's mind churned as she held his arm tight.

10:02 a.m. EDT

Onboard the yacht, the woman was herself recovering from the feedback of the broken connection. *Interesting. Been a long time since someone broke my hold on them. How did she do that? Something I need to find out, I think.* Reaching down into her handbag beside the deck chair, she picked up her cell phone and dialed a number.

"It's Callahan. The tour is leaving... Two to pick up, as we discussed. The yacht will be ready to go in sixty minutes... Yes, payment on delivery, as promised... There's another loose end I need to take care of personally. Just proceed as planned." She closed her cell phone and looked out over the wharf. A moment later, she headed below deck to get ready.

10:05 a.m. EDT

Steve had just led the tour past the cruise wharf gateway when one of his tour members came up beside him. He glanced over at her and details flooded in from his memory. *Karen Bennett. Booking says she's from Michigan. Category 7 cabin — outside with veranda, port stern, on the Athena Deck. Traveling with her husband, Timothy, also taking the tour. Blonde, although it looks like it might have come out of a bottle. Still, for someone her age, she takes good care of herself — tall, thin, awesome shape. Dressed smart for the tour — khaki chinos and a plain white blouse, sun hat, oversized dark sunglasses. Really nice tan.*

Steve had all this info in about a half-second and was still considering it when Mrs. Bennett spoke up. "Sorry to bother you, but can I stop here at the Global Village shops to get some water?"

Steve thought for a moment and nodded. "Actually, that's a great idea." He turned and raised his voice so everyone in the group could hear him. "We're going to pause here for five minutes. I suggest anyone who hasn't brought along a water bottle from the ship head inside and pick up one. It's humid today, and you'll need the fluids."

The Rosens, his family group of five — Mom, Dad, two boys and a little girl — made a beeline for the store. So did the Bennetts. The remaining members of the tour group, consisting of the Naziris, a father and daughter, and Amy and Jason, the couple he'd met earlier, stayed outside, as did Regina. She walked over, a look of approval on her face. "Nicely done. The merchants here have been complaining about losing business when the ships started providing their own bottled water."

Steven shrugged. "Well, we've got time built into the schedule, so five minutes won't hurt us. Maybe they'll buy some souvenirs as well. Help the local economy."

Regina smiled. "As long as no one decides to get a hair wrap now. We don't have time for that."

Steve grinned. "Oh, I don't know. I think I might look good with one. Maybe red, yellow and black stripes. What do you think?"

Regina just shook her head and walked away to chat with Amy and Jason. Steve chuckled and moved across the square into the shade of the covered walkway directly opposite the gaudily painted market. *It's a nice day for this.* A moment later, he was joined by Fatima Naziri.

He'd met Fatima at the teen dance when he'd filled in as DJ — another of Regina's 'convenient' assignments. She had danced for a bit and then just hung around his DJ booth as he queued up songs to keep the rhythm going. After a while, he chatted with her. She was 14, tall and thin, with copper skin and long black hair. Her most memorable feature had to be her eyes — azure blue and very striking. She was also much smarter than him, which really said something. Just as he'd been, she was an accelerated learner. She was already in her final year of high school and looked to start college in the fall — MIT, her father's alma mater, as it turned out.

She came up, looped an arm around his, and smiled. "Good morning, Stevie. I am so excited about you being with me on this trip!"

Ruh-roh, thought Steve. *Better nip this in the bud.* "Thank you, Miss Naziri. But I'm responsible for a bunch of people today."

"Don't worry, Stevie. I'm sure you'll handle it just fine. I can't wait to see you dance the Junkanoo." She squeezed his arm again and lay her head against his shoulder, then started to swivel her hips a little.

"Fatima!"

Mr. Naziri was staring at him, looking none too happy about his daughter's behavior. Steve looked back apologetically and shrugged, then disentangled himself from her hold on his arm. "I think your father wants you, Miss Naziri. Perhaps you'd better go talk to him."

Fatima looked up and smiled. "Whatever you say. Talk to you later, Stevie." She smiled and winked at him and then started walking over to her father. "Really, Daddy, I was just having some fun."

Naziri looked angry. "You call that fun? I call it disgraceful and embarrassing." He grabbed her arm and moved toward the far side of the square, out of earshot. Steve shrugged, and then looked back toward the wharf. Something caught his attention.

That's weird. Is that one of my tour group walking back toward the ship? Steve moved out from under the walkway and watched a woman who appeared to be Mrs. Bennett heading away from him back toward the Goddess. He turned and started to look for Regina.

Steve heard the doors to the market open and glanced over. Through the doors walked both Bennetts.

Steve blinked for a moment in surprise, then looked back at the figure on the dock, who was just boarding a luxury yacht. Within moments, she went below decks and was out of sight.

Steve turned and looked at the Bennetts again. Mrs. Bennett looked directly at him with her big gray eyes for a moment. Steve looked at her and noticed she had a white scar. Something about it looked familiar, but then her eyes seemed to grow bigger and bigger...

After a couple of seconds, Mrs. Bennett put her sunglasses back on.

Steve shook his head, confused. *Huh. What was I just thinking about? Oh, right. Time to get everyone together for the tour.* He called out for everyone to reassemble, waited a moment for the group to join him, and then headed out to start the tour.

Chapter 4

Steve led the group into Rawson Square and turned around. "This statue is a bust of Sir Milo Butler. He was the first Governor-General of a newly independent Bahamas. Fatima, who is the actual head-of-state here?"

Fatima smirked. "Oh, that's an easy one. The Bahamas used to be a British colony and is now a member of the Commonwealth, so the Queen of England is the head-of-state here. But a Prime Minister runs the place."

Steve smiled. "Very good. And over here is the famous 'Crossroads of the Bahamas' signpost. Anyone who wants to get their picture taken, go ahead — I'll pause a moment."

The Rosen family immediately handed him their camera and got together for a family pose. As Steve returned their camera, he felt a tap on his shoulder.

Amy held out her cell phone. "Can you get a picture of us?" She smiled and held her boyfriend's hand.

"Sure. Go ahead and stand in front of the sign." Steve looked at the phone and figured out which control to push to snap a picture. He looked back at Amy and Jason. "Okay, that's it. Now smile and say 'cheese.'" As Steve lined up the shot, Amy quickly turned and kissed Jason on the cheek. Steve clicked the shutter and caught the shot, including the look of happy surprise on Jason's face.

Steve reassessed the couple. *Hmm. They're new at this part of the relationship. My guess is they're still exploring things, from her posture toward him.* Steve smiled. *They do make a cute couple.*

Regina stepped up next to him. "Hmm. They make a cute couple."

"I was just thinking that." He grinned at his boss.

Regina looked at him. "So, anyone making cute with you?"

Steve looked sideways at her, a slight smile curling the corners of his mouth. "No one yet. But someone's putting out feelers, I think. Should I let you know?"

Regina looked at him and raised an eyebrow. "That depends."

"On what?"

"On how well you dance the Junkanoo."

Steve grinned and called out to round everyone up. The Bennetts were talking with a street vendor, who quickly handed them a package. They hurried over and rejoined the tour.

"Ok, next we're heading over to Elizabeth Street. However, rather than a bus, I thought you might enjoy a different sort of ride." Steve whistled, and from around the corner of Bay Street a large surrey wagon drawn by two horses pulled up. The Rosen children got excited at the sight of the animals. Jason put his arm around Amy.

Regina sidled over to Steve and in a quiet voice said, "That's not an official part of the tour."

"Nope. But I thought it could use a little something extra. Don't worry; I'm covering this out of my own pocket."

"But how did you arrange it in less than two hours?"

"I can't give away all my secrets, boss." Steve grinned as he ushered everyone up onto the wagon. The Bennetts sat all the way in the back, then the Rosens, Amy, Jason and Regina, and finally the Naziris up front, with Fatima jumping up right next to him. Her father frowned, but Steve just smiled and shrugged as if to say, *what can I do?*

When everyone was aboard, Steve turned to the driver and nodded. The driver called out to the horses, and they started around the square, then a right onto Bay Street, then a left onto Parliament Street. The horses' hooves clattered on the cobblestones as the tour moved past Parliament Square.

Steve narrated, describing the buildings. "On the right is the Nassau Public Library and Museum. Its unique shape is due to its previous use. You see, this was Nassau's first jail. The cells were set around the perimeter and a jailer could watch all the prisoners at once."

As the surrey wound its way through the streets, Steve kept the group entertained with bits of information — facts about the buildings, amusing anecdotes about the history of Nassau, stories of pirates that had the Rosen kids enraptured. After two more blocks and a quip about the Royal Victoria Hotel, the surrey turned right onto Elizabeth Street, and immediately started climbing up the hill. Steve explained this was one of the oldest roads on the island, carved by hand centuries ago through the limestone.

A half mile later, at the end of the road, the surrey crossed Sands Street and pulled into a large parking lot. The driver pulled back on the reins and called for his horses to halt in front of the entrance to the Queen's Stairs.

"Okay, folks, this is where we get off. Please exit carefully to your right, and wait for me at the entrance." Steve turned to the driver, and the two started haggling. As they did, Regina wandered over to Steve.

"All right, spill it, mate. What's your secret?"

Steve smiled. "What do you mean?"

"I mean, I gave you this assignment three hours ago. You've never given this tour before in your life, and you do it better than Tad Osgood ever did. Paying for a surrey upgrade out of pocket? Those stories about the pirates? You had the Rosen kids eating out of your hands."

He shrugged. "I just want to give the guests an experience they'll never forget. Isn't that what vacations are supposed to be about?" He finished the deal with the driver of the surrey, who shook his hand.

Steve turned back to Regina. She looked at him, slightly frustrated. "I don't understand you, Steven. You're a natural at this. If you chose to stick around, you'd oversee Rec Services in no time."

He shook his head. "You're too kind, Regina. Yes, it's nice aboard the *Goddess*, but it isn't where I belong. I signed on to help a friend of my dad's, and my contract is almost up. When it's done, I'm gone."

"So where *do* you belong?"

Steve's eyes grew distant for a moment. "I don't know yet. But when I find it, I promise I'll let you know." He turned and walked over to rejoin the tour group.

In front of them was a notch, 20 yards across and approximately the length of a football field, carved out of the limestone, with a wide, steep staircase at the far end. Trees overhung the cut, shading almost its entire length. To the left of the stairs was a waterfall, carved in the limestone. The water cascading down filled the space with white noise, blocking out the traffic sounds from downtown Nassau and the tourist buses above. It was busy with sightseers, yet somehow still maintained an air of peace and tranquility.

10:58 a.m. EDT

Amy and Jason walked along the path hand-in-hand. They marveled at the work that must have gone into creating this. But Amy's thoughts right now were more about *who* rather than *where*. As they meandered down the cut, they passed a group of old Bahamian gentlemen, their skin as black as coal, playing a game of dominoes on a picnic table to one side. Two men were studying the tiles, while their friends were kibitzing, offering suggestions and jibes as only old friends could. Up above, at the top of the steps, a bus stopped and disgorged a group of Japanese tourists, who came charging down the steps, talking and smiling and shooting their ubiquitous, globetrotting pictures, holding up their hands in what looked like peace signs.

Amy smiled. *Oh, this couldn't be more perfect. I'm in a fairytale place with my own Prince Charming... and a gaggle of Japanese tourists!* She started to giggle at the mental picture that appeared with that thought. Jason heard her and stopped, looking at her quizzically.

"I'd offer you a penny for your thoughts, but those are worthless these days. Go on, spill it. What's so funny?"

Amy told him about her mental image, and Jason started to chuckle as well. "Oh yeah, that's good. Of course, I'd probably picture you as a princess — only one of those Japanese anime ones. You know, with a vengeful sword and a ridiculously small costume."

She looked back at her boyfriend and wagged a finger at him. "Uh-huh... and those ridiculously large breasts as well."

Jason was suddenly interested in the foliage above him. "I have absolutely no complaints in that department, Ms. Rogers."

She grinned up at him. "Good answer."

Jason looked down at her, then leaned in and kissed her gently.

Amy closed her eyes, then broke off the kiss, rested her head on Jason's chest, and sighed. "Yeah, this is just about perfect."

Jason was thoughtful for a moment and then smiled as well. "Well, you better enjoy it. Carrick is going to push you hard when we get back, and you know I will, too." He backed away a bit from Amy so he could look at her. "You're an incredible swimmer, Amelia Rogers, but last season, it was like you were holding back for some reason." She started to protest, but he put a single index finger on her lips. "Hush, you. You can't talk your way out of this one. I'll know if you're dogging it. Next season, I want to see the real Amy."

Amy looked at him for a moment, defiantly, hands on her hips, and a mischievous glint in her eyes. "As I recall, Mr. Avant, last night you got to see the real Amy. All of her. Just as I got to see the real Jason." Amy giggled again. "I mean, who'd have thought you had a tattoo of—"

Jason blushed, then before Amy could finish that sentence, he rushed in and kissed her again. After a muffled moment trying to speak, she melted into the kiss, her arms encircling him and pulling him close. *Wow,* she thought. *Yep, Amelia Jane, you are in love.*

She broke off the kiss, and snuggled against Jason's chest again, listening to his heartbeat. He chuckled again. "Only you would try to talk about those things with kids around."

"Maybe." She looked up at him, her expression suddenly somber. "Uh, Jason, there really is something I need to talk to you about."

He looked down at her. "Now that's a serious looking face. Is everything okay?"

"Yeah. But there's something about me you need to know—"

Jason put a finger to her lips. "Whatever it is, Amy, it doesn't matter. Simple truth — I love you for you. And nothing you tell me is going to change that." To punctuate his declaration, he leaned down and kissed her again.

When they came up for air, he looked at her and smiled. "Now, here comes the rest of the tour group. We'll talk about it later on the beach."

Amy just nodded, shocked speechless at this turn of events. She'd played out how this could have gone a dozen times in her head. Never once had it turned out with Jason saying it didn't matter.

He loves me. That's all the matters. Amy's hand reached out for Jason's.

11:06 a.m. EDT

Steve walked down the cut slowly with the rest of the tour group. He pointed out certain spots on the walls, talking about limestone and fossils and prehistoric sea life. As they approached the stairs, he stopped for a moment. "Fatima, you're a history buff. When were the stairs built, and why?"

The young lady perked up, but her father was still holding her hand, unwilling to let her go to Steve. She stood there reluctantly. "The stairs were built in 1793 by slave labor to allow British troops, stationed in the newly constructed Fort Fincastle at the top of the hill, a shortcut to the harbor."

Steve nodded. "Very good. That's why the stairs are so wide — to allow the British to march in formation four abreast down the stairs." He then reached into a shirt pocket and pulled out his camera. "And since this place is so full of tradition and history, I'd like to share another one with you."

"On the *Celebration Goddess,* there's a tradition of taking pictures of all our tour groups that come to this very spot. So I'd like you to move over to the stairs. Each one of you pick a step to stand on and then look at me over the railing."

The group murmured happily to each other and moved toward the stairs. They all seemed pleased with the idea — everyone except the Bennetts. *They look pretty serious,* Steve noticed. *I wonder if something's wrong. I'd better ask them on the next bus.*

The couples lined themselves up, with Amy and Jason between the Bennetts and the Naziris, and the five Rosens at the bottom of the stairs. Regina had stepped out of the picture for a moment, but the Rosens cajoled her back into it.

Steve grinned, and then put the camera up to check the viewfinder. He framed the shot, adjusted for the light level, and snapped three shots in rapid succession when no one was expecting. Then he called out to the group. "All right, everyone. Say 'cheese.'" The Rosen kids joined in immediately, and the adults added their smiles. Steve snapped that shot as well and pulled off a few more candid shots.

"Thanks, folks. I'll have prints made up onboard and sent to your staterooms. Now go ahead to the top of the steps, and I'll meet you there in a second." The group started up the steps. Steve took a moment to reach down and retie one of his shoes. When he stood up, Regina was standing there.

"Ship's tradition? Really, Steven. You know as well as I do, you just made that up."

He grinned. "Yeah, but they don't know that. And who knows, maybe it will become a tradition."

Regina just shook her head and started toward the stairs. Steve followed her, enjoying her confusion. They climbed the 65 steps up into the sunlight.

At the top, the group was milling about. The Rosens had stopped to take a picture of the children with Fort Fincastle and the Nassau Water Tower in the background, while Jason and Amy were holding hands and looking at each other. The Naziris were arguing again — apparently, Fatima wanted a scarf one of the vendors was selling, and her father was having none of that. *Poor kid*, Steve thought. *Her dad has her on such a short leash. No wonder she concentrates on school — it must keep her away from him.*

Steve looked around for the Bennetts, but they were nowhere in sight. He walked over to Amy. "Did you see where Mr. and Mrs. Bennett went?"

Amy and her boyfriend glanced around. "Oh, sorry. I wasn't looking."

Steve smiled at her response. "Yeah, I'd sort of noticed that. Thanks anyway."

He grinned at her blush as he looked for and located Regina in the crowd. Steve moved over to her. "Looks like the Bennetts are wandering off the reservation. Should I go after them — or do you want to?"

Regina shook her head. "No. Just because they paid for the excursion doesn't mean they have to stay with it. They can make their own way back to the boat."

"Fair enough." He turned back and called out to the others in the tour group. "All right, folks, we're moving on. We'll visit the Water Tower first — highest spot on the island of New Providence and I'm told the view is spectacular. Then we'll head over to Fort Fincastle. Let's head on up the hill." Raising his leader flag in the air, Steve started up the incline. A few steps up, he turned around and continued walking backward uphill, facing the excursion group. He wanted to be sure he didn't lose any more stragglers.

The group was about to pass the fort when a pair of Bahamian policemen approached them from Steve's left.

Steve smiled at the officers. "Good morning, gentlemen. Beautiful day. Can I help you?"

The lead officer, the shorter of the two men, spoke up. His voice had a clipped accent — not Bahamian, but Steve couldn't quite place it. "Your ship contacted the local police and asked for an escort, due to a past incident at the Atlantis. We are here to provide that escort."

Steve glanced back at Regina bringing up the rear of the group. She shrugged as if to say, News to me.

Steve quickly assessed the situation. *Big guys — a lot larger than any other police officers I've seen on the island.* His ability fed him info right away. *The officer on the left is 6'2", 230. Even worse, on the right is easily 6'4" and almost 280. He's played some sort of sport — most probably MMA because of the shape his hands are in. But something is off about that smaller guy's uniform. Although it might be Park Police... no, something is definitely hinky here. Better play along until I can get a better idea of their intentions.*

Steve looked up at the water tower. "We'll keep moving. Thanks for the escort, officers. Let's head for the water tower, shall we?"

The officer shook his head. "I would recommend we visit the fort first. It is less crowded right now, because of the scheduled repairs."

Steve thought quickly. *No listing of any repairs in any of the data I downloaded when prepping for this tour. Definitely, something's up.* He glanced back at Regina and with one hand surreptitiously signaled her to stay back and separated from the group. He hoped she understood. She nodded and started wandering down the hill toward another group of tourists.

Steve looked back at his group. "Slight change of plans, folks. The tower is a little overcrowded right now, so we're going to tour the fort first. Everyone, follow me." He turned to the officer and gestured for him to lead the way.

The officer smiled and nodded. They started over toward the entrance on the south side. Steve noted as he followed the officer, that there were sawhorses and construction items piled beside the entrance. The officer ducked past the swinging iron gate and headed up the centuries-old stone staircase.

Just as he was reaching the top of the staircase, Steve heard the gate slam shut behind the group. He turned to look and saw the officer below at the back of the group turning away from it, keys in one hand, and a pistol in the other.

Steve turned back to the other officer and was greeted with the barrel of a gun five inches from his face, aimed directly at his forehead. Amy, who was right behind him, let out a yelp. The officer leered at him. "I am afraid we have had a change in plans. This is a robbery. Kindly drop all the bags you are carrying. Then put your hands behind your head, lace your fingers together, and in single file, walk along the wall here to line up by the cell doors."

Steve carefully lay down the leader's flagstick he was carrying and looked back at the group. "Better do as he says. I don't want anyone getting hurt." He laced his fingers atop his head as ordered and climbed out of the staircase. As he hit the top step, he decided this was a situation that needed his unique skills. Reluctantly he activated his Talent.

The world slowed to a crawl as he started surveying the area. In his mind's eye, Steve suddenly saw everything overlaid with data. It was as if a switch flipped and his worldview became an augmented reality

Fort Fincastle, built in 1793, three gun emplacements from the mid-1800s, barrels of bronze, 6 feet, 7 inches long which can pivot 47 degrees of arc, four cells on the top level, three used as static displays, a fourth as a tourist photo opportunity. Iron gates, rusted, but serviceable. Limestone, over 200 years old, cracked, unlikely to crumble, but possible to fracture, new lock on the gate to the fourth cell, Master Lock, key, 2-inch. The hasp is old, though.

He looked at the first robber. *That's what was out of place. Standard issue service revolvers for Bahamian police are Glock 9mm's — they're carrying a modified .22 calibers. The holster didn't fit the gun correctly. Left-handed grip...*

The world sped back up to normal time. He saw the first robber reach into his left breast pocket and remove a silencer. As he attached it to his pistol, Steve snapped his Talent back into place. He saw how the silencer would affect muzzle velocity and sound wave pattern reverberation in the area. But another part of his mind reached a more chilling realization.

A simple robber doesn't need a silencer.

Coming back into real time, Steve reached the fourth cell and then turned toward the attackers. The shorter one motioned with his pistol. "You, big man, kneel down. Same with the rest of you."

Amy had followed Steve in line, Jason beside her. Amy looked both frightened and angry, but as they knelt, Steve heard Jason tell her, "It'll be all right, Amy. Just close your eyes and breathe for a minute."

Next to Jason were the five Rosens, all looking terrorized by the gunmen. The little girl was crying and had her face turned and hidden in her mother's shirt. Steve's heart went out to her. At the far end, Fatima Naziri had just knelt. The second gunmen kicked the back of Mr. Naziri's leg to force him down. He squawked in protest and received a slap to the back of his head for his complaint. "Quiet, you," the second gunmen growled.

Steve considered this for a moment. His accent was weird — not Caribbean at all. *That sounded African of some sort. Here, in a police uniform?* His Talent didn't extend to languages, but he'd traveled extensively. He tried to remember from his travels abroad where he'd heard that accent before.

The first gunman was still pointing his weapon at Steve. "Is that everyone?"

"Yes, the whole group."

"You sure? I thought I saw another with you earlier."

Steve shook his head. "No. She's a local woman I know. A vendor here. We made a date for later."

"Good for you. Do as you are told, and maybe you will get to keep it." The gunman turned back and faced the line of tourists. "Ladies and gentleman, my associate, Francois, will now go down the line and relieve you of your wallets, watches, and jewelry. Kindly do not move, unless he asks you and then only move slowly when he does. If you fail to comply, well..." He raised his pistol and fired a shot that whizzed between Amy and Steve, striking the brick wall behind them. Steve felt the heat from the bullet as it passed by.

"If you understand what I am saying, nod." The hostages all did so. "Good. Francois, proceed."

The sun beat down mercilessly as Francois went from person to person. He was not shy about reaching in and checking pockets or inside bras for hidden items. As he reached Jason, Steve saw him remove the man's watch and then take his wallet and passport.

Francois then reached Amy and started to take the watch off her hand. She had to unlace her fingers to do so. As she did, the first gunmen pointed at her necklace. Amy caught her breath.

"Please. It's all I have left from my mother."

The first gunman walked forward and leered. "That's not true. You will always have your memories." He reached forward and grasped the necklace, yanking and breaking the thin gold chain. Amy stifled a cry as the gunman held it up into the sunlight, admiring it. Steve saw it was a single Australian opal, set in a golden filigree cage on the now broken chain. The gunman dropped it into his left shirt pocket.

There was another yelp. Steve turned to see. Francois had slid his hands from behind Amy inside the halter-top of her sundress and then inside her bikini top, feeling for any hidden items. Finding none, the gunman stopped for a moment and cupped her breasts.

Amy closed her eyes and grimaced in disgust. Behind her, Francois laughed and said something in his native tongue. Whatever he said must have amused the other gunman, as he started to laugh as well.

Jason had heard enough. He jumped up to punch Francois in the jaw. "Get your hands off her!" he snarled, as he started to grapple with the gunman. Francois's pistol flew out of his shoulder holster and landed next to Steve.

As soon as he saw the gun, Steve started to flash over, determined to find the best possible course. But before he could, Remy moved over and placed the barrel of his silencer directly against Amy's forehead.

"Enough! Stop now or—"

Steve's Talent caught him frozen an instant too late. He cursed to himself. A few moments sooner, he might have been able to do something, but now? Running through the various possible options in his head, he couldn't see a way he could use the pistol to free them that would not result in Amy's immediate death.

For a moment, he saw himself five years earlier, helpless as his mother and sister's murderer drove away. *What good is this Talent if I can't stop anything bad from happening?*

Regretfully, he dropped back into real time.

"—or the woman dies!"

Jason stopped, raising his hands above his head. Francois wiped the blood trickling from the corner of his mouth with one hand, then grinned and walked over until he was nose to nose with Jason. He said something in his native language, his voice full of contempt. Without warning, the thug drove a punch into Jason's midsection, doubling him over, and followed with a second driving punch to the back of his head. The young man collapsed to the ground.

"Francois says next time you will die. Since I have never known him to lie, I would stay down, young man." The first gunman looked back at the other hostages. "Any other heroes?" He looked directly at Steve as if he expected some sort of response. Steve schooled his expression carefully, showing no emotion.

Satisfied no one else would fight, the gunman reached into a pocket and threw a key ring at Steve. "Get up and unlock the last cell."

Steve did so, running his thumb over the key for the tumbler setup in the lock. *Four tumblers — neutral-up-down-down. And a master pin — up. I can pick this — if I can find a bobby pin...*

He undid the padlock, swung open the cell door, which screeched on its hinges, and turned to face his captors.

"All right, everyone, get in the cell. Go on, single file, move it. We do not have all day." Amy reached over and helped Jason to his feet, and the two of them shuffled inside. Francois shoved Steve in after them, and then the Rosens.

As the Naziris were about to enter, Francois slammed the cell door shut in front of them. The first gunman turned and looked at them. "On second thought, we will keep these two as insurance. You all be quiet for a few minutes, and let us make our getaway, and we will release these nice people at the bottom of the hill."

Mrs. Rosen was huddled with her children in the back of the cell, as her husband stood to shield them. Jason had collapsed again on the floor, trying to catch his breath, with Amy beside him. Steve watched his captors while studying the details of the cell around him. Outside, Francois was binding the hands of the Naziris with duct tape in front of them. Fatima looked up at Steve, her eyes pleading for him to help in some way.

Steve stood there, his mind racing. One of the answers had dropped into place when Francois had talked when he hit Jason. Now it was Steve's turn. He looked at the big man and spoke to him in fluent Somali.

[You do not have to do this. Let the girl go. Take me instead.]

The look of surprise on their captors' faces was gratifying. The leader turned to Francois, who was glaring at Steve.

[Idiot! Keep moving! Quickly now, we are on a schedule.]

[But, Remy, he could understand us—]

[It does not matter.] Remy turned back to the cell, a cold smile on his lips.

[A neat little surprise. But I suggest you make it your last. Otherwise... well, I would hate for something to happen to the young lady.] He poked Fatima with the pistol and indicated for her to start moving.

Steve watched as they started to walk away, pulling the Naziris along. As they reached the top of the stone staircase, Steve called out.

[I'll see you soon.]

Remy looked back at Steve and frowned.

[No, you will not. Goodbye.]

He fired the pistol at Steve.

Steve saw the gun move and kicked his Talent in gear. The world dropped into slow-time, and he saw the projected path of the bullet, where it would impact and ricochet. Assured no one would be hurt, he switched back to real time and ducked out of the way. The shot hit off the brick near the hasp, nicking it. In the distance, he heard the iron gate to the fort opening and shutting again.

Steve looked around for a moment. Amy moved forward and joined him at the bars. "How long before somebody finds us, you reckon?"

"I have no intention of finding out." He turned and faced the other hostages. "Did those guys leave anyone with a pen? A bobby pin? Any sort of wire?"

All the adults checked their pockets without success. The younger Rosen boy spoke up. "Will this do?" He held up a rigid plastic Popsicle stick.

Steve grabbed it. "It might. Thanks." He looked around again and spied a possible solution — a network of cracks in mortar around the brick where the anchor for the hasp was secured. They hadn't been there before the bullet from the first warning shot had struck the wall.

Steve scraped the mortar along the cracks with the stick, the edges crumbling away to form a small gap. He quickly repeated this in three other spots, creating a network of interconnected gaps around the brick holding the anchor for the hasp. He worked the stick into one of the gaps and started to move it, slowly at first, back and forth, widening the gap a bit more each time, like a pendulum, spreading from both ends upward and downward toward the other gaps.

Amy watched, trying to figure this out. "How is a Popsicle stick going to get us out of here?"

Steve kept working the stick like a wedge in the crack, widening it. "It's not...a Popsicle stick...it's a lever."

Amy looked at him, confused. Steve continued. "Archimedes once said, 'Give me a lever long enough and a big enough fulcrum and, I could move the world.' Same principle applies here. The old mortar is friable — it crumbles. If I can get the gaps to join up, the brick behind the hasp will slide out—"

Jason came up beside her. "And the door will open."

Steve nodded. He almost had it...

The Popsicle stick snapped with an audible click.

11:37 a.m. EDT

Amy looked at the broken stick in Steve's hand with a raised eyebrow. "Tell me, Archie. Was that the lever or the fulcrum?"

Steve glanced back at her and frowned. "Cute, but not helpful."

Jason put his hand on her shoulder. "Honey, let him work."

Steve swore softly for a moment, then reached over and pushed on the bars. The anchor brick wobbled a bit in place as he pushed. He studied it for a moment and Amy saw that weird look cross his face again. "I need more force," he muttered to himself, then turned to the group. "Jason, Mr. Rosen, will you help me, please? On the count of three, we'll shove against the edge of the cell door."

He turned to Amy. "You might want to step out of the way."

Amy took a step back, incredulous. *Oh, so you think I'm weak and helpless, do you? Just you wait, sailor boy. You're in for a rude awakening.*

Steve looked at the other men. "Ready? One, two, three — push!"

The brick slid out a little but the cell door held. The men stepped back, Steve tried kicking the edge of the door, to no avail.

After his third try, Amy shook her head. *Enough of this.* She reached out and put a hand on Steve's shoulder to stop him.

"You're doing it all wrong."

"Oh?"

"Yeah. Step aside, Archimedes." Amy pushed Steve toward the back of the cell and looked closely at the lock.

Looks like it needs one strike, center outside behind the hasp. Fifteen percent of my power should do it. I just wish I'd told Jason ahead of time. But I was going to let him know about my Talent today anyway. Okay, let's do this. Focus...

Amy crouched down and closed her eyes for a moment, as if in prayer.

Breathe...

Her breathing slowed, as she took a long deep breath, held it for a slow five count, and let it out in a rush.

Activate...

Suddenly, she slammed her right fist down against the ground once, twice, three times...

And...now!

With an explosive burst of speed, Amy jumped up and spun into a whirling blur. Her spinning leg kick connected with the door right on the weld to the hasp. The brick at that point shattered, pulling the anchors free from the wall. As she landed in a crouch facing the people in the cell, the door slammed open behind her. She stood and bowed at the waist toward Steve.

Steve hurried out the door. Jason just stood there, his mouth agape. "You never told me you could do that!"

Amy dimpled as she smiled. "You never asked." She turned to the Rosen family. "Stay here until the authorities arrive. Keep the kids safe." Mr. Rosen nodded, the expression on his face a mix of shock and awe.

The Rosen kids looked at her excitedly. The littlest girl came up and gave her a hug. "Go get the bad men."

Amy smiled at her. "Don't worry, honey. I will. I promise."

Amy and Jason hurried out the door, looking for Steve. They heard him call out from above. "Up here, on the observation platform!" Amy ran up the stairs, Jason right behind her. Steve was already scanning the crowds, trying to find the Naziris. Amy and Jason joined the search.

Jason spotted them. "There!" he pointed and started sprinting down the stairs.

Amy started after him. "Jason, wait! They're dangerous!"

11:40 a.m. EDT

Steve watched from the platform as the kidnappers shoved Mr. Naziri into a van just to the west of the fort, hidden among the parked tour buses. He was surprised to see the gunmen get in the back as well.

They're not working alone.

The vehicle headed onto the loop road. Steve activated and saw the path it would take — right past the main gate below. Steve saw he had thirty-five seconds to intercept and stop it. Real-time slammed back into place as he turned to tell Jason and Amy to stay here, but they had already gone.

Oh, God! They don't know there's a third kidnapper.

Steve hurried down the upper stairs. He was sprinting past the cell doors toward the stone staircase when he heard Jason and Amy open the rusty main gate. Steve took the stone steps three at a time, and as he hit the bottom of the staircase, he got his first glimpse outside. Jason and Amy had managed to get onto the road in front of the van and were trying to stop it. Steve looked carefully at the van and saw the driver.

Mrs. Bennett? What the hell is she doing mixed up in all of this?

She stopped the van, opened the door and pulled out a gun. As soon as Steve recognized what was happening, he took off at a sprint, angling toward Amy and Jason.

For him, time stopped again as he willed his Talent into action. He saw rate of closure, likely bullet trajectories, and angles of impact. He knew how slight his chances of success were, but he still had to try. Time slammed back to full speed, much too quickly, as he reached the curb, pushed off with his right leg and leaped at the couple in a flying tackle.

Four shots rang out, and the world erupted into a panic.

Chapter 5

The gunshots threw the surrounding tourists into a panic; people scrambled in all directions in search of safety. Steve hit both Amy and Jason with his flying tackle, and all three fell in a heap to the right of the van. Steve realized with a sickening certainty that he hadn't been shot, although his ears were ringing from the gun's report. He turned to Amy and yelled, "Are you two okay?"

Amy rolled over and looked gratefully at Steve. "She missed, thanks to you. Jason, I take back everything I ever said to you about how brutal tackle football is. Jason? Jason!" She turned to her boyfriend, and her face went white.

Jason's chest was punctured by three bullet holes, and there was a spreading pool of blood beneath him. He was struggling to speak, but there was red foamy blood in his mouth. He looked at Amy, confused and scared, as she knelt by him.

Steve stood up and spotted Regina at the edge of the crowd. He waved and got her attention. "Call an ambulance!" As he turned back, he locked eyes with Bennett, who had calmly put the gun back in the van, pulled her hair back and put on a ball cap. When she did so, Steve noticed a white scar above her eyebrow. Then she turned, and a pair of cold, gray eyes looked directly at him.

Unbidden, his Talent activated as he stared at the woman. As Nassau froze around him, he was back, five years earlier, seeing the face he'd committed to memory — the angular lines of her nose and cheeks, the small white crescent-shaped scar just above her right eyebrow, the smirking curl upward of her mouth on one side...

The images of then and now aligned side by side, then slid together. The realization hit him like a punch to his gut. *She's not Bennett! She's the woman who murdered my family!*

In his mind, Steve saw a third memory of this woman — a glimpse of this her in a black bikini on a luxury yacht at the end of the cruise pier. *I saw her earlier today...*

Steve snapped back to real time to just as those eyes drove past. Bennett smiled at him as she moved through the panicked crowd, making her getaway as calmly as if she was just another ordinary tourist taxi van. It was a predator's smile — all teeth below cold, gray eyes.

Steve watched her for a moment, his fists clenched. He looked back at Amy, who was cradling Jason's head in her lap, stroking his hair, begging him to hold on. "Please, Jason, stay with me! Please. I love you! Oh, God, please don't leave me, Jason. Please!"

Jason breathing struggled, then slowed and a moment later stopped completely. The light in his eyes dimmed, and Steve swore to himself. This murdering bitch had claimed another victim right in front of him again.

At that moment, Steve knew he had to act. He wasn't going to let her get away this time. But how he was going to do it was going to change his life forever.

Steve knelt next to Amy. "I'm sorry, but I have to go. I think they're headed back to the cruise terminal — they have a way to escape down there." He touched her shoulder. "I'll find them and stop them, Amy. I promise you that."

Steve stood up and closed his eyes for a moment. He clenched his fists, and for the first time in his life, willed his Talent to work at full capacity. In an instant, everything around him froze completely solid. The world went silent, except for the sound of his breathing and his heartbeat.

From his vantage point atop the hill, Steve could see much of downtown Nassau. Everything was in sharp contrast, and he could see minute details and zoom in on individual areas at will. It took him a moment to adapt to this, but he quickly did so, even as the world remained frozen around him.

Now he called forth in his mind a map, showing the streets and buildings, and overlaid it on his view. Next, he calculated the most likely path of the kidnappers, and finally, a dozen different routes through the city for himself. Deciding on the most efficient one, he collapsed the map. Steve closed his eyes and concentrated again.

Time resumed its normal speed. Without hesitation, Steve took off running toward the Queen's Staircase. He threaded his way through panicked tourists, milling about as sirens wailed closer to the scene. Behind him, a confused Good Samaritan yelled out, "There goes the gunman! Grab him!"

Ahead of him, a pair of burly men wearing University of Miami T-shirts turned and decided to try to tackle him.

Great, just what I need. He stopped time for a moment and glanced at the vendors ahead of him, calculating on the fly his own speed, the closing rate and size of his tacklers, the angle of the slope, and the likely paths of the contents of each vendor's cart. Using his free-running skills, Steve saw four possible scenarios, decided his optimal choice, and dropped back into real-time, going into action without breaking stride. He planted and pushed off with his left foot, launching into a tumbling run of one-handed back flips, finishing the last with a twist that landed him in a crouch balanced on the front tongue of a fruit vendor's cart.

The trailer tipped forward suddenly with the weight as Steve ducked, launching all the fruit over him and directly at the would-be tacklers. The jock on the left was hit full on by a trio of high-velocity melons and went down. The one on the right bobbed and weaved through the hail of produce. Although he now looked like an ambulatory fruit salad, he kept coming.

Sheesh, all I did was make him madder, Steve thought as he ducked and rolled forward under Mr. Fruit Salad's lunge, making him miss and smash headfirst into the front panel of the cart. Steve sprang out of the roll into a run and danced his way along the curb, weaving through the crowd. The sirens were getting closer, while behind him, he heard the first jock, who had gotten back up and was yelling for people to get out of his way.

Time for a little misdirection. Steve pushed off his right foot and sprang with a set of free-running leaps onto a spare tire on a vendor's cart and then atop an outcropping of weathered limestone. He ran along the top above the crowd for 30 yards, and then somersaulted off it, landing squarely on the running board of an old pickup truck parked along the curb. As people in the crowd reached for him, Steve grabbed the truck cab's window frame, swung himself sideways in front of the windshield and vaulted across the hood. He hit the ground by the left fender, rolled forward and started sprinting downhill past the last vendor. Off this table, Steve grabbed a long wooden carving, about two feet in length, smooth on the back, the front shaped like a mask from a witch doctor. Steve glanced at it — *hmmm, voodoo fertility god* — and then tucked it under his right arm like a football as he covered the last few yards to the Queen's Staircase.

He dropped into slow-time again as he evaluated the scene. A large group of senior citizens making their way down the upper section of stairs; a pair of couples on the lower part waited for the seniors to finish their descent; a half-dozen small clusters of schoolchildren in uniforms along the walkway below. He flashed on the most efficient path and committed himself to it. Time snapped back to normal as he stepped up onto the stones at the right edge of the staircase and placed the flat side of the carving down onto the handrail. He jumped up onto the voodoo idol's face, said a small prayer to the universe, asking forgiveness for any insult he'd just committed, then leaned forward and balancing precariously, did a boardslide down the upper section of the staircase.

He quickly dropped past the senior citizens and at the base of the first railing section, launched into a front flip walkover, holding onto the board with his right hand.

He landed on the left side of the mid-stair landing and ran down the next few steps, passing one couple to the left. He had begun to cut back to the right to pass the other couple when three of the small groups of schoolchildren came running up the stairs. Steve made a quick decision and did a free-running leap directly over to the handrail, balancing over the pool of water. He swung back and forth, trying to find his center of gravity as he slid downhill.

He had made it to within four steps of the bottom, struggling to control his balance, when it happened. Something was on the railing, and the surface wasn't smooth. When his foot hit it, he was launched forward. Quickly, he brought his arms and legs in close, spotted where his arc would land him and went with it. At the last moment, he swung his hands down and rolled through the impact, coming up in a low crouch. His left knee and hand touched the ground, his right arm extended out to the side, holding the board, ready to strike or defend with it.

Kids on the lower steps stared at him in awe. Senior citizens on the upper steps broke out into applause. But the police at the top were less appreciative. They blew their whistles and yelled for him to stop. Steve sprinted north, seeing in his mind's eye the optimal path to take even as it shifted. He covered the length of the Queens Walk in less than twenty seconds, dodging and weaving through the small crowd, and emerged into the parking lot off Sands Street.

He heard more police sirens; based on the change in pitch, they were closing rapidly. Steve realized he'd be stopped if he continued on foot. At that point, a tourist couple pulled into the lot on a rented motor scooter. As they parked, Steve sprinted across the lot, leaped onto the spare tire and then the roof of a Range Rover parked in an adjacent space and launched himself into another somersault, landing squarely in the saddle of the scooter.

The driver turned around in shock. "What are you — argh!" Steve pushed the driver off the still running scooter into the arms of his girlfriend, jammed the idol carving into the carry basket in front, then grabbed the handlebars and opened the throttle. It was a top of the line scooter — 250 cc motor, capable of speeds up to 70 miles per hour. It shot easily over the berm and toward the Elizabeth Street entrance, but a police cruiser slid into the opening directly ahead of him. Steve put his left foot down, leaned hard, and pivoted his ride into a 180-degree turn. He opened the throttle, and in a spray of gravel, shot away from the police.

A second cruiser pulled into the Sands Street entrance, blocking that driveway. Steve aimed the scooter at a small gap on the driver's side. The policeman started to open his door, trying to trap him. Steve sped into the gap and kicked out with his left foot, slamming the door back shut back shut. He swerved as he crossed the street to avoid a van full of tourists and shot up a driveway across the road and onto the grounds of a private manor.

The manor was hosting a wedding, and valets were parking the guests' vehicles. Steve weaved through the line of cars, jumping the curb at the end of the parking lot and onto the large lawn to the east of the manor house. A large tent had been set up for the wedding reception. At first, he tried to calculate a way around it, but he saw private security people were closing in.

A lot of private security people.

Uh-oh. Just whose party did I crash here?

Steve looked around, saw no other option and made his choice. He gunned the throttle and aimed for the tent opening.

In a moment, the scooter was inside, filling the space with the noise of its engine. Steve snapped into slow-time and looked around. The tent was packed with tables and chairs laid out for a wedding reception. *Not good*, he thought. *No way through.* Steve snapped back into real time and felt an arm brush against his back as someone yelled, 'Freeze!'

Someone is not going to get their damage deposit back, Steve thought, as he gunned the engine and made straight for the exit on the north side of the tent. Tables overturned and glass crashed in his wake as he plowed through the scene of chaos.

Emerging from the tent, he looked rapidly left and right, trying to see any pursuers. He spotted the faint traces of a footpath heading along the lawn into the trees beyond, and opened the throttle, speeding across the lawn as the astonished guests stood and stared at the commotion. Security men ran after him as he drove the scooter into the trees and down the slope.

The path down the hill was narrow and rocky, and he had to wrestle the ride to keep it from getting stuck but kept it always moving downhill. After a couple of tense moments, he crashed through the brush at the bottom of the slope and out into a vacant lot. A fence gate across the way was open, and he sped toward it.

Steve dropped again into slow time just as he was about to enter Shirley Street. *Shirley is one-way going east, while Bay heads west. I'm northwest of the wharf, and the van is somewhere west of me. Shirley's going to take me the wrong way. Got to change directions.* Steve let go of time and as it snapped back, steered the bike right without slowing, merging into the traffic flow on Shirley. He cut off one car and weaved precariously across two other lanes of traffic. At the next intersection, he again planted his left foot and twisted the scooter through another 180-degree turn, this time moving up onto the sidewalk. He opened the throttle and gunned it along the covered walkway. Tourists dove on top of cars or into shops to get out of his way.

At the intersection of Shirley and East Street, he stopped, searching for the van with the hostages. Steve hoped he'd beaten the van here, but if not, he'd have to try his luck at the wharf. That would be a much tougher fight.

A few moments later, the kidnappers' van careened onto Shirley from a block west and wove across all lanes of traffic and onto East Street. As it sped past him, he could see Bennett gripping the wheel and the two kidnappers inside pointing their pistols out the back. The rear window had been shattered.

Shooting at someone? But who else could be pursuing them?

Steve was puzzling over that when a blur shot past him — a human figure, moving much too fast for any normal person. It reached the back of the van and leaped onto the roof. Steve dropped into slow-time to get a glimpse of what was pursuing the van, but what he saw didn't make any sense.

Amy Rogers? But...how?

A moment later, it occurred to Steve that his own chance to head off the kidnappers was slipping away. Snapping back into real-time, he opened the throttle and turned in pursuit down East Street. As he closed in, Remy spotted him and fired through the shattered window. Steve's slipped into slow-time and tracked the path of each bullet. He ducked low and gunned the throttle. The shots missed, and he raced past the van on its right.

Steve decided he'd make his stand at the intersection ahead — the corner of East and Bay Streets. He was three cars lengths ahead of the van as he started across the traffic on Bay Street. Steve dropped into slow-time and examined all the vehicles around him, his mind registering their relative velocities and closing rates. He ran through a half-dozen different scenarios, predicted their outcomes and found one that he really liked. Preparing for a few physically rough moments, he took a deep breath, braced himself, and dropped his hold on time.

Grabbing the idol from the basket, Steve dove off the scooter and rolled left. As he came out of the roll, he turned and flung the idol with his right arm in a flat spin behind him.

The scooter wobbled on without him and crashed into the traffic officer's shelter in the middle of the intersection, knocking it over into the path of an oncoming truck. That driver panicked and swerved left to avoid the traffic box. The truck plowed into a series of parked cars, blocking East Street.

Behind Steve, the fertility idol spun through the air like a helicopter blade down East Street and without warning buried itself in the windshield of the kidnappers' van. The windshield became obscured with a spider web of cracks.

When the idol hit the windshield, Bennett slammed on the brakes. Amy Rogers was thrown forward off the roof. She hit the pavement in front of the van, rolling and bouncing until she slammed into the side of one of the parked cars that now blocked East Street. the truck had relocated into the intersection.

Bennett jammed the steering wheel left and drove the van up onto the sidewalk to bypass the accident. She rounded the corner past Parliament House and tried to angle across Bay Street toward Rawson Square. As she came down off the curb onto the street, the front tires on the van burst. Bennett struggled to control the van as it crashed through a line of rental scooters and ran into a planter at the edge of the square.

Steve's shirt was tattered. He had a road rash on his right arm from his landing and his left knee was throbbing, but he wasn't thinking about that now. He looked back to where Amy Rogers had landed against the parked car, but she wasn't there. Steve filed that for consideration later, then turned and ran as best he could across the road, making a beeline for Rawson Square.

The van had come to rest against a wrought iron fence built to protect the landscaping. Inside, the two kidnappers were scrambling to open the doors. As Steve ran up next to a street vendor, the right passenger door slid open, and Remy emerged. He was bleeding from a head wound and had his right arm pressed against his side, but when he spotted Steve, he didn't hesitate to raise his pistol with his good arm, aiming it directly at him.

Without thinking, Steve grabbed three CDs of steel drum music from a vendors table at the edge of the square. A quick moment of slow-time and he saw the angles the CDs needed to move at. He threw them like *shuriken*, ninja stars, one after the other. The first caught the kidnapper on the gun hand, causing Remy to howl in pain and drop the pistol. The howl was short-lived, as the second and third

CDs struck him; one on the face, the other on the right temple. Remy looked dazed for a moment, then his eyes rolled back, and he crumpled to the ground, unconscious.

When Steve looked up again, Amy Rogers was somehow on the other side of the van, yanking open the side door. He was shocked as she almost ripped the door from its track. *How the heck did she do that?* Francois yelled and lunged at her from inside the van, but Amy grabbed his collar and pulled him forward, using his own momentum against him. He almost flew out of the van, and before he could stop, slammed face-first into the base of the statue of Sir Milo Butler, about twenty yards away, and slid down to the ground, out cold.

Amy looked back and spotted Steve through the open van. "Get the Naziris!" she yelled. "Bennett's mine!" Steve nodded and moved to the van as Amy ran north toward the wharf.

The Naziris were huddled on the back seat, the father shielding his daughter as well as he could. They looked relatively unhurt. Steve pulled the duct tape from their mouths. "Can you walk?" They nodded in reply, too shocked to speak. "Then follow me. Quickly now!" Steve pushed down the middle seat and helped the pair out of the van. He hurried them over to the tourist center on the east side of the square and had them huddle down in the doorway. "You two stay here, no matter what!"

Steve went back into the square, quickly surveying the area. He spotted Amy and Bennett fighting at the north edge of the square and moved toward them.

11:51 a.m. EDT

When Amy caught up with Bennett, she saw that the woman now had a cut above her right eye, that white scar pulsing red from a fresh injury. Amy's own clothes were torn, and she was covered with blood. She wasn't sure if it was her own or Jason's. At this point, it didn't exactly matter to her.

Bennett sneered at Amy, her voice thick with contempt as if she was goading her. "Just walk away, Princess, and I promise you, no one else gets hurt."

"You're a murderer! I'm not letting you get away!"

She chuckled, even as she circled around, trying to find a way out. Amy kept cutting her off. Bennett shook her head. "What's the matter, Princess? Did I break one of your toys? Serves you right. Your kind never knows when to wake up and stop playing hero. I think it's a design flaw, myself."

Amy's face contorted in rage as she moved to her right, trying to force the woman back toward the square. Bennett kept backing up, trying to keep some distance between the two of them. It was as if Bennett was wary of physical contact with her. *Does she suspect something about me? It's as if she knows me...*

Wait a minute! She's the bitch from the yacht! The realization hit Amy, and she stumbled. Bennett took advantage and started to run past her. As she went by, Amy reached out and attacked with a series of arm sweeps and fists, followed by a low leg sweep.

Bennett's reactions were good — really good. *She doesn't fight like a middle-aged housewife,* Amy thought. *She's been trained in hand-to-hand combat and is at least a 2nd-degree black belt. But let's see if she knows this move.* Amy flipped backward out of her leg sweep and added a handstand spin with leg extension. The rotation caught Bennett unaware and she was smacked by a foot directly across the jaw. She went flying backward from the impact and landed in the street. Bennett lay there, face down in shock, as Amy walked over, fists ready.

"Jason was no toy! He was the man I loved. Now get up — I'm not through with you yet!"

Bennett got up on her elbows and wiped away blood from a cut lip. "Maybe you're not, Princess. But I am. Fighting you is not on the agenda today." She reached into her breast pocket and pulled out a small black stick with a red button atop. As she rolled over, Bennett looked up at Amy.

"Consider this a rain check. Another time, Princess."

11:54 a.m. EDT

Steve ran up in time to see Amy standing over a prone Bennett. As Bennett rolled over, he saw a device in her hand — a small black stick with a red button. A cold chill ran down his spine. He knew a trigger when he saw one, and he realized the one place she could have put the bomb.

Steve turned back toward the square and yelled. "Get away from the van! It's rigged to explode!" He then turned and took off at a sprint toward Bennett, ignoring the pain in his left leg.

He was five steps away from Bennett when she hit the switch.

The bomb she'd planted inside the taxi van went off with a terrific blast, shattering windows in Rawson Square and in Government House across the street. The concussion wave hit Steve first, sending him flying sideways. He hit a lamppost and crumpled in a daze. Amy took the brunt of the explosion head-on and was thrown back across the walkway toward the wharf, ending up in the shrubs by the market.

Steve came to after the explosion at the base of the lamppost, groggy and disoriented. His ears were ringing badly as he looked around, trying to shake off the effects of the blast. He tried to focus, and for a moment, thought he saw his family's murderer being helped up off the ground. Steve rolled over, nauseous for a moment, and then looked again. He shook his head. He couldn't be sure, but he must have been seeing double. It looked like there were two Bennetts, both helping each other make their way to a yacht.

No, I've got to stop her. I can't let her get away again.

Steve somehow forced his way to his feet and started stumbling after the women. "You! Stop!"

The women glanced back at him, and then one of them stopped. She turned around, took off her sunglasses and stared at Steve.

Steve saw her gray eyes, and suddenly it was as if nothing else in the area existed — no explosions, no pain — just that pair of eyes. He felt eerily empty as his powers slipped away, the constant whisper of data silenced. Then the eyes faded into a darkening haze...

Steve came to after the explosion halfway down the wharf, groggy and disoriented. *The blast must have thrown me farther than I thought.* He tried to focus, but his head rang like a Chinese gong was being played inside it. As he looked around groggily, he saw at the end of the wharf the Bennett woman stepping onto the back of one of the luxury yachts.

Damn it, she's getting away!

Steve started to get up to try to follow but stumbled. The yacht pulled away from the dock, joining the legion of anonymous vessels in the harbor.

Steve shook his head again. *Uh, that...that must have been some crack on the head. I must have been seeing things. For a second, I could have sworn I saw two Bennetts on the back of that yacht. No...there's something...something about that I'm supposed to remember.* Steve glanced around again, spotting Amy across the walkway and limped over to her.

Amy was struggling to get to her feet, looking around, her face contorting with rage. "Where is she? Did you see her?"

Steve put his hands on her shoulders. "She...she ran down the pier and got onto a yacht."

"We have to go after her! She can't get away!" Amy started to lurch toward the wharf, and then stumbled to the ground. Steve bent down beside her.

"You're hurt and in no shape to follow her. I'm sorry, Amy. She got away."

She looked at him, incredulous. "You're sorry? *Sorry?*" Amy started shaking and sobbing. Steve, unsure of what else to do, put his arms around her to comfort her.

She let out a scream of pure primal rage, and collapsed, unconscious.

Chapter 6

May 23, 5:44 p.m. EDT

As jails go, it's not so bad.

Steve lay on the bed in his cell, staring up at the ceiling. His world right now consisted of a 4x8 room with a bed, a sink, and a toilet.

I mean, the walls are cinderblock, and the facilities are, well, less than luxurious. But it's air-conditioned. And quiet — can't forget quiet.

Steve gazed around the room idly. Since he'd pushed his Talent to full capacity, he now saw with each glance calculations on how to leverage his meager resources into a plausible chance at escape. He closed his eyes and rubbed his temples. *Man, I wish I could figure out how to shut this off.*

He'd been in the cell for just over a day. This wasn't based on a watch — he'd lost his in the robbery. But he'd received dinner the previous evening and breakfast and lunch today. He figured that dinner would be along soon.

As he stared up at the ceiling, he thought back again on the attack and its aftermath. Setting off a car bomb in the capital of the Bahamas in front of their Parliament was definitely going to get someone's attention. That was probably Bennett's plan all along.

Bennett. Yeah, right. I wonder what her real name is.

The police had recovered from their shock and cordoned off the area immediately. A pair of the local constables found Steve and Amy on the ground where she'd collapsed, unconscious. Steve was holding her in his arms, trying to find some words, any words, which would comfort her.

The policemen had given him a wide berth at first, probably in deference to Amy. However, word of his escapades on the trip down the hill soon caught up with him. He might not have caused the explosion, but there was damage to property, a stolen motor scooter and two major automobile accidents that could be directly laid at his feet. *Not to mention the little matter of disrupting the wedding of the daughter of the Bahamian Justice Minister,* Steve thought. *That's probably ironic, seeing as how I'm pretty sure he's going to be prosecuting me directly. Somehow, I doubt I'm on his Christmas card list this year.*

He made sure Amy was being seen by a paramedic before he surrendered. *They really must have been worried about what I would do — four policemen with weapons drawn and trained on me, plus arm and leg shackles. Overkill. You'd think they'd never seen someone who could free-run before. Of course, not having any ID didn't help — and all of mine were in that van when it blew up.*

Lots about this just didn't add up and that bothered Steve — in his world, things always added up. His Talent lay in seeing the patterns around him and using chain reactions that produced desired results. *What have I stumbled into here?* He sat up on the bed and closed his eyes.

Steve felt the anger building inside him. *I had her. Somehow, I crossed paths with my family's killer and came this close...*

No, I can't dwell on that. I know she's out there now. She was up to something today. I figure out what, maybe I can find her again.

What, exactly, did he know?

First, the attack. Steve recalled from memory images of the kidnappers, Remy and Francois. He wasn't stupid enough to believe those were their real names. But he studied their faces, their bodies, their clothes, looking for anything that might be clues to their true identities.

Obviously, mercenaries. And they targeted the Naziris. So why them? Now that Steve thought about it, for as much as the daughter had been like a puppy following him at all sorts of recreational activities, he'd rarely seen her old man. *She's a nice kid. I feel bad for her, being stuck with a dad that restrictive on a cruise. Tough to have fun. But her dad's a ghost. Where could you have been on my ship?*

He thought back to the embarkation day when the cruise started. Steve had been wandering down the passageway the Naziris' cabin was located on and noticed some luggage outside it. He'd glanced down, and saw one of the suitcases had a tag with a unique logo — a three-sided Möbius strip and a five-point starburst above it. Below it was a single word — Triangle.

What was that symbol for? For that matter, what was Triangle? The place where he worked? Could they possibly have anything to do with it?

Steve decided he needed more data. It would have to wait until he got out of this jail cell. He tabled the question and turned instead to the day's other mystery — Amy Rogers.

He concentrated for a moment, sorting through his memories of Amy. He considered his first impressions of her — the smiling young woman he'd met on the Promenade Deck, frozen in a moment of joy. His heart ached for her, knowing the loss that she was about to face.

God, do I know that feeling all too well. No one should ever have to go through that sort of pain. I failed everyone yesterday. I need to get out of here and make it right.

He thought through the moments of their capture and attack, looking for clues that might somehow explain how someone that petite could kick open an iron cell door, or rip a car door halfway off its track. It seemed like she had an extra gear that she kicked in at that point. Her face was a mask of pain and rage — maybe adrenaline was affecting her? But between her catching a speeding van, making a 5-foot running vertical leap, and the car door, the easy explanations were quickly exhausted. Still, it was amazing to watch her in overdrive.

It was almost as if she was...but that's impossible. What happened to me is some sort of freak genetic mutation. A pretty useless one, at that. After all, all it lets me do is maybe do some parlor tricks when doing free-running. But to truly do something important?

Steve felt his depression building when he heard a key turn in the lock to his cell door. As he opened his eyes, he saw a pair of Bahamian jailers enter, followed by two other people. The first was a man in his early 40s, fair-skinned with close-cropped silver hair and piercing blue eyes. He reminded Steve a bit of Paul Newman. His bearing and clothing screamed military, probably private security. He was watching Steve like a hawk watches a rabbit, from a great distance, secure in the knowledge that when the time came to strike, he'd be able to.

The other visitor was a female. White, mid-40s, black hair with a splash of blue in the highlights, although that might have been a result of the lights in the cell. Steady gaze with gray eyes, she was conservative in her attire and attitude, although her laugh lines indicated she liked to smile. Under different circumstances, he might even like his fate if this was the woman deciding it.

Still, gray eyes again? Third time in two days? Steve's spidey sense told him this was just too much of a coincidence.

Steve knew he could escape. He'd already figured out twenty-seven successful scenarios, and the arrival of these people had added eight more. However, he wanted answers, and he suspected these visitors were key to finding them.

She studied him for a moment, her head tilted slightly to one side. Then she held out a hand to him. "Mr. Tate, you've been released into my custody. We need to talk."

Steve looked at her as his left eyebrow rose upward. "Oh, really? And who has the pleasure of taking over as my jailer?"

"My name is Dr. Rhonda Watson, and though you might not realize it yet, you very much want to talk with me." She held out a business card to him.

Steve took it and looked at it. His eyebrows immediately shot upward. On it was a peculiar logo — a three-sided Möbius strip, with a five-point starburst above it. Underneath was a single word.

Triangle.

7:32 p.m. EDT

Amy sat in a hospital room at Princess Margaret Hospital. There was a guard posted outside her door, but that didn't matter. She wasn't going anywhere. She didn't want to.

She'd awoken here after collapsing in the street following the bomb blast. For a moment, she was disoriented, not sure of where she was; then the nightmare of the previous day's events flooded back to her. It all seemed so disjointed, so jumbled. One moment, she was in heaven — the happiest she could remember in a very long time. And now...

"Jason."

The word came out as a half sigh, half choked-off sob. She remembered the touch of his lips... and then the sight of the blood, the confused and scared look in his eyes as Jason realized he was slipping away.

I couldn't even comfort him. I never even had the chance to try to save him. It was as if he had gone almost instantly. The doctor who had treated her had talked to the police official outside her door. They either didn't know she could hear them or didn't think it mattered, what with Jason already dead. One of the bullets had pierced his aorta — he was dead within a minute, they'd said; nothing could have saved him.

That's not true, Amy thought. *I could have. I could have shoved him out of the way, instead of being tackled by that jerk from the ship. One split-second more, he would have been safe, and I wouldn't be—*

"Alone?"

The voice startled Amy. She turned and saw a middle-aged woman, black hair, and gray eyes, wearing a conservative dress and a lab coat, standing in the doorway. "I'm sorry if I startled you, Ms. Rogers. The American Embassy called and asked me to come see you. I'm Dr. Rhonda Watson."

The woman stepped inside the room and closed the door behind her. She was carrying a tablet computer. She grabbed a stool, then moved over and sat down beside Amy's bed. "I'm going to ask you a few questions if that's all right."

Amy watched her warily. Something about this woman was setting off a warning inside her. "Who are you, really?"

Watson smiled. "I understand. It's been a traumatic experience for you—"

"You think? Thank you, Lady Obvious. When can I leave? I need to get my things off the boat. I need to get back home. I need to call Jason's..." Amy stopped, swallowed back the sob, and continued. "J-Jason's family. I need to call his Mom and Dad."

Watson nodded sympathetically. "Yes, and I'll be glad to assist you. But I need to get a few answers first."

"Why? What do you need from me?"

"You stumbled into something, young lady. The target of the attack was... well, actually, that's classified. But someone was willing to do anything to get to him — including shoot an innocent bystander in cold blood."

Amy sat up and leaned toward Watson, the anger inside her building again. "If he was so important, where was his security? Why didn't you guys have him surrounded by bodyguards 24-7, Rhonda?" She turned her questioner's name into an insult.

Watson replied, not unsympathetically. "I'm sorry; but as I said, that's classified. And it's not the reason I'm here to talk to you."

"I could care less why you're here to talk to me. My boyfriend was murdered, and the best I'm going to get is

'I'm sorry?' Well, I'm sorry, too, but more than that, I'm angry. Who was she? Do you know?"

Watson waited while Amy vented. Her reply was calm and measured. "What I do know is that I'm sitting in a room with someone who did this." She turned the tablet she was holding around to face Amy. A video window started playing a montage of security camera footage from the previous day's events. The loop started with Amy kneeling over Jason's body. She stood up, spotted where the van was going, and started running after it. After three steps, she became a blur on the video and was gone. Another angle showed her blur catching the van on East Street and forcing it to turn west while punching out the rear window. The third image...

Amy stared at it. "That's impossible."

Watson nodded. "I thought so as well. You appear to have been shot at close range, thrown off the van, and left lying in the street. But thirty seconds later, you stand up, and charge off after the kidnappers again."

"No. I chased the van, caught up with it when it crashed at Rawson Square, and when I tried to fight that Bennett lady, she blew everything up and escaped."

Watson stopped the playback and put the tablet down on the bed stand. She then reached into the right pocket of her lab coat. "Perhaps. But what you say doesn't explain this." Watson held up a small specimen jar containing a bullet. One end was smashed flat.

"We found this in the middle of the road on East Street — in a small puddle of dried blood where you landed."

"But...?" Amy's mind was reeling. Panicked, she looked inside her hospital gown for any bandages.

"Trust me, Ms. Rogers. The exam when you arrived was extremely thorough. Other than some scrapes, there's nothing wrong. Certainly no bullet wounds."

"But, I don't understand..."

"Frankly, neither do we. However, we'd like to learn more. So, I'm here to make you an offer. We'd like you to come back to our facility in the States where we can evaluate what happened, and see if it was you or some other anomaly that caused this."

Amy looked skeptical. "You want to make me a lab rat? No, thank you. Why would you even think I'd agree to this?"

Watson smiled slightly. To Amy, she looked like someone who had just drawn a straight flush and was having trouble concealing it. She picked up the tablet, touching a few controls on it while she talked. "Simple. Amelia Jane Rogers, how'd you like to be part of the team that goes after...this target?" She handed the tablet back to Amy.

The image on it was the one thing Amy wanted more than anything else at that moment.

Jason's killer.

Amy stared at the picture, burning the image into her memory. Then she looked over the top at Watson, who'd been studying her. Amy's eyes were cold as steel. "I'm in."

8:04 p.m. EDT

The woman formerly known as Karen Bennett of Roseville, Michigan, died just after sunset, 40 miles west of the coast of New Providence, as all her documentation, ID and excess baggage of all kinds were dumped overboard. She sighed. This version of Bennett had been a useful cover for years. She'd never thought it would be gone like this.

"No use worrying over it."

"I know, Hannah, but it's been a pain in the ass to reestablish a good cover since 9/11."

"Maybe. A bigger question is what went wrong?"

She walked back into the main cabin of the yacht and poured herself a glass of white wine, then sat down opposite her companion. "Well, at the risk of sounding like an episode of Scooby Doo, I guess we blame those meddling kids. Seriously, I thought they were locked up securely at the fort. How did they break out?"

Hannah shook her head. "No, it's bigger than that. I killed one, but the other two chased me down on foot, despite a big head start in the van amidst all that confusion. You're aware of the implications?"

"What, that Triangle was somehow aware of the op and already had a security team in place? Nope. I'd have known. This was just a coincidence." She stood up and went to the hatch overlooking the rear deck. "Or are you referring to your legacy? Do you think that's what this is?"

"I don't know. But I guess I need to consider it. I was able to establish a rapport with the girl quick enough."

"Then it's something that needs consideration, and eventually to be dealt with. Especially considering our... history, as it were."

Hannah sipped her wine thoughtfully. "Whatever the case, we still have an assignment now." She reached over and pressed an intercom button on the console behind the sofa.

A male voice came over the speaker. "Bridge here."

"Captain, set your course for Miami. I have a plane to catch."

"Very well, madam. Bridge out."

Hannah turned back to her companion. "Since we didn't get to Naziri out in the open, we'll have to go where he feels safe. You know what I'll need."

Her companion laughed. "Of course I do. After all, great minds—"

"—think alike." Hannah joined in the laughter at the private joke as the yacht sailed into the night.

8:24 p.m. EDT

"You know, I'm not really good at this waiting thing."

Steve looked over at his companion. The man in the security uniform from the prison had been introduced to him as Mitchell Williams. Since then, they'd probably shared ten sentences, and most of those on Williams' part were of the one or two-word variety. Short words, too. Easy to understand ones, like 'No.'

Steve went to glance at his watch again, out of habit, but his left wrist was still bare. *Losing that watch really sucks. I mean, a watch is just a watch. But the Thornbush gave it to me before I left for Europe all those years ago. I guess I was sentimental about it.* He sighed again and looked out the window.

He'd been sitting inside the Gulfstream V for more than an hour. Dr. Watson had brought him here, removed his cuffs, and invited him to change out of his prison coveralls into a set of gray sweats, have a seat and wait. "Mr. Williams will keep you company," she'd told him. "I have another errand to perform, and when we... when I return, we can discuss your future."

Since then, it had been quiet — just the interior of the hangar, the closed doors, and the two guards patrolling around the outside of the plane. They each wore uniforms like Williams' — black combat pants, a black long sleeve shirt made of some strange material that caught the light and reflected it in an unusual way, and a squared off hat, like a painter's cap, also black. The only identifying mark was a single patch on the left shoulder — that three-sided Möbius strip again, with its five-pointed starburst directly above the apex.

Triangle again, Steve thought. *And these guys are no mere rent-a-cops, either. They're either trained athletes or elite forces, or both. And those weapons. They look like assault rifles, but the magazines are all wrong — and since when does a magazine have a LED indicator on it?*

Well, whether he trusted these folks or not, they were his ticket out of the Bahamas now. His personal effects had sailed with the Celebration Goddess, on its way to Freeport. He wondered what Regina thought of all this.

Steve started to glance at his watch again and groaned in frustration. "Man..."

Williams glanced up from the tablet he was reading. Steve decided to try yet again to start a conversation.

"Look, Williams, I'm dying here. It's been a long day. Your boss lady is off on this errand, and I have no idea how long we'll be stuck here. Can I at least get something to drink?"

Williams considered the request for a moment, then put down his tablet and walked to the galley at the rear of the plane. He opened a small reefer and pulled out two plastic bottles of water. He tossed one to Steve and carried the other back to his seat.

Steve opened the bottle, took one swig and swished it around his mouth, then took another long drink. "Thanks, man. I needed that."

Williams nodded and went back to reading his tablet, the water bottle untouched beside him. Steve spoke up again. "Could you also possibly tell me what time it is? All I know is that it's dark out there. My watch was never recovered from the bombing, so again, I'm just a little lost here."

Williams considered this, then pulled back the cuff of his sleeve and looked at his right wrist. "It's 2030 hours. Dr. Watson should return shortly, and we'll be on our way."

"I'm in shock. More than four words strung together at one time! And here I was, thinking you were just a high-quality babysitter hired for your good looks."

Williams' brow furrowed almost imperceptibly at the phrase 'babysitter.' *Better avoid that term again*, Steve thought. Instead, he was curious about something else he'd just seen. "That is some fancy watch you have there. That has to be the thinnest band I've ever seen, and there isn't a visible clasp on it. Or a visible face, either. Did you pick it up through Hammacher Schlemmer? How do you know what time it is?"

Williams' left hand slid his cuff back over his watch as if protecting it from something. *Or somebody. Probably me. And he raised an eyebrow there — ever so slightly. He must not have been expecting me to notice so quickly. Well, they already have an inkling about me — Watson hinted at that. Showing off for the rent-a-whatever can't do anything but improve my rep.*

"Look, if you don't talk to me, then I'm just going to do my thing anyway. I mean, let's take you. Late 30s, my first guess, 38. And 6'3", 220 pounds — no, make that 210. That uniform makes you look bulkier than you are, probably due to something in the fabric. I'm guessing a ballistic material to dissipate force, but one I've never seen before anywhere. You have two visible scars — one above your left eye, probably from a fistfight in high school; the other person had a ring or something and caught you with it. The other is 4 inches long on the back of your right hand. The edges are rough, so it's a burn of some sort — most probably a graze from a tracer round. So, you've seen combat of some sort. You carry yourself like an elite forces soldier — my guess is Army Ranger rather than Navy SEAL. SEALS carry their center of gravity slightly different to be ready for a shipboard environment. So... Afghanistan, and afterward, you went into private security, probably for the money. Oh, and you were married, but that ended a while back."

Steve stopped and took a swig of water, then looked over at Williams. "How'd I do?"

Williams stared at him for a moment and then growled. "You talk too much."

"Well, I think he did marvelously."

Steve spun around and saw Dr. Watson entering the plane, accompanied by the two guards from outside and another passenger — a female wearing a matching set of gray sweats, the hood of her sweatshirt obscuring her face. She glanced once in his direction, then moved to the far rear side of the cabin and sat down, facing the window.

Wow, everyone here loves me, Steve thought sarcastically. *And her, huh? I guess I really shouldn't be surprised.*

He looked up at Watson. "Finished picking up strays? Care to tell me what's going on?"

Watson sat down in the seat in front of him. "Certainly. Just as soon as we're airborne."

One of the guards finished securing the cabin door, and the jet's engines spun up to full power. The hangar doors must have been on remote control — they just started to open without anyone pushing them and the jet taxied past them and onto the tarmac. Within moments, they were climbing into the night sky, and a couple of minutes later, Steve felt the plane bank to the right and head north.

"Okay, Doc. Now will you talk to me?"

Watson turned and smiled at Steve across the cabin table. "Certainly. Yesterday, you foiled the kidnapping of the lead researcher in charge of a top security project for Triangle. That was commendable by itself. But it was the way you did it which has us curious. There's more to you, Mr. Tate, than meets the eye."

"Is that who Naziri is? I wondered why mercenaries would be targeting him."

"Yes."

Steve leaned back. "I'm not sure I like this. Am I your prisoner now, or some sort of lab rat?"

"Prisoner? Not at all. When we land, you'll be free to go, if you so choose. We'll arrange to get you replacement identity documents and fly you back to Seattle. But my hope is you'll listen to what I am offering and decide to work with us."

Steve looked around, unconvinced. "Us? Sorry to sound skeptical, Doc, but so far, all I see is you, some mercenaries, and a logo for a mysterious organization I've never heard of." He tilted his head toward the woman in the hoodie. "Or is she a part of your mysterious 'us'?"

Watson looked unruffled by Steve's reply. "Let's leave my other guest out of this for the moment. Let me enlighten you instead." She took out her data tablet and placed it on the table in front of him. She pressed a control, and a series of images appeared.

Steve raised one eyebrow. "You've got a PowerPoint to show me?"

"You were expecting something different?"

Steve shrugged. "Well, sure. After all, you've got all sorts of curious gadgets around here, and you're actively recruiting me — although I don't know what for..."

D. G. Speirs

Watson smiled. "Ah, yes. Let's figure that out. We'll start here. Why did you take off after the kidnappers yourself?"

Steve looked up sharply at Watson, surprised at the question. "What do you mean?"

"It's a simple question, Mr. Tate. Why did you, unarmed and on foot, choose to pursue a trio of armed kidnappers who had already shown no compunction about killing anyone who got in their way? Why not just report it to the authorities?"

Steve considered his answer carefully. "At the time, it seemed like a good idea. I mean, the kidnappers were dressed as Bahamian policemen so I couldn't be sure who was involved, or if anyone I told would be able to stop them in time."

Watson nodded. "A very sound analysis, but it still doesn't get to the core of why you did it."

She just stared at Steve, not blinking, waiting for his reply. Somehow, Steve knew he would not be able to 'aw-shucks' his way out of this. He looked away, avoiding that gaze. *Can I even trust her with the truth? The police never found any trace of this woman years ago. Claiming she was murdered members of my family may convince her I'm some sort of nut job.*

"The truth? Two reasons. Engineering the initial escape from the cell was because of Fatima Naziri. Here's a 14-year-old girl whose biggest worry was probably trying to flirt with a boy without getting in trouble with Daddy, and suddenly her world is being shredded. I knew when they grabbed the Nazaris it wasn't a robbery, and I calculated the odds — they weren't good. I was determined to change those in her favor."

Watson nodded. "And the other?"

Steve opened his mouth to speak — and then stopped. His expression became serious, his eyes downcast. His voice was quiet, without the usual glib tone. "The other is because I'd... already made a fatal mistake." He looked back up at Watson. "I should have been the first one down those stairs, not Jason Avant. I already knew the kidnappers were armed and should have known the driver would be as well. I should have caught up with them in time to prevent him from being shot." He looked away. "I miscalculated. And because I did, an innocent man trying to do the right thing died."

Behind him, Steve heard the woman in the hoodie catch her breath. She stood up and approached him. He waited as she stopped next to him and stood there for a few moments. Silently, she sat down next to him at the table, her head still covered.

Watson said gently, "Mr. Tate, you did nothing wrong yesterday. You acted decisively in a time of crisis with great ingenuity and managed to, somehow, prevent the kidnapping. Your file says you've participated in parkour exhibitions around the world, but what you did yesterday went well beyond that. And you succeeded—"

"No, he didn't."

The woman spoke in a flat monotone that still managed to convey a level of disgust toward Steve. He turned to her. "Excuse me?"

She pulled back her hood and turned toward Steve. It was, as he'd surmised, Amy Rogers. There was a smoldering anger behind her gaze, fueled by grief over her loss. "You let the bitch that killed my boyfriend get away."

Steve looked at her, holding back his retort. *You have no idea what you're talking about. And I'm not about to tell you and make you feel even worse than you already do.*

He shook his head. "No, after the explosion, we were both injured, and in the confusion she made her escape. You know that if I could have stopped her, I would have."

Watson looked at Amy, then back at Steve. "Do you still want to?"

"What do you mean?"

"If you had another chance at her, would you take it?"

Steve's heart leaped inside his chest. He didn't know everything about this organization yet, but they had resources. *The chance to go after that bitch, with these people standing behind me? Really?*

The question hung there in the air between them. Steve was aware that it wasn't just Watson looking at him. Williams and the other two security men were watching him as well. But it was Amy's eyes that were the hardest for Steve to handle. Her gaze seemed to bore straight through him as if she examined his entire being and found it lacking. A moment later, she turned back to Watson. "Forget it, Doctor. He's not worth your time."

Steve's eyes narrowed as he looked back at Amy. Yes, she was in pain, and thus lashing out at anyone she could blame. But calling him a coward?

"Look, you've got no idea about me, lady. You may not realize it right now, but there is no one else in the world who understands exactly what you're going through."

He glanced sideways at Watson. "Yeah, Doc. I'm in."

Chapter 7

After a few more minutes discussing where they'd spend the night, the meeting had broken up. Watson swiveled her seat to face forward and was using her tablet to deal with something business related. Amy retreated again to the back row and took a seat. She stared out into the night, lost in her thoughts. Williams also had his tablet out and was talking with someone via a video link; Steve assumed it was about the Naziris and their protection details. This left Steve alone, his mind churning over what he'd learned.

A highly specialized international research foundation with its own security arm? The implications were troubling to Steve. *Who's to say they'd always be the good guys? That sort of power always corrupts. Always.*

Steve needed to talk to his father. Given his history in the aerospace industry, Grey Tate must have crossed paths with Triangle at one time or another. Maybe this was one time he could trust his father's advice.

Steve unbuckled his seat belt and moved forward to sit next to Watson. "Doc, sorry to bother you, but can I make an outside call?"

She looked up from her tablet, touching a control that blacked out the screen before Steve could see what was on it. "Who do want to call?"

"My father. I need to let him know I'm safe."

Watson considered this and then nodded. "I think we can do that for you." She touched a control sequence on her tablet and handed it to him. It was blank except for a telephone handset icon. "Just press that and dial the number — our private satellite will handle the call. The software will give you an option for an audio or a video link as well. Would you like some privacy?"

Steve nodded. Watson looked through her briefcase and extracted a small plastic bag with a set of ear buds. "There's a built-in microphone on the cables. Go ahead and sit in the rear of the cabin. That should give you some privacy. As to what you'll say..." Watson trailed off, waiting for Steve to fill in the blank.

Steve considered what to say. *Honesty is the best policy, for now.* "I was going to tell him what happened and where I'm headed and ask his advice."

All right, so maybe mostly honest.

Watson nodded. "Fair enough. Just keep your upcoming work with Triangle Ops out of the conversation."

Steve moved to the back of the cabin, plugged in the earbuds and brought up the call icon. He chose a video link and entered a number from memory.

6:41 p.m. PDT

Grey's smartphone software pinged twice on his desktop before he acknowledged it. He glanced at the incoming video call ID and activated the call. Steve's face appeared on the screen. "Steve! Are you okay?"

"Yeah, a few scrapes here and there, a road rash from when I had to lay down a motor scooter, but otherwise, I'll live."

"The news channels had a video of the events. It was incredible stuff. You want to tell me what happened?"

"I will, but Dad, you have to know this up front. I found her."

"Who?"

"The woman who killed Mom and Marie! She's the one who was behind the kidnapping and murder here. And damn it, I almost had her. I let her get away again!"

"Steven, slow down! Start at the beginning and tell me everything."

Steve did so, starting from the moment the tour group left the cruise ship through the explosion and

Bennett's getaway. Grey interrupted him a couple of times, clarifying a point here or there, but mostly just listened and let his son tell the story in his own way.

When Steve finished, Grey looked thoughtful. "The death of that young man was regrettable, son. But I don't see how you could have avoided it."

"Come on, Dad; quit blowing smoke up my butt. You've urged me to use my ability to its fullest potential, but I never really tried until now. If I had, maybe I could have seen a way out sooner, one that would have saved all of us."

Grey shook his head, his words careful and measured. "Steve, you're right in that I've urged you use your talent — but not like this. Not so publicly. Doing so is going to put you on the radar of some people who are going to want to know how you did it, and may not ask you politely for that info." He paused for a moment. "Have you considered the possibility that, on some level, perhaps you had feelings for that woman and subconsciously altered your actions to guarantee her safety, rather than choose the poorer odds to try and save both?"

Steve frowned; then his expression shifted to disbelief. "Oh, no you don't. You are *not* going there."

"It's a very plausible scenario, son, given the way you've described how your talent works."

Steve looked away from the screen. His voice sounded small and hollow. "If that's true, Dad, that makes things worse. It means that I killed Jason Avant."

Grey's tone was sharp. "No! This Bennett woman killed him. You just couldn't guarantee that you'd stop her. You did save one life. That's something to be proud of, son. Don't forget that."

Steve looked back over his shoulder at Amy. She was curled up in a ball, asleep, exhausted from the crying. "I don't think his girlfriend would agree, Dad. And right now, I'm not so sure I do either." He looked back at the screen as he rubbed his face. "Dad, if using my Talent to its fullest extent means I can't stop someone like this from hurting other people — if I can't bring them to justice — then really, what good is it? It seems like a waste to me."

Grey nodded. "I understand, Steve. But you said this was the first time you even tried using your Talent in full. There may be things you can do with it you don't know about yet. You need to explore it." He paused. "I assume this ends your time aboard the cruise ship?"

Steve nodded. "Yeah, the *Goddess* sailed without me. They left word they'd ship my personal gear back to Washington when they reach Miami."

"So when will you be coming home? We can set up the shop here and start exploring the extent of your powers." Grey began to frown as the silence grew. "Son, I asked you a question. When are you coming home?"

Steve stared out from the screen, hesitating to answer. "Uh, that's just it, Dad. I'm not. The man that Bennett tried to kidnap is named Naziri. He's some sort of big-shot scientist at an organization called Triangle, and they've—"

Grey's face grew clouded. "Hold on a second. Did you say Triangle?"

"Yeah. They spotted my talent from the videos and—"

"Son, listen carefully. I don't care what it takes. Make an excuse. Say you're sick. Say I'm sick. But do not, *under any circumstance*, walk in there and get involved with that organization."

Steve was surprised at the vehemence in his father's tone. "Whoa, Dad! Stop! First, you don't order me to do anything. You fought that battle a while back, and if you remember, you lost. Second, please explain why the nice people who sprung me from a Bahamian jail are so bad. Especially when, after you had heard I was in trouble, you didn't do anything about it?"

Grey looked exasperated. "Steven, will you at least accept that there might just be, on occasion, some things in this world I know more about that you do? This is one of them. I've dealt with Triangle before. Oh, they're not evil —

at least, not 'take over the world' evil or 'Snidely Whiplash' evil—"

"Snidely who?"

"Before your time. Never mind. But what they are... they're soulless. Tringle sees everything and everyone as assets to be used and then discarded when their usefulness has ended. And they do destroy people. I've seen it."

Steve considered this. "Look, Dad. Maybe you're right about this. But right now, they're my best bet to find this woman and get her. And I am going to get her, Dad. I want to catch her and see her fry, for what she did to Mom, and Marie, and to Jason Avant, too." Grey started to protest, but Steve cut him off. "Look, Dad, I promise I'll keep my eyes open — and you know as well as I do that I can think circles around almost anyone when I need to. I'm committed to doing this one thing and this one thing only with them. After that...well, I'll re-evaluate the situation."

"Steven, you're making a grave mistake—"

Steve cut him off. "Dad, it's late, and I'm not in the mood to argue. I'll be in touch soon. Take care of yourself." He disconnected the call. The screen went blank.

10:03 p.m. EDT

The tablet returned to its home state, awaiting a password. Steve returned it to Watson.

She looked up at him. "So, did you get the answer you wanted?"

He thought for a moment and shrugged. "I'm not sure. But I'm definitely in."

7:06 p.m. PDT

Grey waited until he was sure the connection was broken before he smiled. He opened the right desk drawer, opened the black box and activated the phone inside. He was joined immediately by his colleague, who spoke first. "Well?"

"Just as I'd predicted, my boy's always been contrarian; the second I opposed him, he walked right into Triangle."

"Excellent work. And on the other front?"

Grey sighed. "Yes, there was a spark of something. He felt the tug subconsciously as soon as he met her. It made him protect her in a life or death situation. I guess I was wrong, and you were right."

"Of course I was."

Grey swore he could hear the smug smile on the other end of the call. "Well, don't get your hopes up — there is still a lot of distance between them."

"Oh? How so?"

"Three words: She blames him."

"Yes, the loss of life was unintended and regrettable. We'll see what we can do to change that."

"Fair enough."

"Remember, Grey, why we started this all those years ago. Don't lose sight of that goal."

The call ended. Grey stared at the phone for a few moments, then swiveled around in his seat and looked out the window at the sunset.

Welcome to Triangle, Steven.

11:02 p.m. EDT

They landed just after eleven p.m. at Dulles International Airport. Instead of pulling up to the terminal, the jet taxied to a remote set of hangars. When it parked, two limousines were waiting for them — and no signs of customs or any other government security people. Just more Triangle guards. Steve shook his head. *That's impressive — in its own, scary sort of way.*

He watched Watson and Amy get into one of the limos as he and Williams climbed into the other. They drove off in different directions. A ten-minute ride in silence brought them to the driveway of a Marriott hotel. As the valet opened the door, Williams handed him a package.

"Here's your room key, identification, and a data tablet. When you get in your room, turn on the tablet. You'll receive further instructions at that time. Get your rest; tomorrow will be a very full day."

Steve nodded and stepped out of the limo. It drove away, leaving him in the driveway. Steve glanced around, smiled at the valet, and opened the envelope. Quickly looking inside, he thanked the universe the folks at Triangle had given him cash for a tip. He extracted a couple of bills, handed them to the valet and headed inside.

Minutes later, Steve was in his room, examining his new driver's license and passport. He was starting to get a feel for just how efficient Triangle was. He had agreed to work for them in mid-air between Nassau and Washington, yet these were waiting for him upon arrival, less than an hour later.

He undid the security seal on the data tablet and flipped the power switch. The machine booted up quicker than any device he'd ever seen before. The design was unique — thinner, constructed of some sort of advanced lightweight polymer. The screen image seemed hyper-realistic — almost like 3-D but without any glasses.

Upon boot-up, it immediately connected a video link to some sort of control room, like where you'd launch a spacecraft from. On the back wall was the now ubiquitous Triangle logo. As he watched, a tall, gangly young man in a white lab coat carrying a mug sat down in the swivel chair in front of the screen. As he took a sip, he looked at his screen and froze. A look of panic spread across his face.

Steve mused to himself. *Poor guy. He just realized this is a live connection.*

The young man on the other end was in his late 20's, with curly red hair like Steve's, many freckles, ears that were just a little too large for him and round wire-rimmed glasses. When he spoke, it was with a distinct accent — *British... no, Welsh*, Steve thought.

"Ah. Oh. Right, they said you'd be coming online. Err. Hello! I'm Percy Lewis, on duty controller here at

Triangle Control. And you must be..." Percy looked down to his left off camera, and then glanced back. "Ronald Tate?"

Steve grimaced. "Well, my name is actually Steven Tate — I dropped the Ronald a few months ago. Please, call me Steve."

"Very well, Steve. Welcome to Triangle. I'm filling in tonight, but I'm here to help you as best as I can. We've set up an e-mail account for you; you'll find the icon on your tablet. Your schedule for tomorrow has been sent to you as well. Now, it says here your belongings are still aboard your... cruise ship? I think you'll need some clothing before tomorrow."

"Thanks, if you could just get me a ride to the local Wal-Mart—"

"I'm sorry, but given your current circumstances, that's not possible. But let me see..." Percy bent over and started typing quickly on his keyboard, then reached forward just out of Steve's line of sight and manipulated something. Steve assumed it must be some sort of data terminal, perhaps with a touch screen interface. "Right. We can deliver you a wardrobe of appropriate clothes to wear for the next few days. We need to get your sizes, and you can enter style preferences on your tablet. We'll send an appropriate outfit for you to wear overnight."

"Right. My waist is—"

"That's not necessary, sir. Would you please set the tablet upright via its retractable legs, step into the center of the room and face it?"

Steve did as he was instructed, curious as to why. When he was there, Percy said, "Good, now please hold your arms out to your side, and pivot in a complete circle." Steve again complied. The device emitted a series of tones, almost a hum. When he finished the circle, Percy nodded. "Scan complete. Thank you. Finally, what shoe size are you, sir?"

"Ten and a half."

"Thank you again. Give us two hours and your clothes for tomorrow will be delivered. In the meanwhile, I recommend you enjoy some dinner and take some time to unwind. It was a long flight. If you need to contact me, press the Triangle icon in the upper right corner of the tablet."

"Got it. Uh, Percy, can I also get some workout gear with that clothing? Kind of a daily ritual with me. I had to miss today, and I'd really hate to skip two days in a row. Can you hook me up?"

"Certainly. Those we can draw from stores directly. Just indicate your preferences on the tablet. We'll have a package at your door when you wake up."

"Great! Oh, one last question. Internet access?"

"Of course. Browser icon is on the lower left. You can use that to access your public e-mail account. However, we ask you be circumspect in telling people about your upcoming assignment. When you accept that, you'll have to go Internet dark."

"I understand."

"Then have a good evening, Steve."

The video link terminated and the screen returned to the home image of the Triangle logo rotating slowly in the background atop a picture of the Earth. He noted idly that the terminator line on the globe between sunrise and sunset was accurate for that date and time.

Walking across the room, he picked up the house phone and dialed room service to order dinner — green salad, roasted chicken breast with red potatoes and grilled asparagus, and a crème brûlée for dessert. He hung up the handset, sat on the bed with the tablet and started researching Triangle.

Let's see...originated as the Robinson-Smythe Memorial Lab in 1897. The bequest of Lord Wellesley Robinson-Smythe, in honor of his late son, an adventurer and scientist, Frederick Robinson-Smythe. Specialized in advanced materials development — weapons work during World War I, specifically lightweight engine components for planes.

Shifted to advanced communications research in the mid-1920s. Patented first designs for portable wireless wrist communication devices — whoa, these guys were the inspiration for Dick Tracy's watch? Steve's inner geek was excited over that little snippet of trivia. He double-tapped the image on the screen, and it expanded full-size to show a line drawing from a patent application of a wristband and gauntlet arrangement. The battery was a unique flat design. If it had been built, Steve doubted anyone would have detected it under the typical clothes of the day. *G-man decoder ring spy stuff. Way cool.*

Let's see. Truman and Churchill negotiate a deal at the start of the Cold War. Lab opens a facility outside Washington. Began working with the new Department of Defense on communications projects — hmmm, a lot of it still classified. That smells like command and control. I wonder... Steve pulled up a second window, this time showing public maps of the area. A few moments of searching and he found his answer. *Yeah, these guys are within 10 miles of DARPA. I'll bet they share the same DNA, given their histories.*

Further down the page, Steve notices a link to a story in an old issue of Business Week about the rebranding of the company. The lab now handles both civilian and military work, and in the mid-1970s merged with two other firms — Whorfin/Yoyodyne Propulsion and Aerospace in New Mexico and Cyberdyne Logic Systems in California. The resultant conglomerate became Triangle Labs. They'd dropped the 'Labs' part five years later.

Hmm. Yoyodyne and Cyberdyne. Those names sound familiar... can't remember where, though. I'll look them up later.

Triangle now was a multipath research foundation with few commercial endeavors, save for one pet project. But they did announce discoveries every few months that were then licensed and shared with other companies.

He pulled up the Moody's business report for Triangle. The current CEO was one Reginald Stevenson III. Tall, blonde, handsome, a British adventurer and playboy straight out of the comic books. He'd attempted to fly a hot air balloon across the Atlantic, won a road rally across the Sahara Desert, and was currently financing the first private commercial spacecraft, a venture that was earning him both acclaim and notoriety. Steve pulled up video news accounts about the man, now in his mid-50s, trim and tan, smiling for the camera. He admired the way he handled himself. His idea of sending one Make-a-Wish child and their companion on every flight his space liner took was sheer brilliance.

OK, onto the new boss. Who is Dr. Rhonda Watson? Steve started searching through her biographical data. *Let's see...a dual doctorate in biochemistry and mechanical engineering, taught at Stanford until '03, then...nothing? She literally disappears off the map. Weird. Nothing in her personal life that stands out. So, Dr. Watson is a cipher — or something more.*

There was a knock on the door. Room service had arrived with his dinner. Steve directed the waiter to put it on the table and tipped him nicely. He sat down to enjoy the meal and over the chicken and asparagus, pondered what he'd learned. *Obviously, Triangle was not everything it appeared to be from the public's point of view. Nothing in Triangle's public business portfolio needed someone like Steve. So why all the secrecy?*

Still, somebody had gone to a lot of trouble for Naziri and was willing to kill to get him. That meant something.

Steve decided he didn't have enough data. Maybe tomorrow things would be clearer. He set his consideration of Triangle aside and used the tablet to figure out what clothing he'd get. He finished his dinner, including a couple of glasses of a decent white wine, then took a quick shower and climbed into bed. Within two minutes, he was asleep.

Chapter 8

May 24, 1:27 a.m. EDT

Amy sat alone in her room.

It was an extremely nice room — almost a suite, really, with a sofa, queen-size bed with luxurious mattress, soft lighting, plasma screen TV and more. The type of room that a high-powered executive would stay in, not a college student from a small school.

Amy felt lost in the room. She'd tried the bed once, but immediately stood up and moved to the sofa — the far end of the sofa, as far away from the bed as possible.

Beds that size were for sharing, not for sleeping alone. The closer she got, the heavier the loss of Jason became, filling her, drowning her, making it so she couldn't even breathe.

The sofa seemed a safer choice. Here, she could be distracted enough by concentrating on the task ahead of her. This afternoon in the hospital, coming here seemed like the right thing to do. Amy had just one thing on her mind — revenge. But the time on the plane had cooled her passion from white-hot to red, and with that came her first doubts.

Will I be able to find this woman? And if I do, will I be good enough to beat her? She's a trained killer, cold-blooded, and she doesn't care who gets in her way. How do I become good enough to beat someone without a conscience?

She looked across the room and caught a glimpse of herself reflected in the television. *What if I do become that good? Would I even recognize that Amy?*

Would I want to?

She closed her eyes for a second. At least, that's what she intended. When she was awoken by her cell phone ringing, it startled her. And when she saw daylight peeking around the curtains, she swore softly.

She got up and crossed the six steps to the dresser, glanced at the caller ID, and accepted the call. "This is Amy."

Rose's voice on the other end was full of concern. "And good morning to you, roomie." She paused, as if not sure how to proceed. "It's been two days, Amy. I've been worried sick. You called me, and then you disappeared after all that commotion. Where are you now?"

Rose. Dear God, what do I say to her?

"Rose... I appreciate your concern. But I needed the time and space. I needed to be alone. I just... can't be at ASU. Especially not right after..." She trailed off as thoughts of Jason started to overwhelm her again. *Get a grip, Amelia Jane. Focus. Breathe.*

"Amy, I understand. When my mom was killed by a drunk driver, I know how devastated I felt. Your world crashes in; nothing feels safe. But you won't bring Jason back by hiding from the world."

"I'm not hiding—"

Rose's voice was gentle but still firm. "Honey, yes you are. I know your whole story, remember? You were adopted as a baby. Your parents died in a car crash when you were fifteen, a crash where you were the only survivor. The whole survivor's guilt thing, alone in the world. Living with your grandmother. You buried yourself in athletics and schoolwork, held the world off at arm's length, let no one get close, and found out, somehow, you were different, too. Really, really different. You managed to keep it secret, and figured out a way to use it to help people, for the most part. Then, here, at ASU, somebody else found out found out your secret — me. But for the first time, you realized someone could share and guard your secret, be close to you and be safe. So, you went out, you tried to have a normal life, to be open to possibilities... and just when you were really happy for the first time in God knows how long, that's been taken away from you again — violently, suddenly, right there in front of you."

Rose took a breath. Her voice was quiet and gentle. "I understand, Amy. You think it's your fault. You think, somehow, you're cursed, that if you get close to someone, they are going to get hurt. So now you're planning to retreat back into a cave as fast as you can crawl."

Amy stared at the phone for a few seconds, speechless. She coughed and cleared her throat, stifling another sob. "I'm...I'm really that easy to figure out?"

"Hey, why do you think I took a psych elective last semester? No, silly. I've been your roomie for three years. Or, in other words, I've had three years of 'Amy 101.'" Rose laughed once at her joke on her end of the phone. "But you're trying to change the subject. I know you're hurting, Amy, but you shouldn't be alone."

Amy considered what to tell her friend. *I'll be exposing her to danger if I tell her about this place. But if I don't tell her something, she's just going to keep hounding me and get in the way of what I've got to do—*

"Amy, are you still there?" Rose's voice snapped her out of her reverie.

"Oh, yeah, sorry. Look, Rose, I appreciate the concern. But I'm not alone. I'm at..." She thought fast for a plausible excuse. "At a corporate retreat, here in the Bahamas. The cruise line put me up here, and they're bringing in a grief counselor to work with me. They've really been very attentive, given the circumstances."

Amy hoped her excuse held up to her roommate's scrutiny. But her roommate sounded skeptical. "So, you're all alone with a grief counselor in the lap of luxury? That doesn't make any sense—"

"I didn't say I was alone. The other kidnapping victims are here as well, including that tour guide who let... who let..." She let her grief wash over her and started to cry.

Rose rescued her from the moment. "Amy, it's all right. If they've brought in a grief counselor like you say, that's good. Work with them. They'll help you through this so you can accept what's happened and understand it isn't the end of your world."

Amy gulped back a real sob. "I'm doing that, Rose. But you know it's going to take some time."

"Yeah, I know, hon." Rose paused a moment, sounding hesitant to continue. "I thought you should know. Jason's parents are having a private, family-only memorial tomorrow. He's to be cremated and his ashes scattered over the Atlantic."

"That's appropriate. They didn't know that Jason and I..."

"Yeah." Rose's silence was awkward. "There's going to be a public remembrance, too. Here at ASU. They haven't scheduled it yet, but it'll probably be soon." Rose paused for a moment, presumably waiting for Amy to say something, but she just stood there numb and silent. Finally, Rose added, "Do you think you'll be here for that?"

"Rose...I hate funerals. You know why. I...I don't think I'd be able to handle that, either."

Rose sighed. "Yeah, well, a girl can dream. Seriously, come home soon, roomie. Even if it's just to pack up your stuff so you can start over. But know this, Amy — I don't want to lose you."

Amy smiled wanly. "Don't worry, Rose" she lied. "I'm perfectly safe here. Nothing's going to happen. But I need to get going. I promise I'll be in touch soon. Take care of yourself."

Amy cut off the phone call, and then she stood up and faced the mirror. *You just lied to your only friend in the world. Better make this count, Amelia Jane.* She headed into the bathroom to take a shower and get ready for the day.

6:41 a.m. EDT

Steve was in many ways a creature of habit. Even when his surroundings changed, he tried to stick to his usual morning routine: Up at five a.m., thirty minutes of yoga, then a thirty-minute run, incorporating as many *parkour* elements as he could on the fly. Back for a shower and then a breakfast of yogurt, granola, fruit, and coffee. The normality of the routine, no matter where he was in the world, helped him face the day.

As he sat down to breakfast, he used the tablet to check on the news. He pulled up a Bahamian regional news site and read the accounts of the incident from two days earlier. Surprisingly, the attack was now described as the work of a previously unknown terrorist group. The two false guards had been identified as Somalis; concerns were raised it was the vanguard of a new wave of terrorist attacks.

Give the public has a boogeyman, make them to blame for what happened, right? I'll give it to Triangle — that's efficient.

A little further down, the article mentioned there were no fatalities. That brought Steve up sharply.

Huh? That's wrong.

He started searching through the news archives from the day and found a separate news story on Jason's death buried deep inside one of the Bahamian papers. It hadn't even been picked up by any of the American media websites. Steve's brow furrowed. The story said it was a mugging and robbery gone tragically wrong. It also didn't mention that he'd had a companion. It did say, however, that the perpetrator was seen running from the scene, dodging and weaving through the crowd shortly after that.

That's just perfect. Triangle buried Jason's murder and threw me under the bus in one fell swoop.

Steve started looking for video reports. There was a BBC story about the shooting — but it bundled it in briefly as part of a wave of crimes that day, all committed by this one suspect. Theft, murder, mayhem — this unknown person cut a swath from the water tower to Parliament House.

At least they didn't tie me directly to the bombing, too. And that sketch is generic enough.

Steve ran a search on YouTube to find any raw footage from tourists and got an inkling of just whom he was going to be working for. Every YouTube video that claimed to be from the Nassau chaos came up with a screen stating the file was corrupted. Not blocked, not file-restricted for copyright. Just corrupted and no longer available. Steve whistled softly. *Wow. They managed to spike the event on YouTube? I didn't even think that was possible.* If they had done this, he wondered how they handled other social media that might have been posted.

How did they handle the people involved? I guess a lot of the eyewitness reports could be dismissed as confusion and chaos. But what about someone like...

Steve grew alarmed as he made a connection. He quickly scanned the media reports for a particular name. It wasn't in any of them. He brought up a communication interface and through it, dialed a phone number from memory. It rang once, twice...

"*Celebration Goddess* switchboard. How may I assist you?"

"Hi. Sorry to bother you. Did you make port this morning?"

"Yes, sir. We docked in Miami an hour ago and are completing passenger debarkation. Are you looking for a particular passenger?"

"Can you connect me to the Recreation Services office?"

"Please hold, sir." The line switched to hold music — the Celebration Cruise Line theme song from their commercials, and news of their new ship, launching next year. It cut off abruptly as a male voice came on the line. "Recreation Services. How may I assist you?"

"Dave? Is that you? It's Steve Tate."

"Steve! Are you okay? We'd heard you were injured in the bombing."

"Yeah, a bit scraped up, but I'm good."

"Well, that's good to hear. Steve, things are a bit crazy here, so I need to—"

Steve stopped him. "Dave, listen. I need to get in touch with Regina. Do you know where she is?"

Dave got very quiet. "I guess they wouldn't have told you. Regina was severely injured in the explosion. She... she didn't make it."

Steve stared at the phone. After a moment, Dave's sounded concerned. "Steve?"

"Uh, yeah, Dave. Are you sure about that?"

Dave sounded indignant. "Yes, I'm sure. Look, I should go. Steve, you take care, okay?" The phone line disconnected.

Steve furrowed his brow. *Regina was heading to the police office at the foot of the water tower to call for an ambulance right after the shooting. She was nowhere near the car bomb when it went off.* He went back to the news reports, looking through the stories. The words stared back at him again.

No one from the cruise ship listed as injured or killed.

He stood up and walked to the window. As he stared out at the woods beyond, his mind was churning. *Then where's Regina? For that matter, what about the Naziris and the kidnapping? What about the Rosen family?*

Steve felt a chill roll down his spine.

The tablet chimed, and a message window popped up on the screen. *Your limo is waiting at the lobby entrance. – R. Watson.*

Steve looked over at the outfit he'd ordered — khaki slacks, a navy blue knit shirt and black Nike running shoes — and decided it was time to get some answers. He walked over and tapped the screen to acknowledge the message. Moments later, he was changed and headed out of the room.

7:29 a.m. EDT

Amy stared out the window as the Virginia countryside rolled by. She had been greeted by Mitchell Williams, who was now dressed in a black suit and tie and Ray-Ban sunglasses. *Great, I'm joining the MIB*, she mused, as she climbed into the limo. She felt underdressed next to him, in her jeans, sky-blue Converse All Stars and a Rascal Flatts T-shirt they had sent over. *I still can't believe they even had clothes like these in their catalog.* Still, clothes that looked like they came right out of her own closet (only less wrinkled) helped her feel a little more normal this morning. And right now, she needed a little more normal.

During the ride, Williams watched Amy carefully, never saying a word. *Not sure if I'm an asset or a threat, are you?* She thought glumly. *That's probably fair. Right now, I'm not sure myself.*

The limo crossed under a freeway and turned onto a two-lane road. On the left was an 8-foot-high stone wall. *Somebody really likes their privacy.* A few minutes later, the limo turned into a wide driveway with a modest sign proclaiming it the home of Triangle.

Williams stirred. "We're here, Ms. Rogers."

The limo rolled up to a guard shack, and a pleasant-looking older security officer walked over to the window. Williams lowered it. "Good morning, sir. IDs, please." Williams flashed his security credentials while Amy fished out her new driver's license from her purse.

"Thank you, sir. Dr. Watson passed through five minutes ago and left word for you to proceed to the ground floor secure conference room. Oh, and welcome to Triangle, Ms. Rogers."

Williams grunted in acknowledgment and raised the window. A tall gate, made of a metal lattice, rolled sideways, and the limo started through. Amy was surprised at the size of it. *Just what are they trying to keep out — or keep in?*

The grounds looked like a championship golf course — rolling green lawns with trees and paths crossing the occasional stream or pond. After a couple of minutes, they came to a T-intersection. The limo turned left and pulled in front of their destination.

Williams exited the limo first and held the door open for Amy. She stepped out, looked up, and stopped in awe. The complex was five stories tall and shaped like the curve of a smile. The wings to the left and right curved away from her in both directions for the length of two football fields. The face of the building was covered with a reflective glass that shimmered like a bronze mirror. The clouds and sun behind her were reflected off the surface, and where the sun hit the glass, the effect was breathtaking.

Williams waited a moment, then said, "This way, Ms. Rogers."

Probably used to newbies gawking when they arrive, she thought as she followed him up a wide, shallow ramp to the entrance. As they reached the doors a sensor activated and they slid open. They passed through a second set of doors and into the main lobby.

The lobby itself seemed as wide as a football field, but it made great use of that space. The back wall, all five stories of it, curved from window to window. It was a single large high definition display screen — probably the largest in the world. It showed a blue rippling pattern that reminded Amy of sunlight reflecting off the water. Periodically, large display windows would appear, displaying three-story-tall images of famous pieces of art. Benches were set against the glass facade behind her, so one could sit and watch the display. It was hypnotic and tranquil.

Williams was oblivious to it. He'd proceeded to a circular desk of black granite in the center of the lobby, where he signed the two of them into the building. He turned and again said, "This way, Ms. Rogers." He walked toward a spot midway along the base of the right curve of the wall. A set of inset doors, hidden until that moment, slid open for him. Amy hurried over to catch up with him.

The corridor beyond was luxury office space — indirect lighting, sounds dampened by the thick carpet, furnishings of dark wood and brass. The space was all about wealth and power and the confidence to show it tastefully. They walked past three doors on each side of the hallway. Amy noticed there were no doorknobs anywhere;

instead, a small black plate was installed on the wall next to each door.

At the end of the hall, they stopped in front of a pair of solid French doors. Williams stepped to the right and placed his hand on the black wall pad. A bar of light appeared on the pad and quickly scrolled up and down. He stepped back as a warm contralto voice from out of nowhere said, "Good morning, Mr. Williams."

Amy jumped back, startled, and looked around for the source of the voice. It seemed to come from everywhere at once. Williams grinned slightly. "Good morning, Savannah. I have Ms. Rogers here, to see Dr. Watson."

"Yes, I see that, Mr. Williams. Identity confirmed. They're expecting you inside. Please proceed."

Williams nodded. The two halves of the door slid into the frame on each side, revealing a conference room that could easily seat 30 people. Williams walked in, and Amy followed. They were greeted by Dr. Watson, who was already seated at the table.

Steve Tate walked over from a coffee service set on the far side of the room. He had a half-eaten pastry in one hand, and a cup of coffee in the other. He grinned when he saw Amy and put the pastry down on the conference table. In an overly polite manner, he said, "Good morning, Miss Rogers. Enjoy your beauty sleep?"

Jerk.

Amy decided again that she really didn't like this guy and walked away with a disgusted shake of her head. She sat down in a seat opposite Dr. Watson. "So, what's this meeting about?"

A clipped Oxfordian accent came from the head of the table. "This meeting is about what we can all do to help save the world, Miss Rogers." The high-backed chair swiveled around, and a tall, thin, blond Englishman with a goatee and mustache looked at her over steepled fingers.

Amy caught a glimpse of Steve. He looked absolutely shocked.

"Allow me to introduce myself. I am Reginald Stevenson III. Welcome to Triangle."

Chapter 9

8:01 a.m. EDT

Steve worked hard not to look surprised when the chair swiveled around, but he doubted he was succeeding. *The Stevenson, the actual man who runs Triangle, here, in the room, meeting with us? Capital-H 'hinky' here.*

He glanced over at Amy. *Smooth move, Tate. First chance to talk with her in a semi-social setting since the Bahamas and what do I say? Beauty sleep? What the heck was I thinking?* She was ignoring him now, focused intensely on Stevenson.

Steve turned backed and realized his host was talking about him. He tuned back into the conversation.

"—you did in Nassau was extraordinary, Mr. Tate. I'm not just being complementary." Stevenson picked up his own tablet and tapped a couple of controls. The painting behind him faded out of existence — *ultra-high definition monitor*, Steve realized — and displayed a tourist video of the events in Nassau, taken from the water tower. He saw his leap, the gun go off, the three of them hitting the ground. He glanced over at Amy, who stared at the screen, her jaw set as she relived the moment.

The van drove away, and Steve watched as his image took off down the hill around the corner; the crowd identified him as the shooter and tried to catch him. He engaged in his series of free-running maneuvers to escape them.

Without thinking, Steve activated his Talent and time slowed to a halt in the conference room. He studied the screen carefully, as this perspective gave him a different overview of the entire scene. As Steve reran his calculations and examined the path he took compared against other the possible options available to him, he spotted three new variations. A closer look showed they wouldn't have been any more efficient. *No, I made the right choices.* Satisfied, Steve dropped back into real time.

Stevenson stopped the video. "Did you see that, Doctor?"

Steve noticed Watson was observing him, not the screen. "I did. Steven, what did you just do?"

Steve glanced around the room. Everyone was suddenly staring at him.

Busted.

He cleared his throat. "Umm, I was... that is... I was reevaluating the path I took through the crowd, to see in retrospect if the choices I'd made in real time were the most efficient. I was in a bit of a rush at the moment, and bystanders were affected by what I did, even if it the only thing I hurt was their pride."

Stevenson rewound the video, placed a timer on the screen, and restarted it. It played out, showing that Steve had gone from the shooting site to the Queen's Staircase in fifty-seven seconds. Stevenson nodded, "That, lad, was impressive. More than you realize."

Steve frowned. "I admit, I pulled off a couple of crazy maneuvers in there, but nothing an elite level free-runner couldn't handle."

Stevenson grinned. "Watson, care to elaborate?"

Watson nodded and tapped a control on her tablet. The display broke into a series of video windows, showing a similar scene — people running on Fincastle Hill. "Yesterday, we had an operative start at the location of the shooting and run in a straight line through a dense crowd as quickly as possible to the stairs, at various times during the day when the attractions were open. No detours, no zigzagging, no jumping. Fastest possible route: One minute, twenty-five seconds."

"We then had our computers analyze the footage of your run, and try to duplicate it for our training facility downstairs. Per their analysis, the best possible time using your moves in that crowd would be one minute, ten seconds."

Steve shrugged. "Different times, crowd reaction, et cetera. There are a lot of factors to consider—"

"Oh, yes, we're aware. The simulation took seven hours and a team of programmers and scientists to prepare."

Stevenson looked at him pointedly. "Whereas you, Mr. Tate, did it alone, on the fly, in real time, thirteen seconds faster than the best-case the computer or experts could devise."

Steve saw Amy looking at him, a curious expression on her face. "Look, I just tried to do the right thing and stop a murderer—"

Stevenson leaned in. "Mr. Tate, it's not what you did. We're all grateful you chose to intervene. Much more so than you know. But how you did so was uncanny. Tell me, have you ever heard of hyperkinesthesis?"

Steve froze in place. *They know. I'm not sure how, but damn it, they figured this out. He glanced from Stevenson to Watson. Well, I'll be damned if I'll give my secret up to anyone that easily.*

Steve took a deep breath and answered cautiously. "Yeah. I've heard of it. There was an article in a runner's journal, something about the theory where you are hyper-aware of all the factors in your environment, and can process them in such a way that your physical actions can produce the exact desired results." He looked around the room for a moment and then decided to continue. "It's, um, it's also rumored that someone with an ability like that could quickly evaluate and start a chain of events using the interaction of objects in their environment to also produce the same thing."

Amy stared at him in disbelief. "It's not a theory, is it? You can actually do those things?"

Steve put his hands up in front of him. "Hey, now, I'm not admitting to—"

Amy frowned. "Don't deny it. You are too this hyper-whatever it is. If you could change events..." Her voice trailed off for a second. Then her face clouded with anger, and her voice became strident. She stood up and slammed the table in front of her. "You could have stopped them all. You could have changed things! He didn't have to die. You son of a bitch!"

Steve stood up and yelled back. "I already did!" change things!"

Amy stopped, breathing heavily. The silence in the room hung between them. After a moment, Watson looked at him and asked quietly, "What do you mean, Mr. Tate?"

Steve brushed his hands back through his red hair and turned around. Closing his eyes, he swore softly once to himself, and then looked out the window. "When I reached the bottom of the steps in the fort and came out of the gate, Amy and Jason were sprinting and had reached the curb to stop the van." He closed his eyes again, and in his mind replayed the scenes and his calculations. His face became emotionless, but his voice was still thick with pain. He turned back and looked directly at Amy. "I saw the gun already coming up, and looked for a solution. Time stopped, and what I saw was an 85% chance that both of you were going to be killed. I chose the one option where there was a chance you survived."

Amy stared at Steve. Her voice was shaky. "You... you saved my life?"

He paused. "No. I tried to save both your lives. The bullets... the bullets were supposed to hit me." Steve sat down, deflated. "Something went wrong. I still don't understand what. Maybe I wasn't fast enough..."

Dr. Watson glanced at Stevenson. "I am sure you tried your best, Mr. Tate."

Amy was just staring at him. Her mouth was moving, as if she was trying to say something, but no words came out.

Stevenson cleared his throat. "You've never told anyone about this ability before, have you, Mr. Tate?"

Steve shook his head. "No. I'd...use parts of it at a time. But until two days ago, I'd never even tried. Not at full strength like that" He took a deep breath and blew it out slowly. "Look, you don't know the circumstances of how this showed up. Let's just say I wish I'd never found it. Now all I want is to be normal, you know? You saw how people reacted out there when I tried to stop Bennett. Hell, I see what happens when people realize I'm the smartest guy in the room and can think circles around them–and that isn't even related to my Talent. I'm just a really smart guy. No, if folks figure out I can manipulate cause and effect, they'll start treating me like some sort of freak. Or worse, start looking for torches and pitchforks. Occasionally, I slip up. Like I just did. That's when I move on."

He looked at Stevenson. "My father thinks I'm a flake because I never stay in one spot. He doesn't understand that I need to move just to stay safe. The irony is that he's the only one I've told about my Talent. He's always bugging me to use it a lot more. But I never wanted it. The cost was too high."

Stevenson nodded. "Mr. Tate, I believe we can help you. Triangle does many things and could find a place for an asset like you. We've been an advanced R&D lab, first for His Majesty's government during World War II. Now, we've been here in Virginia since the start of the cold war. We develop a lot of technology as an offshoot of our Red Labs."

"Red Labs? What's that?"

Stevenson nodded to Mitchell, who went to the door and pressed a control. A yellow banner lit up across it with two words on it – SECURED COMPARTMENTALIZED. Mitchell nodded back at Stevenson.

"What you're about to hear is not just highly classified. Many senior members of your own government don't even know of its existence. The founders of this organization determined that as technology advanced, the ways it could be misused would advance as well. They knew that given time and imagination, people who wanted to would find the means to unleash unspeakable harm on others. Why? For profit, for power, to right some imagined ideological wrong. In a few cases, just for the sheer fun of it. Those are the ones that concern us the most — psychopaths with unlimited power."

Amy and Steve glanced at each other uneasily. Steve spoke up. "So, cue the mad scientist vibe. I get it. But what does that have to do with your Red Labs?"

Stevenson looked over at Watson. She continued the briefing. "At Triangle, our philosophy is that the best defense against such threats is to be proactive rather than reactive. We do this in two ways. First, we identify, through scientific and behavioral analysis, likely targets that could develop such antisocial behavior and intervene early enough to prevent them from reaching a point where they could truly cause harm."

Steve smirked. "Yeah? Looking at the world over the last two decades, I've got to ask — how's that working for you?"

Dr. Watson replied. "Surprisingly well."

Steve looked at her earnest expression. *She really means that*, he realized with surprise. *Just how bad might things be if these guys hadn't intervened?*

Amy asked, "What's the second way?"

Stevenson smiled. "Simple. We hire our own mad scientists."

The screen image shifted to show a secure military-style facility in the middle of a desert. Steve looked incredulous. "You guys are Area 51?"

Stevenson chuckled. "No. You're looking at Triangle's New Mexico facility. Ostensibly, they still do there what we originally did a century ago — materials testing on new metal alloys and the like, evaluating them for use in future military projects. However, that's just the top floor." He touched his tablet, and the image shifted to a three-dimensional cutaway of the base. "As you can see, we've built extensively underground. The basement is where the real fun happens. That's where Red Labs is located."

Amy looked at the design. "You went to a lot of trouble to hide it. Why?"

"Because that's where we're creating doomsday every day."

Steve did a double take. "Say what?"

"Red Labs works every day to imagine and create worst-case scenarios. Pocket nuclear bombs. Weaponized custom viruses. Attacks on data infrastructure. Things like that."

Steve smirked. "Right. And next, you'll be telling me that you have plans for zombies and alien invasions in there." He chuckled and looked at Stevenson and Watson. They weren't laughing. In fact, they looked deadly serious.

"Wait. You *really do* have plans for zombies in there?"

Watson continued as the screen shifted to images of things that seemed to come from horror movies. "Red Labs team members try to imagine the worst possible things that could happen. Then we develop the systems and technology needed to create the specific chaos and mayhem their scenarios require."

"This is going to sound like a really stupid question — but, why?"

Williams spoke up from the far end of the table for the first time. "To stop it."

Watson nodded. "If you know how something can happen, you can then reverse engineer the technology and techniques needed to prevent it. Make sure raw materials or components are always in short supply or difficult to acquire, or have the parts on hand that could build a device to neutralize that type of threat. Ideas like that."

Steve leaned back, still trying to wrap his mind around the concept. "Wow. Okay. So, if I believed any of this — which, I've got to tell you, I'm really not sure I do at this point — how often would you even need to intervene?"

Watson looked at Williams and nodded. Williams replied. "Last year, Triangle Ops was called on to stop twenty-seven different events at what we call Stage Four — within two days of causing significant damage or loss of life. Nine of them directly related to Red Lab related scenarios."

Amy looked stunned. "Tw-twenty-seven? That's, like, every other week. Who are these bad guys?"

Stevenson looked at her. "As I said before, it varies. Foreign governments, corporations whose leaders forget their place in the world, terrorist factions, and, of course, the occasional megalomaniacal psychopath. There seem to be enough bad people to go around."

Amy put her hands on the table in front of her. "All right, you've convinced me. There's some sort of shadow war going on out there, and we need something like this. But how do you keep people from finding out about it?"

Stevenson leaned back in his chair, fingers steepled in front of him. "I'm afraid that's still classified. Let's just say we can be very...persuasive."

Steve thought about what he'd seen so far, how they had obviously manipulated the press and the government over the events in Nassau. That's probably an understatement. "I'm sure. But, again, how does this involve us?"

Williams came to the front of the room. The image on the screen shifted to a pair of pictures. "You two were in the wrong place at the wrong time. The targets were Dr. Rafiz Hamid Naziri, and his daughter, Fatima. Dr. Naziri is one of our leading scientists at Red Labs. We believe the attack was an attempt to force the doctor to build something based on his current project there. You got in the way and foiled the kidnapping."

Steve smirked again. "What kidnapping?"

Amy looked at him, confused. "What do you mean?"

Steve replied, "Well, all the news reports about the incident, as well as the official Bahamian government statements, paint this as a terrorist attack on American citizens in a foreign port. I believe they say it's a new Islamic extremist group." He looked at Williams. "Convenient boogeyman, right?"

Williams glanced at Stevenson and Watson. "We thought it best to steer attention away from Dr. Naziri and his daughter, rather than have the media speculate as to why someone would want him."

Steve nodded, but his tone was caustic. "Sure, that makes sense. Even spinning Jason Avant's death as an unrelated robbery works, too. Oh, by the way, nice job planting the story that makes me the prime suspect in his murder. Although the sketch really doesn't do me justice."

Amy looked at him, surprised. "They're blaming you? How could they do that?"

"Ask our friends here, the ones who want our help. Oh, and that was a nice touch, after letting the real murderer get away and disappear. After all, you had your scapegoat. But you have other problems — you left holes in your stories. What about Regina Folkes? And what happened to the Rosen family?"

Amy's eyes grew wide. "Oh, my God, I'd forgotten all about the Rosens and their kids! You mean they aren't all right?"

Steve shrugged. "I haven't a clue. They're not mentioned in any news coverage, and all the private video from that day has been spiked online — your doing as well, I presume. And when I called the ship, I'm told Regina was somehow injured in the explosion and isn't expected to live." He stood up and leaned forward on the table. "Except *I know* she went to get medical assistance for Jason before I left Fort Fincastle, and unless she grew wings, no way she could have beaten me down to the square..."

Steve's voice trailed off. Suddenly he looked over at Amy and broke into a wide grin. "Oh. Oh! It's so obvious — right there in front of me." He turned away toward the window and started laughing. "Now this all starts making sense. Wow, I am so stupid sometimes!"

Amy smirked at him. "So much for you being the smartest person in the room, hotshot."

Steve wheeled around and leaned in on the table, directly across from her. "Really, Princess? I'm sorry, but you and I share a lot more than just tragic backstories, don't we? I'm not the only one in the room with an extra ace up my sleeve, am I? Care to play show and tell?"

Amy looked at him defiantly for a moment, then turned away and settled back into her chair, arms crossed, avoiding his gaze. "Not right now, no."

Stevenson looked at them. "Mr. Tate, I assure you, the Rosen family is fine. They were unaware of the shooting until they were rescued by authorities and returned to the ship. We casually inquired as to what they saw regarding your Talent. They thought you were clever in figuring out about old mortar."

Steve looked at him, his eyes narrowing. "And Regina?"

"Miss Folkes is also fine. As soon as you... displayed your abilities in a positive manner, she moved on to her next assignment. The confusion of the events served as a perfect way to cover her identity."

Steve looked at the Englishman. "Of course. Regina works for you. She was on the *Goddess* because of me?"

Watson nodded. "As we noted, when someone with an extraordinary ability and a particular set of... behaviors outside the norm—"

Amy snickered at that. Steve glared at her.

Watson continued. "As I was saying, when someone fits our profile, we evaluate them. That often requires an operative on the ground."

"Just how long have you been studying me on the ground?"

Williams spoke up from the corner. "Six months."

Steve whistled softly. "You had someone in Nice?"

Watson nodded. "Snohomish, too. He jumped regularly at your school."

Amy started to snicker again, but then Williams turned to her. "And we've had someone monitoring Ms. Rogers at college for twelve months as well."

The smile on Amy's face disappeared like a bargain item at a Black Friday sale - there one second, then replaced by something empty and bitter. Steve watched her and started to chuckle. "Busted, huh?" He turned back to Watson. "Look, you folks know I'm a Talent. You made me admit it in front of her. Now you've just all but admitted she must be some sort of Talent." No one said anything. "Oh, come on, I saw what you did in Nassau. You ripped the door of a van next to me! Don't you think it's time I'm in on the joke?" He looked pointedly at Amy. "Or would you rather just have them tell me, Princess?"

Stevenson and Watson glanced at each other, then turned to Amy. After a moment, she crossed her arms and said "Fine! Go ahead." She avoided eye contact as she swiveled her chair away from Steve.

Watson looked at him directly. "Ms. Rogers seems to store and amplify kinetic energy, then retrieve it on demand."

Steve considered that for a moment. "So she's what, the human equivalent of a super ball?"

There was a small bark of outrage from Amy as she swiveled her chair back around.

Watson quickly intervened. "In a broad sense, but that's really not how it works so I wouldn't go around thinking of her that way."

"Not if you want to have all your teeth after you wake up." Amy glared at him. Steve narrowed his eyes and returned the stare, not backing down from the challenge.

Stevenson raised his voice. "That's enough out of you two! Suffice it to say, you're both possess unique Talents, and are deeply motivated to find this woman." The screen image dissolved into a passport photo of Karen Bennett.

Williams referenced his tablet. "Her real name is Hannah Callahan. We don't have a lot on her. Public records show she was born in the Detroit area, studied medicine, moved to Portland and was living an ordinary life — married, two kids, house in the suburbs, SUV, mortgage, RN at a hospital. But thirteen years ago, something happened. She divorced her husband, and with the kids in the back seat, appeared to commit suicide by driving her car off the Astoria Bridge over the Columbia River. When the car was finally fished out of the river, the kids' bodies were recovered. She never was. It was assumed her body washed out to sea."

The screen changed, showing a split of four security camera images of Callahan in different environs.

"Four years ago, her image began to show up in the intelligence around high-profile assassinations in South America and Europe. Interpol has code-named her 'Ghost.' Here, there, then nowhere. It took two years of sifting to find this." The two images of the old and new Callahan came up side by side.

Steve looked at them, committing them to memory.

"Uh..."

Williams looked at Steve. "Yes, Mr. Tate? Something on your mind?"

"Callahan's been active longer than four years ago."

Williams looked at Watson, who raised an eyebrow. "How do you know this?"

"I saw her walk away from the scene of a murder five years ago."

Williams frowned. "There's was no evidence of her being active at that time—"

"Trust me on this. She was there. I know."

"Who was her target?"

"Target? No clue. But as for her victims..." Steve took a deep breath. "Marie and Rose Tate."

Amy looked at Steve in shock. The room was silent for a moment. Stevenson steepled his fingers and looked down at the table. "Your sister and mother. So, the real reason you pursued her in Nassau?"

Steve nodded. "One of them. The woman's a cold-blooded killer and needs to be stopped. I almost had her this time."

Williams nodded in agreement. "Nassau was the first time she's even come close to being caught. She typically kills any witnesses, yet you two managed to disarm her before she made it back to her yacht." He looked directly at Amy.

Amy glanced over at Steve, then back to the screen. "But this doesn't make sense. She's an assassin. What did this woman want with Naziri?"

Steve spoke up. "She was hired to do a job for someone else, right?"

Stevenson nodded. "Indeed."

"Great. Add ruthless mercenary to her resumé. It was probably payment on delivery. Get Naziri, use his daughter as leverage to spill his secrets, then dispose of the two of them, probably at sea. Until we threw a stick in the spokes." Steve glanced at Watson for a moment and turned to Williams. "On board ship, she used the name Bennett, traveling with someone posing as her husband. Both took the tour that morning. He seemed nervous, as I remember."

Williams nodded. The image changed. "The passport read Charles Timothy Bennett. But the fingerprints came back Nathan Walling, out of Miami. Small-time crook. Did a five year stretch at Everglades Prison in Florida on a burglary charge, released early this year. No idea how he hooked up with Callahan."

The image shifted again. It was the remains of a body. The sharks had eaten well. "What's left of him washed ashore near Key Largo last night. As I said, no witnesses."

Stevenson looked at the two recruits. "Triangle Ops is always looking for people with specialized skills to work with us. Your actions in Nassau show you can do the job. Plus, you both want this woman, almost as badly as I do. And your unique abilities make it, well, difficult for you to blend in outside. Our organization can help keep you hidden, keep you safe. So, will you join us, become part of Triangle, and stop this woman?"

Amy looked at Steve, narrowed her eyes, and nodded. "I don't know if I want to do this forever. But if it means catching that bitch and making her pay, then I'm definitely in."

Steve shrugged. "You folks recruited me. I'm flattered. And honestly, I could use your tools. But I don't appreciate being turned into a murder suspect. I want that cleared up immediately. Understood?"

Stevenson nodded. "I will personally see your name is cleared before the day is over, Mr. Tate. Having you wanted for murder would make it difficult for you to be effective as an operative." He stood and faced the two of them. "Mr. Williams will take you to our Headquarters facility and get your training started. Welcome aboard, and good hunting."

Chapter 10

Stevenson and Watson exited the conference room, leaving Williams behind. He waited at the wall screen. Steve grinned as he turned to Amy. "Let's go save the world, shall we?"

Amy groaned. "Great. Just perfect."

Steve ignored her and turned to Williams. "So, do we need to go back to the hotel? Are we flying somewhere secret?"

Williams sighed, shook his head, then turned and pressed a hidden control on the wall screen behind him. The screen slid aside, revealing a hidden corridor. It had black walls, a black tile floor, and indirect lighting at both the floor and ceiling levels. "Follow me." He entered, expecting them to be right behind them.

As Steve and Amy walked down the corridor, he looked over at her. "Is there a problem, Princess?"

She stared straight ahead. "First, don't ever call me Princess again. Not if you want to keep that pretty boy smile afterward. Second, in case you hadn't noticed, this is serious. So, will you kindly stop goofing around?"

Steve shrugged. "Well, if I can't call you Prin—"

Amy glared at him, and Steve put his hands up. "All right, all right. If I can't call you that, what should I call you?"

"Call me Rogers."

Steve shook his head. "Rogers? Nah. Way too formal. I hate being called 'Tate.' I go by Steve, or Steven if you must be formal. Can I call you Amy? It's how you introduced yourself on the cruise ship, after all."

"That was a different time. I'm a different person now."

"Suit yourself. But you're still way too cute to be just a 'Rogers.'"

They reached the end of the corridor. There was a tall marble desk, almost like a podium, on the left. Centered on the opposite wall was another pair of doors with one of those ubiquitous black pads to the right. Williams pressed his hand to the pad, which scanned him. "Good morning again, Savannah."

"Good morning, Mr. Williams."

Williams turned to Amy and Steve. "Savannah is the advanced AI that runs the facility," he explained. He looked back at the podium. "Savannah, we have two new agents. Please print and ID them into the system now. Authorization Williams four-two-two-nine."

"Authorization confirmed. Good morning, Agent Rogers, Agent Tate. Welcome to Triangle Ops. I am Savannah, and I am here to assist you. Who shall go first?"

Amy and Steve glanced at each other. Steve bowed slightly. "Ladies first, by all mean. My mother raised me to be chivalrous."

Amy raised an eyebrow. "Really. Too bad she stopped when you were four." She stepped forward. "All right, Savannah, what do I do?"

"Relax, Ms. Rogers. My sensors indicate your heart rate is slightly elevated. This process is painless and will only take a few moments. First, place your hands, palms down on the display as indicated." The top of the podium lit up, showing the silhouette of two hands. Amy walked over and placed hers atop them.

"Excellent. Please hold still." A bar of light appeared beneath each hand and moved from fingertips to the base of her palms and back again, twice. "Scan complete. Proceeding to step two."

A device that looked like a pair of high-tech binoculars emerged from a panel at the top of the podium. "Please take the visual probe and look through it." Amy picked up the device and placed it to her eyes. "Thank you. Are you wearing any corrective lenses?"

"No."

"Again, thank you. Please hold the device still and look through it. You will see a bright light. Try not to react to it."

"Thanks for the warning," Amy muttered.

"Testing in three, two, one, mark." The light inside the device grew intense, but not blinding, and it was over in a few moments.

"Thank you. Please return the device to its holder. Proceeding to step three. Voiceprint. Please step up to the podium, and when indicated, state your full name and read the sentence displayed."

She stepped forward. The display changed, showing the sentence and a ten-second countdown. When the counter reached zero, the word RECORDING appeared in red.

"My name is Amelia Jane Rogers. Now is the time for all good people to come to the aid of their fellow man."

When she hit the last word, there was a chime and the recording indicator went off.

"Thank you, Miss Rogers. How would you prefer I address you?"

She looked at Steve and frowned. "You can call me Amy, Savannah." She looked over at Steve. "But, only you."

"Thank you, Amy. I look forward to working with you. Mr. Tate, it is your turn."

Steve was chuckling as Amy moved back to where he was standing. "Amelia Jane? Somebody have a Jane Austen fetish in your family?"

"Oh, knock it off."

"Whatever you say, A.J." He smirked as he walked past her to the podium.

She glared at him and said sharply, "Don't you ever call me that!"

Steve went through the series of steps without incident until the voice recognition phase. As he finished, the recording light went out, but the panel turned red, and a loud buzz sounded. "I am sorry, Mr. Tate, but there is an error. Your name does not match."

Williams looked at him in surprise. "Savannah, what do you mean, his name doesn't match?"

"Mr. Tate's full legal name is Ronald Steven Tate."

Williams' eyebrow rose at this. Steve smiled ruefully. *Man, is anybody ever going to get the memo on this?*

"Savannah, please check the Lexus database, legal filings for Snohomish County, Washington for November last year." He turned to Williams and shrugged. "I had it changed legally."

"Savannah?"

"The information is correct. There is such a document on file. I have amended Mr. Tate's personnel record to his correct legal name of Steven Tate. Voiceprint accepted. Welcome, Mr. Tate."

"Please, Savannah, call me Steve. I have a feeling we're going to be great friends."

"Thank you, Steve."

He grinned at Williams and said, "Lead on, sir."

Williams' left eyebrow rose once more as he turned and touched the hand plate again. The doors opened showing the interior of an elevator. They entered, and turned around facing the door. Williams said, "Level two."

The doors closed and the elevator started to descend smoothly and rapidly. Steve leaned over to Amy and in a quiet voice said, "Definitely a theme going on with all these underground lairs."

Amy just sighed in disgust and shook her head. The indicator above the door changed to a numeral '2'. The doors opened, and they entered Triangle's Operations Headquarters Base.

The hub corridors were circular, like a large tunnel. The walls on both sides arched up and met overhead. It curved gradually out of sight thirty yards away in either direction. There were circular openings along the corridor. According to the diagram in the elevator, there were concentric hub corridors on each of the five underground level

Steve was grinning from ear to ear. "Oh, man! I can't wait to get hold of a map to this anthill. Built during the cold war, I'll bet — that'd explain the retro sci-fi design. Everyone wanted to be on Star Trek, I guess."

The elevator was located on the inner side of the hub. Williams turned left and started around the circular corridor, then turned right at the first outward branch corridor. Steve noticed it was painted a deeper shade of blue than the inner hub corridor. *I wonder why — maybe for navigation?* he speculated.

They approached a door in the left wall which slid out of their way automatically. They walked into a room that looked like it shared DNA with the workshop in Steve's hangar back home — neat, organized workbenches, modern shop equipment, electronics gear and parts storage containers. Waiting for them were three men. In the center of the room was a portly African-American man in a white lab coat at a workbench with two stools. Two others in white knit shirts and khaki pants were seated at a table in the corner, chatting quietly. Their shirts had the Triangle logo embroidered in blue on the sleeves. They stood up and walked over to the table.

Williams turned and indicated the gentleman in the lab coat. "This is Dr. Quincey. He's head of the Operations Support division — the tools of the trade, so to speak. And this is—"

Steve interrupted him as he stepped forward to shake hands with one of the gentlemen in the white shirts. "Percy! Nice to see you in person. So, what's going—?"

Williams cleared his throat. "As I was saying, this is Percy Lewis and Ethan Nowitzki. They will be your controllers."

Amy raised one eyebrow. "Controllers? I'm not sure I like the sound of that."

Percy crossed over to Amy's side. "Oh, not to worry, Miss Rogers. It's nothing quite as sinister-sounding as all that. Dr. Quincey can explain it to you."

Steve smiled. "See, A.J., nothing to worry about."

Amy turned on him sharply. "I said don't call me that!"

Steve shrugged and moved over to the table. "So, Dr. Quincey. 'Tools of the trade,' huh? Does that mean you're called 'Q'? Is the workshop here 'Q-Branch'?" Steve was grinning as he looked around.

Quincey had a shock of gray hair and a large bushy mustache that made him look like a walrus when he frowned. Steve thought he looked distinctly walrus-like right then as he shook his head — specifically, a bull about to attack. "No, they don't, and neither will you. Now sit down, shut up and pay attention, or I'll have to show you just how effective some of my gadgets are at dealing with immature people."

Steve stopped, gulped once, and sat down. "Yes, sir."

Williams smiled slightly. "Looks like you have them well in hand, Doctor." He turned to Amy and Steve. "Get settled in. I'll contact you with instructions for your first training session." He turned and exited.

Quincey nodded at him, then walked over to a shelf and picked up a tray with a surgical drape. He placed it on the table in front of Amy and Steve. "Welcome to Triangle Ops, Agent Rogers, Agent Tate. We're going to get you set up right now with some basics. First, communications." He removed the surgical drape, revealing two Petri dishes with a silver disc the size of a button in each and a device that looked like a bulkier cousin of an air needle gun, like the type used to give inoculations.

"These are your commlinks. They transmit sound through bone conduction, so you can both hear it and communicate back to us. It also has a GPS locator and basic biomonitoring functions so we can keep track of you on missions. Mr. Tate, you wanted to get up close and personal with the technology. You'll go first."

Steve stood up and walked over to the doctor, who was putting on a pair of surgical gloves. "So, what do I do? Swallow it?"

Amy chimed in from her seat. "No, Tate. It needs to be near your brain, so in your case, they'd shove it up—"

Dr. Quincey interrupted her. "We attach it to your skull, behind your right ear."

Steve stopped. "My skull? Uh, isn't that a surgical procedure?"

Quincey smiled. "It used to be, but we use a laser injection method now." He took an alcohol pad and swabbed a spot behind Steve's ear, then loaded the commlink into the gun. He checked the power setting and aligned the device against the correct spot behind Steve's right ear. "This will take about three seconds. Try not to move."

Steve tried to sound more confident than he felt. "Okay, Doc."

"Oh, and it might hurt just a little bit."

Before Steve could react, the doctor pulled the trigger on the device. Steve felt a brief burning flash, and then something slammed into the side of his head. It was as if he'd been kicked during a rugby match. He bent over double as the doctor put down the gun and picked up a gauze bandage covered with gel. He placed it on the insertion site and Steve felt the gel mold to his skin and solidify. Quincey peeled back the bandage.

Steve stood up and looked at the doctor, his eyes filmy with tears. His voice was unsteady as he stammered out, "A-a little?"

The doctor grinned and shrugged. "So, maybe more than a little. You survived." He turned to Amy. "Next."

Amy passed Steve and muttered, "Serves you right."

Steve just smirked at her. *Oh, yeah? Just wait until you get clobbered, A.J.*

Dr. Quincey reset his injector and prepped her ear. He looked at her. "Ready, young lady?"

"Bring it on, Doctor."

Steve watched as Amy braced herself for the impact. Then Quincey pressed the trigger. It hit her, and she barely moved a muscle.

Steve stared at her in shock.

Quincey slapped on the bandage and smiled. "I'm impressed. Typically, that practically kicks people out of their chair."

She smiled at him, and then looked at Steve. "It's what I do."

Quincey grabbed his tablet. "Let's plug you two in." He brought up a diagnostic screen and entered a series of commands. "Savannah, activate their commlinks. Give us a tone."

Savannah's voice filled the room. "Yes, Doctor. Parameters, please."

"Let's go with 800 hertz, quarter-second duration, three-second intervals, and 65-decibel equivalent, please."

"Acknowledged. Stand by."

Steve listened carefully, anticipating. Then suddenly, his thoughts weren't alone anymore. First, there was a brief burst of static, and then an electronic tone started beeping every three seconds. He smiled and gave a thumbs-up to Dr. Quincey. Amy seemed to be having a little bit of an issue for a few moments; then her signal cleared and she nodded as well.

"Ms. Rogers, we'll take you first. Please start reciting the alphabet." Amy started doing so. Quincey's tablet displayed a waveform showing the sound, but what came through the speaker on his tablet sounded like the adults from the old Peanuts animated cartoons — a series of 'wah-wah-wah' sounds. Steve looked over at Ethan and Percy, a puzzled look on his face. Ethan walked over.

Steve leaned in and asked Ethan quietly, "What's with the cartoon sound?"

"Bone conduction microphones work differently based on varying bone densities. The lighter the bone, the better the transmission. But the commlink and computer need to be trained on what it should sound like. Hence, reciting the alphabet. Watch; by the third time through, it'll be passable, and it gets better as your training goes along."

"Thanks, um, Ethan, right?"

"That's right."

"Interesting accent. Like Percy's. Not standard British. Welsh?"

Ethan raised an eyebrow. "Nicely done, mate. Not many catch that difference on the first try."

Steve smiled. "I free-run, so I've spent a lot of time in Europe over the past 3 years. You learn to acquire an ear for that sort of thing."

"Good skill to have in this line of work."

The tablet started sounding like Amy's voice, garbled at first, but clearer with each passing letter. Finally, Quincey stopped her. "That'll do, Miss Rogers. Savannah will monitor your everyday conversations and use them to improve the communication filter. And now, for incoming..." Quincey turned away and walked to the far wall. He pressed a control, and then spoke quietly into the tablet. "Miss Rogers, come here, I need you."

Amy jumped. "My God, it's just like you were in my head!"

"Not too loud?"

"Not at all. Just... wow. I've never experienced anything like that before." She was grinning.

Quincey nodded. "Very good. You can adjust the volume by flexing your jaw forward or backward. You can also mute and turn off your commlink by pressing on it directly, but I'd let the biogel heal the injection site first before you try that. Give it a day or so." Quincey turned to Steve. "Mr. Tate, let's get you taken care of."

Steve walked over and sat down at the table, then started to recite the alphabet. It took the computer a little longer to understand him — he had a bad habit of slurring the occasional letter. By the fifth time through the alphabet, the speaker was passably reproducing Steve's voice. He was also ready for Quincey's voice in his head, but even so, he was surprised at how amazingly clear it was. "Wow. This is great. So, do you just communicate back to the base or can we communicate with other agents in the field? I can think of some great tactical ways to use these—"

Quincey cut him off. "We can discuss those another time. Ms. Rogers, please sit down here at the work table."

11:22 a.m. EDT

Dr. Quincey put away the first surgical tray and brought out another. As Amy sat down, he removed the surgical drape, revealing a pair of 5-inch wide silver bracelets. Steve grinned. "Let me guess — they deflect bullets."

Amy groaned and put her head down on the table. *Does he ever stop?*

Percy and Ethan started snickering in the corner. A glance from Dr. Quincey silenced them quickly. He just shook his head. "No, Mr. Tate. Nothing as simple as anything worn by an Amazonian warrior princess. Instead, allow me to introduce you to your SAVANTs."

Quincey reached down and pressed each device twice on the left edge and then once in the middle. A narrow slit appeared in the device, and then it popped open, hinged in back.

Wait — I didn't see a hinge a second ago, Amy thought. On the outer surface, she saw a faint bluish glow.

"Are either of you left-handed?" Quincey asked. Amy raised her hand. He nodded, made a notation on his tablet, then reached down and carefully rotated one bracelet so the opening now faced left instead of right.

"Ms. Rogers, please put your right forearm inside the first SAVANT. That's good. Now, Mr. Tate, if you please, do the same with your left forearm inside the other bracelet." The two of them placed their arms as instructed. Amy's was icy cold to the touch. She suppressed a shiver

Quincey nodded and grabbed his tablet. "Excellent. Now, this may hurt a bit."

Amy watched Steve glance at the doctor as if to say, *really? Again?* But before he could speak, Quincey touched a control on his tablet screen. Both gauntlets closed around their forearms like a trap snapping shut. Amy gasped in surprise and looked down.

At first, the device still just looked like a large metal bracelet. But then the curious blue glow Amy had noted seemed to intensify and the seam between the two halves grew smaller and fainter until it was indistinguishable. Moments later, Amy felt as if a thousand tiny needles were pricking her underneath the bracelet. As she started to raise her arm, she felt the device *move* by itself, sliding down her forearm and closer to her wrist. Somehow, it squeezed in tighter, flattening out and becoming thinner, and more flexible. Within moments, it had become like a metallic skin around her wrist. The prickling sensation stopped, and the blue glow dimmed.

Amy lifted her right forearm and watched the light play off the metal. In the reflection, she saw Steve was admiring his own new device. When he glanced at it like a watch, a local time display appeared in a faint blue glow that seemed to hover slightly off the surface of the device. He whistled in appreciation. "Wow. You definitely don't see something like that every day."

Amy stretched her right arm out and flexed it, feeling how the device affected her balance. *Not bad. It won't throw me off when fighting.* She turned back to the table. "All right, Dr. Quincey. I'll bite. What, exactly, is a SAVANT?"

Quincey was looking down at his tablet, monitoring the initial readouts from the devices. He nodded at what he read and then looked up at her. "It's an acronym — Standard Agent Variable Activity Nanite Technology. We developed them to function as an enhanced communications and data interface with Ops Control, as well as a flexible tool for agents in the field."

"Adaptable? How so?"

Quincey smiled. "Your devices are now voice-coded to respond to you. Tell yours to switch to Mode 3, Ms. Rogers, and observe."

Amy looked at him quizzically. "How do I do that?"

Percy spoke up from the corner. "Say 'SAVANT, Mode 3.' It will interpret and comply."

She glanced over and nodded. Taking a deep breath, she said in a clear voice, "SAVANT, Mode 3, please."

In her head, Amy heard a female voice very much like Savannah's say, "SAVANT, acknowledged." The bracelet on her right wrist glowed bright blue and began to morph, flowing like liquid metal around her hand and fingers until it covered them like a second skin. The feeling as it flowed was disquieting. It was as if a million small bugs were marching over her hand. When the coverage was complete, the coating solidified into a metallic gauntlet; flexible in the joints, but rigid on hard surfaces. The blue glow dimmed, and the voice in her head said, "Mode 3 complete."

Amy held up it up, turning it to and fro. The glove's metallic surface reflected the light, even as it continued to glow a faint blue.

Steve's was beaming with awe. "That has to be the coolest thing I've ever seen. Living metal. These nanites — how are they powered?"

"Solar collectors."

"Nice. So, what does this Mode 3 do?"

"Well, let's see..." Quincey looked on the shelf behind him and found a rock. He tossed it to Amy. "Here, hold this in your glove and analyze it."

She looked at the rock for a moment and then grabbed it with her right hand. "SAVANT, analysis?"

Inside her head, the voice replied after a slight pause. "Rock, basalt, 570.6 grams. Indigenous to this region."

She tossed the rock back to Dr. Quincey. "Any limitations on the SAVANT that I should know about?"

"The nanites are thermal conductors, so avoid temperature extremes. Corrosives are also bad. Surprisingly, though, they're not an electrical conductor — the nanites absorb and store electrical energy. They do it quickly, too. But you'll be scheduled for a full briefing on the use of all four modes of a SAVANT as part of your training."

Steve nodded. "Okay, Doc, but what about our friends waiting quietly over there. How does the whole controller thing fit into this picture?"

Ethan stood up and walked over to the table, Percy following close behind. Amy mused as she watched them. *Well, this Percy guy is tall and thin, and Ethan is shorter, stockier, and balding while sporting a pencil-thin mustache. Who do these guys remind me of?*

Ethan spoke up as he walked. "It's shorthand. The technical title is SAVANT Interface Controller. Those things are marvels of technology, but they have limits. They're designed to connect back into the mainframe at Triangle Ops via a secure satellite linkup to a series of consoles located at the facility here in Virginia. When an agent is on assignment, a member of their controller team mans the interface console. We monitor the data flow to and from your SAVANT, answer your requests from the field, monitor your progress and physical status, and coordinate actions with the other agents in the field, as well as appropriate civilian or military authorities as needed."

Steve grinned. "So, you guys are the Jarvis to my Iron Man?"

Ethan grinned back. "In a manner of speaking, yes. Quite a good reference, actually."

Amy looked at the three of them. "Unbelievable. Is everyone in this place a comic book geek?"

They all turned and looked at Amy. Ethan grinned. "You don't have to be — but it seems to help."

Amy stared at them. The flash of recognition hit her.

Oh, my God. I'm working with Laurel and Hardy.

Quincey finished checking his tablet and looked up at them. "Right. The telemetry from your SAVANTs indicates they are functioning properly. Ms. Rogers, please return yours to its default state — Mode 1. Any questions?"

Steve nodded. "Yeah, I have one — how do you take it off?"

Quincey looked surprised. "Our agents usually don't do that. They find it is useful to be ready to go into mission status instantly."

Amy snorted. "Yeah, well, you can bet Tate here isn't going to be like most agents."

Steve looked over at her, his expression one of false sincerity. "Why, A.J., I'm touched you've noticed." He turned to Quincey. "Seriously, Doc, can it be removed?"

"Yes, either by voice command or a touch code sequence—"

"Oh, you mean like this?" Steve touched the left edge twice, then touched and held a third spot one-third of the way down the length of the SAVANT, just as Amy had seen Quincey do earlier. His device quickly flowed back into its default neutral configuration, the seam reappeared and the bracelet popped open, slipping off his left forearm. Steve caught it deftly with his right hand, snapped it shut and slid it into his pants pocket.

Everyone in the room looked at him in shock. He smiled and said, "Anyone else hungry? I could sure go for some lunch."

Chapter 11

Steve changed into his workout gear after lunch in his new quarters. There were all sorts of enticing gadgets in his room, but he resisted the desire to explore. *Time for that later; it'll all be here when I get back.* He finished tightening the laces on his running shoes and checked the fit on his workout gear. He had selected a set of running tights and a tee this time, both in black. They were made using high technology compression fibers, close fitting, moisture wicking — like what he wore when free-running. He grabbed a loose pair of cargo shorts, also in black, and a nylon web belt from the gear locker and slipped those on as well. *Knowing this place*, he thought, *I suspect this gear has other tricks hidden up its sleeves, so to speak.* As he looked in the mirror, he grinned at his reflection. *I'm looking forward to finding out.*

He grabbed his SAVANT, thought about putting it on, but decided against it and slipped it into the right front pocket of his cargo shorts instead. One more quick glance to make sure his quarters were squared away. Satisfied, he headed out the door and down the corridor.

Steve traced his path back to the elevator, quickly moving down the corridor toward the central hub ring. As he exited the doors that designated the corridor as staff housing, he started to turn left toward the elevators, but then stopped. Grinning mischievously, he leaned against the wall and waited.

Steve was feeling competitive now that they were moving into training. Amy's attitude toward him about Callahan bothered him more than she knew. Yes, he was goofing off a bit, but it was his way of staying loose.

If I let the enormity of what I'm trying to do here get to me, I'll turn into a basket case — or worse, start doubting myself. And with this target, there can't be any doubts. Callahan's a stone-cold killer, ruthless. She doesn't make mistakes.

No, I've got to show little Miss Perfect that she's wrong about me. I must set the tone. If I'm ready, right from the start, and already two steps ahead of her, she's going to have to play catch up. Besides, I want to see her A-game before I trust her in the field.

So, game on, A.J. Let's see who's ready to play.

Two minutes later, Amy came striding down the corridor and walked right past him, wearing blue running tights, a white singlet, running shoes, and her hair in a ponytail. If she'd seen him, she gave no indication. In fact, Amy seemed a bit lost. She glanced about for a second, confused, then looked at her SAVANT. A little indicator arrow appeared projected on the wall, and she followed its guidance.

These things can function as a wayfinder? Interesting. He decided to follow her. He fell in two steps behind her and waited for her to notice him. Surprisingly, she didn't. *Hmmm. Oblivious, or deliberate?*

Steve cleared his throat.

Amy didn't turn to look. "How long have you been stalking me, Tate?"

Steve grinned. *Game on.* "Not stalking, A.J. Just admiring the scenery."

She wheeled on him immediately, blushing and angry. "I told you, don't call me that! And you...you keep your eyes where they belong!"

Steve looked at her piously. "And where might that be?"

"Anywhere but looking at my ass!" She turned and stomped off around the corner. Steve grinned as he watched her leave, admiring how her hips did sway just so as she walked. *One point for me.*

He caught up with her at the elevator. She avoided making eye contact with him, her arms crossed, her foot tapping impatiently. She reached out and pressed the elevator call button again. Steve decided to try a different tack.

"You know, for a high-tech underground lair, you'd think they'd have a better lunchroom."

Amy's foot stopped tapping. She turned to him, an incredulous look on her face. "What?"

"I'm just saying, I would have thought they'd have better food. But it was pretty typical cafeteria." He sighed. "I guess some things are just a universal constant, resistant to even the newest technological advances."

"I'll be sure to pass your opinion on to the executive chef. Of course, since he's a graduate of the Le Cordon Bleu, he might not give yours any credence."

Steve was doubly surprised, not just by the fact that Amy wasn't speaking, but also that the dulcet tones of Ethan's Welsh accent were in his head. "Ethan, you sly old dog. How long have you been listening in?"

"Long enough to know you appreciate your new partner's... assets."

Steve chuckled. "What are you doing in my head? I'm not wearing the SAVANT."

"Not your SAVANT, mate. Your commlink. Even without the SAVANT, we can still talk. Speaking of your jewelry, are you planning on putting it on soon?"

Steve took a couple of steps away from Amy down the corridor. "Actually, I'm trying to see how long I can go without one. Plus, I want to finish ahead of Miss Perfect over there during the session, and if I do it without using the SAVANT, that's even better."

He actually felt Ethan's sigh over the audio. "Steve, training's not a competition. You both need to be able to handle what might happen, and the SAVANT is a valuable tool—"

"You're so wrong, Ethan. Everything in life is a competition, eventually. You get ranked somewhere. You fight for a promotion. You try to defeat the bad guys and save the world before someone else does it. I might as well recognize and acknowledge that in my training. Besides, what did you guys do before you had SAVANTs?"

"We... made do."

"So, consider me making do."

"Steve, don't take this lightly. Mitchell Williams is a professional. He is not above letting you get injured to make a point."

Steve's smile grew bigger. "Bring it."

The elevator arrived. Steve followed Amy onto it.

1:55 p.m. EDT

In the Interface Control Center (ICC), Percy sat at the console next to Ethan's. Because of his experience, Ethan had been assigned to Steve, while Percy had the privilege of being Amelia's controller. Percy was happy for the assignment. He considered Amelia Rogers a fascinating figure — gifted, yet touched by tragedy. He was glad she'd taken Mr. Stevenson up on his offer to be part of the team. It was a sign she was willing to start pushing back against the hand she'd been dealt by fate.

Ethan hit the mute on his console. "Oh, for the love of God!" He threw a stylus down on his console.

Percy glanced over curious. "What's the matter?"

"It's Tate. The bloody fool's about to learn a very painful lesson."

"Oh?"

"Yeah. He's arrogant. Going to try the training room without a SAVANT the first time out."

Percy whistled. "How long do you think he'll last?"

"Three minutes, top."

Percy raised an eyebrow. "That long, really? Care to place a wager on that?"

Ethan glanced over at Percy. "What do you have in mind?"

Percy considered this for a moment. "A glass of the 15-year single malt at Sullivan's."

"And you're taking what, the under on this?"

Percy grinned. "Most definitely. No SAVANT? I think you're optimistic at three minutes. This is Mitch Williams. He'll be dead in a minute, tops."

"You're on, my young friend."

A female voice issued from Percy's console. "I'll take some of that action."

Percy turned white as he looked over and realized he had left the connection with Amelia open. Closing his eyes, he swore silently and said, "Sorry, Amelia, it's a private wager. But you're my gal — I know you'll do better than him."

"Hmph. There's no doubt about that. And Percy, I'm nobody's 'gal' — understood?"

Ethan and Percy winced at her frosty tone. Percy nodded, although there was no way Amy could have seen it. "I understand, Amelia. I'll keep it professional from here on out."

"You do that. Oh, and knock it off with the 'Amelia,' will you? It makes you sound like my grandmother. Call me Amy."

Ethan made a cut sign across his throat, and Percy hit the mute button. "You'd better be careful with that one, mate. Sounds like working with her is going to be like dancing in a minefield."

"Message received and acknowledged, chief."

They turned to their consoles and set to work.

1:57 p.m. EDT

Steve and Amy rode the elevator to the bottom level of the Operations Headquarters complex. Level 5 was the largest on the base. It spread out in three concentric rings and housed numerous training and storage facilities. As they exited, Steve remembered the directions he'd been given. *Counterclockwise out of the elevator, second exterior corridor, another right into the middle ring and the door to Training Room 3 is two down on the left.* Steve turned to Amy. "This way."

Amy pushed him aside brusquely. "I know where I'm going, Tate."

Steve chuckled as he followed her. Oh, yeah, she's rattled. That's two points for me.

Amy reached the door to Training Room 3 first and activated it. It was dark inside, but as they entered, automatic lighting overhead came on, illuminating the room in sections. Steve's eyes grew wider as more and more sections were lighted.

Amy looked over at Steve. "Just how big is this place?"

Without stopping to think, Steve slowed time for a moment; the data sprung to him, unbidden. He sped back up and replied, "One hundred twenty feet tall, 2,140 feet long and 400 feet wide."

Amy whistled. "That's just less than 20 acres. The engineering involved in building this—"

"Oh, my God, they actually built one!"

Amy gave him a confused look. "Built what?"

Steve ran another half-dozen steps into the room and turned back toward Amy, grinning like a 6-year-old on Christmas morning. "Don't you get it? These folks actually went and built themselves a real-life Danger Room."

"Yes, that name sort of came naturally to this place."

Steve glanced back and saw Williams approaching them.

2:01 p.m. EDT

Williams strode across the floor, confident and relaxed. He was now dressed in a paramilitary uniform, combat boots, and a crossdraw weapons harness with two PK-93 hand weapons. He saw Steve examining the weapons. *Good, rookie. Pay attention.*

Williams looked at them. "It's actually called an Automated Interactive Trainer. It can be programmed to present all sorts of different scenarios and conditions." He smiled slightly and wryly added, "Although we typically don't use a lot of buzz saws or spinning tops of doom, and stuff like that."

He walked around them in a circle, stopping so that most of the room was behind him. "Today, we're going to evaluate your current skill set and how you use them in a pressure situation. It's a bit of a familiar scenario — simply get from here to there, through the obstacles, in a limited amount of time." Williams held up his SAVANT and pressed a pair of controls.

"Hello again, Agent Williams." Savannah's voice filled the space around them but not the entire room. Williams smiled as the two rookies looked startled. *Another neat parlor trick — localized projected sound wave technology.*

"Savannah, please put Training 3 into configuration Bravo Seven."

"Complying."

The room started to reconfigure itself. The AIT floor was made up of a series of interconnected hexagonal blocks whose height could be varied and surfaces tilted to form a variety of slopes, valleys, steppes, and small chasms. Williams turned back to Steve and Amy. "The room will be looking to stop you. It's equipped with an adaptive artificial intelligence. It learns from your actions and choices, so what you see at the beginning won't necessarily be how it looks by the time you are halfway through the course. The only thing that stays the same is the basic topography. The obstacles can and will change. Do you understand?"

Steve and Amy nodded. "You'll have twelve minutes to reach your goal. You can work independently or together, but one of you must reach it in the time allotted, or you both fail this test. Do you understand?"

Steve and Amy both answered affirmatively. Williams looked at Steve. "Where's your SAVANT?"

"In my pocket."

Williams looked carefully at Steve for any signs of insincerity or challenge, then shrugged. "Your funeral." He turned and walked over to the wall next to the door, then stepped onto a platform that quickly rose to the observation level. As he stepped into the observation booth, he said, "Savannah, please bring the training AI online."

"Confirmed. Training AI is online."

"Good. Set it to level 3."

Savannah sounded hesitant. "Agent Williams, are you sure you want that level of difficulty with new recruits?"

"Please do as I say, Savannah."

"Yes, sir. Training AI is at level 3, awaiting your commands."

Williams reached for the console's PA button. His voice filled the cavernous space. "The target is a flag at the far end of the room. You have twelve minutes. Starting in three, two, one..."

Chapter 12

In the first minute, Steve had a sneaking suspicion the Danger Room was trying to kill them.

By the third minute, he knew it for certain.

While Williams rode the platform up to the observation level, Steve used the time to examine the layout of the room. He concentrated for a moment and time slowed to a bare crawl. The target flag had just appeared at the far end of the room atop a promontory that rose 75 feet in the air. Steve looked at what lay between him and that flag — rolling hills in front leading up to a 25-foot drop into a 30-yard-wide depression at the 300-yard mark that filled with water from wall to wall. Then back to dry land, flat and featureless, until it reached a sheer cliff wall, 40 feet tall. Beyond the top of that cliff was a 15-foot-wide gap filled with a low-lying fog and then, finally, that promontory — a single raised hex on the far wall.

His Talent engaged and started providing him all sorts of additional data about the space. He immediately knew the promontory hex was 6 feet across at its widest point, angled down at a 20-degree tilt to the left.

Steve was considering all of this. *Yeah, the terrain is not quite a walk in the park. And I'm betting there'll be some hidden surprises as well.*

He glanced up at Williams, frozen in the observation booth. That's when he noticed the ceiling. In the shadows, above the lights, hexes in the ceiling were in the process of opening their irises. A couple had completed the process and devices that looked like cannons were lowering into place. *That's more like what I expected.*

Steve looked back at the training room as his mind went into overdrive. He saw the river's depth, temperature, and current, the angle of the ground, the fire alleys set up by the cannons. He determined three dozen possible paths through the course and their success probabilities. As his mind ranged over the final chasm, he found another nasty surprise – a large turbofan, rated at just over 60 miles per hour.

When it triggers, there's going to be a severe downdraft. If you're not flying quickly past it, you'll be slammed into that chasm.

He made an initial decision, then snapped time back to normal, and activated his commlink. "Ethan, you still with me?"

"Yes, Steve. Although I do wish you would put on your SAVANT for this test."

Steve shook his head. "Sorry, buddy, not yet. I told you, I want to test myself, unaided against your systems. Maybe I'll retake the test with it later, and we can compare notes. You know, to see if it really does provide any sort of assist."

"That sounds logical. Painful, but logical. Well, mother always did say painful lessons are best remembered."

Steve frowned. "Gee, thanks for the confidence. I could use some intel here, though. The room is deploying a series of cannons across the ceiling. What sort of projectiles am I looking at?"

He heard Ethan typing at his console as he pulled up the information. "Ballistic spheres."

"What the heck is a ballistic sphere?"

"Rubber core spheroids with a fabric cover approximately 2½" in diameter."

"Tennis balls?"

"In a manner of speaking, but these have a solid core. Think of them more like fuzzy baseballs."

"Then they're your basic evil robotic pitching machines. Muzzle velocity?"

"Variable, between 25 and 60 miles per hour."

Steve gulped. "Ouch. Get hit in the wrong spot by one of those, it'll ruin my day fairly quick. Hell, getting hit anywhere is going to hurt. You guys play rough."

He turned and looked over at Amy. "Uh, Ethan, has anyone briefed A.J. on what to expect?"

"A.J.?" Ethan sounded puzzled. "Oh, you mean Ms. Rogers. No, she's been quiet and hasn't asked."

He shook his head. *She has no idea what she's getting into.* "Do me a favor. Have Percy talk to her. Tell him to say he overheard us or something. Don't bruise her ego, but get her the same intel you've given me."

"Are you sure?"

Steve nodded. "Yeah, I'm sure. I want to win, but I want her to at least have a chance, too."

Williams' voice rang out over the PA system. "—commencing in three, two, one, mark!"

At the far end of the room, above the promontory, a twelve-minute countdown clock appeared and started marking off the seconds. Steve saw a series of red laser dots spring to life, roaming about the landscape, seeking a quarry. *Targeting for those cannons, no doubt.*

For the first minute, Steve stood and studied the course one more time.

2:06 p.m. EDT

As Williams' voice rang out over the PA system, Amy slowed her breathing.

It's just another race, Amelia Jane. Just like hundreds of others, only drier. Relax. Focus. Breathe.

The clock appeared on the back wall, and Amy hesitated a moment, then glanced over at Steve. He just stood there, that same strange look on his face as she'd seen in the conference room earlier.

Master of cause and effect, huh? Trying to change things in your favor, Tate? Won't matter if I'm there first.

Percy's voice crackled in her ear. "Amy, you should know, there are several hazards coming online—"

Amy's reply was sharp. "Stop it! I need you to be quiet. Don't say anything to me unless I ask you a question. Do you understand? Just let me concentrate on beating this thing."

"But, Amy—"

"No buts. Now butt out!"

She furrowed her brow in concentration as she bent down in a sprinter's crouch. The mantra filled her mind. *Focus. Breathe. Activate.* She slammed the ground with her fist once, twice, three times. She felt the energy inside her open, and touched it, then burst out of the crouch and took off at a sprint into the course.

Within ten seconds, she was 150 yards downrange, zigzagging along a narrow path.

As soon as she'd started, the red dots on the ground arrowed right in on her. Moments later, something that looked like a tennis ball fired downward and hit the ground just in front of her. She glanced up and saw the cannons.

A trio of balls hit her. She stumbled a bit as she absorbed the impact energy and let them roll off her harmlessly. She changed direction and angled toward a hex that looked like a small outcropping with an overhang. *They might not be able to hurt me, but I don't need the distraction. I can take shelter there and plan my next move.*

A trio of balls came down in a grouping just in front of her, forcing her to juke to the right and then cut back left. That's when the course decided to fight back.

As she cut left, the hex in front of her changed. The floor seemed to ripple as a bed of pressure switches suddenly appeared just as she put her weight down. Amy thought she heard a warning yell over her commlink as the world literally went sideways when her foot touched one of the switches.

The hex abruptly sprung upward and tilted right, like a stuntman's launch-board, throwing her off balance. To her right, another hex retracted into the floor, leaving a 10-foot-deep hole that she slid toward. She clawed at the edge, trying to escape the trap. *Come on, Amelia, pull yourself—*

Three balls slammed against the side of her head, one after the other. Dazed, she let go and dropped into the hole. An inch-thick Plexiglas cover slid in place above her, sealing the chamber.

The sudden quiet was eerie. The cannons sounded muffled and distant as Amy hit the bottom of the dark tube. She stumbled as she tried to stand and heard a rumble. The hex slowly rose out of the floor, revealing a six-sided cage with alternating metal and Plexiglas sides. She stood up and looked at the trap, grimacing. The lid was 10 feet above her.

She accessed her commlink. "All right, Percy, I need you now." All she heard in reply was static.

"Come on, Percy, this is no joke. I need your help now!" Still no reply.

It dawned on Amy that the trap might be jamming communications. *All right, Amelia Jane. Looks like you'll have to figure a way out yourself.* She checked the walls of the container, banging at the seams, looking for a weak spot. Finding none, she started to punch one of the Plexiglas panels.

After four punches, she stopped, frustrated. She'd felt each punch, stronger than the previous, hit the same spot on the wall. *Something should have happened.* She punched it again, to no avail. It was as if it absorbed the energy as she hit it.

Amy could feel the anger building within her. *Nobody cages me!* She decided to change her tactics.

Focus.

She looked carefully again at the same spot she'd punched, then knelt reached down and slapped the floor of the trap.

Breathe.

She took in a deep breath, held it and let it out over five seconds. Then she flamed her fist down into the floor a second time.

Activate!

Amy felt energy course through her muscles. It was as if she were suddenly supercharged. She leaped up and whipped into a spin-kick that hit the targeted spot.

The cage shuddered with the impact, but the panel held. This time, though...

A crack! Yes! I can break this thing! Nodding to herself, Amy knelt on one knee and launched into another spin-kick. This time, a spider web of cracks appeared where her foot impacted the Plexiglas. *Yeah, one more should do it.* She moved back in place to launch one more attack.

This time, as she slammed the floor and started to leap, high-pressure jets of ice-cold water shot from one solid side of the hex, slamming her against the Plexiglas panel opposite it. She raised her arms to block the spray hitting her in the face and knelt into a rising puddle.

Damn, that's cold! Wait, it's filling the cage. It's filling the cage! I can't get out!

The water level rose rapidly. Within moments, Amy had to start treading water. It was so frigid it quickly sapped her strength. Amy kept tapping more energy from her reserves, but the cold drained it right away. The water level pushed higher and higher, bringing her close enough that she could push against the lid. In desperation, she repeatedly pounded against it. A web of cracks appeared, but the lid still held, and the water continued to rise relentlessly. Amy was forced to stop, unable to gain enough leverage to strike the lid with any force.

Still, the water rose higher. The gap shrunk smaller and smaller. Panic rose in Amy. *Oh, God, I can't die. Not like this. Not drowning. Somebody, please, help!*

"Help me, please!"

She hadn't meant to cry out, but as soon as she did, the water stopped rising. It was barely 9 inches from the top. She found she could breathe if she held her head sideways. But she had no leverage to push against the lid, and the limited air was going to run out quickly.

Amy realized she was going to drown.

2:10 p.m. EDT

Steve had seen Amy fall into the trap. But she had made it clear she didn't need his help. He was determined to study the course and see how it would change before he started down it.

That all changed a minute later when he heard Amy's cry for help. He snapped into action.

"Ethan, Amy's trapped! Is there an external release for that cell A.J. is trapped in? And I need rope – about 50 or 60 feet of it."

Ethan's voice was calm over the commlink. "There's a 50-foot coil of rope in a wall locker to your right. I'm authorizing you access." Steve heard typing in the background for a moment. "The cell has an override switch — north side, 4 feet down on the external panel."

"Can you walk me through activating it?"

"Of course, but if you'd prefer—"

"Hold that thought, Ethan." Steve turned, spotted the locker Ethan mentioned, and palmed the black control pad. It responded to his palm print and swung open. He looked inside, quickly found and grabbed the rope. Slinging it over his left shoulder, he turned and started to thread his way across the floor toward Amy.

He was cautious in his movements, evaluating the landscape and the weapons firing at him. *The cannon reload cycle is 4.6 — no, 4.4 seconds,* he noted and added that to his calculations. He took three steps left, then five forward quickly. He started to step forward but then froze in place. The same pressure switches that had triggered Amy's trap had just appeared where he was about to step. Carefully, he pulled his foot back and eyed the wall to his left. Turning toward it, he leaped over the trap, landing one foot on a hex that sloped upward to the right. Transferring his weight, he used a set of free-running moves to conserve his momentum, leaping sideways from hex to hex along the wall.

More cannons in the ceiling started to track his movement and change the angles of their shots. Steve ducked down to avoid two shots, and barely dodged a third on his right. He yelled out, "Ethan, these shots are getting a little too close for comfort. Can you do anything about the cannons?" He dodged again to his left.

"Like what?"

"I don't know. Maybe hack into the control programming? Tell them I'm a rock or something?"

"Let me give that a shot."

"Quickly, please! Ouch!" Steve shouted as he again tried to move closer to Amy's cell. Almost all the cannons were tracking him now, and he was hard-pressed to avoid all the balls fired at him. He threw himself quickly into a left cartwheel to avoid three shots and was about to execute a forward somersault that would take him out of another cannon's range when he was hit from behind by a ball from a different cannon.

He staggered forward, his right arm numb from the impact, then looked around for the weapon — and found himself staring directly into the muzzle of the cannon that had just emerged from the floor and was tracking him for another shot.

Aw, come on, really? Steve thought, as he ducked and rolled, then instinctively swept his right foot out in a circle kick. Somehow, this managed to knock another two balls out of the air, but the maneuver threw him off balance, and he landed hard on his right shoulder. The impact sent an electric jolt through his body, and he lay there for a moment, unable to move.

Steve waited for the impacts of multiple shots he knew were coming, but miraculously, nothing happened. He glanced up and watched as half the cannons withdrew into the ceiling. The remaining cannons started moving and targeting each other. They opened fire, and in short order, the remaining weapons were damaged and disabled.

Steve breathed a quick sigh of relief. "Thanks, Ethan!"

"No problem."

He stood up and quickly covered the remaining distance to the trap. As he circled it, looking for the override switch, he could see Amy through the Plexiglas, struggling to keep her head above water.

The switch was right where Ethan said it would be. "Okay, smart guy; the switch has two buttons — red and blue. Which one is it?"

There was a pause. "Ethan, which one? Red or blue?"

"Steve, my notes don't indicate that — it should be three yellow switches."

Steve looked quickly around the edges of the cell. "No dice, Ethan. Nothing with three yellow switches. Any other ideas?"

Frustration showed in Ethan's voice. "Sorry, Steve. I'm coming up blank here. None of the schematics show anything different. They must have redesigned the shells and not filed the plans."

Steve silently studied the cell for a moment, then reached up and without hesitating, pressed the red button.

The cell immediately started sliding back down into the floor.

Damn. Guessed wrong. He watched with a growing sense of helplessness as Amy, still struggling to stay above the water, slid past him and disappeared into the floor. Through the Plexiglas cover, he saw her starting to panic as the cell darkened.

No! I won't fail again! Only one thing to do. Steve reached into his pocket, grabbed the SAVANT and slapped the bracelet on his left arm. It immediately started its initialization process. As it did, he called out. "Ethan, does the SAVANT have any weapons capability?"

"Yes, it can generate plasma bolts effective at short ranges — 20 meters or less. But you're not trained—"

"We can argue about that later. This is an emergency. How do I access it?"

"Mode 3, say 'weapon,' aim your fist at the target and fire."

"But how do I trigger it?"

"Squeeze your fist tighter."

Steve lifted the SAVANT and murmured to it. "Right. Time to join the party. SAVANT, Mode 3."

In his head, he heard the SAVANT acknowledge his order and watched as the device morphed into a gauntlet, covering his whole hand. As it finished, he thought, *here goes nothing.*

"SAVANT, weapon."

"Acknowledged."

Forming his left hand into a fist, he aimed at the closest edge of the lid and squeezed his fist tight.

The gauntlet glowed bright blue and a ball of flickering blue-white energy, too bright to look at, formed briefly along the front edge of his fist and then shot forward. Steve braced for recoil, but there was none — the ball of energy just leaped from his fist and struck the edge of the lid. The plasma blew a hole in it the size of a basketball.

Steve could see Amy gasping as the fresh rush of air filled the small breathing space. He yelled down to her. "Are you okay?"

She looked up him with disbelief. "Really?"

"Yeah, well... Never mind. Just get to the far side of the hex and duck underwater. I'm going to blow the lid open."

She nodded and moved over to the edge. Steve called out again. "Ethan, can I increase the strength of the plasma bolt?"

"Yes. It defaults at 30 percent power. But at a higher setting, you risk injuring Miss Rogers."

"What, as opposed to letting her drown? I think she's willing to take that chance." Steve said. "SAVANT, increase plasma bolt power to 50 percent."

"Complying."

Steve took aim at the cover and watched as Amy ducked below the surface. After a quick, silent prayer, he fired.

This time, the bolt was much bigger, and when it left his fist, there was a recoil. The bolt hit the lid dead center. There was a bright flash and loud bang. He was temporarily blinded, but when he blinked he saw a hole melted through the lid, large enough for Amy to escape the trap.

He ran over to the edge, but she hadn't surfaced. He called out her name, but there wasn't a response. Steve looked quickly, then reached down and put his arm into the water. He swept it back and forth, and a tense few seconds later touched Amy's hand. He yanked her upward to the surface and pulled her to the edge of the hole.

Amy could drag herself partially out, but her strength was giving way. She held onto the edge, her lips blue, shivering. "Can't do it, Tate. C-can't get out. Too tired. N-need to rest." She laid her head down, her eyes starting to close.

Steve shook his head. "No, no, no, A.J. You need to stay awake and work with me here. I'll get you out." He took the coil of rope and quickly fashioned a loop on one end. "Here, slip this on, under your arms. By the way, what do you weigh?"

Amy struggled into the loop. "One...one-ten."

Steve looked at her and grinned as he continued working. *Liar,* he thought. *125, easy.* He fashioned the other end of the rope into another loop and worked it over his left arm and shoulder. "Be ready to start climbing." Turning, he sprinted up the 30-foot slope in front of him. Reaching the crest of the hill, he tugged on the line, then turned around and fell backward toward the water.

After dropping five feet, the rope went rigid and Steve swung inward at the wall, catching it with his feet. He hung there agonizingly for a few seconds, then slowly started to slide lower. *It's working,* he thought. *My weight is counterbalancing A.J.'s, lifting her right out of that trap.*

When he had dropped ten feet toward the water, he yelled out, "Ethan, is she safe?"

"Ms. Rogers is out of the water and secure on the slope."

"That's grea — ahh!"

Steve gasped as he suddenly dropped another ten feet and jerked to a stop. *Oh, crap!* He glanced at the churning water of the artificial river below. *I'll pull her right over the cliff with me.* Quickly, he aimed his SAVANT at the rope and fired.

The plasma bolt severed the rope. Steve fell backward the remaining few feet into the water below.

The initial plunge was an icy shock; every muscle spasmed. But Steve soon touched bottom and pushed off, rising back into the turbulence of the stream. He swam with the current, angling toward the far shore. Spotting an eddy, he pushed his way into it. The current swirled and then calmed as the water became shallower. Quickly, he stood and walked the final few yards to shore. He collapsed to his hands and knees, trying to catch his breath.

"Ethan, time check."

"You have two minutes, twenty-three seconds remaining."

"A.J.?"

"She is recovering and has started climbing the slope behind you."

"Thanks." Steve rolled over and looked at the rock wall looming 100 feet in front of him. He got to his feet and started forward again, wondering what else the room might throw at him.

Twelve steps later, he got his answer. A small vent opened on the floor next to him, and a plume of high-velocity steam shot upward. He barely rolled out of the way in time.

Geysers. Just ducky. And they're using real steam, too. Points for authenticity. Steve waited until the geyser stopped, then sprinted forward, dodging right fifteen yards away when another geyser went off, then straight ahead fifty more to the cliff wall. Just before he reached it, something inside warned him, and he stopped short. The floor at the base of the cliff rotated and a set of five steam jets went off all at once. They fired for five seconds and stopped.

"Time?"

"One minute, twelve seconds."

Steve looked for a path up the cliff, but the lower hand and foot holds were too far apart to allow for a rapid ascent. He couldn't use parkour skills to climb it, and regular rock-climbing skills would get him parboiled. He needed another option.

And he needed it fast.

He activated his Talent again and time slowed to a crawl again. He studied the vents and the area around him. Every scenario he could see led to failure. He just couldn't ascend fast enough to get away from the steam...

The idea came to him from nowhere. Suddenly, he was calculating the velocity of the steam and variable weight ratios. The best numbers he came up with gave him a 60/40 chance — at this point, as good as he was going to get. He spotted what he needed, and snapped back into real time.

"Man, do I hope you guys grade well for creativity," he muttered.

Ethan sounded confused. "What are you doing?"

Steve grimaced. "What I always do — I'm making this up as I go along." *That always sounds so much better in the movies,* he thought, as he backtracked across two hexes and found the maintenance panel to access the steam cannons. It was approximately 2 feet square, mounted on a pair of hinges. He raised the panel.

"SAVANT, decrease plasma bolt power to five percent."

"Complying."

He aimed his gauntleted fist and quickly fired at both hinges. The maintenance panel fell over and landed on its back. He grabbed it, turned and started sprinting toward the cliff.

"Time?"

"Forty-three seconds."

In a smooth motion, he lay the panel down, so the flat outer surface was face down toward the floor, then sent it sliding toward the base of the cliff. He ran close to it, and just before it hit the cliff face, he leaped forward and landed atop the panel. He quickly crouched down and grabbed the interior handle. The five steam cannons shot off, launching the door panel skyward, with Steve atop it — he was now a human projectile.

He arced through the air, over the top of the ridge and toward the back wall. Just before he hit it, he dove left off the metal plate in a somersault, landing unsteadily on his feet atop the promontory just above the flag. He had to windmill his arms to keep from falling backward into the crevasse.

Ethan's voice sounded in his head. "Thirty seconds."

At that moment, the turbofan in the overhead kicked on. The blast of a gale force wind blew straight down at Steve. The surface of the hex detached itself and started to slide down the slope, dropping to his left into the mist-filled chasm below.

Steve didn't think; he just reacted. Rolling to his right, he went over the side of the pinnacle, catching the edge of it with his right hand. His momentum carried him in an arc downward and sideways along the cliff face. His left hand brushed against the flag. He grabbed it.

He hung there for a moment by his fingertips, fighting the gale trying to push him into the chasm. He took a deep breath and then yelled, "Ethan? Time check!"

The elation in his controller's voice was evident. "There were fourteen seconds left when you grabbed the flag, Steve. Congratulations, you've beaten this test."

Steve grinned and stuffed the flag into his pocket, then reached his left arm upward to get a purchase on the edge of the pinnacle. He was barely able to grasp his fingertips onto the edge and hung there for a moment before his left hand lost its grip again. He scrambled to find a foothold and push himself upward, but the surface was totally smooth. *I can't get a good grasp on anything.*

He glanced over his shoulder and saw Amy at the top of the cliff opposite him. He waited a moment to see if she was going to do anything to help, but she just stood there, watching him. *Gee, thanks for the assist, A.J.*

Looking up at the top of the pinnacle, Steve grimaced. *This is going to hurt.*

His right shoulder screamed in pain as he did a slow one-armed pull-up. Finally, he could hook his left elbow, and then his right, over the edge. He hung there for a few moments, breathing heavily. "Ethan," he said wearily, "I think I'm just going to hang around here for a while."

The turbofan cut off. Steve glanced up to see Williams rappel quickly down from the overhead, braking when he was suspended in the chasm between Amy and Steve.

"That's not an option, rookie."

In a single, smooth motion, Williams quickly drew the pistols from the crossdraw holsters and fired at the two of them simultaneously.

Steve recognized the plasma bolt just before it hit him. Unconscious, he fell backward into the chasm below.

Chapter 13

Steve came to on a stuntman's air pad that had been hidden by the mist. All around him, the Danger Room reconfigured itself back to its neutral state — hexes retracting into the floor, mist venting, water draining, automated equipment collecting the ballistic spheres for reuse. The pad deflated and rolled him off to one side, depositing him onto the floor, and retracted into the side wall.

Steve rolled over on his back and stared up at the ceiling. He groaned and said, "Ethan, tell me you got the license plate of whatever ran over me."

Ethan chuckled inside his head. Steve decided it was a particularly evil sound. "Oh, that's right. Laugh it up at your nice cushy desk job."

"I did warn you that you might get hurt."

"I'm sorry, I missed the part where you cautioned me Williams was *going to shoot me.*"

He glanced to his right and spotted Amy lying on the floor 40 feet away. She must have fallen forward when she was shot and landed on another pad. She looked cold, wet and miserable.

Williams walked over to Steve and looked down at him. "Good job, rookie. Damned impressive. Too bad you died." He held out a hand for Steve, who grabbed and pulled against it, rising unsteadily to his feet.

Together, the two of them walked over to Amy, who lay on her side in a fetal position, shivering. Williams knelt in front of her. "You'll live, rookie. Let's get you up." He nodded to Steve, and together the two of them helped her to her feet.

As soon as she was up, Amy shook off Steve's assistance. "I don't need your help. Get away from me!" she growled, punctuating it by shoving him in the chest. Steve held up his hands and backed away.

Williams shook his head. "Really? The man saved you from hypothermia, possibly saved you from drowning, and that's the thanks he gets? You disappoint me, Rogers. Of course, you at least had your SAVANT on and working, which Tate didn't, initially. That's a point in your favor." He started to walk away but then turned back.

"No, I take that back. Here's a question for you, Rogers. If your SAVANT was working, why could Tate use his to get you out of that trap and you couldn't?" He sighed and shook his head in resignation. "Come on, let's get you two cleaned up and debriefed." He turned and walked to the exit.

Steve looked at her for a second. Quietly, he said, "Seriously, Amy, are you okay? Do you need a hand?"

Amy sounded humiliated and angry and in no mood to accept his charity. "Just get away from me, Tate."

Steve shrugged. "Suit yourself, A.J." He turned and started toward the exit, rotating his right arm to work out the soreness in his shoulder.

Amy leaned over and put her hands on her knees, trying to catch her breath. She looked up at him walking away. "Don't call me...ah, just screw it." She followed them toward the exit.

2:40 p.m. EDT

Williams' debrief was simple, short and to the point. "You both ultimately failed because you didn't work together. First mistake — you assumed it was a timed test."

Amy protested. "But you said it was timed!"

"No, I said you had to reach your goal in twelve minutes. I did not say the exercise was over when you reached it. Do you understand the difference?"

Realization dawned for Steve. "I think I do. Missions often try to avert something that's deadline-based. But even if you succeed, bad guys are still around, and are still able to hurt you."

"Very good, Tate. You get a gold star on your report card. Maybe even an extra cookie if you behave." He turned to Amy. "Look, at times we talk in here like it's a game, chalking up wins and losses. But out there, wins and losses mean lives. For us, training must be about wins and wins. And sometimes, winning means changing the game that's being played."

"But know this, rookies: In the end, it's not a contest. It's not a game. It's life and death — and the people you'll be up against will be trying to kill you. Your skills will give you an edge in trying to stay alive. So will our tools and training. But if you don't use 'em, you're just asking to be a statistic." He looked over at Steve. "That's why you wear your SAVANT. You should have set it up to display life signs in the area. That way, it would have let you know I was dropping in for a visit, possibly in time for you to do something about it."

"I didn't know it could do that."

"Then how did you know to use it as a weapon?"

Steve shrugged. "Lucky guess?"

Williams rolled his eyes and then turned on Amy. "As for you, Rogers, I'm trying to decide if you're naive, stupid or were just being deliberately cruel out there. Tate and his controller were distracted by reaching the flag and surviving the downdraft trap. But you knew I was coming. I monitored your transmissions. I know your controller warned you. I know your SAVANT was active. I know you could have seen me visually." Williams dialed up the sarcasm as he pointed at Steve. "So why didn't you tell him that?"

Amy looked like she wanted to be a million miles away from that room at that moment. She nodded tentatively, plainly fearful of what might be said next. "I...I didn't think he could hear me if I yelled—"

Williams slammed his hands down on the table in front of her. His eyebrows were raised, and his face seemed like the poster definition of disbelief and derision. "Yelled?

Excuse me, what did you two *already have installed* today? How were you talking to your controllers?"

Steve glanced at Amy. "Through our commli... oh." He looked sheepish.

Williams nodded. "Yeah. 'Oh' sums it up really good. The reason you communicate in the field is so you can coordinate your actions. There wasn't a lot of that going on in there, was there? Actually, the answer was none."

He turned back to Amy. "But it's you, Rogers, that has me truly concerned. Your controller tried to pass you vital intelligence from the moment I said go, and you shut him down. Do you know where that came from?" Amy shook her head. "From Tate here. And then, when you managed to almost get yourself killed, who was there to blast you out of that trap and then use his own body to keep you from drowning? Seems to me he at least tried to make this a team effort."

Steve interjected. "Look, Agent Williams, I didn't mean to—"

"Shut up, Tate. I'm talking here." Williams turned back to Amy. "I know you want this really bad, and my bosses are jonesing for your Talent. But if what we just saw is an indication of how you'll perform in the field, I'm going to tell you now — go home and get on with your life."

Amy stood up, anger flashing in her eyes. "You can't do that to me!"

Williams walked around the table and faced her down. "You think not? You had a man out there, depending on you. He was in a vulnerable position, hanging off the side of a cliff by his fingertips after coming to your rescue earlier. Someone who's shown, both here and in the field, that given the opportunity, he'll have your back. Yet you just stood there and made no attempt whatsoever to help him."

Amy's voice was a whisper. "That's not true..."

Williams didn't back off. "But what really put the nail in the coffin was when I arrived. His back was turned; he was hanging on for dear life, exposed, defenseless. Yet you stood there and just watched. You left him there to die." Williams moved even closer, leaning down until his nose was only an inch from hers. His voice dropped to a hiss. "Can you afford to make another mistake and get someone killed — again?"

Amy opened her mouth, but no sound came out. Her face screwed into a mask of pain as she turned and ran out the door and into the corridor.

Steve was on his feet immediately. "Amy, wait!"

Williams stopped him. "Leave her be. She needs to think this through."

Steve turned to the senior agent, his eyes blazing with anger. "Maybe so. But what the hell was that? The love of her life died in her arms two days ago. The guy bled to death as she was holding him. Don't you think that last bit was maybe, just maybe, a little bit below the belt?"

Williams eyed him critically and then shook his head. "Nope. Not at all. Yeah, she's been through hell, but she wants to go after someone who isn't going to bat an eye when it comes to playing head games with her. And if she folds like that under pressure, she won't be any good to you as a partner. So we break her now and rebuild her. Trust me, you two are gonna need each other."

Steve raised an eyebrow. "Oh?"

"Yeah. With that Talent of yours, you may think great on your feet, but you're only above average on reaction speed — and you're not bulletproof."

"Gee, you make that sound like a bad thing."

Williams sat on the edge of the table near Steve. "Sooner or later, you're going to go up against someone who's faster, stronger or smarter. That's why we never send an agent out there solo. The trick is making sure the bad guys won't be all of those things at once against the two of you working together."

Steve cocked his head to one side. "Then where's your partner?"

Williams looked at the wall behind Steve. "She... left this line of work. Found a better place to go." A pained expression shadowed across his face for a moment. Just as quickly, it was gone. He turned back to Steve. "Not using your SAVANT right away and not establishing comms with Rogers were your sins this time, Tate. Hubris is an ugly way to die. So, swallow your pride, slap on the jewelry right from the start, and use it correctly next time."

Steve tossed Williams a mocking salute. *"Oui, mon Capitaine."*

"I'm serious, Tate! You did a lot of good, smart things in there. Getting intel from your controller — exactly how that's supposed to work. Having him hack the systems — again, smart use of your resources. They will do that for you in the field. But that rescue — using yourself as a counterweight when Rogers was hypothermic — was a brilliant piece of improvisation."

Williams sat on the edge of the table. "Tate, you have good instincts, but you're used to doing things your own way. That's probably a legacy of your time in free-running. But I told you. We don't send out agents solo — ever. You two better start learning to play as a duet."

He stood up and walked to the door. "Go clean up and get yourself to medical to have that shoulder looked at. Then get yourself a meal and some sleep. Report back here at 0900. Tomorrow, we'll run the two of you through the paces on your SAVANTs, followed by hand-to-hand training."

Williams stopped at the door and turned back, a thoughtful look on his face. "Oh, and be ready to spend a lot of time flat on your back tomorrow."

"Why?"

"Rogers is a black belt in three martial arts disciplines. I have a feeling after today she plans to take a lot of her frustrations out on her new sparring partner." He turned and exited the briefing room.

Steve raised an eyebrow. *A.J., a stealth ninja master type? Who'd have thunk it?* He decided to be more careful when teasing her from now on. He called out after Williams, "Thanks for the warning...I think."

4:37 p.m. MDT

Twenty-five hundred miles away, Dr. Rafiz Hamid Naziri was in a foul mood.

He sat at his desk, reading the message again from his daughter. The tone was scathing and sarcastic.

Fatima was back safely at her boarding school in Connecticut, weeks away from her graduation. Naziri was grateful she was safe, but Fatima didn't see it that way. Despite her brilliance, she was emotionally immature, so she saw certain things in simple terms. Her shiny bauble of the Bahamas trip was cut short, so it must be her father's fault.

My first vacation in three years, and it turns into a fiasco. And all because of an Ops decision not to send security with me. Who exactly was behind that?

Naziri groaned.

"Trouble?"

Naziri looked across his office here at the Triangle New Mexico underground facility. Seated on the sofa, watching a video on his tablet, was Matt "Rock" Stoneham, his new babysitter from security. Late twenties, African-American, 6-4, built like a football linebacker. Naziri caught a glimpse of his tablet. He was watching an animated program about giant robots. *Typical.*

"Bah. Only trouble caused by you and your cohorts in the security branch of Triangle Ops. Thanks to your decision not to provide me and my daughter protection during our trip, I'm back here much too soon. Back in the middle of this wasteland, virtually chained to this desk."

Stoneham didn't look up from his video but nodded. "Hey, it wasn't my call about being there in Nassau, but I'm here now, and that means keeping you safe. So here you are, nice and safe four levels underground in the middle of our little patch of nowhere, back at work."

Naziri's eyes narrowed, and the words became clipped. "Fine. But there are limits. Must you even follow me into the bathroom and wait outside my stall?"

"Yeah."

"Even down here?"

Stoneham paused his video and glanced up at the scientist. "What part of 'yeah' didn't you understand? It's one of the less pleasant parts of my job, but I still have to do it."

"I can't think with someone like you hovering over me all the time."

Stoneham stood up and walked over to Naziri's desk, his face clouded. "What do you mean, 'someone like me'?"

Naziri was having none of this. "Exactly what I said. Someone like you — a security drone, a living weapon, full of menace, ready to be violent at a moment's notice!"

Stoneham stared at the scientist for a moment, then started to chuckle. The sound reminded Naziri of gravel rolling around in a barrel. "You think I'm full of menace? Means I'm doing my job right, Doctor." He pulled over a chair and sat next to the desk. "Seriously, what's got you so upset? We have your daughter secure—"

"It's not that. It's the whole attack itself. I can't figure out why anyone would have attacked *me*."

"What do you mean?"

"Young man, while my project is interesting, it is nowhere near as bad as the most dangerous ones in the vaults down below."

"Oh, don't sell yourself short, Doc. Although..."

"What?"

"I've never been briefed on your project, so I'm not exactly clear what you're working on."

Naziri smiled. "You have no idea?"

"Nope. I was in San Jose at the engineering facility when the call came - get wheels up pronto to protect a very important personage. This is my first time down the rabbit hole, so to speak."

"What's your clearance level?"

"Delta two. Don't worry, Doc. I'm authorized to know. Otherwise, they'd never have let me down here."

Naziri nodded. "Very well. My project is a weaponized version of something I call a quantum data projector."

Stoneham nodded. "Of course it is."

"You have no idea what that is."

"Not a clue." He grinned innocently. "But I have a feeling I'm about to find out."

"Perhaps the best way would be to explain how I came up with the idea."

"Sounds reasonable. So where did it all start?"

"I can still remember the day the idea first occurred to me. Red Labs is a competitive environment. Each month, scientists from satellite facilities around the globe meet via teleconference to discuss ideas with each other for potential study and review."

"Yeah, I've heard of those! The monthly Mad Scientists' Balls."

Naziri looked at the bodyguard sternly over his glasses for a moment before he continued. "As I was saying, it was at one of these scientific conferences three years ago when another scientist from the Red Labs facility in Florida presented a project she'd been working on. What was her name again? Hinden? Harden? Ah, yes, Henderson. Cute woman. Short hair, somewhat thin, if I remember—"

"Doc, you're drifting off course."

"Oh, right. Anyway, Henderson had been researching stealth masking technology on an advanced hunter submarine. She'd created a data probe that could hack into an enemy's sensor data. She called it a 'whisker' probe—"

"A whisker? That's a weird name."

"It was an acronym. WSKR. I think it was short for Wireless Stealth Kinetic Reconnaissance or something like that." Naziri looked at Stoneham, who was staring at him in disbelief. "What?"

"You're kidding, right? A 'W-S-K-R'? Let me guess. She was testing these things on a DSV? A deep submergence vehicle?"

"No, on a hunter submarine. I told you that. May I continue?"

"Sure, Doc. Sorry I said anything."

"Right. Henderson explained her probe would maneuver stealthily into position near a target submarine, hack into its internal data network and then edit any sonar tracking data in real-time to eliminate all traces of the hunter submarine it had come from. The idea was to dynamically paint a 'hole in the water' until it was too late for the target to do anything."

The bodyguard nodded. "Electronics jamming and spoofing. Don't aircraft already do that in combat?"

"Primitively, yes, but not in that sort of environment, or with that level of precision. Anyway, as Henderson presented her project, it got me thinking. How easy could you spoof any other sort of data on the fly in real time?"

Naziri stood up and walked over to a white board on one wall of the room. He erased a list of names, the grabbed a pen. "Now, I had to determine parameters for the project. Ideally, the target would see the modified data, but it would also need to be masked in such a way that the originator of the source data would still believe it was successfully reaching its target."

Stoneham studied the diagram Naziri just drew. "Was such a transaction possible?"

Naziri smiles. Not only possible, but it turns out, it had already been done — albeit on a small scale."

"Huh?

Naziri pulled out his cell phone and tossed it on the desk. "Turns out that tools have existed for years that can spoof caller ID information, although they've been illegal since 2011 under federal law."

"So what did you do?"

"I did what any man with multiple advanced degrees would do. I built upon the genius of others. I constructed my own spoofing device from scratch, using plans I bought off the internet. Of course, my box was a lot more advanced – I managed to reduce the form factor so it could be disguised as a wrist watch. I successfully field tested it at the Federal Building in Albuquerque."

"How long did that take?"

"About ten weeks."

"What was the next step?"

"Caller ID was one thing. But the internet is a different story – a distributed data network, multiple simultaneous real-time data paths. I needed to work on a quantum level to succeed, but after three months, I had a prototype. So, I decided to go after a larger target – Fox News."

Stoneham stared at him. "You didn't."

"Why not? A popular cable news website, regularly updated on an hourly basis. Large traffic numbers. If it were going to work, this would be the place. And besides, you know what Stevenson says – go big or go home."

"So, I went to Washington and stationed myself across the street from their headquarters, and monitored them for two hours. Finally, I targeted the story. You might remember it – Congressman Evans, the freshman congressman from Ohio who'd chosen to embarrass the president at a White House Rose Garden event."

"Oh, yeah. He later apologized — said he'd made a terrible mistake in misjudging the president..." Stoneham trailed off and looked at Naziri. "That was you?"

Naziri smiled. "Well, when I activated my device, anyone visiting the Fox News site saw on their front page a story about Congressman Evans endorsing the president for re-election."

"What?"

"Yes. Of course, all the Fox News folks saw when they pulled up their site from inside the building was the original story they'd loaded — the congressman publicly criticizing the president. And so, for fifteen long minutes, their switchboard was barraged with calls as angry readers demanded to know why this maverick young leader had suddenly betrayed their political cause. If you watched the comments section, you could see people getting spun up and arguing back and forth, about what had actually been said."

"After fifteen minutes, I pulled the plug on my device and allowed the website to revert to its original appearance. Fox News immediately denounced the attack as the work of liberal hackers, and promised that computer security experts were working to track the perpetrators down."

"Never got near you, did they."

Naziri shook his head. "I monitored both communications and internet tracking efforts and dodged around them easily. Their search efforts were clumsy at best. No, for all intents and purposes, it was completely untraceable."

"What did you do next?"

"I took what I did at Fox News and presented it as proof of concept for my project at the next scientist's conference. And then I announced my goal for the next step – insertion and modification of any data stream, including video, at any bandwidth. I believed it was possible to insert false images seamlessly and undetected into real-time streaming video."

"Stevenson himself was chairing the meeting this time. When I presented my conclusions, he became very agitated. 'My God, Naziri. The implications are horrifying. Insert a false image into a stream from a trusted intelligence data source and governments could react to the data violently. Once that happened, you'd never put that genie back in the bottle.'"

His bodyguard gave him a measured look. "I'm with Mr. Stevenson on that. It sounds pretty dangerous."

"Oh, it gets worse. Think about it. The tech could falsify financial transaction data and force the markets into a panic. I remember the look on Stevenson's face when I told him that. 'If that happened and your device was discovered, people would never trust any electronic transaction ever again. The entire electronic financial infrastructure would be destroyed!'"

"And that's why you're down here.

Naziri smiled wryly. "Yes, young man, that's why I'm down here. As I understand it, destroying the world economy fits nicely under the heading of 'doomsday' scenario. Stevenson elevated the project to Level One status and assigned it a code name: False Mirror. And for the last eighteen months, this has been my life."

"Eighteen months?" Stoneham whistled once in appreciation. "Long time in the hole, especially all by yourself."

"The data stream issue has proven a harder nut to crack than I first thought. Part of this was the nature of transmission signals. The transition from analog to digital signals helped, but it wasn't complete. I've had to design technology to determine the source signal type. Then we have to consider the best possible location to insert the false data. I've even considered building a large-scale, launchable prototype that could hijack and take over an intelligence satellite. But that must wait."

"So, where are you?"

"Three weeks ago, I finally submitted Phase One of the project, detailing how such an attack could be made, including the necessary programming and hardware needed. That earned me a break."

"That's when you went on the cruise?"

"Yes. It was a last-minute decision, booked just a week before sailing. It was as much a birthday present for Fatima as a chance for me to recharge my own personal batteries. Besides, I barely see my daughter anymore."

"Why's that?"

"Since her mother died of cancer five years ago, she's been at her boarding school in Connecticut or at her grandparents' in Stratford. Frankly, I've been like a ghost in her life. I'd really hoped the trip would help us bond again."

"Did it work?"

"I thought we'd started to. But since the kidnapping attempt, we're separated to opposite corners of the world again, and Fatima blames me for all that happened. In a way, she might even be right. So, in the end, no, it didn't."

Naziri walked back and sat down at his desk. "You're in security, Mr. Stoneham. Tell me this. If my security is covered by Level One protocols, and I only scheduled my trip at the last minute, how did the kidnappers find my daughter and me?"

The bodyguard frowned. "I'm just muscle, Doc. You need someone with a much better view of the situation advising you."

"Now who's selling himself short? Knowing how Triangle works, there's more to your story than you're letting on."

Stoneham grinned. "Maybe. But that's a story for another day. But I will tell you this. There's something suspicious about the fact you were unaccompanied on the cruise ship. There should have been an asset with you — or at least undercover." Stoneham thought about this for a few moments. "If an asset was already in place for another reason—"

"Bah. What does it matter? The kidnappers failed, and I'm chained to this desk for Stevenson once more, with no idea if I'll ever escape from this prison again."

"Now, Doc, that's not the way to look at this—"

Naziri arched an eyebrow at him. "Oh, really? I tell you, young man, sometimes I wonder if I was rescued by the right side in all of this."

His computer terminal chimed three times. The video link icon popped up on the screen. Naziri glanced over at it and groaned. *Stevenson again. Sometimes that man could be a positively infuriating pain in the—*

"I'll let you take this call in private, Doc. I'll be just outside your door."

"Thank you, Mr. Stoneham."

The bodyguard nodded and exited the office. Naziri settled himself, assumed a calm manner, and opened the channel. "Good evening, Director."

"And you, Dr. Naziri. I need a status update."

What, beyond the one you called for four hours ago? Naziri's smile was plastered in place. "The plans for the phase two prototype were completed and sent to your office for approval. Component fabrication and acquisition has started. If you sign off on the design tonight, we can build within ninety-six hours, and start testing defensive measures shortly after that."

"Very well, Doctor. Is there anything else you need? This is the highest priority Red Labs project right now."

Naziri considered this for a moment. "Another fabrication tech in the shop would be helpful. Although it would be nice if this one were a little more... pleasing on the eyes. You keep sending me wrinkled, old men or young, inexperienced boys."

Stevenson looked as if he had just turned over a rock and found a particularly ugly insect. After a moment, he let out that exaggerated sigh of his and said, "Doctor, I had Watson and Williams do a little research, in anticipation of just such a request." A second window opened, showing a picture of a woman with red hair, angular features and a peculiar white scar above her eyebrow.

Stevenson continued. "This is Karen Railson, one of our leading fabrication techs from Triangle Silicon Valley. I will have her report to you in the morning if she meets with your approval."

Naziri looked over the woman's curriculum vitae. "Stanford. Caltech. Hewlett Packard. Yes, I'd say she would do quite nicely, Director."

"Fine. She'll be there in the morning. And Doctor, try to keep your mind on your data curves, rather than your new assistant's." He reached up and terminated the video link.

Naziri rubbed his hands in anticipation. *Oh, you'll get your device, Mr. Stevenson. The sooner I finish it, the sooner I can celebrate with this woman.* He smiled as he walked over to his workbench. *I wonder if she'll like alternative jazz.*

Chapter 14

Ethan and Percy carried their trays from the serving line and sat at a table by the cafeteria's video wall. Today it was tuned to a camera set back among palm trees on a deserted beach. They stared for a moment, imagining a warm tropical breeze blowing past them.

Ethan closed his eyes and leaned back. "God, what I'd give for a week in a place like that. Especially after these last few days."

Percy smiled. "Mine has a lot more people in bikinis on it. And a bamboo beachside bar, where both the libations and the morals are liberal."

Ethan chuckled and opened his eyes. "True. True. But, alas, reality intrudes. Tough to maintain the illusion when you're facing this." He pointed at the wilted salad in the center of his tray, dotted here and there with chunks of canned chicken, mandarin oranges and chow mein noodles.

Percy looked at his simple ham and cheese sandwich and smiled. "You're braver than I am, mate."

Ethan stabbed at a leaf of lettuce and piece of chicken and started to chew. "Eh, I've had worse." He swallowed and took a swig of water to help it down. "So, Percy, me lad, what can we do to help our two young charges survive their trial by fire?"

Percy considered it as he bit into his sandwich. "I'm not sure. Seems to me they're learning important lessons. Sometimes painfully, but they're learning."

"But the process is tearing your young lady apart. She's comfortable with hand-to-hand, but she is having major trouble mastering the SAVANT, and the mission sims have been disastrous. She's died, what, six times now?"

"Not quite that bad. Four-for-six. But those other two times were only because Tate saved her." He took another bite of sandwich and talked around it. "There's no way we send her out in the field. She'll fold up and be useless. Worse than useless."

He washed down the sandwich with his drink and leaned back in the chair, admiring the beach for a moment. "Honestly, Ethan, I don't think there's anything you or I can do. I mean, I admire her pluck and determination, but she's getting worse at this, not better. I think perhaps it's time we admit that we may be just wasting our time here."

Percy glanced back to Ethan, expecting a reply. But Ethan had stopped with his fork midway to his mouth and was staring behind Percy. "What's going on? Something on the monitor—"

Percy turned and found himself looking right at Amy's midsection, six inches from him. He gulped and looked up. Amy's jaw was set as she looked directly at Ethan.

"Tate and I wanted to schedule an extra practice session this evening and were hoping you two would work us through a few scenarios. But since I'm just 'wasting our time,' I'll be in my quarters."

She turned to leave. Percy reached out and grabbed her right wrist. Amy stopped and glared at him. "You have to the count of three."

"Listen, Amy, I'm sorry you had to hear that. It's—"

"One."

"—just an assessment of where you're at now, not what your full potential is—"

"Two."

"—as a Triangle agent. I know you're better than this!" Percy snatched his hand back quickly as if he'd been shocked. Amy just stared at him, her eyes narrowing.

"Three." Somehow, she made the one word convey all her frustration and anger toward Percy, Triangle, and her entire life as it stood. She turned her glower toward Ethan. "Tell Tate that I won't be joining him tonight. Or perhaps ever again."

She turned and stalked out of the room. In the corridor, people who saw her backed against the wall to get out of her way.

Ethan pushed his salad away and glared at Percy. "Brilliant. Just flippin' brilliant. Damn it, man, can't you pay attention to what's going on around you?"

Percy looked hurt. "Me? Couldn't you have given me some sort of warning?" He looked back at the entrance. "So, what do we do now?"

Ethan reached for his tablet. "Damage control. Hopefully, there's something to salvage here." He tapped a control. A comm window opened. "This is Nowitzki in Ops. I need to talk to Dr. Watson immediately."

June 1, 9:12 a.m. EDT

As Rhonda Watson sat at her desk, the beginning of a headache throbbed in her left temple. *Actually, the beginning is sitting across from me. This is just a manifestation*, she thought.

Amy Rogers had spent the night in her quarters, refusing to speak to anyone. Her commlink was off, her SAVANT shut down, and her door secured. Watson herself had gone this morning and tried to get her to open the door and talk without success. Luckily, it was a scheduled rest day so she wouldn't miss any training activities. But isolating herself was not a good sign.

"Mr. Lewis, you're aware of how much trouble you've caused, right? Ms. Rogers arrived at Triangle in a fragile emotional state. She's been drastically challenged from her first moments here. What she needed was an ally, someone to encourage her to keep striving. Not someone acting like a judge on one of those TV talent shows."

Percy fidgeted in the chair. "Yes, ma'am. I mean, in my defense, all I was doing was being honest in my assessment. I guess she might have overreacted to it as overly harsh..." He slowed to a stop under the woman's glare.

"It's blazingly intuitive insights like that which got us into this mess." Watson rubbed her temple and closed her eyes. "There's just no way she'll ever trust you now."

"If I could just talk to her—"

"And do what? Apologize? She'll never be sure if you're telling the truth or just flattering her. No, you're finished with this agent, Mr. Lewis."

She typed a command on her tablet. "I'm reassigning you. You're to catch the first transport to New Mexico, to the Red Labs facility there."

Percy blanched. "New Mexico?"

"Yes. You're to report to Dr. Naziri. His project is a Level One priority and has reached a prototype build stage. He could use an extra set of hands. And you just happen to have a pair we won't need around here anytime soon."

"But...New Mexico?"

"Yes. I hear the weather's been lovely there the past few years. I recommend sunscreen. Dismissed."

Percy opened his mouth to say something else, thought better of it, stood up and left the room.

Ethan silently watched him go and then turned back to Watson. "A little harsh there, don't you think?"

Watson closed her eyes and rubbed her temples again. "Not really. I should have fired him." She looked over at him. "Would you be able to handle controlling both?"

"Oh, sure. No problem. I can do it if you don't go real world with them on anything more complicated than say, oh, buying a newspaper."

Watson sighed, then swiveled in her chair and looked out the window behind her. "I see."

"What do you plan to do?"

"Given the circumstances, Ms. Rogers needs special handling." She swiveled her chair back and typed a series of commands into her tablet. Amy's file came up on her desk monitor, and Watson scanned it, moving through pages, looking for something she'd seen. "I have an idea. If it works out, you'll be back working solo with Tate in short order. But I'm going to have to really do some convincing..."

"Ma'am?

"Ethan, I really do need you to hold down the fort for a day or so. Contact Williams and have him move tomorrow's morning session back by two hours. Have Savannah monitor Amy's commlink and SAVANT. If she comes online, attend to her needs immediately. Be gentle and give her anything she wants, within reason. Most importantly, she's under no pressure to perform any tasks or training. Understood?"

Ethan nodded and stood up. "Right. I'll take care of it, ma'am. Good luck, and good hunting, too." He walked out.

Watson looked over the data on her screen, rubbing her chin. She found the page she was looking for and expanded it, then nodded. "Savannah?"

The AI answered immediately. "Yes, Dr. Watson?"

"Public access — I need a video call window. Put it on the wall screen. Oh, and order a personnel pickup team in transit immediately."

"Yes, Dr. Watson. Where shall I route the team to?"

"Central Florida. Have them await further instructions."

"Yes, Dr. Watson."

"As for the video call, place it to the following number..."

June 2, 9:47 a.m. EDT

Steve waited alone at the entrance to Training Room 3. *Great. No A.J. After all the crap from two nights ago, I wonder if she's even going to show up. Better call and find out.*

"Ethan, are you online?"

"Just plugging in. Had a bit of a late night."

"Oh? Anything you'd care to share with me? I could use a good laugh this morning."

"Nothing so exciting or noteworthy. Just catching up on paperwork."

Steve smirked. "Wow, Ethan. This life of international intrigue you live is fascinating."

He expected another droll reply, but instead all he heard was some muffled voices — one of which had a distinctly female timbre. Intrigued, Steve asked, "Ethan did you bring a lady into the bat-cave? Do you need some alone time, big guy?"

Ethan's sigh was so large and long that Steve swore he could feel it across the commlink. "Steve, it's the SAVANT Interface Control Center — there are fourteen different stations here. I'm just assisting a new controller to get set up. It's called being polite and all that. You might want to consider trying it some time."

"Fine, fine, don't get your panties twisted — or hers, for that matter. Uh, speaking of twisted panties, where's A.J.?"

Steve's SAVANT flared to life, projecting a small schematic of this level onto the wall next to him, complete with icons for himself and Amy. Steve had instructed Savannah to modify his SAVANT map interface, so it always changed Amy's icon to a tiny pink crown. Now her icon was at the central hub ring, moving toward the nearest branch corridor.

Ethan commented, "Amy is at Level 5, Ring 1, B corridor. At her current rate of speed, she'll join you in approximately forty-seven seconds."

Steve grinned. "Now you're just showing off for the new lady controller. In fact, if I didn't know better, I'd say you were flirting."

Steve again heard a distinctly feminine giggle over the commlink as he shut down the SAVANTs projector. *At least someone appreciates my humor this morning.* But there was something familiar about that giggle. It tickled a memory at the back of his brain.

Right on time, Amy rounded the corner at a sprint and pulled up next to Steve.

"Morning, A.J. Oversleep?"

She glared at him. "As the matter of fact, Tate, yes I did. Damn that Percy. I had a wake-up call scheduled with him for training days. He must have blown it off. I swear he's out to sabotage me."

"Whoa, slow down, A.J.! I heard about what happened, and he'd be stupid to do something like that. More likely the guy's just scared of you."

Amy's glare ratcheted up two levels. "What do you mean, scared of me?"

Steve backed up a step, thinking, *Boy, am I glad her Talent isn't shooting laser beams out of her eyes.* He put his hands in front of him. "Well, if right now's any indication, when you want to you can be pretty damned intimidating."

Amy took a deep breath and forced herself to calm down. "Fine. But someone in the ICC should have picked up the slack or at least responded to me via my commlink. No one did." She looked at her SAVANT and shook her right arm as if to test it. "Maybe this thing is busted."

"Let me check." Steve focused on his SAVANT. "Ethan, is Percy around?"

Steve could tell that Ethan was hesitating. "I'm sorry, Steve. Percy's not here right now."

Hmm? All right, Ethan, I'll go along for now. But what aren't you telling me?

"Can I get an assist here? It looks like Amy's SAVANT might be down. Is there a way to use mine to run a diagnostic on hers here in the field?"

Instead of Ethan's voice, there was a very familiar female chuckle over the commlink. "Well, if you'd rather go outside and find a field before you run that diagnostic, I guess you could do so. But I swear, Stevie, you always want to do things the hard way."

The look of surprise on Amy's face showed she'd heard the voice, too. Together, they simultaneously exclaimed, "Rose!"

Then they looked at each other in shock and simultaneously asked, "Wait a minute! How do you know Rose?"

Chapter 15

Rose grinned at her station in the ICC as she sprang the surprise on her friends. She hit the mute on her mic pickup and turned to Ethan. "That was fun!"

"Yes, well, playtime's over." He pointed to the monitor. On it, Amy and Steve were arguing vehemently.

Rose frowned. "I see what you mean."

8:54 a.m. EDT

Amy pushed Steve away. "You're the guy back home? You're nothing like what she talked about."

"Yeah, well, if you're the roommate she told her dad about, that sure explains a lot."

Over the commlink, Rose tried to interject. "Uh, guys, there'll be time for this later—"

Amy glared at Steve. "What did she say?"

Steve shrugged, trying to think of a quick comeback. "Oh, just the usual tales of girls gone wild—"

The roundhouse kick caught him completely off guard.

Note to self — do not forget how fast she is, he thought as he spun through the impact. He rolled and came back up in a defensive stance. Her next attack was already underway — a leg thrust and snap kick toward his head — when he threw his Talent into gear.

Time slowed, and Steve evaluated her attack and his potential defensive responses. He decided on one with a higher risk of failure, but which would have a particularly nasty and painful result if successful. *This'll teach her to sucker punch me,* he thought, as he flashed back into real time.

Steve thrust up his arm into an arc that deflected her kick at the last moment. As her foot brushed past his ear, he pivoted, grabbed her leg and continued rolling left. Amy slammed hard into the wall and screamed in pain as he twisted her knee and threw his full weight down on it. They went down together into a heap.

The Danger Room door slid open, and Williams ran out into the corridor. "Knock it off!" he yelled at them.

Amy kicked Steve off her to disengage from the pile, then rolled to her right and stood up quickly. Her face contorted in anger, and she looked ready to strike out again.

Steve pushed away from the kick into a twisting back handspring and came down in a defensive stance, ready for her next attack. He took note that she was favoring her injured leg and knew he had the upper hand. His lips curled into a nasty smile. "Come on, A.J. Bring it."

Suddenly, both their commlinks overloaded with a high-decibel screech. Steve and Amy grabbed their heads in pain.

8:56 a.m. EDT

Ethan covered his ears as Rose blew the referee's whistle for another three seconds. "All right, you two. Stop this right now! I know both of you can hear me. We'll have time to sort out who said what to whom later. It's been a sleepless night, I've traveled a long way, and I'm exhausted. So right now, I talk, you listen."

"Amy, you're the reason I'm here. They tell me you need help. Well, roomie, guess what? I'm it. I don't understand the full scope of this place yet, but I know my way around cyber tech, and more importantly, after three years of being in your life, I know my way around you. I already know both who and what you are. More importantly, I know exactly what you've lost. More than almost anyone else here, I know what it's cost you."

"So you have an agenda now. Yes, they've let me know all about that. Amy, these people can help you achieve that. So can I. But you are going to have to learn to work with the folks here, including your new partner there, for that to happen. Otherwise, you're going to blow your best, and possibly your only chance, to catch this woman."

Rose paused for a moment, watching Amy on the monitor. Slowly, Amy unclenched her fists and relaxed from her fighting stance. She leaned up against the wall, getting weight off her injured knee. *Atta girl,* Rose thought and turned her attention to Steve.

"Steve, Steve, Steve. You know, when they told me you were here, I wasn't sure how I felt. I mean, my heart leaped at the chance to be near you, to work with you again. At first, I considered it the perfect bonus to this assignment. But when they told me what happened, I realized that it's happening all over again for you, too. You're reliving it all again. Your mom, Marie, and a woman who's been like a ghost, haunting you. But it's not the same this time, Steve. This time, you have a chance to catch her. But it's not going to happen if you push folks away like you did with me five years ago."

"Rose, that's not true—"

"Stop. Remember, me talk, you listen. You may have this 'hero saves the day' stuff down to an art, Mr. Tate. Working day-to-day with people? Not so much. This is your chance to change that. Amy is going to be the first real working partner you've ever had - if you can learn to work with her instead of competing against her. Besides, she's the only one who's going to understand, perfectly, your need to find Callahan."

"But Steve, I also know the head games you play as well as anyone — no, scratch that; given our history, probably *better* than anyone. Get this straight — Amy's going to be your partner, so she sure as hell had better be able to trust you — completely, totally, implicitly. The games stop. Right now. Do you understand? All of it, right now. Stop busting her chops and start helping her help you."

"Now you two have a training session. I suggest you go train," Rose said.

She cut off her mic and sat back in her chair. Ethan gazed at Rose, impressed. "Why haven't we recruited you before?"

She smiled. "Who says you hadn't? Now, I'd like a little privacy with my girl, if you don't mind."

Ethan nodded, and turned back to his console, muttering, "Oh, yeah, this is definitely going to be interesting."

8:59 a.m. EDT

Steve straightened up from his combat stance, his eyes still watching Amy warily, reluctant to turn his back on her. He felt a hand on his shoulder and turned around. It was Williams. His expression was grim.

"You two are a waste of my time."

Steve's eyes narrowed. "Excuse me?"

"She's a wreck with all the emotional strength of an eggshell — one severe test in the field, and she'll fold like a bad poker hand. You... you're all computer and no heart, brain boy. Yeah, you can think your way through situations and do amazing stuff, but deep down, I don't believe you care about anyone except yourself."

"That's not true—"

"Really? You've completely missed the point — that you two are supposed to be a team. You think this is some sort of race, and you've done everything to come in first — including submarine Rogers' confidence. You, of all people, should have been helping her — after all, don't you share a parallel history with her? Yet you're as much the reason she's failed as the ghost of her boyfriend." Williams looked away, disgusted.

"The worst part of this is I should have been out in the field, doing my job. Pursuing this target. Protecting this organization. Instead, I'm stuck down here, wasting my time with two useless, untrainable wannabes. Watson and

Stevenson must be out of their minds thinking you two could ever be successful agents."

He turned and stalked off into the Danger Room. Steve stared, unsure whether he wanted to follow and continue the argument. As he considered his response, he felt a hand on his right arm.

Amy's hand.

Instinctively, Steve snatched his arm away, whirled to his right and dropped backed two steps into a defensive stance. "What, now you want to come after me, too? Tell me how I'm screwing up your life?"

Amy held up two hands in front of her in a gesture of apology. "Look, I, uh, want to say I'm sorry. I took a cheap shot at you just now. I was wrong."

Steve looked at her, genuinely surprised. He relaxed out of the stance.

Okay, genius, your move. Are you man enough to admit you're made a mistake? After all, she's suffered just as much as you have. You don't know her whole story. That might be a good place to start.

He took a step toward her, looking down at the floor for a moment, then glanced up and met her gaze. "Umm, yeah, about that. Look, Amy, you don't have to apologize. I haven't been as supportive as I should have been. Truth is, I've avoided it, playing head games since we started training. I guess part of it was a way for me to avoid dealing with my own past. But that wasn't fair to you."

Suddenly, Steve felt awkward around Amy. His stomach doing a slow flip-flop. *What the heck...?* He stalled, looking around to avoid eye contact as he took a deep breath. He blew it out slowly, filling his cheeks for a second as he did so. The moment of awkward silence grew longer. He looked again at Amy and cleared his throat.

"So, umm, how about we clean slate it now and start all over between us? What do you say?"

Amy considered Steve's offer. *A new beginning? With Rose guiding us? This could work.* She nodded slowly. "Sure, Tate. It's a deal."

The look on Steve's face surprised Amy. It was a goofy smile, mixed with the relief of someone who had been hoping for a result. "Thanks, A.J.!"

He turned and rushed into the Danger Room. Amy started to growl, but inside her head, Rose quickly said, "Chill, Amy. He didn't say that to hurt you deliberately."

"But he knows I don't like being called that."

"Yeah, but that's not why he did it. Remember, Roomie, he might be one of the smartest kids in the room, but in some ways, at times he's just an overgrown 6th grader."

"Meaning..."

Rose sighed. "Wow. Really? If I have to spell it out for you, maybe you're still a 6th grader, too. Think it through, Amelia Jane. But do it later. You need to get into the Training Room. You're in for another surprise."

Fine, Amy thought, with a puzzled frown. *I'll deal with it later. But not too much later.* She turned and walked into the Danger Room.

Amy was surprised to see Dr. Watson and Williams at the far side of the room, near the maintenance hatch, out of earshot. It looked like they were having a very intense discussion. Williams kept gesturing angrily, while Watson just stood her ground, arms folded, and shook her head. Her replies were short and direct. Finally, she cut him off, and a set of data appeared in mid-air between them. Williams grabbed it and sweep it onto his tablet. The image of Dr. Watson flickered once and nodded — *a hologram,* Amy realized — as Williams walked over to her and Steve. His attitude was stiff and formal, and he avoided making eye contact with her.

"Something has come up, and I've been... reassigned. You two are to continue your training without me." Without saying another word, Williams exited the Danger Room.

Steve and Amy glanced at each other, confused.

Amy broke the silence. "Who trains us now?"

"An excellent question, Ms. Rogers. And the simple answer is each other."

Steve and Amy turned and looked at the hologram of Dr. Watson. It had reappeared, ghostlike, behind them.

Steve frowned. "Excuse me, ma'am, but I don't see how either of us is qualified to train anyone to be an agent or a spy — or whatever you folks call yourselves."

"Those lessons will come as we need them. We can bring in other instructors for specific skills. But the first lesson you need is how to work together. How to trust each other. So now you're going to teach each other."

Amy's eyes narrowed. "I don't understand."

Watson referred to her tablet. "Miss Rogers, you're an elite-level swimmer and hold black belts in three martial arts disciplines. Mr. Tate here is an expert in skydiving, gymnastics and a leading competitor on the European FreeRunning circuit." She looked up. "The only thing you both lack is some sort of handheld firearms training—"

"Excuse me, Doc, but my father made sure I knew how to use a pistol and a rifle after my mother was killed. I'm not qualified to be a sniper, but I can hold my own."

Watson nodded. "I see. And you, Ms. Rogers?"

"I've handled a pistol before, but I've never felt the need to fire one."

"Understood. Well, we can bring someone in to train you on that. Besides, you've already shown an affinity with your SAVANT, Mr. Tate."

Watson's hologram gestured at the two of them, urging them together. "Do you understand? Each of you is already an expert. So now, I want each of you to start teaching your partner to be proficient in one of your areas of expertise." Watson looked at Amy. "That means you, Ms. Rogers, are going to teach Mr. Tate advanced hand-to-hand combat." Amy glanced over at Steve, a Cheshire cat grin forming on her face.

Watson gestured to Steve. "Meanwhile, Mr. Tate, you will train Ms. Rogers to become proficient at parkour."

Steve nodded. "Actually, this sounds kind of fun."

Watson looked at him. "I'm serious, Mr. Tate. There's a target out there to stop, and Mr. Stevenson thinks you're the right tools for the job. However, Williams was correct — so far, you've been wasting our time. That stops now. Negotiate a schedule amongst yourselves, but by the end of the week — that's four days from now — I expect to see real progress." Her hologram winked out.

Steve rubbed his jaw where Amy had clocked him earlier. He looked over at her. "You game for this?"

Amy was leaning down, massaging her right knee. She looked over and nodded. "Yeah. Callahan's still out there. We both want her, right? Let's get to work." She stuck out a hand to him. "Partner?"

Steve shook it. "Partner. Ladies first?"

Amy thought for a moment. *Repeatedly thumping him to the mat from the start might not be the best way to cement our partnership.* "Why don't you show me how to make some of those free-running moves?"

Steve grinned. "Okay." He looked up at the ceiling. "Savannah, got your ears on?"

The base AI answered him smoothly. "Certainly, Steve. How may I assist you?"

"Please configure Training 3 for me. I need a free-running course. Let's start with a set of four blocks, eight-foot square, concrete, brick or similar, set in a square, with a four-foot gap between each block to start."

"How tall?"

"Vary the heights between 3 and 6 feet. Be random about it."

"Complying." The floor in the center of the room started to move, reconfiguring itself to create the blocks.

Steve looked over at her. "You have any gymnastics training?"

"I competed for all four years in high school. Balance beam was my specialty."

"Nice. You'll get this down in no time." He started walking toward the blocks. Amy fell into step beside him. "All right, A.J. — er, Amy, let's get started. Parkour started in France a few decades back..."

June 3, 11:46 a.m. MDT

Traffic on the two-lane road was sparse under the midday sun. To Percy, it seemed as if even the cars and their drivers were trying to avoid the heat.

But not me. No, I had to go open my bloody mouth and shoot if off. Now it's ended me up out here, smack in the middle of nowhere.

The 'middle of nowhere' was in reality about sixty miles west of Albuquerque. His plane had arrived at midday and a car was waiting to pick him up. As he sat in the passenger seat, watching the miles of empty terrain pass by, he couldn't help but think, *my life is ruined.*

The woman driving the car glanced over at him staring out the window. "It can't be that bad."

"Yeah, well, forty-eight hours ago, I had a plum job, and now..."

She chuckled. "And now, welcome to the backside of hell, right? But it's not so bad. Dr. Naziri's actually really glad to have you working with him."

Percy glanced over at the driver. "Oh? He said that?"

She pursed her lips for a moment. "Not exactly. But the doctor sent me to fetch you directly from the airport and said we're to go straight to the lab. This project's very high priority, so anyone they bring in to work on it has to be top notch, right?"

Percy nodded, warming to this woman. "That's true."

"He said you were an MIT hotshot with a degree in electrical engineering. Since he's MIT as well, that works in your favor, too." She paused and glanced over at him again. "But he definitely didn't mention you'd be cute."

Percy perked up and looked at the woman. *Hmm, early 40s, reddish-blonde hair, kind of tall, nice figure, great tan...maybe she's feeling a little cougarish today. Well, if I'm going to be stuck out here in Purgatory, it might be nice if it had a reward or two like this.* "That's very kind of you to say, Ms..."

"Karen Railson. But my friends call me Hannah." She smiled at him and lowered her sunglasses to reveal a pair of striking gray eyes.

Percy stared at those eyes, They were beautiful, so beautiful he wanted to sink into them, get lost in them as if they were the only things in the world. Moments later, he smiled, suddenly so happy to be near her. "I'd very much like to be one of those friends, Hannah."

"I thought you might."

The car turned onto a dirt road, passing a simple wooden sign with a Triangle logo.

Chapter 16

Watson sat at her desk, reviewing reports. The late afternoon sun angled through the trees, throwing a golden tint into the room. One shaft of sunlight glanced off the inch of scotch in the glass on her desk, scattering amber reflections.

She put down the tablet and stood up. She grabbed the drink and walked over to the windows, gazing over the landscaped grounds. Taking a sip, she savored the burn of the single malt as she congratulated herself. *Bringing in Johannsen was a stroke of brilliance. She's settled down Rogers to where she's making real progress. The two of them will be field ready within another two weeks.*

She stared past the manicured grounds at the distant hills beyond the Triangle property. *Now if I just had somewhere to send them.* She glanced back at the desk. On her tablet were the latest intelligence reports. They all boiled down to a single sentence — no sign of Callahan anywhere.

No one disappears that thoroughly by themselves. Somebody's cleaning up after her, erasing every trace of Callahan as quickly as she makes any. And they're good, too, Watson thought grudgingly. *We could probably learn a trick or two from them, whoever they are.*

Savannah interrupted her. "Excuse me, Dr. Watson; you have an incoming call from Rose Johannsen."

"Put her through, Savannah. Wall screen, please." Watson put the drink down and walked over to the wall. The image shifted from a copy of Van Gogh's *Sunflowers* to Rose at her console in the ICC.

"Miss Johannsen. I was just thinking about you. You've made quite a positive impact since your arrival."

Rose nodded. "Thanks, Dr. Watson. But I have a favor to ask."

"Go ahead."

"The public memorial for Jason Avant is at ASU tomorrow morning at 10 a.m. I'd like to go, and I want to take Amy with me."

Watson stared at her. "You're joking."

"No, ma'am, quite serious."

"Why? What good will it do?"

Rose sighed and looked at her boss. "Ma'am, sometimes I am amazed that, for as smart as you people here are, just how... clueless you seem to be as a group about certain things." She shifted in her seat and faced the camera directly. "While you're thinking about Amy as a potential asset, I'm worried about her as a person, as a friend. You've never given her a chance to say goodbye to Jason. You swept her straight from the hospital into training, and she's been underground and incommunicado ever since."

Watson sputtered angrily. "That was for Ms. Rogers' own good—"

"Bull."

Rhonda Watson stopped short and stared at the screen. Very few people had the temerity to even consider using such a tone with her. "Now you listen, Miss Johannsen. I—"

Rose glowered at Watson. "No, you listen. You can claim all of this was in Amy's best interest, but we both know you've got another agenda, Dr. Watson. And believe it or not, I'm fine with it. If I weren't, I wouldn't have signed on to be part of your little clambake here. But you need to remember something. Amelia Jane Rogers is a person, not a tool. A grieving young woman who found the love of her life and on the very day she figured that out, lost him forever."

Watson opened her mouth as if to protest, then stopped. A strange look came over her as if a long-forgotten memory was forcing its way to the surface.

Rose continued. "Funerals aren't for the dead, Dr. Watson, they're for the living. And Jason was a popular figure at ASU. People there need to say goodbye. Amy more than most."

"Won't her reappearance just raise more questions?"

"Jason and Amy had just started their relationship when he was killed. I don't think many people knew they were romantically involved. She'll be just another emotionally devastated athlete in the crowd, deeply affected by his loss." She held up her forearm. "If you're worried about her, um, jewelry, she could leave her SAVANT behind."

"You really believe the trip is necessary?"

"It is. But, hey, what do I know?" Rose paused a moment. "Oh, that's right; I'm the person you brought in to make her whole and useful to you."

Watson sighed and smiled ruefully. "When you put it in such a charming way, how can I possibly refuse?" She walked back to her desk. "But I want backup along, just in case. Take Steve Tate with you."

Rose frowned. "Um, I don't think that's a good idea—"

"I disagree. He's her partner now. He should be there to support her. Given his history, being at the funeral will probably strengthen the bond between them."

Rose opened her mouth to protest, but Dr. Watson cut her off. "And it is not up for discussion."

"Yes, ma'am."

Watson typed quickly on her tablet and pressed send. "There, your travel orders are on the way. Draw whatever civilian clothing and supplies you need from stores. Transport is awaiting your call."

"Thank you, ma'am."

"I'll expect them back in training the next morning."

"They'll be there. Thank you." Rose cut off the transmission and the image again shifted to Van Gogh's Sunflowers.

Watson took another sip of her drink, then picked up her tablet and pressed a couple of controls. A file folder opened, and a series of thumbnails appeared. Watson scrolled through them, found the one she was looking for, and tapped it twice.

The Van Gogh faded and in its place, a photo appeared. Eight friends, at a beach, posing around an old station wagon with a pair of surfboards on top. Watson moved closer and ran her finger over the face of a blond young man in the middle of the group. Next to him were younger versions of Rhonda Watson and Mitch Williams.

God, Clay, I still miss you. You have no idea how much I do. She finished her drink, then sighed. *I'm not sure I can do this without you.*

A small chime sounded. Watson swept the image off the screen. It returned to the default Van Gogh. "Yes, Savannah?"

"I am sorry to disturb you, Dr. Watson. You asked me to contact you when Agent Williams arrived at his assignment."

"Thank you. Send him a message to contact me in sixty minutes."

"Acknowledged."

"And leave me alone for ten minutes. No interruptions."

"Acknowledged."

Watson took her glass to the window again and stared once more at the distant hills. She took another sip and felt the burn.

"Where the hell are you hiding, Hannah?"

June 13, 5:57 a.m. MDT

The monitor showed a series of images of the desert — dry, flat, empty of anything resembling civilization. The pre-dawn skies were gradually lightening from navy to azure.

"Test confirmed. You've negated all live transmissions from the cameras on the network." Percy looked at the doctor over his monitor, all smiles. "Even the commercial EarthSat that just overflew the site shows nothing! For all intents and purposes, Dr. Naziri, Triangle New Mexico just disappeared from the face of the Earth."

On the main workbench, the False Mirror prototype hummed softly, emitting the faint blue glow typical of all Triangle technology. Percy asked Naziri about that earlier and was told it had something to do with the power source for the nanites used in much of Triangle's tech. "That, young man, is the real secret behind Triangle. Now, if you could somehow turn off the nanites all at once... Hmm, I wonder if anyone's ever proposed that to Red Labs. Percy, remind me to check the database."

"Yes, Doctor."

They had returned to fashioning the prototype, and now, four days later, their tests confirmed it was working. Naziri turned around, frowning. "Now, where is Ms. Railson? Ah, there you are, my dear. Kindly terminate the test circuit. Let's show our face to the world again, shall we?"

She smiled, and on a small remote pressed a control sequence. The lights on the prototype flared briefly, then faded to black. Onscreen, a very brief burst of distortion appeared, and when it cleared, the monitor image again showed the base from various camera angles. One moment it was gone; the next, it was simply there again.

Percy looked again at Naziri. "Test terminated successfully. Congratulations, Doctor."

Naziri nodded. "What do you think will be the after effects of the test?"

Percy considered it for a moment. "Well, if the EarthSat was recording for any commercial mapping sites, then Google Maps may have problems finding us when they release their next update. I'm not sure Mr. Stevenson would consider that so bad."

"Yes, well, he might not consider it so good, either. I will include that in our findings." Naziri glanced at the clock. "Let's see, 6 a.m. here...yes, I can call. I must report on this immediately. Ms. Railson, kindly put the prototype back in its storage unit. Mr. Lewis, please assist her, of course. Then both of you get some rest — it's been a long night. I will see you both here tomorrow morning."

Percy nodded. "Thank you, Doctor." Railson waved as Naziri exited the lab and headed for his office.

Percy started shutting down the test station and coiling up the associated cables as Railson undid the power and data relays into the device. Powered down and inert, the device wasn't very impressive — just two offset rectangular blocks on a tubular aluminum base, with a pair of carry handles on top. It weighed all of 15 pounds; she picked it up easily and placed it in a padded fiberglass storage case.

As Percy coiled the custom data cables he'd constructed (complete with his own invention, a nanite-based 'skeleton key' adapter to fit it to any system), he glanced over at Railson. "So, Hannah, do you have any plans?"

"After an all-nighter like that? Steak and eggs sound good."

"Actually, that does. Where's a good place to get some around here?"

Railson walked over to Percy and smiled. "My place." She leaned in and kissed him, slowly, carefully and very, very thoroughly.

Percy tried to say something, but suddenly he wasn't thinking clearly. The cable he was coiling dropped to the floor. "Uh..."

"Of course, if you have other plans..." She walked away, grabbed her leather jacket off the back of a chair and headed for the door.

Percy fumbled for the words. "N-no... nothing I can't... Hey, wait for me!" He grabbed his own jacket and ran out of the lab.

1:14 p.m. EDT

Amy, Rose, and Steve strolled across the campus of American Southern University with the crowd leaving Jason's memorial service. There had been tears and hugs, but everyone was surprisingly upbeat. Despite the tragedy of Jason's death, it had been a celebration of his life, of the good works he had done — his time in the service in the army before coming to school, his love of swimming, the joy he took in teaching.

As they walked away from the auditorium, anonymous among the crowd, Amy hadn't let go of either of her companion's hands. Silently, she led them through the campus's signature esplanades, heading somewhere specific. Rose and Steve followed her willingly.

They rounded a corner and stopped. In front of them was a large circular pool, teal in color. Moments after they arrived, 75 jets lining the edges leaped to life, all aimed toward the center. In seconds, they'd formed a canopy, a dome of mist and spray over the pool that the sunlight played through, sparkling and jumping. The sight was breathtaking.

Amy spoke quietly. "It was my first day on campus. I'd just come around this corner, and the fountain was running. I was mesmerized. I had never seen anything so amazing, so..."

"And then this guy walks up and stands next to me. He doesn't say a word; he just stands there, looking at it. Just like I was. We must have stood there for fifteen, twenty minutes."

"Finally, the fountain shuts off, and he starts to walk away down the hill. Doesn't say a single word, just walks away. So, I have to know. 'What did you think of it?' I call out to him."

"He glanced back at me, smiled slightly and said, 'Second most beautiful thing I've seen today.' And then he turned and kept going."

"Six weeks later, I was at the swimming pool, doing laps, and when I stopped, here is this same guy, standing at

195

the end of my lane, grinning down at me. Just a little half-grin, somewhat timid. But all for me. He introduced himself that time — Jason, a graduate student here who was also helping coach the swim team. The whole time, he's polite and respectful, and never once made a move. Flirts, but doesn't follow up."

"He helped coach me through three seasons here... and finally, a couple of months ago, I got up my nerve and I made the first move. And we had seven wonderful weeks..."

Amy's breath caught. Steve and Rose didn't say anything. They just held her hands as the fountain ran in the background. Amy stared at it.

"The night before the ship pulled into Nassau, we were strolling on the deck of the cruise ship. There was a full moon out. It was a perfect night. Well, we stopped along the railing and watched the moon silently for a few moments. Then, without a word, he just turned to me and kissed me, and, well, one thing led to another. First time ever for us, and everything I ever could have wanted. Afterward, he smiled at me, that same half smile."

"'What are you smiling about?' I asked him."

"'I was thinking about the full moon tonight,' he said, brushing the hair away from my face."

"'Oh?' I said, thinking to myself, 'How could you be thinking about the moon after THAT!'"

Rose broke up, giggling, Steve smiled, and Amy nodded. "Yeah, I know. But then he looked at me... and he laughed and said, 'Well, it was the second most beautiful thing I saw tonight.'"

Amy's voice faltered. Steve nodded. "Sounds like Jason was a very wise young man."

"He...he was." Amy turned, buried her head on Rose's shoulders and started sobbing. Steve let go of her hand as Rose encircled Amy in a hug. The tears flowed as Amy finally let herself cry freely. Rose held her, stroking her hair, murmuring to her that it would all be okay, and encouraging her to let it all out.

Steve opened his mouth to say something, but Rose caught his eye and shook her head slightly. He stopped and took a step back. With a tilt of her head, she signaled for him to go get the rental car. Steve nodded, touched Amy lightly on the shoulder, and left.

Amy continued sobbing quietly as Rose held her close. Slowly, the sobs subsided, and Amy caught her breath. She lifted her head and looked at Rose. "I'm sorry."

"What, for getting my dress a little damp? Eh, it's Florida. It happens down here."

Amy laughed at that. "I don't know what I'd do without you, Rose."

They started walking to the edge of the fountain. "Same as you always do, Amy. Survive. You'd pick yourself up, move forward and make the best life possible."

Amy sat at the edge and started playing her fingers through the water. Rose sat next to her and smiled, then bent over, touching her forehead to her friend's. In a low voice, she asked, "So, did he ever find out about your... you know..."

"My Talent?" Amy looked away for a moment and then shook her head. "No. I started to tell him, but I never got to finish. But I think he may have already known, Rose. He would have been okay with my being special."

Rose considered this and nodded. "Well, we've still got unfinished business. We're going to find Callahan, Amy. And I promise you when we do, I'll let you have five minutes alone with her." Rose dipped her hands in the fountain and rinsed them off.

Amy smiled thinly. "I'll only need two." They shared a quiet laugh.

Rose stood up and stepped back. "I'll give you a moment." She moved a respectful distance away.

The fountain had stopped, and the pool had smoothed to a mirror. Amy lay down at the edge and looked at the water. It seemed to stretch on forever, into infinity. For a moment, Amy felt if she just dove in and swam to the other edge of that infinite pool, Jason would be there, waiting for her, to take her in his arms again.

I love you, Jason. And nothing will ever change that. I promise you.

She dipped one finger into the water, and then on the gray concrete next to her traced the letters 'JA' and a heart around it. Closing her eyes, she brought her fingers to her lips and pressed them there, and then, reluctantly, took the kiss and touched it to Jason's initials.

Goodbye, Jason.

She stood up and wiped away another tear, then walked over to Rose, who stood vigil for her. With a nod, they turned and headed back down the hill toward the rental car.

Behind her, the letters, the heart, and the kiss slowly evaporated and disappeared, gone forever.

Chapter 17

They flew back to Washington in the Triangle Gulfstream V. Rose pulled out a blanket and covered Amy, who looked as if she was getting her first restful sleep in quite some time. Steve was staring out a window when Rose carried her cup of coffee and joined him up front. "Penny for your thoughts?"

"Yeah. When did you get so good at this?"

"I was always this good. You were just too distracted to notice." She looked back at Amy. "What does she know about us?"

"I've never said anything. But you two were roommates, so who knows what stories you made up." Steve chuckled. "Does she know you once called her 'The Little Mermaid'?"

"No, and I'd prefer you let that one pass unmentioned, thank you very much." Rose grinned back. "Not quite my finest hour, I admit, but we'd just met."

She sipped her coffee and glanced over Steve's shoulder at her sleeping friend. "I tell you, Rusty, she had it bad for that guy. At least she got her man in the end, even if it was tragic. Better to have loved and lost, right?"

"So, what about you, Thornbush? What's your story these days?"

"Who, me? Why, I'm as innocent as a newborn lambkin, Mr. Tate," Rose said with a wolfish grin. "Come on, you know me; never one to pine over the one that got away. But, as for my latest? His name was Raoul. Sadly, emphasis on 'was.' Foreign exchange student from Paraguay. Very wealthy father, very expensive tastes, and unfortunately, very easy to distract, too — in his case, a blonde. A shame, really. He played water polo. Had the most amazing breath control when he—"

"Whoa! Too much information, Rose!"

Rose giggled. "I do love watching you squirm, Rusty."

"Sorry, can't call me that anymore. I had my name legally changed. I dropped the first name altogether. It really is just Steve now."

Rose stared at him. "You're kidding, right? You actually spent the time and money to do that?" Steve nodded, and she whistled. "Bet somebody was not happy when that happened."

Steve shrugged. "My life, my name."

"Well, you can change the label but it doesn't change the man." Rose moved to the seat next to him and leaned in. "Or does it? R..." she touched him on the nose with her forefinger.

"Rose..."

"S..." She quieted his protest with a single finger on his lips.

"Don't."

"T..." She leaned in and kissed him gently, lingering for a moment. "My, I have missed that."

Steve backed away, and then moved into a seat in the row opposite her, putting distance between them. "Well, I haven't. That was a lifetime ago. And it stops now, understood? We have a job to do. We go back, we train, and we take out Callahan."

Rose pouted as she looked at him. "When did you start to care?"

Steve looked back at Amy. "When I realized just what she'd lost." His voice became quiet, strained. "Callahan took half my family but she stole Amy's future from her. I try to imagine how I'd have felt if..." Steve's voice trailed off.

"If it had been me?"

Steve's eyes met hers. "Yes." His voice became quiet, distant, as his mind raced back to the shooting. "I should have been able to stop her, Rose. The odds were bad, but I've seen worse at other times and still made the stunt."

"Oh, really? I'd love to know where."

Steve looked at Rose, trying to decide how much of his past he could really trust her with. "Umm. Well, you know how I've been in Europe doing freerunning for the past three years, right?"

"Of course I do. You're kind of good at it."

"Well...during my time there, I haven't always been *in* Europe."

Rose looked at Steve and raised an eyebrow. "Do tell."

Steve looked out the window, avoiding her gaze. "One of the guys on the circuit needed help with his family. So I went to help them out of someplace that was, well..." He trailed off for a second, unsure how to continue.

"Let me guess. Not in Europe."

"More like *way south* of Europe."

Her eyes narrowed. "How far south?"

He glanced back at Rose. "Very. What I did there doesn't matter. The point is, Nassau wasn't the first time I'd been on the wrong end of a gun. I knew how to handle it. But something went wrong. Jason shouldn't have taken those bullets — they should have hit me."

Rose's frowned. "Yeah, knowing you, that's definitely the choice you'd make. Of course, if you succeeded, what would have been the outcome?"

"Jason Avant would be alive, and Amy wouldn't be in so much pain."

"Good answer. But you only get partial credit, Brain Boy."

"Rose, there's no need to be—"

"Oh, just shut up and listen, will you? Yes, you didn't save Jason. A tragedy, to be sure. But if you succeed, then you *don't stop* Callahan."

Steve blanched. "What?"

"You heard me. Callahan gets away with the Naziris. Steals his secrets, then kills them and tosses them overboard for the sharks to snack on. Finally, she uses the secrets from Naziri to build her own doomsday device and presto – end of the world."

Steve stared at her, silent for a few moments. "I hadn't considered the implications..."

"Of course not. At the time, you were just trying to save someone. You were working from incomplete data when you made the calculation about your jump. If you go back now and look at all the implications, the logical conclusion is that what happened, however painful, might have been the best possible outcome. But maybe you need to start asking a different question."

"What's that?"

"Given what I understand now about your Talent — oh, and by the way, nice job hiding that from me; don't think I'm ever going to forgive you for keeping that secret from me. Anyway, given what I understand, you absolutely knew, without a doubt, what the result would be when you leaped. You knew you were going to eat a bullet and most probably die, right? Except, somehow, you didn't. So what did you miss?"

Steve frowned at her. "What do you mean?"

"I'd have thought it would've been obvious to you by now. You missed something, another factor, which somehow affected the situation, yet was beyond your Talent to detect, identify, quantify and measure." Rose stood up and walked over to Steve. "So, tell me, Steve. What is it you *can't see* with your Talent? Figure that out, and a lot of other questions might start finding their answers as well." She kissed him on the cheek. "And if not, well, the least you can do is recognize and enjoy the time you were never supposed to have."

Steve looked at her, surprised. "Meaning?"

"Well, if you'd done the math right, we wouldn't be having this conversation. You'd have never known you'd found Callahan. Instead, she'd have killed another member of your family."

Steve started to reply, and then stopped, staring at her, his mouth agape. Rose smiled slightly, leaned over and with one finger closed his jaw. "Instead, you now know who she is. Instead, now you and Amy have a chance to catch her, bring her to justice, and live happily ever after. Look at that as a final gift Jason gave Amy and you. I'd suggest you two try to make the most out of it."

She stood and kissed Steve gently on the forehead, then walked back and sat next to Amy. Steve watched her, then turned back and stared at the clouds, lost in thought.

3:57 p.m. MDT

Percy was awoken by repeated knocking on the hotel room door. *Man, they are persistent, I'll give them that.*

"Go away. It's my day off."

The knocking continued, more urgent. Percy groaned. "All right, all right, give me a sec, will you?" He looked around, found his pants on the floor and slid them on. He padded over to the door and opened it a crack.

Dr. Naziri was standing there, accompanied by two Triangle security personnel. "Mr. Lewis! Why haven't you answered your phone?"

"It hasn't gone off. Here, I'll show—" Percy reached into his pocket. His phone was missing. "Huh, that's weird."

"May we come in?"

"Uh, yeah... sure." Percy opened the door wider. Naziri and his two guards pushed past him and started searching the room, checking in the bathroom and the closet.

Percy's mind was starting to clear up. "Hey, don't, she might still be—"

"Who might still be, Mr. Lewis?" Naziri's gaze was intense.

"Umm... Hannah. Ms. Railson. She invited me up for some steak and eggs... and..." Realization dawned on Percy. "How did you know to look for me in her room?"

"We weren't looking for you, Mr. Lewis. We were looking for your companion. And what she took."

"What she took?"

"She walked out of Red Labs with the False Mirror prototype three hours after we finished the last test. She came back with an authorization form, loaded it into a car and drove away."

Percy blanched. "That's impossible, Doctor."

"Oh, and why is that, Mr. Lewis?"

Percy gulped once and pointed. "Because, three hours after we left the lab, the two of us were in that bed!"

June 14, 7:55 a.m. EDT

Amy's head was pounding as she walked into the shower and closed the glass door behind her. *Too much*, she thought, as the water cascaded over her. *Too much grief, too much sleep... and too much tequila.*

After they had landed, Rose had suggested that a night out for the three of them would help bond the team. Steve went right along with it, and Amy, grateful for their support earlier, had agreed.

"What was I thinking?" she said to the shower, which had no answer other than a spray of water. *I was already an emotional wreck. No way should I have gone out drinking. And then they had me sing karaoke? Ugh.*

Eyes closed, she grabbed the bar of soap from the dish and started to lather up.

Huh. That's weird. It smells funny.

As she moved it around to her left side, she felt a flare of pain. She carefully examined the injury — a deep bruise on her left side. *What the...? Oh, my God. Did I get in a bar fight?*

The commlink chimed in her head. The sound made her wince. She finished rinsing off her body, turned off the water and said, "Acknowledged."

"Amy?" Rose was talking quieter than normal.

Either she's being very nice, or she's as hung over as I am. "Uh, Rose, did we get in a bar fight last night?"

Rose chuckled. "Ah, so you do remember some of it. That's good; Steve was afraid—"

"Steve? What does he have to do with it?"

"You mean you don't remember what you and—"

"Good morning, Ethan, have you seen Amy — AUGH!"

Steve walked around the corner into the bathroom, wearing a towel wrapped around his waist, and found Amy standing in the shower.

Wearing nothing but a smile.

Amy shrieked.

Quickly he shut his eyes and turned his head away. Blindly reaching onto the linen shelf by the door, he grabbed a towel and tossed it in her general direction.

"Never mind, Ethan; I found her. Give me thirty minutes. No, you don't want to know."

Amy looked at him, petrified. "What are you doing in my quarters?"

He kept his head ducked away as he answered her. "Uh, yeah, about that. Actually, you're in my quarters."

"Your quarters?" Amy suddenly felt a chill. She suspected it wasn't related to her lack of clothing.

"Yeah. It's...complicated. Look, can you, uh, put that towel on? It'll be easier to explain if I can look you in the eye."

Amy, mortified, opened the shower door and grabbed the towel. She quickly wrapped herself in it and then turned, so her back was to him. Quietly, she said, "Rose, if you knew about this—"

"Hey, don't look at me. It was your idea."

"My idea? How—"

"Look, I was calling to tell you we're on alert. Dr. Watson wants to see you, pronto. I'm stalling for you now."

"Not helping, Rose."

Rose sounded hurt. "Amy, I've got your back through just about anything. But sometimes you've got to learn things on your own. I'll leave you two alone."

"Rose? *Rose!*" There was no response. Her friend had cut off the comm channel, leaving Amy alone in Steve's bathroom.

Well, alone except for Steve.

Amy took a deep breath and turned around, still inside the shower. Her blush circuit was still working in overdrive. "You can turn around and look now. So, how is it that I'm in your bathroom?"

Steve turned around, cautiously opened one eye, and relaxed when he saw she was decent, or at least covered. "Your idea. You wanted us to spend some time alone and quote, 'bond together,' unquote." He walked to his sink and started getting ready for the day as if she wasn't there.

Or as if she belonged there as a regular part of his life, she mused for a moment, then shook it off. "And did we... uh... 'bond,' as you called it?"

"I guess you could say that." He lathered up and started shaving. "Although, I think it's probably a lot less complicated than you make that out to be, sometimes."

Amy blushed yet again. "Look, Steve, I... I mean, you and me, we... us..."

Steve was chuckling. "Relax, Amy. What happens at Triangle and all that."

Momentary panic seized her. *No. I'd remember if I... if we... wouldn't I?* She tried, but last night was all a jumble to her.

He'd finished shaving and was rinsing off his face. "Are you okay, A.J.?"

She nodded. "Yeah, it's just—" She pulled up short and stared at Steve. "Wait a minute. You called me A.J." She opened the shower door and walked over to him at the sink. "Just what exactly *did* happen last night?"

Steve smiled as he got out his toothbrush. "We went to the bar, you sang karaoke — nice voice, by the way; no one will ever mistake you for a ship's horn."

"Gee, thanks."

"Yeah, well, after that, a nice young man came over and asked if you wanted to dance."

"Go on."

"You said no, he took offense, and a bit of a scrap started. Rose and I got you out of there before anything too bad happened."

"Define bad."

"Amy, you're a black belt in karate, judo, and aikido. In a fight, you're the textbook definition of 'bad happening.' We got you out of there before you took the guy *and* the place apart. After all, we might want to go back there someday."

"Well, as long as..." That's when Amy noticed the cut on his left forearm, where his SAVANT would normally rest. It was cleaned and stitched — she counted five of them. "You got hurt?"

Steve saw her looking at his arm. "What, this? I had to deflect a bottle in mid-air. Damn thing shattered instead of bouncing."

"This still doesn't explain why I'm in your quarters."

"When we came back to base, you insisted on dressing the wound yourself. I think you were maybe a little drunk, but you absolutely insisted. Said it was necessary for field training." Steve shook his head. "Since I'd already been drinking, I wasn't thinking any better. I agreed to this harebrained idea of yours. You grabbed a field med kit from mission supplies, we came here to my quarters, and you did this."

"I sewed you up?" Amy was incredulous.

"Sure did. Lidocaine shot, the whole nine yards. Afterward, we talked for a while about... well, a whole lot of things, and then you passed out on my sofa. I covered you with a blanket and went to bed. By myself. In my own bed. Alone. With the door closed and locked."

"When I woke up, the couch was empty. I figured you'd gone back to your quarters. When I got Ethan's call, I headed back in here..." He shrugged and grinned.

"Ah... well... and all we did is talk?"

"No, we played spin the bottle."

Amy gasped. Steve sighed, shook his head, and turned to face her. "A.J., relax. Despite what you think about me sometimes, I am a gentleman. My mother raised me to be respectful of women, especially in these circumstances. Besides, you're my partner. That would be..." He paused to take a breath and sighed. "Look, taking advantage of a moment like that, even if someone is saying that they want you to...that would just have been wrong." He walked over to the door.

"I'm going to get dressed and head over to medical to have them approve of your handiwork. We need to meet with Dr. Watson — something's happened that has everyone on edge. Just call Rose when you're ready and we'll meet at Watson's office." He turned to leave.

"Steve," Amy blurted out.

He turned around and looked at her. His expression surprised her. Gone was the relaxed, young man with the humorous outlook. His guard was down and in his look she saw a glimpse of just how much she meant to him. For the first time, Amy realized she didn't need to guard herself from Steve. She realized he would protect her, no matter what. Something inside her stirred at that realization. She started to blush and turned away for a moment, then looked up at him shyly.

"Just... thanks."

"No worries, A.J." He started to go again and then stopped in the doorway. He took a deep breath as if debating whether to say something.

"Steve? Is everything all right?"

Without turning around, he nodded. "Yeah." He hesitated a moment, then added, "This might not matter to you, but in case you're wondering, everything else today is going to be the second most beautiful thing I see." He left the room.

Amy stood there, blushing furiously and wondering just what it was she'd said to him last night.

8:50 a.m. EDT

They met up again outside Dr. Watson's office. Amy and Steve had both chosen mission wear, in case they needed to head out immediately on assignment. Steve pressed the door panel. It identified him and opened. Inside, Dr. Watson was on a video link with someone. She waved them in as she completed her conversation and indicated for them to take a seat.

Amy glanced over at Steve. He'd noticed it, too. The man on the video link was Dr. Naziri, the attempted kidnap victim. *Naziri. That means Red Labs is involved. And maybe they have a lead on Callahan.* She felt a mixture of dread and excitement.

Dr. Watson completed her conversation and closed the video link, then turned to them.

"Tate, Rogers. Good morning. We've had a development. Callahan's resurfaced."

"What?"

"Where?"

Watson held up her hands. "I'll answer your questions in due time. Let me explain. She infiltrated the Red Labs facility in New Mexico, took advantage of Mr. Lewis'... proclivities and made off with the False Mirror prototype."

Amy grimaced. "Percy? He's at Red Labs? Is he all right?"

Watson nodded. "He's fine."

Steve looked over at Watson. "So, what exactly happened?"

Watson pushed a series of still images from her tablet onto the wall display. "Dr. Naziri's team, including Mr. Lewis, successfully tested the False Mirror prototype just before dawn yesterday. After the trial, Dr. Naziri left to report the results, leaving behind his two assistants to secure the equipment."

"Two assistants?"

"Yes. Mr. Lewis and another woman named Karen Railson out of Triangle's Silicon Valley facility. Well, after supposedly securing the equipment, Percy and Ms. Railson went off for coffee and a tryst."

Amy snorted. "Yeah, that sounds like Percy."

"Indeed. Approximately three hours later, Dr. Naziri's lab assistant returned to the facility and took the prototype. When Naziri found out, he went looking for the assistant. Instead, he found our Mr. Lewis. Unfortunately,

Mr. Lewis' alibi for his companion means she couldn't have been the one taking the device."

Steve looked at her. "Are you sure it was Callahan?"

"See for yourself." Watson pressed a control and a surveillance video from the front gate showed a woman driving in, time-stamped at 9:10 a.m. She had reddish-blonde hair now, but the white scar above the eyebrow was unmistakably Callahan's.

"So what's the story on this lab assistant?"

"We're still working on it. She wasn't with Mr. Lewis when Dr. Naziri arrived, and we haven't been able to locate her since."

Steve shared a worried glance with Amy. "Then what you're saying, Doc, is that Callahan's had access to Red Labs the whole time?"

"I'm not sure. But I fear she used this lab assistant as sort of a Trojan horse. Given her history, three real Ms. Railson is probably already dead."

Amy frowned. "Wait. If you've known this since yesterday, then why only tell us now?"

"You three were... otherwise occupied. And we only knew where she was, not where she is. At least, until an hour ago."

Part of the screen expanded to form a map as Naziri explained. "For security purposes, my workspace had a sealed backup security system that only three people were aware of: Agent Williams, as head of Triangle Security, Dr, Watson as head of Triangle Ops division, and myself."

"How did it work?"

"Every day, anyone entering and leaving the lab passed through a passive nanite mist. If a particular code signal is sent, these nanites then go active, locate each other and assemble a signaling device. It's a sophisticated radio-frequency identification tag, designed so that it could broadcast a signal we could monitor through the commercial cellular network. Not as elegant as a GPS tracker, I admit, but when you're looking to design a powered hidden tracking device the size of a grain of rice, you have to make the occasional compromise."

Steve frowned. "I don't know, Doc. I'm damn impressed and disturbed at the same time by some of the implications. But we can debate those another time."

Watson nodded. "I agree, now is not the time. As soon as Dr. Naziri became aware of the theft, he sent the code for yesterday's RFID nanites, activating any that were outside the base's perimeter."

Amy stared at the map on display, showing a pulsing yellow blip. The implication hit her, and her own heart started racing. "You have a signal?"

Watson nodded. "We have a signal. An hour ago, Callahan was in Alameda, California, located on the old navy base there."

She turned and faced them. "You two aren't fully trained for field service, but I promised you a shot at this target. So here it is. I'm authorizing you as provisional agents, under Agent Williams' control. He was already in the field on assignment. He will meet you in Oakland. Assemble your gear for a stealth urban assault and extraction. Your plane leaves in ninety minutes."

Steve nodded and turned, squeezing Amy's shoulder once encouragingly as he left. Amy lingered, staring at the map for a moment before she spoke up. "Dr. Watson, thank you."

Rhonda Watson smiled. "Just get her this time."

Amy nodded. "Count on it."

She glanced once more at the map.

I'm coming for you, Callahan. You're mine.

7:00 a.m. PDT

Hannah was whistling tunelessly as she lay out the supplies. The phone call came as expected. "They're on the way."

"Alone?"

"Nope. Williams is running the mission."

Hannah smiled. "Just as we figured. Is everything rigged where you are?"

"Just finishing up. You all set?"

"Oh, yeah. Between the police and Triangle, no one here is going to know what hit 'em." She started laughing, and it echoed back through the phone.

Chapter 18

The elevator doors opened, and Rose stepped in and said, "Level 3." Quickly the doors closed behind her. As the elevator slid smoothly down the shaft, she kept rubbing her palms against her slacks, trying to dry them. *No need to be nervous,* she tried to convince herself. *This is just like every other day. Just another day at the beach.* Her pep talk didn't seem to be working.

The elevator's chime signaled its arrival as it slowed to a halt. The doors opened again, and Ethan was waiting there for her. "Ah, just who I was looking for. Come, walk with me."

They started left, counterclockwise around the hub corridor. She fell in beside Ethan, matching him stride for stride. After a moment, Ethan glanced over at her. "I wanted to explain how this works before we reach the Secure ICC."

"I appreciate that. I keep trying to convince myself it's just another simulation—"

"But it's not." Ethan looked sympathetically as they passed a branch corridor. "I remember my first op, too. I was nervous as hell the first time I walked into the SICC. Felt like I wanted to chunder the whole time. Luckily, that op wasn't very involved. It gave me the chance to learn and grow into the job. That was eight years ago, and I'm still here, so I must still have the right of it."

Rose tilted her head and looked at him. "Eight years? You've already run another agent."

"Two of them, actually. Though not at the same time."

"So, who were they? And what happened?"

Ethan paused, and a small smile crossed his features as he remembered. "The first one retired from field work after five years. She wanted to start a family. Triangle understands that sort of thing. I hold out hope she'll come back someday, though. May was something special. You'd have liked her, I think." Rose thought he sounded sort of wistful as if missing a long lost friend.

"And the other?"

Ethan's face grew clouded as he started walking again. "There was this pair of agents. They were already sort of freelancers before Triangle recruited them — built their own support system and everything. Not as sophisticated as here, but still damned impressive."

Rose raised an eyebrow. "How could anyone *freelance* at what we do?"

"How, indeed. Let's just say this woman and her partner are...unique cases. Anyway, when they came under Triangle's umbrella, the previous operations chief wanted to integrate them into our system here. You know, one agent to a controller—"

"Wait. That's not what they had?" Rose's eyebrow notched a level higher.

Ethan shook his head. "No, their whole team coordinated with a single person at a base station. And as far as I could discern, this guy never slept. He just stayed at his console 24/7/365. I could see a few advantages to that, but it's also damned dangerous — single point of failure and all. Anyway, after this team had joined Triangle, they shifted the male agent of their team over to me."

Rose waited for him to continue, but he just walked in silence. Finally, she couldn't stand the suspense. "Ethan, what happened?"

"Let's just say it was a spectacularly unqualified failure." He glanced sideways at her, still not breaking stride. "It's important to have a good rapport with your agent. Really, it's more than important. It's vital. Well, Rob Frederick and I never had that. Hell, we didn't have any kind of rapport. I think he expected me to be just like the previous controller he and his partner had. At least, that's all I ever heard out of him. 'Dale would have figured that out quicker,' or 'Dale could access that data,' or 'Dale was way smarter than you.'"

Ethan sighed. "I'm good at what I do, Rose, but I'm no genius like Dale Johnston, their old controller, apparently was. So, we never clicked. And the distance between us kept getting worse. It escalated to the level where he made it a point of pride not to listen to me and the data I provided him on missions."

"What? That's crazy, or stupid, or both!"

"Yes, well..." Ethan trailed off, his steps slowing. He turned down a branching corridor and stopped. "On this mission, I warned him that he and his partner needed to evac the building they'd just rescued their objective from. Frederick told me to stop worrying so much — just before their adversaries deliberately collapsed the building on top of them."

"God, no!"

"Fortunately, they barely escaped being seriously injured. The young lady they were rescuing, however..." He trailed off again, then took a deep breath and started walking once more.

"After that, I offered to step away and allow them to rebuild their original team. Tiger Team is back to being semi-independent, using Triangle resources as a backup for their own."

"And this actually works?"

"It seems to so far. But, as I said, the Tigers have a unique dynamic. Once this is over, I'll introduce you. You and Dale might have a lot to talk about." Ethan glanced at his watch and picked up his pace a little. "But I still need to discuss today with you."

"Okay, shoot."

"First thing — this is a covert field op, so we'll be using the Secure ICC. It can handle four agents, but we're only going to need three."

Rose looked up sharply at that. "Three?"

He nodded. "Yes. You, me and Christine Merrimac. She's Agent Williams' controller. The two of them have been a team for almost a decade now, and since he's lead agent in the field for this op, she'll take the lead in the SICC."

"Ethan, what exactly does 'taking the lead' mean in there?"

"At Triangle, it's usually a one-on-one relationship between agents and controllers. However, when multiple agents work an op, we need to coordinate their actions. Usually, this means the controller whose agent is senior in the field acts as the functional lead back in SICC, whether they're the most senior in the room or not. But we're not a military outfit, Rose. You'll find our command structure's not that rigid."

Rose looked at him askance. "You want to define 'not rigid' a little better. I don't want to step on any toes in there."

He shrugged. "We keep our eyes and ears open. We listen to each other, for the most part. Good ideas come from all corners. But someone must be in command. Otherwise, things devolve into chaos, and we duplicate our efforts, wasting time and resources — or worse, we don't get vital information to our agents promptly."

She nodded. "So it's like a quarterback in the huddle."

Ethan grimaced. "You know, even after a dozen years on this side of the Atlantic, I'm still amazed that you Americans seem to define everything in relation to your version of football."

"Hey, if the shoe fits..." she smiled. "What's this woman like to work with?"

He tugged on his chin. "Well, she and Williams are a matched set, you might say. She's no nonsense, although I think she has a sense of humor buried in there somewhere. But when we're on a mission, she's all business. She, uh, might not appreciate your originality of idiom when describing situations."

Rose rolled her eyes. "Oh, one of those. Great. My first live mission, nervous as hell, and now I've got to be careful about stepping on a verbal landmine."

Ethan reached out and clasped her shoulder. "Relax, Rose. Just do your job. You'll be okay, and I'll be there to help you out if you need it."

"Fair enough. All right, let's go meet the Dragon Lady."

He sighed. "It might help not thinking of Controller Merrimac that way, Rose. She's on the same team as we are — and we're all trying to stop a madwoman from making things very bad for a lot of people."

"You're right. Lead on, Controller Nowitzki."

He grinned, and they picked up the pace again. Two minutes later, they turned a corner and reached a set of doors with a pair of security guards outside it. Rose wasn't sure what surprised her more — that actual people were guarding the room, or that they were doing it this deep inside the base.

Ethan nodded to them, and then went to the ID pad. In a moment, it had verified his identity and opened to admit the two of them.

If the main ICC reminded Rose of a mission control center, then this Secure ICC room was more like something from the bridge of a starship. There was a large wall-sized data screen — she guessed it was easily 25 feet wide, running from floor to ceiling. In the middle of the floor, were two pairs of interface consoles, each with additional clear liquid crystal displays set atop them. A jump-suited technician was sitting at one console, with his tablet plugged in. As he worked, the screens cycled through a series of video test patterns.

In the middle of the room was a tall, brunette, middle-aged woman, dressed like Rose in black tunic and slacks, with a Triangle logo on her collar. She was already wearing her interface control headset, the lightweight frame barely visible as it balanced on her ear. She seemed to be in a conversation with someone, so they waited patiently just inside the door.

"No, Max, I need as much real-time satellite data over the region as you can get me. If you need to piggyback off a covert bird from someone who's less than friendly, then do that. Be discreet, but get me the images." Christine Merrimac reached up to her ear and disconnected the link, then turned and faced the two of them. "Ah, Ethan, right on time. And you must be Rose Johannsen. I've heard nothing but great things about you from Agent Williams. Trust me, he doesn't say anything like that very often, so it must be true." She waved them over to her in the center of the room.

Rose found herself liking this woman despite her initial trepidation. She seemed to be no-nonsense, but not cruel about it. Efficient she could work with. "Any change since the last briefing?"

Merrimac nodded. "Right to business. Good. Agent Williams was already in northern California on another lead when this came in. He's handling ground logistics. He has a surveillance and assault vehicle lined up from the Silicon Valley depot on the tarmac at Oakland International, just waiting for our two trainee agents to arrive."

Ethan nodded. "So where do you want me?"

Merrimac pointed at the left island. "I want you on station one, on the outside. Put Ms. Johannsen on station two next to you. I'll take station three." She indicated the inner right console on the pair across the gap, where the technician was running a diagnostic.

Rose walked over to her station and sat down at it. It sensed her presence and immediately powered up. She grinned. *Oh yeah, most definitely Star Fleet time here.* A virtual keyboard hovered in the air in front of her. She reached out and typed in her identification sequence, and the console completed booting up, showing a standard set of interface icons. She put on her own headset, quickly tested the audio link, and then pressed an icon on the console's main screen.

All right, Rose. Let's get to work. She quickly keyed in a set of commands. A data window opened on the main screen — the locator signal from Amy's SAVANT, overlaid on a map of the western US. It showed Amy in mid-air over Utah, moving westward.

"How do I switch what display this data appears on?"

Ethan walked over to her. "It's a touch-sweep move — here, let me show you." He reached over, touched the right side of the tracking display, and then made a right sweeping motion of his hand. The image immediately swept over to the right screen. He touched it again and swept left. The image returned to her main desk display. A third touch and a sweep upward with his fingertips shifted the image to the clear LCD display atop her desk. Finally, he moved that, pushing it away with one hand. It faded on his display and appeared instead on the large wall display.

Rose grinned. "Oh, I definitely like the toys in here."

Merrimac's voice was stern in her headset. "Not toys, Ms. Johannsen. Tools. Get that straight right away. Take fifteen minutes to familiarize yourself with this set-up, and configure it to your satisfaction. Your display there indicates our agents will rendezvous in just over an hour, and I want us ready for them to hit the ground running."

Rose looked sheepish. "Yes, ma'am. Any particular data you want displayed when they arrive?"

Merrimac looked thoughtful. "Yes, let's do an analysis of the signal output from the micro-RFID to see if we can deduce anything special about where Callahan has taken the device."

Rose looked at Ethan. "While I'm configuring this, could you pull and feed me all the real-time telemetry data from the RFID since it came online?"

"Sure thing." Ethan leaned down and in a semi-whisper said, "You're doing great, Rose. Keep it up." He walked around in front of the workstation to his own console and started logging in.

Rose glanced over at Merrimac, who was on the communication link with whomever 'Max' was, arguing again about satellite coverage. *Hmmm. Maybe I can find an alternative there as well...*

As she worked on configuring her station, she sent out a query to find all active surveillance cameras in the Bay Area.

4:21 p.m. MDT

Amy watched as the Wasatch Mountains slowly passed beneath the left wing of their jet. There was a broken cloud layer below them, and she was concentrating on the white fleecy behemoths. In the clouds, she saw shapes, her mind trying to put pattern to chaos. Quite often, the image resolved into an image of Jason, but more than a couple of times, it seemed just as easily to be Steve's face grinning back at her. The third time that happened, she groaned and pressed her forehead against the window.

You need to stop thinking with your glands, Amelia Jane, and start thinking with your head. You're on a mission to stop a madwoman and a murderer who has stolen a piece of technology as dangerous in its own way as an atomic bomb. You need to stop her and bring her to justice. Otherwise, all this training has just been a waste of time.

She glanced across the aisle at Steve, who was also staring out the window on his side of the plane. He'd said maybe a dozen words to her since they'd taken off. She guessed he preferred sleep or the company of his tablet to her. Not that she could blame him. After all, she'd been a mess last night and almost gotten them both in trouble. By all accounts, he'd been a gentleman, and her response? She blushed as she remembered how she'd yelled at him in his bathroom. Even then, he had still paid her an incredible compliment afterward.

But he'd used Jason's own line. *Why did he do that? What exactly did that mean?*

She groaned again in frustration. *Maybe when I find Callahan, I can get her to shoot me and put me out of my misery — after I kick her butt.*

"I'd offer you a penny for your thoughts, but those aren't worth much these days."

The voice startled Amy. The choice of words, even more. *There is no way he could have known Jason said that to me in Nassau...could he?* She looked up and saw Steve standing next to her seat. He indicated the seat across from her. "May I?"

She nodded, and he flopped down in the seat. "You know, with my Dad's job, I must have flown across the country a couple hundred times over the years, but it still sucks when you're a passenger. Five hours in an aluminum tube, just waiting for life to begin again on the other side. Too much time to spend alone, up inside here." He tapped his own head.

She looked at him. *Oh, come on, Amelia Jane. He'll have your back out there. He's not going to bite.* She took a breath. "So, your father was into flying?"

"You could say that. Grey Tate. As in, Tate Aerospace?" Steve looked at Amy for some sign of recognition at the name, but she just shrugged. Steve whistled. "Wow. A few years ago, Dad would have been wildly disappointed. Now, though..."

"Now?" Amy realized that, in all her grief, she'd never really thought about Steve and his life, beyond his Talent.

He looked out the window at the clouds. "Yeah, well...things change. He used to be the CEO of one of the largest aerospace firms in America. Now, he's up in Washington, running a little aviation shop and skydive place at an out-of-the-way airport north of Seattle that no one's ever heard of."

"And you're not."

Steve's usual grin faded. He was silent for a few moments before he turned back toward her. "Let's just say I'm not exactly the prodigal son."

Amy nodded. "Who is?"

From time to time, Amy had seen this look on his face — a grudging half-smile, almost forced, with real pain lurking behind it. It was like a scar that had never really healed but was masked and hidden behind a drapery of smile and bravado. "Not is. Was. That was supposed to be my sister. Marie." He swallowed hard once and continued. "Twin sister, actually — although I was older, by all of six minutes."

"What was she like?"

"Oh, everything I'm not, if you take my Dad's word for it. Smart, responsible, a pain in the ass about following the rules. Meticulous in everything. Oh, and as good as I am up *here*," he said, tapping his forehead, "she was better. More organized. Dad had her pegged to take over the family business. A lot better choice than the screw-up son."

Captain Obvious wasn't always perfect. How interesting. "Steve, what happened that day?"

Steve turned back toward the window. The expression on his face changed and for a moment, Amy thought he was using his Talent again. But now Steve seemed to be suffering, almost in agony. Concerned, Amy moved over and sat next to him.

His eyes focused someplace else only he was seeing, another time, another place. "Mom and Sis and I had just gone out for pizza. I was supposed to make dinner, but I got distracted by something stupid and ended up burning the meatloaf. Set off the smoke alarm, scorch marks on the stove, the works. Instead, we drove into town to Giorgio's. Dad was going to meet us there."

Steve gulped again, and something inside made Amy instinctively reach over and hold his hand. It was icy cold. Oblivious to her touch, he continued. "When we got to the restaurant, I got a call from Rose, so I stayed outside to talk to her for a moment.

Steve seemed to notice Amy's hand and gave it a small squeeze as he turned to her. "I'm not sure how your Talent works. But mine comes with certain...side effects. Like I can't erase or forget moments, memories. They don't dim with time. For me, they are as fresh and raw five years later as the moment they happened." He swallowed hard. "So, as much as I want to, I can't forget the moment I saw those bright flashes go off inside the restaurant. Or how loud the gunshots were. Or that the first time I saw

Callahan, how she bumped into me and I kept going by as I ran for the restaurant."

Steve looked up at Amy. "She ran into me, Amy. She was literally as close as you were, and I didn't stop her. I went inside and saw Mom and Sis. So much blood. And when I went out..."

Amy finished softly. "You never found her."

Steve shook his head. "No, that's just it. I did. She started to drive by. But as she did, suddenly, the world *froze*. Everything stopped moving how it all fit together. I could see the exact distance I was from the car and how fast it was moving and how fast I was running and that, no matter what I did, I wouldn't be able to catch it. And then, just as suddenly, the world started back up. And she was gone. But her face was an indelible memory."

"My father pulled up right after the shooting. I saw the look on his face — it was as if his world had collapsed. But the thing is, sometimes it seems like it isn't Mom's death but Marie's that bothers him the most. And when I finally got around to telling him about my Talent, he's acted like..."

She just sat there, riveted. Steve looked at her. "I don't know, Amy. It's like every time he looked at me, I knew he was blaming me. If I hadn't screwed up, we wouldn't have been at the pizza place when Callahan was there. So, it was my fault. And somehow getting this power seems like I got rewarded for screwing up so...so incredibly badly..."

Steve's voice faltered for a moment. Amy squeezed his hand tighter, anchoring him back to this moment, this reality. "You know why I hate my Talent? Because if I didn't have it, somehow, my mother and sister would still be here today."

Amy realized she'd stopped breathing for a moment, lost in the tragedy of his story. *He's been carrying around that kind of guilt all this time? His family gunned down like that? No wonder he went after Callahan that morning.* She met his gaze and asked gently, "What did the police say about the murders?"

He shook his head. "Just another tragic, unsolved Seattle murder. I gave them her description, but this woman was like a ghost — and you heard what they told us when we got here. Callahan is an assassin. She knew how to cover her tracks. After that, Dad sold the company. Now he works on puddle jumpers. A lot simpler life, one more appropriate for a screw-up son to take over someday."

Amy looked at Steve and realized she had him all wrong. This man cared very deeply, and yet, for all his skills, judged himself a failure, because he hadn't prevented a death that almost no one else in the world could have foreseen, let alone tried to do anything about. Yet, despite that, Steve kept trying. Maybe he was seeking redemption. Whatever the cause, she was alive as a direct result of Steve not giving up. He needed to see that.

"Steve, you're a lot of things. Pain in the butt to be sure. But a screw-up? Sorry, I don't see it. You saved my life in Nassau. You saved my life again the first day of training, and you've had my back repeatedly since then. If you're a screw-up, what does that make me?"

He looked at her and ran a hand through his curly red hair. "I'm tempted to make a comment, but you know way too much kung fu. I really shouldn't start my first mission with a broken wrist." He smiled wryly at her and looked at the death grip she had on his hand. She released it and grinned back.

"See, that's an intelligent decision. And you're so much better than 99% of the population at making those. So knock off this whole idea that you're a screw-up. You're smart, you've got a tolerable sense of humor and..." She trailed off, not sure how to say what she felt.

"Oh, come on, A.J. You're not going to leave me hanging here like that, are you?"

Amy grimaced at his use of that nickname for her and looked at him, determined. "Yeah, for now I am. When we make it through tonight, then I'll tell you. Deal?"

He looked at the hand she offered him, reached out and shook it. "You're on."

"Good. But something about your story is nagging at me, Steve."

"What?"

"The briefing we got about Callahan when they were recruiting us into Triangle. They told us she'd been an assassin for at least four years, and with your case, that makes it five, right?"

"Yeah?"

"Well, if she's an assassin, who was she targeting?"

Steve started to say something, then stopped. Amy nodded once. "Right. Something doesn't add up. Given the confirmed targets Callahan's has gone after, the wife and daughter of the CEO of a mid-size aerospace company are small potatoes. What was really going on?"

He looked at Amy, his face growing grimmer. "Well, Dad did some DOD contracting and sold off the business afterward. Could it have been some sort of corporate conspiracy? Blackmail? Someone playing hardball?"

She shook her head. "No. After all, killing family members like that is a desperation ploy — if it doesn't work, what would they have left they could do? I think there was something else in play."

Amy watched Steve close his eyes for a second. She could just imagine the tumble of confusing thoughts racing around in that supercomputer brain of his. He took a deep breath, let it out slowly, then opened his eyes and looked at her. "We just don't have enough data."

"Agreed. Well, then, there's only one thing to do. We need to ask the other person who was there why she did it."

Steve stared at her as if she'd suddenly grown a second head. "You're kidding, right? This woman killed two members of my family and your boyfriend. She's killed dozens of other people, evading capture every step along the way. She's been a ghost as far as authorities were concerned for the better part of a decade. So now the two of us, rookies at this game, are going to outwit her, capture her, and get her to tell us everything?"

Amy nodded. "Yeah, pretty much."

Steve looked at her, then down at their hands. She had reached out and taken his again, their fingers intertwined. He grinned.

"Well, then. Why the hell not?"

Chapter 19

The Triangle jet landed at Oakland International just after sundown and taxied to a remote portion of the airfield. Williams was waiting for them. Like them, he was dressed in standard mission gear — black pants, turtleneck, and combat boots. Instead of a gear vest, he had his sidearms in his signature set of crossdraw, in addition to his SAVANT.

The breeze carried a chill off San Francisco Bay as the pair descended the steps from the jet and met Williams on the tarmac. He nodded at them. "How was your flight?"

"Long. So where's our chariot?"

Williams pointed a thumb over his shoulder. Amy and Steve looked at what appeared to be a black cargo van. Steve nodded. "Stealthy. But isn't the van equivalent of a black helicopter going to attract attention around here?"

Williams' mouth twitched up at the corners. "You forget who you're dealing with, Tate." He raised his SAVANT to his mouth and whispered something. Behind him, Amy and Steve watched in amazement as the surface of the van seemed to ripple and shift. Within moments, it morphed into a Pacific Gas and Electric service van, complete with ladders and a five-gallon water bucket attached to the tail end.

"All right, rookies, close your mouths before the flies get in. We don't normally do that out in the open — no need advertising this technology in public yet. But you might see a small subset of it available on cars soon — the ability to change paint schemes on the fly. The legal folks are wrangling over whether to release it, though — it could make life easier for the bad guys. We work very hard not to do that."

Williams headed around to the driver's side. Steve looked at Amy and smiled. "Shotgun."

She rolled her eyes. "Whatever."

Williams' voice was clear over their commlinks. "Tate, up front with me. I want you handling nav and tactical. Rogers, you manage communications and intel in the back. Let's move it, people."

The two of them headed to their respective seats.

Steve opened the passenger door and paused for a moment in amazement. The interior was as much a cockpit as any advanced aircraft he'd seen. The windshield was a smart LCD screen, with heads-up displays for the vehicle condition. In front of him was a small membrane keyboard, which allowed him to enter queries through the Triangle data net. That reminded him—

"Control, this is Tate, do you copy? Have your ears on, Ethan?"

"I read you five-by-five, Steve. Welcome back to terra firma."

Behind him, he heard Amy and Rose initiating their link as well. He looked over his shoulder at Amy. The midsection of the vehicle had a computer console like a SAVANT Interface Station set behind the driver's seat; in the rear of the van were two shelves of devices that Quincey's tech branch had developed for Triangle field agents over the years. Amy took a quick glance back, and Steve could tell she hoped accessing any of that gear wouldn't be necessary — like him, she was still unfamiliar with most of the devices and their functions. From the expression on her face, he guessed she thought she'd end up doing more harm than good back there.

Steve lifted his wrist to his mouth and murmured, "SAVANT, Mode 3." The device started to morph, expanding from a bracelet to a gauntlet on his left hand. After a few moments, a series of readouts appeared on the device, indicating its charge, location and communication status.

Williams entered the vehicle, climbing into the driver's position. "Christine, we're all secure on board. Start the briefing, please."

A section of the windshield turned opaque, and a video feed of Christine Merrimac, Williams' long-time controller, appeared. To her right, a second data window opened, showing a graphic of the San Francisco Bay Area.

"Early yesterday, tracking nanites released when the False Mirror lab was breached activated and managed to form a RFID transmitter. This indicates the location of the intruder who removed the missing prototype. We believe that the device will be close to this individual, or that they will be a source of intelligence to its location."

"The signal was initially distorted and intermittent, but approximately twelve hours ago, it finally cleared up enough to pinpoint a location. The target is currently in a vacant hangar at Nimitz Field on the old Alameda Naval Base."

Steve looked at the aerial image of the base. "I remember my Dad talking about this place. It closed, what, a couple of decades ago?"

Ethan chimed in from off screen. "1997, to be exact. It's one of those limbo places from the drawdown at the end of the Cold War. Relatively isolated. Some parts of the base are in use, but many buildings are still abandoned. The hangar in question is slated for demolition, but with no scheduled date."

Amy examined the pictures of the building. "I see two vehicles parked out front. Have we been able to guess what kind of opposition to expect?"

Rose's voice came in from off screen. "Unfortunately, no. That picture's six months old. For some reason, we can't seem to get eyes on the building with a satellite. The last four passes of friendly satellites have been diverted."

Merrimac interjected. "We expect a Chinese Intel satellite to be doing a fly-by in a half-hour, and we don't think they'll notice if we 'piggyback' their signal. Passively, of course. And there's a commercial asset coming online in an hour. Not as high resolution as a MilSat, but any port in a storm."

Steve looked over at Williams. "Anywhere we could go to get eyes on this building from the ground without getting noticed?"

Williams eyed the map. "I don't think so. Whomever Callahan is working with picked this location well. Look here. Because of the previous demolitions on the base, the target hangar is now isolated, clear for two city blocks on all four sides.

Amy piped up from the back. "What about a drone aircraft?"

Merrimac replied. "No good. The base airspace is now in the flight corridor for Oakland International. Even a stealth drone would get noticed and waved off."

Amy shrugged. "Why not just send the locals in to capture Callahan and the device?"

"We won't send anyone blind into a situation like this. Not even the locals."

Williams rubbed his face with his hands. "So, we've got a lock on a signal, but no one can actually tell us anything for sure until we walk into the building?"

Merrimac nodded. "That's the gist of it. It sucks."

A new, smaller window appeared in the upper right corner of the windshield — Dr. Watson. "I know it doesn't look ideal, but time is of the essence here. Use extreme caution, but we need to recover the prototype, or destroy it, if necessary."

Williams looked at the director's image. "Acknowledged. We'll proceed north to get closer to the target. When the satellite images come in, we'll formulate our assault plan."

Watson nodded. "Mr. Tate, Ms. Rogers, I know I promised you a crack at Callahan, but please remember, recovering the prototype is our priority." Watson paused a moment, then added. "Of course, capturing her alive would be a nice bonus."

Steve glanced back at Amy, who nodded. "Understood, Director. We'll do our best."

"I'm sure you will. Ms. Merrimac, keep me apprised of the mission's progress." She reached forward, and her window blinked off.

Williams looked over at Steve. "Let's get going. Find us a nice, slow route. Bring us to the edge of the base."

Steve nodded and brought up the GPS tracking and real-time traffic maps. "Let's see. It's just after 7 p.m. Head out of the airport and onto California 61. That takes us right to the old east gate of the base. We can figure out our plan from there."

Williams pressed the ignition button and the electric motor of the vehicle hummed to life. He wiped down Merrimac's video link to a small LCD screen on the center console between Steve and himself. The windshield switched to an augmented reality display.

Steve studied the windshield, fascinated. It was the first time he'd seen a real-life display that came close to what he saw in his mind's eye — constant calculations about locations, waypoints, items, angles, etc. Just observing, he already noticed a half-dozen ways it could possibly be improved. Steve made a mental note to talk to Quincey when he returned to base.

As Williams made his way through the hangars and onto the service road at the airport, Steve thought back to the briefing. Something was already bothering him about this, other than the bad onsite intel. He had a nagging feeling he'd overlooked something mentioned in passing that was critical.

The van made its way north, across the inlet and onto Alameda Island. The speed limit was 25, but the traffic was stop-and-go at the tail end of rush hour. This was not a problem, as the team was counting down the minutes until the Chinese Intel satellite passed overhead and gave them a real-time look at the target.

He glanced back at Amy. As they bumped along, Steve couldn't help but muse on how useless their Talents were against a simple delay like a traffic jam. *Yeah, some super powers these turned out to be.*

Powers... power...

The hairs stood up on the back of his neck. "Amy, can we get access to the smart power grid here in Alameda?"

Amy looked at him. "Rose, can we get that?" she called out, unsure how to access the data.

Rose's voice was calm over the commlink. "I'm on it. And stand-by. The Chinese satellite fly-by starts in three, two, one..."

On their windshield, a video window popped up in the lower right quadrant, displaying in real time the feed from the Chinese spy satellite. On the map display, a tracking line showed the flight path of the bird as it overflew the Bay Area, and a circle showing the image coverage. Its focus was north — UC Berkeley and the Lawrence Livermore Laboratory, but the bottom edge of the image caught the Alameda base for all of twelve seconds. As it streamed by, Steve noted a large central hot spot in the room, and a small number of human body heat signatures. Then the fly-by moved out of range.

10:12 p.m. EDT

Merrimac looked smug. "Data capture complete. Field team, stand by. Ethan, enhance and analysis."

Ethan quickly racked up the video on his screen, and then trimmed out the sections they didn't care about. The remaining twelve seconds was copied six times and handed off to different sets of analysis tools — each looking for a story to tell. Weapons imagery, energy signatures, different human identifiers from vibration to heat. Quickly, an image was emerging.

Ethan used the data to assemble a three-dimensional briefing, based on the original building schematics and the new intelligence data. Once completed, he turned to Merrimac. Three minutes had elapsed.

"I have the briefing ready for the team."

Merrimac nodded and pressed the mic button on her headset. "Field team, Ethan has your briefing."

Ethan brought up a three-dimensional representation of the hangar. "Based on the look-in, we have five confirmed hostiles, with a sixth possible at the edge of the observed scan. Assume six hostiles. They are broken into teams of two. The first pair is located in a fixed position on the upper level, northwest corner, armed with appears to be an automatic weapon. The resolution at that height isn't perfect, but from the layout, it's probably a .50 caliber machine gun."

"Standard machine gun nest," said Williams. "Nothing we can't handle."

"There other hostiles are on the ground level, in two teams. The first on a single roving guard on the perimeter. I assume the other at the edge was the partner. This hostile was at the southeast corner of the building, proceeding in a clockwise patrol. Silhouettes suggest both automatic weapons and handguns. There is also one small, energy-based weapon — possibly a Taser, although the signature for those is always sketchy."

Amy looked curious. "A Taser? That's a capture weapon. Everything else is lethal force. Seems out of place."

"I know," agreed Steve.

"Almost finished," reminded Ethan. "The final team is stationary in the office complex, north center of the hangar. This is where we have the one confirmed target and a second possible. The reason we're not sure is that the last hostile's data was corrupted by an unusual energy signature. If I were a betting man, I'd say it's probably the False Mirror prototype."

He looked directly into the camera pickup. "If so, that's definitely bad news — it means they intend to deploy it — and soon."

7:19 p.m. PDT

Steve turned to Williams. "This isn't right."

Williams glanced over at him from the wheel. "What do you mean?"

"I mean, it's too easy. You said it yourself. Whoever picked this location did so very well. It's extremely defensible, with open ground in all directions, so you'd easily see an enemy coming in."

"Go on."

"Well, that sounds like they're expecting a fight. So how come there are so few guards when they know we'll be coming?"

"Maybe they're expecting reinforcements."

"We don't even have any idea who *they* are."

"Probably more mercenaries Callahan has brought in."

Steve shook his head. "Amy, what about signals intel. Have we heard a peep out of whoever they are — either on radio or cell frequencies?"

She shook her head. "Nothing I've been able to figure out.

Rose spoke up. "But that could mean they're extremely disciplined — or they have some other ways to communicate."

Merrimac looked smug on the video link. "It could also mean we have the jump on them—"

Steve looked at him. "Do we, really? That sounds like wishful thinking, ma'am." He turned around again. "Amy, did Rose get us access to the smart grid data yet?"

Rose's voice was back again. "Here it is, Steve. But what exactly are we looking for here?"

Steve thought furiously. *How to explain this?* "Look, in the early part of this decade, they had an initiative to start converting the power grid in California to a smart grid, which would allow people to better monitor their power usage remotely. I guess people all remember being screwed by Enron at the turn of the century. So, the

Feds threw a ton of money at smart power grids, and installed pilot projects in about 100 towns and cities."

Merrimac interrupted him. "We don't have time for a history lesson."

Steve snapped back. "Just listen, ok? Alameda was one of those towns. I remember reading they replaced all their power meter some years back. Now using a smart meter lets them remotely monitor the power usage of any building in the city limits, and plan for it accordingly. So..."

"So," Amy picked up on what he was saying, "if anyone is using an unusual amount of energy to power up the False Mirror prototype, we can spot it that way!"

Steve started typing and brought up with a graphic display of the old military base. The street and buildings were in blue and gray, and each building had a color assigned to it, from black through red based on the level of power consumption. He scrolled the focal point across the base, finding the occasionally occupied building. Finally, he reached his needle in the haystack. "That's what I thought. Williams, Amy, look at the map. What do you see?

"A bunch of gray blocks of buildings with black readings," Amy said.

"Exactly."

Merrimac glanced at the duplicate of graphic on the display wall in the SICC, then back at the camera pickup. "What's your point?"

"So, if our bad guys are in that building, why are all the lights out, so to speak? Especially since the Chinese satellite says there's a power spike from the False Mirror in progress?"

For a moment, you could hear a pin drop inside the van. Rose's voice held a touch of awe as she said, "Son of a... you know, you are still a piece of work, Steven Tate. What tipped you?"

"The briefing mentioned the signal from the RFID strengthened thirteen hours ago, after being erratic and all over the place. Maybe it was erratic because Callahan and her team couldn't figure out how to neutralize and spoof the signal until then."

Williams nodded. "That makes sense. But if that's true..."

Amy looked at her teammates. "We need to pull over."

Williams scanned ahead and found an abandoned gas station on their right. He pulled in and put the van in park.

10:23 p.m. EDT

Back in the SICC, Merrimac glanced over at Rose. Clicking the mute on her mic, she looked over at the younger controller. "How did he know that?"

Rose smiled. *Way to go, Steve.* "It's what he does. He's really good at finding things that are hinky that way."

Merrimac looked over at Ethan, one eyebrow raised. "Hinky?"

Ethan grinned. "Early *Scooby Doo,* I think. I believe Tate was raised on cartoons. It means something needs investigating. I'm learning to trust his intuition."

Rose shrugged. "I've learned to trust his hunches — sometimes the hard way."

Merrimac raised an eyebrow. "Oh?"

Rose glanced sideways at Ethan and blushed. She turned to the senior controller. "Bobby Reynolds. Junior prom." She shuddered just a bit. "Although how he knew about—"

Williams growled out, "Anyone still awake back there?"

Merrimac clicked on her mic. "Sorry, Mitch. We were just discussing approach here."

"Well, let's cut the chatter. Tate, lay this out for me."

On the primary display, Steve looked into the video pick up. "Think about it. High-value target, yet very few guards, and almost no power? Then there's the type of weapon it is. False Mirror is basically a data bomb — it needs to alter a data stream to do damage. Well, that's an abandoned hangar — I'll bet the site's Internet dark as well.

No, this has trap written all over it. The False Mirror prototype isn't there."

Shauna looked at her camera pick-up. "What about a wireless network signal?"

"Even the largest, most advanced wireless pipeline isn't broad enough to transmit data at speeds False Mirror would need to work undetected. It requires a hardline."

Ethan looked again at the trace data on the wall display in the SICC and bit his lip. "Steve, are you sure? The nanite-RFID trail ends at the door to that building. That's where Callahan went."

"'Went' is probably the operative word, Ethan. As in 'been there and done that.' And the trail ends there? I doubt Callahan would stay in one place for that long, knowing we'd be coming to look for her. No, I'm willing to bet you she's long gone."

Ethan and Rose shared a look. Rose was the one who broached the question.

"Steve, these were nanites. How in the world would Callahan have figured out that they were on her, spoofed them and gotten them off herself?"

7:26 p.m. PDT

"**I don't know**."

Think, Steven. He closed his eyes for a moment, and the answer was right in front of him.

"Actually, yes I do." He turned and looked directly at Williams. "But you're not going to like it."

Williams' eyes narrowed. "Spit it out."

"It's really obvious if you think it through. We missed it because we haven't seen this as a series of connected actions from all the way back at the beginning of this. But ask yourself, how has Callahan known about this project? How did she know Naziri would be in Nassau? How did she know the prototype was finished? How might she have known about the nanites?"

He ran one hand through his hair nervously and took a deep breath. "I'm sorry, Agent Williams, but

Triangle's security's been compromised. It has been all along. That's probably why she's been so hard to find — someone's been erasing her data from the inside. And that's why this is a trap. Because she already knows we're coming."

Williams' hands tightened on the wheel. "Damn it. You mean I've been chasing my tail in circles all this time because of a mole? When I find him, I'm going to—"

Merrimac interrupted him. "Mitch, we don't have time right now."

She opened a window to Watson and brought her up to speed on Tate's theory. She nodded, her face grave. "Mr. Tate, those are serious accusations. I hope you can back them up."

"Sorry, Director. But it's the only theory that fits the available evidence."

Merrimac peered at Steve through her video link. "Say you're right, Tate, and the navy base is a trap. Where are Callahan and the device really hiding?"

Steve considered this for a moment. "Amy, I need a map of the central Bay Area on the main display." The LCD shifted, and a satellite image of the Bay Area zoomed in.

"Controller Merrimac, when the RFID signal was initially being tracked, was precise geotag information included?"

"Of course. We triangulated it based on the closest cellular towers."

"Good. Can we plot a complete trace of those tags, from the moment the RFID came online, overlaid on the display map?"

"Certainly, but it will take some time—"

Rose cleared her throat. "Excuse me, ma'am. I took it upon my own initiative to have the entire data stream of RFID data downloaded and compiled on my console. I have the plot ready for you."

On the video link, Steve could see Merrimac quietly grinding her teeth. Dr. Watson came to his rescue. "Well done, Controller Merrimac. Nice to see your team taking initiative."

Merrimac nodded, although her smile looked a little forced. "As you said, ma'am, we try to be prepared. Tate, sending you the data now."

Rose started sending the data, a smile forming. "Clever boy. I see where you're going, Steve. I'll add another layer to your map. Buildings with large data pipelines."

Amy sounded confused. "Why would you need that?"

Steve turned and looked at her. "Remember, False Mirror needs a hardline to work."

Merrimac interrupted. "Your data's now ready." On the map, an icon appeared, winking in and out of existence as it threaded a path unsteadily northward from Oakland Airport. It passed through Alameda and stopped briefly at the hangar they had found. But then it moved again, heading through Oakland and up to Berkeley, where it stayed for a half-hour. Then it headed across the Bay Bridge and halfway across, exited onto Yorba Linda Island. From there it went down to...

"Treasure Island."

Amy pointed at that. "What is that?"

Steve smiled. "My second needle in the haystack. Amy, can you expand and recenter the image?" She worked on her keyboard momentarily, and the map zoomed out, showing all of San Francisco Bay. In the center, the Bay Bridge cut a path across from Oakland to San Francisco, and midway, on Treasure Island, the RFID icon blinked erratically around the island and settled jumpily on a building there. Per the time display, it flickered unsteadily in that one spot for six hours before the signal became strong and steady. Then it headed back to Alameda. Steve froze the image and pointed.

"If I had to wager anything, I'd say that's where we'll find the prototype."

10:32 p.m. EDT

Ethan frowned as his monitor displayed a 3D image of the layout of the Treasure Island Naval Training facility. Decommissioned a decade ago, it lay there abandoned, stuck in a bureaucratic limbo as different governmental organizations fought over its carcass like vultures in a desert. Add in the unique activist communities that the Bay Area fostered, sprinkled liberally with lawyers, and you had a recipe for the perfect bureaucratic Gordian knot. He shook his head and whistled softly. "How the heck did he peg that one spot in this mess as Callahan's bolt hole?"

Rose shrugged. "As I said, it's what he does. He sees connections faster than anyone I know — sometimes faster than computers can analyze the data."

Merrimac stared at the image on the screen. "Right. Do we have any real-time satellite image?"

Rose checked her monitors. "Son of a... Negative. The CIA just received another retask order and is again moving their bird. It'll be out of area for at least another orbit. Our next possible real time pass will be in... thirty-four minutes." She looked back at Merrimac. "We still have the data from the Chinese intel satellite pass, right? That had to have given us something."

Merrimac growled, "Damn it. Who keeps ordering all these satellites rerouted?" She looked at the camera pickup. "Mitch, we may have avoided the trap, but we're still blind. No real-time satellite assets. I want you to hold position—"

Rose piped up from her console. "Uh, that might not be such a good idea. I'm monitoring increased message traffic on the civil authority frequencies." She pressed a couple of controls and tapped into the conversation. A look of concern spread across her face.

"Agent Williams, someone called in a bomb threat at the base in Alameda. The locals are rolling a full tactical response." Rose looked at Merrimac. "It's our target hangar."

7:36 p.m. EDT

Amy looked at Steve from the back of the vehicle. "That makes no sense. Why bring the police to your front door?"

Steve thought furiously. "Yes, it does. They still believe we're headed to Alameda. But it was a setup and just as we arrived we would have been caught with it by the locals." He turned to Williams. "Look, we've got maybe twenty to twenty-five minutes before they figure out we didn't put our head in the trap. After that, they'll know we're not playing, and the prototype will be in the wind again."

Williams looked at the time display on his SAVANT and pulled up a GPS map. He touched it in the holo display and slid it onto the smart windshield, then sized it out of his direct field of vision. "Ethan, plow the road for me. You have us on GPS; make sure there are no delays getting us onto the Bay Bridge and to the island. Rose and Christine, you have five minutes to determine best entry points into that building—"

Rose spoke up. "Actually, I have an idea about getting you real-time surveillance before the satellite arrives. Permission to work on that?"

Williams considered this. "Everyone's an overachiever today. Fine. New plan. Christine, feed the plans to Tate and Rogers, here. I'll let the new brain trust figure out a way to open the front door while I play chauffeur. Christine, you take care of the traffic lights, keep my way clear. Johannsen, you do... whatever it is you're going to do. Ethan, can you delay the locals any?"

"Working on it."

"Now we get to work." Williams looked at the small image of Dr. Watson. "Nothing personal, Rhonda, but stay the hell out of the way until we finish." He closed the video link window to her, then put the van in gear and pulled out into traffic. Ahead of them, the traffic lights started changing to green, one after another.

10:40 p.m. EDT

Back in the SICC, Christine turned to her console, opening multiple different command windows. She tapped into the California Highway Patrol regional patrol network and located all their patrol cars.

"A speed trap during rush hour? Naughty, naughty, CHP. I can think of a more productive use of your time."

Inside the CHP cruiser, the alert came up for a silent lights-only response across the bridge in the Embarcadero district of San Francisco. The state trooper put down the radar gun, flipped on his lights and pulled into traffic.

7:41 p.m. PDT

Williams spotted the highway patrolman as he pulled out in front of the van, lights flashing, but no siren. As the other cars on the road pulled aside for it, Williams smiled. "That's my girl."

"Thought you'd like that. He's heading for the Embarcadero — straight across the bridge. ETA — seventeen minutes. Just slot in behind the patrol car — but not too close."

"Relax, Christine. It's not my first time doing this—"

"—and it won't be your last. I know, Mitch. Just be safe."

Williams pressed a control on the console. The vehicle's exterior rippled, and it transformed into a California Highway Patrol van, complete with grill mounted red and blue flashing lights. He pulled the van into traffic and closed the gap with the CHP cruiser, monitoring his heads-up display. Williams pulled out into traffic and closed the gap with the CHP cruiser as he monitored his heads-up display. Steve and Amy were belted in and holding on, going over the schematics of the building Merrimac had sent. Williams spoke up. "SAVANT, add a countdown timer to the heads-up display — nineteen minutes. And start." In the lower center of the windshield display, four ghostly white numbers popped into existence, resolved into a digital counter reading *19:00* and started counting down.

7:45 p.m. PDT

The ride behind the CHP cruiser went smoothly. They glided through the Posey Tube connecting Alameda to Oakland, and then onto the Nimitz Freeway heading toward San Francisco. As they cruised along the freeway, Steve glanced left toward Alameda and watched as helicopters started circling the old naval facility. "Looks like we're running out of time."

Ethan's voice sounded tense with frustration. "Still working on it. I'll say this – these folks are single-minded when it comes to a bomb threat."

Williams glanced over. "So, what are we looking at?"

Steve shook his head. "Nothing easy. While the base was decommissioned, the brig was left behind intact. That's where the Defense Finance folks decided to put their off-site storage — an already secure building. They closed it and moved out a year ago, but I'm guessing a lot of hard points and data conduits were left for a decommissioning team to strip out. Plus, by design, you can easily control access — only three ways in or out."

Amy chimed in from the backseat. "I'm thinking Callahan, or whoever she's working for, wants a payday. My best guess is she plans to spoof the military into emptying their piggy bank."

Williams took the turn off onto Yorba Linda Island. "And how do you plan to stop her?"

Steve thought quickly. "Amy, a 10-foot fence with razor wire — how fast can you deal with it?"

She considered this for a moment. "Over, or through?"

"Over."

"With a running start, three seconds. Standing still, maybe six."

"Here's the problem. Again, this building is in the middle of nowhere. The nearest structure is 200 yards away, and there are no taller structures less than a half-mile away. They'll be expecting a frontal assault on the main entrance. Maybe if we could reroute a helicopter from the bomb response—"

Williams interrupted him. "A helicopter? Kid, we're almost out of time!"

Merrimac chimed in. "Sorry, Tate, but Agent Williams is right. The police are going to launch an assault on the hangar in Alameda in five minutes. When they do, your enemy will know for sure you're not there." She paused for a moment, and then looked again at the camera. "I'm sorry, but at this point, Agent Williams you need to abort the assault and gather intelligence on where they might be moving the prototype next."

Steve looked down for a moment, then at the countdown clock — 4:53.

"No, wait! Don't you see? This is even better! We time our assault simultaneously with the one at the Alameda base. The confusion will give us a few extra moments to find the prototype, grab it and go. Of course, if we make that frontal assault they're expecting, we're going to need to make a sacrifice."

Williams looked at him. Merrimac glared at him from the screen.

Ethan piped up. "Well, you are definitely making an impression on your first mission, Steve."

Williams nodded grimly as he turned drove onto Treasure Island and headed down the Avenue of the Palms. "You'd better be right, Tate."

"I am. Cut over to 11th Street and Avenue I and hold there for thirty seconds." Steve looked back at Amy. "Look, the south side exercise fence mounts flush with the wall, but curves over to prevent prisoners from climbing out. Use it to get up on the roof, then head over to the west side, drop onto the exercise balcony and get inside. The

Plexiglas is a half-inch thick — it'll stop most people, but I know you can get through it. That's cellblock C, above where they did data storage and retrieval. From there, follow the right corridor to the end, down one level, and then left. The main control room should be there. That's my best guess where they've plugged in the device."

"What about you?"

"When we drop you off, count to sixty and start running. Another twenty seconds after that, our distraction will kick in. Trust me, it'll work."

Amy's eyes narrowed. "Trust you? That's the best you've got?"

Steve looked up at her and smirked. "Oh, I've got better, but that should wait until after the mission."

"If you two lovebirds are done, might I remind you we're on the clock?" growled Williams. "We have three minutes until a SWAT team hits that hangar in Alameda and our little surprise party goes pear-shaped."

Steve looked at him. "Right. Sorry." He glanced back at Amy. "The sun will be setting behind you as you come in, so they'll have a problem tracking you with the glare. But even so, be careful — we want you back in one piece. And remember, first we grab False Mirror, then we grab Callahan, and if possible, make her talk."

Williams pulled up to the intersection of 11th Street and Avenue I. "Time to go, Rogers."

Amy nodded. "Right."

She opened the door and exited the vehicle. Steve looked at her for a moment through the window and nodded. Over the commlink, he said, "Sixty seconds — mark!" And with that, the van turned left onto Avenue I and drove away.

8:01 p.m. PDT

Amy glanced at the faint blue countdown and the reading showing the energy status of her SAVANT. She took a deep breath, thought about her target, and focused on her run. *Two blocks, followed by the razor-wire fence* *and a two-story climb. I'll need twenty-five seconds.* She closed her eyes again, visualized her path, and willed the information to her muscles.

The countdown on her SAVANT moved onto single digits. Inside, Amy felt the warm glow that came when she tapped into her Talent. She crouched down, waiting for the beeping as the timer reached zero.

Breathe. Focus. You can do this, Amelia Jane.

When it came, she slapped the ground and triggered her Talent. Within a second, she felt the energy stored throughout her body coursing into her muscles. She felt vibrant, alive, almost exhilarated for a moment. Then she focused back on her task, willed herself into her mission and launched forward. Within three steps, her extra gear engaged and she was a blur.

8:02 p.m. PDT

Williams stopped the vehicle and idled for a few seconds at the corner of 13th Street and Avenue I. He looked over at Steve. "Ready to open the front door?"

"Yeah."

"Quincey is going to be pissed. He hates it when we break his toys."

Merrimac's voice came over the commlink. "Most definitely. I've arranged for a replacement ride. It will be there in twenty minutes — north shore boat ramp."

Steve nodded. "Got it. Tell them to reserve me a chair on the Lido Deck."

Williams grumbled, "Let's get this over with." He reached over and undid his seat belt, then pressed two controls on the dashboard. The heads-up display on the windshield flashed bright red letters.

WARNING: Self-Destruct Activated.

Williams glanced over at Steve. "This thing uses a cold fusion core. When it goes, it's going to be...spectacular. So be sure to shield your eyes. Otherwise, you'll be useless inside. And remember; be at least thirty feet away from it when it goes."

Steve looked at Williams, confused. *Cold fusion? But, I thought that theory was disproved?*

His thoughts were interrupted by Williams. "SAVANT, shut down all displays. We're going in dark."

All the displays powered down inside the vehicle. On a silent electric motor, it shot forward, quickly building speed. Williams cut across an abandoned lot used now for staging construction supplies as he angled the vehicle toward the front opening arch. As the vehicle shot across Avenue M, Steve's door popped open.

"Now, Tate! Out!"

He rolled out as he'd been trained, taking the impact on his right side as he landed. Something went crunch, and a pain shot through his side as he took a breath.

Damn, cracked a rib.

He rolled into a crouch and shielded himself from the blast as the SUV impacted the main doors.

8:03 p.m. PDT

On the south side of the building, Amy had dashed in, a complete blur of motion, planted with her right foot and leaped upward. She landed one foot on top of the outer perimeter fence and used that to launch herself onto the security fence. It buckled a bit beneath her and then recoiled. She used that energy to launch into a somersault and land at the edge of the roof in a crouch, right arm extended, ready to fire her SAVANT.

8:04 p.m. PDT

At that moment, Williams' vehicle impacted and the cold fusion core of the engine expanded quickly into a sphere approximately 3 times the size of the car. For three seconds, it was the hottest, brightest thing on the planet. When it winked out, the van, the entrance to the brig and anything else that had been in contact with that fusion bubble was simply *gone.*

Steve's commlink overloaded with the burst of static. He reactivated it. "Wow, Williams, when you said it would be spectacular, you weren't lying."

There was no reply. "Williams?"

Again, silence in reply. "Mitchell, can you hear me? Mitch? SAVANT, locate Agent Williams."

"Unable to comply." The SAVANT's warm female contralto was matter-of-fact.

Steve fought a sense of panic. "Explain, unable to comply."

"Agent Williams' SAVANT is no longer broadcasting, and his passive locator signal is deactivated."

He felt a cold trickle of sweat slide down his spine. "Ethan, what do you have back there in Control?"

Ethan's voice was careful and measured over the commlink. "Steve, Agent Williams is offline. You need to assume command of the mission and complete it. Do you understand?"

Chapter 20

Silence filled the SICC as first two seconds passed, then three, and then five more. Ethan looked over at Merrimac, who was staring at her dead console, and Rose, who was focusing exclusively on hers, her jaw tense, and her fingers flying over the virtual keyboard.

Steve's voice when it came was terse. "I understand. I assume we still don't have any better satellite intel?"

Ethan looked over at Rose who shook her head. "That's a negative. And Rose's other plan still isn't ready."

8:06 p.m. PDT

Steve looked at the devastated main entrance to the brig and held his side. "Ethan, put me on a private channel for a moment?"

"Stand by." A brief pause. "Go ahead."

"How's Christine holding up?"

"She's in shock. She and Williams go back a long way."

"Will she be able to do anything to help with the rest of the mission?"

"The truth? I don't know."

He considered this a moment. "I'm in way over my head, Ethan. You know that, right?"

"Don't worry, Steve. We'll be here to support you. I've placed a call to Dr. Watson. She's on her way down."

"Good. Link me back to everyone."

There was a momentary pause. "Go ahead, Steve," replied Ethan.

"Team, I'm going to need your help. Christine, that flash was sure to get someone's attention. We don't need to borrow trouble with the locals, especially with them already on alert with the Alameda bomb threat. I need you to monitor the local law enforcement agencies and alert us when the resources they are sending to investigate get here. Can you do that for us?"

There was a long pause before Merrimac answered shakily. "Yes, Agent Tate. I've got it covered."

"Good. Give us a two-minute head start before they arrive. Also, if you can, find out what's happening at the Navy base across the bay."

"I'll work on it."

"You can do this. Ethan and Rose, your job is to have Amy's and my back. Full sensor sweeps with the SAVANTS. Tell us what's around us, and if anything is hinky, say something – don't wait to be asked. Understood?"

"You got it, Steve. I'll tell Amy."

"You do that Rose. Ethan, I need the analysis on the Chinese flyby of this site. How many hostiles am I facing here?"

There was a moment's pause. "The computer identifies thirteen possible human signatures. However, due to the thickness of the building's walls, it couldn't get a good handle on potential weapons or energy signature. And Treasure Island isn't a smart grid site, either."

"Yeah, I didn't think I'd get that lucky twice. Okay, I'm moving into the brig to sweep for the device."

"Acknowledged."

Steve brought his gauntleted fist up and aimed it in front of him as he sprinted across the parking lot and into the mangled main entrance.

The fusion bubble had destroyed a sphere about 30 feet in diameter. Everything it had touched simply ceased to exist. This included the main doors and most of the lobby. Steve threaded his way through the half-remains of chairs from the waiting lounge that must have been stacked in the area.

The first security door into the brig was still intact. Steve took aim and blew open the lock, then pulled open the door and came in low through the entrance.

As entered the space he swept his SAVANT around the room. The control room was empty, and the far door was open. There were neither guards on duty–nor any evidence there were any nearby. He pressed a control on his SAVANT and a wireframe map of the building interior flashed on the wall for a second, along with the icon for Amy.

But no other life sign icons.

"Ethan, is that right? I'm showing zero people here?"

"That's what we show on this end as well. Both your SAVANT and Amy's show the building is empty."

Steve frowned as he turned the corner, finding the base of the stairs to rendezvous with Amy. "But that's—" He glanced up at Amy, who appeared at the top, sweeping for targets. "Ethan, how many men did that satellite scan say were in here?"

"The computer identified thirteen probable hostiles inside the building."

Steve looked at Amy, who was coming down the stairs now. "That was less than thirty minutes ago? Where did they all go?"

8:10 p.m. PDT

Amy continued walking down the stairs toward Steve, scanning her surroundings. She shook her head. "I've got a bad feeling. When that bubble went off, I got a good look at the rooftop. No one's been up there in a while."

As if on cue, the lights in the brig began to flicker back on. Steve closed his eyes and swore. "Damn it! This was another feint, and I bit on it!"

Amy shook her head in disgust. "You know, as much as I hate Callahan, I have to admit she is damned good at what she does."

He sighed and ran a hand through his hair. "Well, let's find out what we can. Try to find where they were supposed to have put the False Mirror prototype. Maybe they left behind a clue."

They headed down the corridor toward the old Solitary Confinement section, still sweeping the area with their SAVANTs. Something was bothering Amy, but she was having trouble making the connection. "Rose, what are you showing back there?"

"Your building is deader than a doornail. No data, no telecomm; heck, even the power is shielded."

Amy frowned. *The power is shielded? But — oh, God, no!* "Steve, freeze!"

Steve was halfway down the corridor and stopped on command, in mid-stride. "A.J.?"

Amy slowly reached down and grabbed a handful of dust. She tossed it into the air over Steve, and it drifted past him and toward the floor. Three inches in front of him, the motes started to sparkle, as they passed through some type of photo or laser electric alarm.

"Ethan, Rose, listen carefully. We're being hacked. Someone is hacking the SAVANTs right now, in real time."

11:12 p.m. EDT

At that moment, Christine's console reset itself in the SICC.

She'd been monitoring the frequencies as requested when the application window dissolved into static. The next moment, all three of her screens showed the same image — a live video image of Amy and Steve down the long corridor to solitary confinement.

Christine exclaimed, "Ethan, look!" and pushed the image from the top monitor onto the wall screen. As they watched, additional SAVANT data started to augment the picture.

This SAVANT was operating outside of the hack, for it showed a complete tactical scan of the room.

Christine's heart sank when she saw the image. Columns of shaped explosive charges lined the interiors of the corridor walls on either side of Amy and Steve, and laser triggers had sprung to life both around them. They were trapped.

Ethan was quickly on the commlink. "Amy, Steve, whatever you do, don't move. The corridor is booby-trapped."

Over the audio link, they heard a chuckle, and Ethan went white. He looked over at her.

She shook her head in disbelief. "No, it can't be!"

8:12 p.m. PDT

Amy and Steve turned slowly toward the sound. Rounding the corner and walking into the doorway was Mitch Williams.

Following directly behind him was Hannah Callahan.

Steve looked surprised. "You seem awfully chipper for someone who's dead."

"You know, Tate, for someone so smart, you can be a bit thick at times."

Amy nodded. "I've been telling him that for weeks now."

Steve glanced over at Amy and said in a semi-whisper, "Not helping, A.J."

Ethan's voice came over the commlink. "Keep him talking. We have a trace on the hack and Rose is working to break it and disarm that booby-trap."

Amy looked at Williams, then over at Callahan, her eyes narrowing. "So, False Mirror works."

Williams smiled. "Now, Miss Rogers, don't play games. Remember, I wrote the playbook. By now, Ethan's called in the cavalry and wants you to stall. Of course, you're going to try to get me to provide you with additional intel."

Callahan grinned. "Oh, we can give them this one. After all, they'll deduce it soon enough anyway. And they did try so hard. Yes, it works. Quite spectacularly. After all, it brought you here."

Steve looked at their captors. "Dude, why? That's what I want to know."

Williams shrugged. "Initially? Money. Lots and lots of money. Think about it, Tate. Do you even understand the implications of False Mirror? You can never be sure about any electronic data stream, anywhere, ever again. It's the ultimate hacker's skeleton key. Any system, any display, anywhere in the world, in real time. Governments will pay top dollar for it — corporations, even more. But in the end, if everyone knows about this, then no one can ever trust their electronics again." He shook his head and chuckled. "The Flat-Earthers should love me. I now hold the key to the destruction of modern computerized society — and I plan to use it wisely."

Steve shook his head. "Williams, you are seriously screwed up. No one ever uses ultimate power wisely. You can't escape human nature."

Williams opened his mouth to reply, but Callahan coughed once and whispered something in his ear. Williams grinned and nodded. "I would love to debate this with you, Tate, but I don't have the time. I need a bit of a head start." Callahan handed him a control box with two switches.

Steve's eyes went wide. "Williams, you'll be killed in here along with us if you set those off." As he spoke, he was looking at the angles to see if he could figure out a move to get them out of this.

"Oh, I agree. But not quite yet." He raised his voice. "Ethan, I know you can hear me. Sorry, but it's nothing personal. It's just business."

"Christine, you were right, this won't be my last time doing this. But it is yours."

"You're fired."

He pressed the left button on the control box.

11:14 p.m. EDT

Ethan and Rose shared a glance as they realized what he'd said. They dove for the floor while Christine stared in horror at her screen as shaped explosive charges behind their consoles exploded.

8:14 p.m. PDT

Steve and Amy heard a brief wash of noise; then their commlinks went silent. They looked at each other for a moment. Amy mouthed the word "Rose." Steve shook his head slightly. They turned back to face Williams and Callahan.

Steve's voice took on an edge. "If you just hurt my friends, there is no place in this world you can hide. I will hunt you down. I will find you and believe me, I will kill you."

Callahan grinned. "Such brave words. Too bad they're your last—"

With a yell, Amy leaped at Callahan. Without looking at her, Williams raised a pistol with almost superhuman speed and fired. The bullet caught Amy in mid-leap and threw her against the wall. She slid down into a heap next to Steve.

"Amy! No!" Steve bent down, afraid to touch her. Please, God, not again! She was unconscious, breathing slowly, her face already pale and ashen.

"Now you made me go and show what got me recruited to Triangle in the first place." Williams chuckled. "What's the matter, Tate? You really didn't think you two were the only ones, right?"

Steve looked up in shock at Williams. "The only what?"

"The only ones with powers, or skills, or as we're called, Talents. You and Rogers are just the second batch. Or in her case, were."

Steve glanced at Amy, who seemed to have stopped breathing. He turned back to Williams. "You're lying."

"Am I? Think about it. How else could Callahan here have gotten away with what she did? Let's just say she's very...persuasive. Me? I'm a human ballistics calculator — I never miss."

Steve stood up and faced Williams, a cold fury building inside. He let the anger build, blue hot inside him, as he spoke in a low growl. "You think so? Give it your best shot, dickhead."

Williams shook his head and looked back at Callahan. "Tsk, tsk. Swearing in front of the lady? Not very nice. As you wish." With an inhuman swiftness, his pistol whipped into position and a shot fired.

Steve tapped into his power. The world slowed to a halt, and he saw the trajectory of the bullet. But this time, instead of a way around it, he felt rage build inside him, and he pushed back against the bullet. The world sped back up as the air around him thickened into a wedge. The bullet deflected harmlessly past him, striking the wall down the corridor.

The look on their faces was worth it — utter shock and disbelief from Callahan, sheer joy on Williams'. "Brilliant! No one ever could dodge me before. I wondered if your Talent would allow that. Nicely done." His face then drained of all emotion as he turned and faced Steve head on. He continued, "Of course, one bullet is easy."

This time, Williams tossed the detonator into the air as a distraction. With his left hand now free, he brought out his second gun and proceeded to empty both clips at Steve.

Steve smiled and slowed time again. All the trajectories became apparent. He channeled more of his energy, shaping it in front of him. He envisioned the air forming not a wedge, but a ramp, a crystalline wave that curved and channeled the bullets. As time sped back to normal, the flying lead struck the wave and rolled and danced in it, tumbling over and over until their kinetic energy dissipated. With a clatter, they fell to the ground in front of him. As they did, he used the distraction to reach behind him and pull a pair of shuriken off his belt. The ninja stars flew, one striking the detonator and knocking it to the floor. The other buried itself in Williams' left shoulder.

Callahan stared at the bladed triangle jutting from Williams in surprise and disbelief. "You actually brought a knife to a gun fight?"

"Amazing what you can learn after a month in Somalia." Steve stood protectively over Amy, his SAVANT raised, a *shuriken* in his other hand, ready to defend her from Williams.

In the distance, sirens could be heard approaching. Callahan and Williams shared a glance. Callahan took off around the corner, while the senior agent looked at Steve and shook his head. "I underestimated you, Tate. Well done. You earned your life tonight — if you can figure a way out of that trap." He pulled the *shuriken* out of his shoulder and let it clatter to the floor. "Another time, Tate. But don't think I'll make the same mistake with you twice." With that, Williams slid around the corner, and the lights in the building went out, plunging it into darkness.

Steve waited a moment and collapsed to his knees, drained. He'd never used his Talent like that before; certainly, never for that long or that intensely. Frankly, he hadn't been sure he'd be able to stop all those bullets. *But what choice did I really have, right? It was either figure that out or die.*

He looked over at Amy's body. He felt utterly deflated and helpless. *Oh, God, I couldn't stop her again. Callahan's killed again, and I couldn't stop her.* In the faint blue glow from his SAVANT, she looked so pale and fragile. He reached over and brushed some hair from her face. "I'm sorry, Amy."

"You should be," she replied, ever so faintly.

Steve looked at her in shock. "Amy? Amy! You're alive!"

She opened her eyes and started to sit up. "And you are still Captain Obvious. Or, to put it in smaller words that even you can understand, 'Duh.'"

"But, how? You took a bullet in mid-flight."

She winced as she touched her side. "I didn't say it didn't hurt, brainiac. Remember what they said about how my Talent worked?"

"Yeah. Something about kinetic energy."

"Well, it turns out a bullet has a lot of it. So, it hurts." She reached inside her top and pulled out a flattened bullet. "Here. Have a souvenir."

Steve stared at her. "You knew?"

Amy shook her head. "No, but I suspected. Something happened in Nassau. They have footage of me getting shot, but I don't remember it." She started to try getting up. "Look, can we talk about this later?"

"Deal. Meanwhile, we need to get out of here. Hopefully, our ride is still waiting by the north shore of the island. Can you walk?"

"I might need a little help at first."

He nodded and lifted Amy into a fireman's carry. She squawked at being manhandled. "Not what I had in mind, genius."

"You know, you are pretty ungrateful for someone being rescued. Just shut up, until I get you out of the building."

He started to take a step forward when she yelled. "Wait!"

"What?"

"What about the booby-traps?"

Steve triggered his Talent and focused his attention on the corridor. There were none of the tell-tale signs of active laser receptors. He snapped back into real-time. "All clear."

"You sure?"

"Well, if I'm wrong, this'll be a really short rescue."

She grumbled but settled down as Steve maneuvered by memory through the pitch-dark building to the maintenance and service entrance. He aimed his SAVANT at the door lock, and a plasma bolt shot out, breaking it. Gently he put Amy down, then swung the door open and looked through it, his SAVANT out, checking for any life signs ready to attack them as they stepped through. The loading dock was clear.

He walked back to her. "How are you doing?"

"I'll live."

"Good. Can you make a run for it?"

She stared at him for a second. "What?"

"Seriously, can you run?"

Amy tried her legs, taking a couple of tentative steps. "Not my usual running style, but fast enough. No extra 'go' gear, though."

"I can work with that. Look, the boat ramp is 450 yards northeast. Just stay close. Oh, and last one there's a rotten egg." Steve grinned at her, then bolted out the door and turned left into the darkness.

She shook her head as she followed, muttering to herself. "A child. I'm working with a child. I'm not a secret agent, I'm a babysitter!"

Steve sprinted across a parking lot and access road, dodging around deserted road maintenance yards toward the water. Behind him, he heard sirens growing closer as emergency vehicles responded to the report of the mysterious bright flash seen on the island. He yelled to Amy behind him. "Follow the water's edge. The boat should be just to the east of the Treasure Island light."

Amy sped up her pace and quickly closed ground on Steve, then fell into stride beside him on the left. "Are we sure it's going to be there? Won't Williams have taken it by now?"

"Maybe. But if it is, then we can duck into the neighborhood on that side of the island and try to find a vehicle to borrow."

"Let's hope not. This island has only one way on or off it by land. If they suspect a bombing, they'll be sure to have a roadblock up soon."

They fell silent as they ran, passing the old waste treatment plant and an abandoned warehouse. As they rounded the corner, they saw the north jetty into the bay, with its 30-foot metal tower and the white Treasure Island light slowly cycling on and off every five seconds. As it came up, they saw a small speedboat carrying Callahan and Williams pull away from the jetty.

Amy pointed at the departing craft. "Dang it, he's getting away."

Steve looked around. He spotted a small trailer with a tarp over the back in the parking lot. "Maybe not. Come on." He ran over to it and pulled back the tarp. Underneath it was a pair of WaveRunners. He looked skyward for a moment and thanked whatever guardian angel was on duty at that moment, then started examining the watercraft.

Amy's smile when she saw the WaveRunners was almost dazzling. "Nicely done, Tate!" She scrambled up onto the craft and checked the fuel tanks. "This one's half full... the other is on fumes."

Steve thought about it as he watched William's boat dwindle in the distance. Two of them on one ski would be too slow to chase him, and if they divided the fuel between the two craft, there would be no guarantee either would have the range to get to shore. He ran through the numbers in his head and came to a reluctant decision.

"We're letting them go."

"What?" Amy climbed down quickly from the craft. "We just caught a break here! We can catch them!"

Steve shook his head. "And then what? We're outgunned, we have no logistical support, and no idea where they're going or who's helping them. We may not have enough fuel to make it to shore, and in case you hadn't noticed, that water's damned cold. We've both been injured — we're in no shape to handle hypothermia as well."

Amy's voice was rising, becoming more emotional. "Steve, we can't let him get away. The bastard shot me, for God's sake! He tried to kill me!" She paused, turned away. "And he's killed our friends back at Control."

"We don't know that yet."

"But I can take him, Steve! He won't surprise me the next time. You can guard me—"

"No."

"But you can't let another chance get away. Not again!" Her voice was bitter.

He turned and yelled at her. "You think I like doing this? Watching them sail away? Do you, really?"

Amy stepped back, surprised at the anger and anguish in his voice. He turned and walked over to the front of the trailer. "Do you really think I'd choose this if there were any other way to catch them? You haven't learned anything about me at all, A.J." He grabbed the tongue of the trailer and started to lift it.

"Steve—"

"No! We're going back to Triangle now. We'll regroup, and then we'll find them again. Now, help me get this trailer to the boat ramp and into the water before we get caught."

He strained to push the trailer slowly out from its parking space. Amy watched the receding lights from Williams' boat on the bay for a few seconds, biting her lower lip. Then she lowered her head and turned back to help him.

They cut the lines holding the WaveRunners to the trailer and pushed it down the ramp. As it hit the water, the WaveRunners floated away from it. Steve grabbed the bowline for the one with fuel and called over to Amy. "Want to drive?"

She looked at him, surprised. "Uh, sure. You don't?"

He replied as he pulled it over to the jetty. "I trust you. Besides, I need to try to contact Triangle to activate our contingency plans. So, I need you to drive. Besides, you're from Florida. I thought you loved water."

"Why, Tate, you surprise me. You are learning." She ran along the top of the jetty and leaped over his head, doing a forward somersault and landing in the driver's seat. She reached out her left hand and offered it to him.

"Show off," Steve grumbled as he grasped her hand and started to climb aboard. Amy leaned hard to the right and pulled up with her left arm. Steve was lifted into the air so quickly that he momentarily felt like he was levitating.

He fell hard across the rear seat, wincing as pain shot through his right side.

"Better work on that landing, ace. Let me know when you're ready."

"Funny." His pride kept him from saying anything more. Moments later, he was seated behind her on the watercraft as it bobbed in the waves of the bay. "Head south under the Bay Bridge. And watch for wakes — the ones from cargo ships will swamp us if we don't take them head on."

"Aye, aye, captain. South it is." Amy flipped the power to the ON position and pressed the electric starter. The engine roared to life, and after a moment, she engaged the impeller and opened the throttle slowly. They made their way out into the open channel and headed south.

Steve closed his eyes for a moment, trying to gather his thoughts. *Priority one — re-establish contact with Triangle.* Since Williams had been the lead agent on this mission, they'd entrusted him with all the primary and secondary contact data. He was just a trainee agent so none of that data would be in his SAVANT. *Still, I could hack it, especially if I get help from Rose...*

Rose.

My God. Ethan and Rose.

Steve's face went ashen. The realization sent a shudder of dread throughout his body.

No, Steven. Concentrate. Focus. We will get back to both of them. But they're 3,000 miles away, and you can't do anything for them right now. His inner sensei was doing overtime work dragging his mind back to the task at hand.

Amy felt Steve shudder and turned her head slightly. "Is everything all right?"

Steve looked grim. "I don't know yet. I'm still trying to get my commlink to talk to me."

She looked up at the Bay Bridge as they passed beneath it. "Well, with no police boats chasing and no snipers in the girders, I'd say we made a clean getaway."

"Don't be so sure yet. There's still a lot of helicopters over the Alameda base."

Steve looked to his left. The decommissioned naval base was just coming into view past the Port of Oakland's loading facilities...

His mind went numb. *The police response is there, but the hangar...* "Amy, look over there."

"Where?"

"At the base. The hangar's gone."

"What do you mean, gone?"

"I mean it's a smoking pile of rubble. Lots of police. Lots of fire trucks. But no hangar."

Amy was quiet for a moment. "What about the police? The SWAT team that went in there?"

Steve shook his head. "From the look of that response, we have to assume the worst. Williams and Callahan must have rigged it to explode."

Amy looked up. "Hang on!"

She opened the throttle full and leaned hard right. The WaveRunner bucked and then dug in, carving a new course directly toward Yorba Linda Island."

"What the...?" Steve's protests cut off when he glanced behind and saw a searchlight from a circling helicopter illuminate the spot they'd been in just seconds earlier. A Coast Guard patrol boat sped through the light, cutting across their wake in an obvious search pattern."

Steve looked at Amy. "Sorry I said anything."

"Yeah, well, it's not the first time I've had to avoid interacting with friendlies. But it's getting too hot out here for my liking. So where to now, genius?"

"We'll have to be careful wherever we go. Callahan and Williams rigged this whole mission as a double cross, no matter what we were going to do tonight."

He thought for a moment and then looked over to his right. The San Francisco skyline was lit like a string of jewels along the water's edge. He zeroed in on a cluster of lights south of downtown. "How do you feel about baseball?"

"It's long, boring, and no one understands the infield fly rule. Why?"

"Cute. Head west and aim for those lights. That's AT&T Park. The Giants are playing tonight — it's a good place to come ashore and get lost in the crowd."

"All right."

"We'd better ditch these vests while we're still near the bridge. Mission gear will be too conspicuous at the ballpark, especially if the authorities are on the alert. Better put our SAVANTs in Mode 1 as well."

She idled the WaveRunner while they removed and tossed their gear into the water, then opened the throttle and set course toward the lights.

Thirty minutes later, she steered the WaveRunner to an open mooring at the end of the dock in the public marina and tied up there. Steve made a quick note of the craft's registration number. He'd make sure that Triangle would compensate the owners for 'borrowing' it. No need to ruin that guys' day any more than it already was.

Amy was already at the end of the dock, waiting impatiently. "Come on, Tate. Was that necessary?"

"Yeah, it was. Good guys, remember?"

"Fine. So, now what?"

"Well, my SAVANT's uplink to Triangle is still down. I can use general data retrieval, but all the internal classified files and secure data comms are shut off. Whether that's due to what we heard back at Control..." Steve trailed off.

"So we go to plan B?" Amy looked grim. "Do you even *have* a plan B?"

"Me? Come on, A.J. We were on this assignment as provisional agents. Neither of us was fully read in. Williams had the plan B, and probably plans C and D, as well. And knowing him, he'd probably set those up so they would fail — or worse, trigger a thingamajig that would do something catastrophic if we use them."

"What we need now is another way inside Triangle. I need to think." Steve closed his eyes for a second, remembering everything he'd read about Triangle.

Suddenly, a picture he'd seen three weeks before flashed in his mind.

Yeah, that'd work.

He opened his eyes, turned and headed toward the stadium.

Amy hurried to catch up. "Wait, Steve! Where are you going now?"

"Me? Well, three places. First, the little boy's room — nature calls—"

"TMI, Steve!"

"Then, the street vendors in front of the stadium."

"Because someone there is a source, right?"

Steve glanced at her. "Of information? No. But neither of us has had a meal for almost eight hours, and we're running on empty. We need to eat something."

As if on cue, Amy's stomach rumbled in response. Ignoring the sound, she looked at Steve. "You said three places."

"Yes, I did." He kept walking, toward the right field wall of the stadium.

One of the unique features of AT&T Park were the archways in the waterfront concourse. They allowed people walking on the concourse to step up to wrought iron fences that looked into the stadium. You could see directly onto the ballfield and the stands beyond.

As they approached the first arch, Amy saw Steve look carefully through the fence for something among the stadium crowd. Not seeing it, he turned and headed toward the next arch.

Amy followed him, puzzled. She cleared her throat. "And?"

They moved over to the second arch. Steve again moved around folks, still searching for something specific. When he didn't find it, he started toward the next archway. On the way, he turned back to Amy. "And what?"

"Where's the third place you were going?"

As they approached the third archway, he began to search the stadium crowd again. After a moment, he stopped and smiled. He crossed to Amy, stood behind her, and taking her hand, pointed toward a spot inside the stadium. "There."

Amy followed Steve's aim and found a luxury box along the third base line. Standing silhouetted in the light was a man with his back to her, wearing a Giants jacket and holding a beer in one hand. Even from this far away, she could tell the man was tall and thin, with blond hair. He carried himself with an air of distinction. As he turned and was momentarily lit inside the box, she was surprised she recognized him.

She'd had no idea that Reginald Stevenson III even liked baseball.

Chapter 21

The Giants had recently installed a set of self-service ticketing kiosks, allowing fans who had preordered their tickets to swipe their credit card and pick them up at the ballpark. Now, six innings into the game, the devices stood alone in an alcove next to the Will Call booths.

Steve crumpled up the wrapper to his last hot dog and tossed it in a trashcan as he walked up to one of the kiosks. He smiled mischievously. "Okay, baby, let's dance. SAVANT, Mode 2."

The SAVANT morphed its configuration, becoming a wrist mounted tablet computer. As it finished, the small screen powered up and displayed its status.

<DEVICE READY. TRIANGLE NETWORK UNAVAILABLE>

"Yeah, tell me something I don't know. We need to tap into the data network here and get two available seats."

<ACKNOWLEDGED. REMOVE DATA TAP AND APPLY TO NETWORK TERMINAL>

He reached on the side and pulled out a thin cable attached to a small metallic square. He attached that to the credit card swipe reader on the ticketing kiosk.

"Right, it's attached."

<ACCESSING...CONNECTED...SPECIFY LOCATION>

"I need two seats, Club Level, third base side. Section 220 or 221."

<ACKNOWLEDGED...WORKING>

His SAVANT went to work, interfacing with the computerized ticketing system. A moment later, the kiosk spit out two tickets — Section 220, Row 2, Seats 3–4.

Steve smiled and detached the cable, which retracted automatically back into the SAVANT.

"Good job. Switch to Mode 1."

<ACKNOWLEDGED>

The device started to morph as he grabbed the tickets and started walking toward Amy. She made eye contact and headed over toward the gate, where they were scanned in and through the turnstiles.

"Two points for you, ticket geek. But these are club level — one level below Stevenson's suite — if it even is his suite."

"One step at a time, A.J."

"Tate, stop calling me A.J.!"

"As you wish, Amelia Jane." He grinned and sprinted up the staircase to the Club Level. He heard Amy follow him as she groaned in frustration.

They settled into their seats just as the Giants were coming up to bat in the bottom of the seventh. It was a tie ballgame, 2–2. Steve looked around for a second, to see if anyone was watching them, then activated his Talent.

The world took on its familiar blue tinge as he examined the stadium. He concentrated on the luxury box area, looking for ways to contact or access the suite Stevenson was in. It wasn't looking good. He slipped back into real-time, frowning.

"Damn. I was hoping we could hack his cell signal from this close, but Stevenson's using a shielded phone. Given what he does, that makes sense..." he trailed off, looking at the field again. Suddenly he smiled. "Moonlight Graham."

Amy looked confused. "Who's Moonlight Graham?"

Steve looked shocked. "Didn't you ever watch movies as a kid? No, scratch that; of course, you wouldn't have. Look, ever hear of a film called *Field of Dreams*? You know, 'If you build it, he will come.'"

"I'm familiar with the phrase. But how does it apply to us?"

"Well, in the movie, the 'voice' tells the hero to go to Fenway Park on a certain day, because something's going to happen there. Well, he does, and in the middle of the fourth inning, the scoreboard suddenly flashes up the words 'Moonlight Graham.' It's a sign for the film's hero, telling him where to go next. And only the hero sees the message."

Amy looked out at the scoreboard, and then back at Steve. "You're kidding, right? That's your plan? You're going to hijack the AT&T Park scoreboard in the seventh inning of a game to send a message to Stevenson?"

"Well, if you've got a better one, I'd love to hear it."

"Yeah. We settle down here, wait, and at the end of the game, catch Stevenson on the way out of the stadium."

"No good. The suite level has its own private exit. We'd never see him, and since we don't know what vehicle Stevenson's riding in, it could be any of a dozen limousines waiting underground. No, this will get his attention enough to call you and then—"

"Me?" Amy's eyes got wide. "You're going to broadcast my digits to the world on that scoreboard?"

He nodded. "I'll be handling the actual hack using my SAVANT. I figure I'll have thirty seconds before security shuts me down, and then another two minutes to get out of Dodge. So, you need to be the one he'll call."

He told his SAVANT to switch to Mode 2. As it morphed, he looked at Amy. "Relax; these won't be your personal digits. We'll use the dummy cell phone line we set up for your SAVANT back at training. I'm hoping a Virginia area code will make him curious."

Amy looked around nervously. "Are you sure this will work?"

Steve keyed in a series of commands on the SAVANT and looked up at her, smiling. "Trust me, A.J. What could go wrong?"

"Do you really want me to start listing all of them?"

"Not particularly. We don't have the time. Okay, be ready for the message in five, four, three, two, and one."

On the field, the Phillies' pitcher had just released a fastball toward the plate as Steve touched a control on his SAVANT's screen.

The entire ballpark immediately plunged into complete darkness.

"Tate!"

Steve looked around at the pitch-black stadium.

"I did not see that coming."

9:26 p.m. PDT

On the suite level, Reg Stevenson was standing in place, waiting for some sort of lighting to kick in. *Well, that's curious. Not an earthquake. So, where's the emergency lighting?*

He became aware of a faint glow on one of the video monitors above him. On that screen, and that screen only, the message popped up:

Reggie, A.J. loves you.
Please call home. Save Aunt.

Below it was a phone number with a Virginia area code and a Loudoun County prefix.

After eight seconds, the image blinked out, and every light came back on in the stadium.

On the field, players milled about as the umpires and managers quickly met at home plate to discuss the issue and whether to continue the game. Security guards quickly ran out onto the field and ringed the perimeter. The public-address announcer called for the crowd to remain calm as an uneasy murmur rolled through the stadium.

Stevenson reached for his cell phone.

9:27 p.m. PDT

Steve hadn't realized he'd been holding his breath, and let it out slowly.

Amy turned to him and growled in a low voice. "Of all the stupid ideas! How did you black out an entire major league ballpark? And where was the message? I didn't see anything on the Jumbotron out there — did you?"

Steve shook his head. "I would have sworn that would work. Maybe if I—"

Amy put a hand over his mouth. "Maybe, nothing. Now we do it my way. Let's head for the staircase, and figure a way to the secure exit for the suite holders and their guests—"

Amy was interrupted as the incoming call signal vibrated on her SAVANT. She looked at it, slaved Steve into the commlink audio and answered the call. "Hello?"

There was no mistaking the voice on the other end. "Hello, A.J. This is Reggie. I love you, too. But we really do need to talk."

9:35 p.m. PDT

Stevenson arranged to meet them at the corner of 3rd and Brennan, just west of the stadium. They left the stadium immediately and walked along 3rd, trying to look like a couple out on a date. Steve sought to embellish the point by holding Amy's hand, but she shook it off. "Better to have them both free, in case we need to defend ourselves."

"From whom?"

"Me, for starters, if you keep trying to hold my hand."

Just before they made it to the corner, a black stretch SUV pull up alongside them. They immediately climbed in and found themselves face-to-face again with the man himself.

Amy spoke up as soon as she got in. "Thank you, sir, for your help. I'm—"

"I remember exactly who you are. The more important question is what's happened that you had to black out an entire baseball game to get my attention? A neat trick that was, by the way."

Steve blushed at the unwarranted praise. "Uh, thanks, I think."

"Sir, Triangle's been compromised. The theft of False Mirror was an inside job. The lead out here to find the device was a trap — it's still in the wind."

Stevenson steepled his fingers and looked at Amy carefully. "That's a serious charge, Ms. Rogers. What are you basing this on?"

Steve spoke up. "Mitch Williams leading Amy and me into the trap and trying to kill us, for a start. Plus, the SICC in Virginia is offline. I haven't been able to raise anyone since the ambush, and our SAVANTs are on independent mode."

Stevenson looked distressed. "Off-line?" He reached over and pressed a button on his console. A male voice came over the speakers in the limo. "Triangle Comm. How may I be of assistance, Mr. Stevenson?"

"Put me through to the Duty Office at Triangle Virginia. And locate Dr. Watson for me."

"Working." There was a brief pause. "Sir, all comms with Triangle Virginia are down."

"What do you mean, all comms?"

Amy and Steve shared a glance. *Not good.*

"Sir, satellite and fiber optic channels are both non-responsive. Additionally, the data feed from the Virginia computing center is silent."

Stevenson thought for a moment. "Any word on Dr. Watson?"

"She hasn't responded, but her locator shows she is in the Triangle Virginia complex." There was a pause, and then the voice continued. "Sir, I have intercepts of multiple 911 calls regarding a series of explosions in the Loudoun County area, centered on our facility. Civilian fire and police have responded to the scene."

Stevenson nodded and looked at his passengers. "That's probably why Watson isn't taking my call yet — she's handling the response to what's happened." He looked up at the speaker comm. "New instructions. Contact our hangar at SFO; tell them to get Firebird prepped for immediate takeoff. I want to be wheels up in twenty minutes."

"Yes, sir. Anything else?"

"Get a message to Dr. Watson that I'm en route. She's to contact me at the earliest possible moment."

"Yes, sir. San Francisco reports Firebird will be ready on time."

Stevenson nodded. "Well, at least that's one thing working right." He cut off the connection and then pressed the driver intercom button. "Johnson, new destination. Our hangar at SFO. Speed is of the essence."

"Yes, sir."

Steve and Amy sank back in their seats as the limo accelerated quickly. Satisfied, Stevenson turned to them. "If you're right, this is going to be a problem. Mitchell Williams was one of the best operatives Triangle ever had. When we get aboard Firebird, I'll want a full debrief from you two so you can bring me up to speed."

The limo hit a bump and Steve winced. "Sir, are there medical supplies aboard? Between Amy being shot and me cracking a couple of ribs, it's been a rough night."

Stevenson looked at Amy in surprise. "Good Lord. Shot? Shouldn't you be in a hospital, young lady?"

Amy shook her head. "No, sir. It seems to be part of my skill set to be...well, bulletproof."

The magnate took that news in stride. "Of course, we should be able to take care of you en route aboard Firebird. I'll have Medical stand by in Virginia as well." He looked at Steve again. "You're Grey Tate's boy, right?"

"Yes, sir."

"Then you're in for a treat."

The limo pulled off the freeway and into the private aviation area north of the main airport terminals. There an ordinary unlabeled hangar, large enough to house a Boeing corporate jet, at the far end of the flight line. The limo pulled up next to it. Johnson jumped out and opened the door. Stevenson led them inside.

10:03 p.m. PDT

After entering the building, they started through the offices toward the hangar's interior. Steve immediately felt the hum of an aircraft power plant idling. But there was something different — the frequency was lower pitched. *Some new sort of power plant?*

As they reached the door, Stevenson handed them each a set of earphones. "Put these in until we board the plane. I'm afraid Firebird is a wee bit noisy." He opened the door, and a wall of sound hit them. Steve found himself taking a step back against the pressure wave it generated. Once he had adjusted, he stepped into the hangar.

And stopped.

And stared at a thing of beauty.

Firebird was pure black and about 120 feet long. She had a delta wing formation, with the main engines mounted underneath, close inboard, with squared-off exhausts. Instead of a traditional tail stabilizer, it had dual upsweeps on the ends of both wings. A truck was pulled up behind, loading it with fuel. There was frost on the fueling hose, and when Steve saw that, he realized what they were flying on.

"Oh, dear God. You built one."

Stevenson clapped him on the shoulder, grinning. "I thought you might recognize it. But you can gawk later. We need to get in the air now." He headed for the boarding ladder.

Steve just continued standing, frozen in awe. Amy turned to him. "Tate, snap out of it. We need to focus." Still no response. She grabbed his arm and started to pull him toward the boarding ramp. "Steve, come on!"

He followed her but kept looking at the plane, muttering the whole time. "I can't believe he actually built one." They reached the boarding ladder and climbed up the stairs.

As soon as they entered the plane, a flight crew member closed and sealed the door behind them. They entered the main cabin, and Steve felt like he'd walked onto the set of some science fiction series. He stopped and stared again, his mouth agape.

Amy waved her hand in front of his face. "Hello, Earth to Steve. Come on, we need to sit down." She headed for a quartet of seats around a table on the left side of the compartment.

Steve sat down next to her and looked at the table. It was a SMART table, a computer interface. When he touched his hand to it, it lit up and did a scan of his handprint. The scan box blinked red, and a female voice said, "Tate, Steven. Unauthorized."

Amy smirked. "Well, at least it knows the real you. And it's a good judge of character."

Steve frowned at her. "Hilarious, A.J. You try it."

"Don't call me — oh, never mind." She reached out and put her hand on the table.

"Rogers, Amelia Jane. Unauthorized."

"Caroline, authorize Tate and Rogers, here. Full access." Stevenson had entered from the flight deck and sat down in one of the seats opposite them.

As he buckled in, the computer responded, "Very well, Reggie. Welcome aboard, Steven. May I call you Steve?"

Steve's grin grew even larger. "Sure."

The computer continued. "Welcome aboard, Amelia Jane. May I call you A.J.?"

Steve tried unsuccessfully to stifle a laugh, while Amy looked nonplussed. "Uh, Caroline, is it? I'd prefer Amy."

"Response noted. Welcome, Amy."

Stevenson nodded. "Once we get airborne, we can get to work. We'll have ninety minutes to figure things out."

Amy looked at him with a confused expression. "Ninety minutes? But it's a six-hour flight to Dulles. Where are we going?"

Steve looked at Amy. "You really don't know what he's got here, do you, A.J.?"

"It's a private jet. A little fancier and more dramatic, but I figured that's your style, Mr. Stevenson. No offense intended."

Stevenson smiled. "None taken, Miss Rogers. But you're a little bit off the mark."

Steve smiled. "Amy, remember what I said in the hangar? If I'm not mistaken, you are sitting inside the world's only operational spaceplane."

Amy stared at Steve, speechless. Stevenson nodded. "Actually, one of four. Firebird, Thunderbird, Songbird and Sunbird. And the reason Mr. Tate was so excited, is because he's seen it before."

Amy looked at Steve again. "But you said—"

"The prototype model is sitting on my father's desk back in Snohomish. You see, he designed this plane early in his career, but the project was killed off decades ago. The cold war ended, and it had no place in the 'New World Order.'" Steve turned to Stevenson. "Does my father know you built it?"

Stevenson nodded. "I should think so. He built it himself, on contract for us four years ago."

Steve's brow furrowed. "Four years ago? You're serious?" He looked around the plane, emotions warring on his face. "That's interesting. I guess I'm glad he knows how to keep a secret."

From behind him, Steve felt the engines pitch up. Stevenson pressed a control on his chair, and it swiveled 180 degrees to face the front.

Amy leaned over to Steve and asked him quietly, "Is everything all right?"

"Oh, uh, yeah. I just... I'll tell you about it some other time. You might want to lean back right now, though."

10:08 p.m. PDT

Amy raised an eyebrow at Steve's warning. "Really? Why?"

Suddenly, the engines roared to takeoff power behind her, and the plane leaped forward. Amy was pushed back into her seat, which must have used some sort of reactive cushioning to support her. After twenty-five seconds, the plane rotated and left the ground. She glanced out the window and saw the lights of the city and the bay below her. Suddenly, the plane aimed its nose skyward, and the engines throttled up to full power. Amy felt as if a small elephant had suddenly sat on her chest.

Steve glanced over at her and yelled above the engine noise, "That's why!"

Chapter 22

When Firebird reached cruising altitude, Stevenson turned around and started to debrief Steve and Amy. He was meticulous, walking them through the events forward and backward, looking for details about Williams' behavior. When they concluded, Stevenson sat back, his fingers steepled in front of him. "He must have a vendetta of some sort, but I'll be hanged if I can place what we've ever done to earn that level of ire."

Caroline interrupted the conversation. "Excuse me, Reggie. Dr. Watson is attempting to contact you. Shall I put her through?"

Stevenson stood up and moved to the console on the starboard side of the plane. "Yes, please, Caroline. Holopresence." A blue circle on the floor lit from beneath and Stevenson stepped into it.

A blue circle on the console lit up, and a three-dimensional hologram of Dr. Watson sprung up in front of him. "Rhonda, are you all right?"

She looks exhausted, Steve thought. Her voice matched her appearance. "It's not good. Mitch — I mean, Williams knew exactly how to cripple us. He set explosives that destroyed both the main and backup satellite uplinks, the fiber-optic hardline, and..." She paused and swallowed hard. "And in the SICC, he booby-trapped the SAVANT Interface Consoles and set them off mid-mission."

Steve and Amy gasped. Stevenson closed his eyes and pinched the bridge of his nose. "Casualties?"

"We had three controllers on duty. One dead, two injured. One severely."

"Specifics?"

"Christine Merrimac, Williams' controller, was killed instantly. Ethan Nowitzki managed to get down and avoided most of the blast. He's got a ruptured eardrum and some shrapnel in his right arm."

Steve and Amy looked at each other. Amy called out. "What about Rose?"

Watson looked up, surprised. "Was that Amelia Rogers?"

Stevenson nodded. "Yes. Rogers and Tate managed to find me after this whole thing went sideways. That's why I'm en route in Firebird."

Amy and Steve stood up and walked over next to Stevenson. The blue circle on the floor expanded to encompass the three of them. Steve looked at the hologram. "Doctor, you haven't answered the question. What about Rose?"

Dr. Watson took a deep breath. "Rose Johannsen suffered a severe head trauma because of the explosion. She underwent surgery to treat a subdural hematoma. She's alive but in a coma. The medical staff is unsure if she'll survive the night."

Amy turned and buried her head in Steve's chest. He just stood there, numb.

Stevenson looked at Watson. "We arrive at Dulles in forty-two minutes. Have ground transport waiting. I also want you to activate Tiger Team. Bring them in on this. They have Songbird on loan. Use it, and get them to Virginia now. We have to find Williams, and quickly." He glanced at his watch. "We'll see you within the hour."

Stevenson cut the connection and turned to the two agents. "I take it Ms. Johannsen means something to both of you?"

Steve nodded. "We grew up together in Washington. She's..." He couldn't finish the sentence.

Amy's voice was subdued. "Rose was my roommate. I'm the reason she came to Triangle." Her voice broke. "I'm the reason she's dying."

Stevenson put his hand on Amy's shoulder. "Rogers, the reason she's in a coma is that an enemy with a vendetta and no conscience attacked us. Not because of you. If anyone's to blame, it's me. And trust me, this will not stand. He will not get away with this."

Stevenson walked back to his seat then turned to face her. "I'd like you two to be there at the strategy meeting. But only if you can focus. I know what I'm asking is rough. But now we've got to stop a pair of cold-blooded killers armed with a devastating weapon and you two may be my best option to do so." He looked at Steve. "I know I've asked you this before, but I have to again. Are you still in?"

Amy and Steve looked at each other. She nodded, her face grimly determined. Steve turned back to Stevenson. "We were never out, sir. We both have unfinished business in this case. We just have two targets now, not one."

Amy nodded agreement. "I'm with Steve on this. But both Callahan and Williams have brought up something. They referred to other Talents. They implied there are a lot more people besides Steve and me out there with abilities."

Stevenson looked at them, his face a mask. "While Triangle is always looking out for individuals with unique abilities, I've never heard of anything like that. He probably said it to distract you. I'd concentrate on trying to figure out his next move instead."

Steve and Amy glanced at each other. "We plan to."

Stevenson nodded. "Then take a seat. We'll be landing soon."

June 15, 2:40 am EDT

Compared to the violent nature of the takeoff, the landing was as smooth as silk. Firebird glided in and quickly taxied to the Triangle hangar on the west side of the airport. Once inside and safe from prying eyes, the engines cut off and the three deplaned. They climbed into a waiting black limousine and drove out the gate, where an escort of four motorcycle policemen waited. They positioned themselves, two in front, two behind, and escorted the limo through the back roads of northern Virginia to the facility's main gate. A uniformed Triangle Security officer waved them onto the property.

The limo pulled into the underground parking level and stopped next to the elevators. Stevenson exited first and pressed his palm to the ID pad. The biometric sensor confirmed his identity and the elevator opened. Steve and Amy followed him, and the doors closed behind them. Stevenson ordered it to descend to Level 3, and it quickly did so.

When the doors opened, Steve caught the acrid scent of smoke and fire retardant. He looked at Amy who was wrinkling her nose. Stevenson looked grim. "This way," he said.

They walked into the hub corridor and turned left, heading toward a secure briefing room. They saw only a few base personnel; the ones they did looked grim and determined. No one said a word as they turned right and entered a branch corridor.

Ahead on the left was a second branch corridor, darker than night because its overhead lighting wasn't working. Emergency light stands had been put in place, and in the harsh white light Steve soon could see why. Much of the ceiling was discolored by smoke. Large fans and hoses had been set up to ventilate the spaces.

As they reached the corner, Amy slowed to a stop. "My God," she whispered.

A few yards down the corridor, the doors to the SICC were twisted and crumpled, canted at an angle. Through their broken frames, they caught a glimpse of the devastation inside. The wall screen was shattered; portions of the ceiling had collapsed. Conduits and cables were hanging down. The interface consoles were obliterated; only the pedestals remained. There was blood spattered on the walls. A lot of blood. A team of damage control technicians in red coveralls were documenting the damage.

"Tate, Rogers, this way, please," Stevenson called out to them. Steve started again down the central branch, pulling Amy along with him.

They entered the briefing room and were surprised to see Dr. Naziri on a video screen. Dr. Watson was at the head of the conference table, talking with another pair of operatives — a redheaded female and a blond male, both in their early 20s. They wore matching black turtlenecks and green combat pants and looked like they'd just returned from a mission. Steve thought he'd seen them before around the base and tried to recall their names, but he wasn't sure.

Seated at the end of the table, looking much worse for the wear, was a sight for sore eyes — Ethan Nowitzki, his right arm bandaged and in a sling, a second bandage covering his right ear. He looked grim.

Amy ran over to him. "Ethan!" Her arms were around him instantly in a hug.

"Easy there. Amelia. Good to see you made it back."

"Sorry. Are you hurt badly?"

"I'll survive. But it's been a long night. Williams and Callahan have hit us hard."

Stevenson immediately took charge. "Status report?"

Watson opened a set of data windows on the wall screen. "We've managed to splice in a repair on the fiber optic ten minutes ago. That's how we have Dr. Naziri. Communications reports that repairs to the satellite link are underway and we should re-establish a connection with our birds in an hour."

Stevenson nodded. "Good. At least we won't be blind anymore." He turned to the two other agents in the room. "Tiger Team, thanks for reporting in so quickly. You'll take point on this op when we've prepared a response."

The female agent with the red hair looked at Stevenson. "If you say so, but I think you've already got the team in place." She pointed at Steve and Amy. Watson and Stevenson looked at her, surprise on their faces.

"Are you sure?" Stevenson looked skeptical. "When it comes to field experience, they're pretty green. You two have been at this for years."

3:05 a.m. EDT

Amy was curious about that. *Years? She looks like she's barely out of college. Of course, so do Steve and I. Still... years?*

The other agents looked at each other, and then at Ethan, who nodded grimly. The blond spoke up. "Oh, yeah, Lucy's sure. Besides, if I inferred correctly from the briefing, these two each have an extra ace up their sleeve. Williams could plan for us, but can he plan for that?"

Watson turned to Ethan. "And do you have anything to say?"

"Only that I concur. Even though Williams sprung a trap on them, they held their own and made it back, bringing vital intel on the situation. I believe they've proven their worth to the organization."

Watson cleared her throat. "That's all well and good, but we've still got two problems. How to beat False Mirror, and figuring out where Williams is. And now that we know that Callahan is working with him, we need to find out what their connection is, too."

Ethan nodded. "As to the where, Max in Intel thinks they have a lead on them." He pressed his hand to the SMART table. A virtual keyboard appeared. Using his good hand, he typed a command and opened a window, scrolled through a message, then grabbed an image and flicked it sideways. It slid off the table and appeared on the wall screen. "Amy, would you mind?"

Amy walked over to the image, touched the corners and pulled it apart, expanding the window. It showed a still image from a red-light camera. In the picture, a tall blonde woman in sunglasses was behind the wheel of a late model sedan. In the passenger seat was a Caucasian man, early 40s, with close-cropped gray hair and dark glasses. Ethan ran a quick facial recognition comparison and five seconds later confirmed it. *Williams.*

Steve looked grimly at the screen. "Callahan's with him."

"Yes."

"Where was this taken?" Stevenson asked.

"San Francisco International. The timestamp indicates 2155 local time."

Stevenson swore under his breath. "Bollocks. You mean we were at the same airport at the same time?"

"Yes. Intel reports that they boarded an international departure that took off just thirty minutes after you left."

Watson turned to Naziri's image. "Dr. Naziri, how could he have gotten the device through security?"

Naziri looked at them, his lips pursed for a moment. "If the device was active, it has a self-masking capability. It would have actively avoided detection."

Stevenson swore. "Whatever possessed you to actually build the thing, Doctor? Especially in light of what happened in Nassau?"

Naziri's brow furrowed. "You ask why? What is my role here in Triangle, Mr. Stevenson? I take your worst-case scenario and figure out how to stop it. After Nassau, I knew I had to determine that quickly for False Mirror since there were people willing to kill to get the design. So, I built the prototype, to find the defense for it. And I did so under your direct orders, sir!"

Stevenson stared at the screen. "Dr. Naziri, I gave no such orders."

Naziri shook his head. "Of course, you did. Right after I returned from the kidnapping, you contacted me via video link and..." Naziri slowed to a stop. "You gave no such orders? Then did you order a young woman to my lab to assist?"

Watson checked her tablet. "Dr. Naziri, the only personnel transfer order is the one I made for Mr. Lewis that you rerouted to my office—"

Naziri went pale. "I rerouted it? Not possible. Mr. Stevenson always told me he sent them personally, at my request for additional assistance."

Steve and Amy looked at each other. "Sounds like you've been compromised for quite some time, sir."

Stevenson nodded. "Indeed." He turned to the red-haired agent. "I need to know just how bad this breach is. How quickly could your colleague, Mr. Johnston, look into it for us?"

The Tiger Team agents shared a glance. "If you're willing to give him full access this time, Dale should be able to get you something fairly quickly."

Stevenson nodded. "Ethan, coordinate this with the Tiger Team personnel. Dr. Naziri, I need you to find your archival recordings of all the video calls and forward them to Mr. Nowitzki here."

Watson looked exasperated. "Reggie, I'm sorry, but that seems a lot like closing the proverbial barn door. Instead of a set of plans, now they have a working device. And we don't have a solution."

"Oh, but I do."

The briefing room went silent for a moment. Stevenson looked up sharply at the screen. "Excuse me?"

Naziri looked smug. "I said I have the solution, the way to defeat False Mirror, right here." He held up a pair of portable USB drives.

Watson looked amazed. "But...how?"

"Well, once we knew the device was stolen, I knew that Phase 3 would become the highest priority, So I decided to work on it, rather than wait for you to send word. I thought it would be nice to be ahead of these people for once."

The red-haired agent smiled. "Dr. Naziri, that's wonderful. So how does it work?"

Steve and Amy looked at the pair of drives, then at each other. Amy spoke up first. "Let me guess. This is somehow like those old nuclear launch codes — you know, two different sets of keys, where both have to be inserted at the same time?"

Naziri smiled. "Not quite, but close." He held up a red USB drive. "This contains a new coding for the False Mirror device — an operating system update if you will. It must be uploaded first to the device." He then held up a second, green USB drive. "This one is a command search pattern which the False Mirror device will interpret as an attack and act to defend itself. However, the new operating system instructions will cause the device to instead build up and fire off a tuned electromagnetic pulse."

Ethan's head shot up at that. "Oh, now wait a minute. That sounds familiar."

Naziri nodded. "Yes, it was actually Mr. Lewis who provided me with the inspiration for how to defeat the device. You see, what we need it to do is not just turn it off — if the components, even disabled, are left behind, there is a possibility it could be duplicated."

Amy looked at the senior Triangle personnel in the room, who didn't seem too happy about Naziri's solution. "So what? He uses a tuned EMP and the device burns up and goes poof? Big deal."

Steve looked over at her. "A.J., if I understand our tech correctly, it *is* a big deal, because a strong enough tuned EMP will permanently deactivate and destroy the nanites that Triangle uses." He held up his left arm and tapped a finger against his SAVANT.

Amy opened her mouth to reply, then stopped as that sunk in. She turned to the screen. "Dr. Naziri, what's the range of that EMP pulse when it goes off?"

"On a prototype? Anywhere from 200 to 300 meters."

Ethan looked up at Naziri. "Can't we program our satellites to broadcast the command search pattern and ensure the device is disabled?"

"Unfortunately, no. The device's defense protocols are different for a satellite-based signal. This needs to come from a computer on the same local network the False Mirror device is connected to."

Stevenson looked up at the screen. "Still, Doctor, while it's not a perfect solution, that's probably the first piece of good news we've had all day." He looked over at Watson.

She stepped forward into the video pickup. "I'll have two couriers there in fifteen minutes. Please duplicate the devices and give one set to each."

"I'll get to work on that. And Dr. Watson?"

"Yes?"

"Good hunting." Naziri terminated the connection.

Stevenson walked over to the wall display and tapped a control. "Now we have a way to beat this blasted thing. Next question: Where the devil is he going with it?"

Ethan looked up from his virtual terminal. "Well, one of Williams' registered alias' shows on the passenger manifest for a United flight to Tokyo. And there's more. The same manifest lists a Karen Callahan as a fellow passenger in first class."

Steve frowned. "Karen Callahan? A new alias?"

Watson looked at Stevenson. She hesitated just a moment. "Let's assume so. It can't be a coincidence. We've got to intercept them when they land in Japan."

Lucy, the red-haired agent, looked at the blond. "Japan. You've got some influence with people you can count on there, don't you, Rob?"

Rob looked slightly uncomfortable, pulling at the collar of his black shirt. "Well, um, yeah. At least, sort of. I'm not sure this is up their alley, but I can ask." He looked over at Stevenson. "If that's all right, sir."

He folded his arms and stroked his chin for a moment. "We could do with some extra eyes on the ground. Are they discreet?"

Rob and Lucy shared a look. "Uh, you could say that."

Stevenson's eyebrow shot up. "Care to elaborate?"

Rob looked even more uncomfortable. "Not really."

He shook his head. "I give you two far too much latitude sometimes. Fair enough. Go ahead and talk to them. See if they can get a bead on our lost targets. I'd like to nail their hides to the wall."

Rob nodded, and he and Lucy exited the briefing room. Stevenson looked over at Steve and Amy. "You two look like hell. I want you to go see Medical to get your injuries treated. Then get some sleep, and a good meal, and be back here in twelve hours."

Amy protested. "But sir, they're out there—"

"They're flying to Tokyo, Miss Rogers. They'll be in the air at least another eight hours. We're going to try to apprehend them quietly upon landing. If not, well, I'll need you two rested and recovered if you're going to go up against them. So, go to medical, get something to eat, and get some sleep."

Steve nodded and tugged on Amy's arm. "I don't think it's up for discussion, A.J. Let's go."

Amy turned on him. "Will you please stop calling me that?"

Steve smiled and shrugged. "Maybe." He headed out the door. Amy groaned and followed him.

3:12 a.m. EDT

Stevenson turned to Watson. "Are you sure about those two?"

Watson replied, "Yes." She turned to the screen wall and contemplated the map. *At least, I hope I am.*

12:05 a.m. HADT

Dinner in first class is superb, Callahan thought, as the United flight attendant cleared her tray and refilled her glass. It was a light white wine, crisp and refreshing.

Williams turned to her and smiled. "How's the wine?"

"Quite nice. But even in first class, I'm not happy that I'm on a commercial flight. I'm used to flying privately. It allows me to avoid...certain entanglements."

"Ms. Callahan, I've been assisting you remotely for months now. You think that when we finally meet in person, I'd allow us to be put in harm's way?" He smiled and sipped his wine.

Callahan frowned. "I'll bite. How are you going to pull this off? Triangle's going to be all over us when we arrive in Tokyo — like, if you'll pardon the expression — white on rice."

"No, they won't. You see, Triangle thinks we're going to Narita. But the advantage of this device," he patted the duffle bag on the floor beneath his seat, "is that it specializes in the art of misdirection. So, when our pilots received their instructions to divert to Osaka because of weather twenty minutes ago, well, that's part of it."

"And the other part of it?"

"Well, sometimes, sacrifices need to be made. And if they think we're already... well..." He took off the Triangle collar pin he was wearing and dropped it, from a height, into his water glass. He turned and grinned at her.

Callahan smiled back, practically purring at him. "Such a bad boy, Mitchell. And brilliant."

"Yes. Stevenson never understood that. When he passed on me as Operations Director and chose my ex-partner instead, he made the biggest mistake of his life."

"So, what now?"

"A couple of quick strikes that will ensure that I am set for life. The chaos will be epic, and at the height of it, I'll leak the reason for it and the whole story behind Triangle. The real story. Stevenson will be exposed and ruined, we'll be rich, and then your employer and I can discuss my new working arrangements."

Callahan raised her glass in salute. "I think you'll find working for us to be very profitable, Mitchell."

Williams raised his glass as well. "Then here's to profit."

12:45 p.m. EDT

As much as he had wanted to keep going, Steve had to admit that the boss was right. He'd first checked in with Medical, where they'd applied a bio-gel patch to his right side. Thirty minutes later, his ribs were well on their way to being healed. He checked down the hall, but Rose was still in recovery after her surgery. He offered up a little prayer. *Please, God, look after her tonight. Get her through the night safely.*

A few hours of sleep and a nourishing breakfast put him in a better frame of mind. He called down to Medical for an update on Rose. She was now in the ICU, holding her own — still in a coma, but her vitals were stable. *I know Rose; she's tough. If anyone can come through this, she will.* Still, before he exited his room, he said another little prayer. *Thank you, God. If you've assigned Mom and Sis as Guardian Angels, keep them on the job with her today, please? Just one day at a time, that's all I'm asking.*

He headed down the corridor on the Level 2 and stopped by Amy's quarters. He pressed the door panel, and a chime sounded. A slightly groggy voice emerged from the speaker. "Who is it?"

"Rise and shine, A.J. Time to save the world."

He heard a groan. "Go away."

"No can do, A.J. Let me in."

A few seconds later, the door slid open, and Steve walked in. Amy was seated on her bed, wearing a pair of blue yoga pants and a white tank top. Her eyes were red and puffy, and she was hugging a pillow. Steve had never seen her like this before. Even disheveled, though, she was beautiful.

Snap out of it, Brain Boy. Not on the menu.

"Wow. Did you get any sleep?"

She looked up at him and frowned. "A little. I kept thinking about Rose, about Williams, about Callahan... and about Jason." She sniffled and grabbed a tissue. "I am so tired of losing people and getting hurt, Steve. What did I do to deserve this?"

He looked around and found a chair. He brought it over, turned it around backward and sat on it across from Amy. "The truth? Nothing. I used to ask myself the same question. After all, if I hadn't burnt dinner, wouldn't Mom and Marie still be here? But I'm getting the feeling that from minute one, you and I have pretty much been in the wrong place at the wrong time. But you knew that when you went after Callahan in Nassau. So, the question is — do you still want to? This is a much bigger fight than we ever knew, and we're just pawns in the game. Nobody will blame you if you back out now. You've already been through a lot. But I'll say this." He looked down at the floor for a moment. "There's no one else I'd rather be out there with. I may give you a lot of grief, A.J., but the truth is we make a great team. Together, we're going to catch both these bastards and bring them to justice."

Amy looked at him. "I'm really not going to get you to stop calling me A.J., am I?"

Steve shrugged. "I think it fits you. It's tough sounding and I don't know anyone tougher than you."

Amy smiled at that. "You have no idea."

"Actually, I sort of do. You've taken a bullet, what, twice now? Any idea how that works?"

Amy shook her head. "It really wasn't something I was looking to figure out."

"Yeah, but think about it. You'd activated your Talent both times. I mean, in Nassau for sure, and while you were behind me, I assume you activated your Talent in the brig?" Amy nodded, and Steve continued. "Yeah, but you're not always active, just like I'm not. It's too exhausting. So here's a question — when you're Talent isn't engaged, are you still bulletproof?"

Amy opened her mouth to answer and then stopped. A frown creased her brow. "I'm not sure I want to find out the answer to that question."

Steve nodded. "Agreed. But someone else out there might. Again, this whole Talent thing keeps getting bigger by the day."

"Do you think Stevenson was telling us the truth?"

Now Steve became thoughtful. "I doubt it. His answer seemed just a bit...nuanced to me."

Amy looked at him. "But if it's not true, then just what the heck are we, Steve?"

"I think that's a discussion for another day." He stood up. "If you feel frustrated, let's work off a little of that. We're not supposed to report in for another couple of hours. Meet me in the Danger Room after you've eaten and we can do a little sparring. I even promise not to kick your butt too badly."

Amy smirked at him. "You're on, Tate. But remember, you asked for it."

"Just bring your A-game, A.J." Steve turned and started to leave, then paused for a moment. He looked back at her.

"A.J., back on the plane, you said..." His voice trailed off.

She looked up at Steve and cocked her head to the side. "I said a lot of stuff."

"No, you said there was something more you'd tell me when we made it through last night."

She nodded, her face grave. "Do you still want to know?"

"Well, I was sort of curious."

Amy closed her eyes, buried her head in her pillow for a second, and then looked back up at him. "Yeah, you would be."

She put the pillow down, stood up and crossed over to him at the door, then took his hand.

"The thing is..." she hesitated as he looked down at her.

It's all right, A.J., he thought. *I won't hurt you.*

She cleared her throat for a second and started up again. "The thing is, Steve...is that with you...for the first time, I feel safe. And I'm still trying to understand what that means."

He smiled slightly. "I make you feel safe? Seriously? You can go rabid ninja on almost anyone, Amy. As I said, you're tougher than anyone I know."

"I know, but it's what I feel, okay?" She turned away.

Steve hesitated a second, then put his hands on her shoulders. "I'm flattered, Amy. No one ever said that to me before. You do know I'll always be there for you, right? If you ever need me, no matter what — I will be there."

She turned and looked at him, her eyes flashing angrily. "Don't make a promise like that! You could never keep it!"

"Amy—"

"No." She walked back to the bed and sat down with the pillow again. "You'd better go. I'll catch up with you in Training 3."

12:55 p.m. EDT

Amy hugged the pillow tightly and closed her eyes. She heard Tate cross to the door, heard it slide open, and then a pause and a sigh.

"You're wrong, A.J. I will always be there for you."

She felt her heart leap in her chest with those words. She opened her eyes.

"Steve, wait..."

The doorway was empty. A moment later, it slid shut with an audible click.

She shook her head. *Girl, don't even go there.* She pushed the pillow aside and got up to change.

Chapter 23

The sparring session was vigorous, but surprisingly, neither had been able to land a serious blow. Steve had taken the hand-to-hand combat lessons to heart and his improved ability to read and adapt counteracted Amy's speed when she attacked; her quickened reactions and new moves utilizing her environment made avoiding Steve's counterattacks relatively easy. After thirty minutes of even sparring, they decided to call it a draw.

Stevenson and Watson were looking at the data table when Steve and Amy walked into the briefing room. The two Tiger Team agents were back, as was Ethan. In a video window on the wall screen was a new team member.

"Hello, Percy," Amy said as she walked in the range of the pickup. "How's New Mexico?"

"Oh, Amelia! Good to see you. Surprisingly, it is quite nice. I've discovered this quaint little—"

Watson cleared her throat. "Sorry to interrupt your visit, but we've work to do. I hope you two got some rest because there have been developments." She turned to the other two agents in the room. "Report please, Ms. Tyson."

Got it, Steve thought. *Now I remember who they are. Lucy Tyson and Rob Frederick, based out of somewhere in the Rockies... Denver?* His thoughts were interrupted as Tyson brought up a series of images on the wall display.

The images were of news coverage of a plane crash in Tokyo Bay. Rescue ships on the water were picking up pieces of wreckage. The United Airlines logo appeared on a piece of fuselage that floated on the choppy waters.

Amy looked at the redheaded agent. "What happened?"

"Rob got in touch with his... friends. They made sure Tokyo authorities were ready for the plane to arrive. Unfortunately, it never did." Her face was grim.

Steve froze in shock. "He didn't."

"Yeah, he did. The flight went down on approach six hours ago. Communications with the ground indicate the pilot was disoriented. Up until he hit, he kept reading off his altitude as 3,000 feet higher that what his flight level actually was."

Frederick interrupted. "But then things got stranger. Ninety minutes later, relatives who'd just been informed of the accident started getting phone calls from their loved ones."

Steve looked up sharply at that. "What?"

"That's right. Suddenly all our supposed victims are standing around the airport in Osaka, trying to arrange for transport home to Tokyo while coverage of the crash is playing on the news channels and the names of victims start scrolling across the bottom of the TV screens. Imagine the surprise when the relatives started getting those phone calls."

Steve shared a look with Amy. "False Mirror."

Frederick nodded. "Had to be. Our best guess is the flight crew received a message diverting them to Osaka because of the weather at Narita, and then the transponder was reset to squawk United 478's call sign."

"Then that's really United 478 in Tokyo Bay?"

"We think so, but until we can check the airframe number, we can't be sure."

Tyson looked grim. "What's troubling is that he was able to do this in mid-flight. For someone not involved in the design and testing, he knows this device's capabilities all too well for my liking."

Stevenson nodded. "Agreed. So, did Williams and Callahan end up in Osaka?"

Frederick pulled up Osaka security camera footage of the United gate as Williams and Callahan deplaned. "My friends had authorities alerted to look for our targets at Narita. No one was looking for them in the south. By the time anyone realized what happened, the two of them were long gone and authorities had no idea where to look." Frederick stopped at this point, but he again looked nervous. Steve and Amy shared another look. *What about Japan has him on edge? It's as if he's afraid of revealing too much. Something predating Triangle?*

Watson looked at the two senior agents. "Anything else you care to share?"

Tyson shared a glance with Frederick. He looked over at Watson. "The authorities may have lost these two, but my friends spotted Williams and Callahan, and are tracking them. They're on a bullet train, heading to Tokyo."

Watson's brow furrowed. "And will your friends assist us in apprehending them?"

Frederick looked more uncomfortable by the minute. "Uh, I don't think so. They answer to a different authority. As it is, they're doing me a huge solid just tracking our bad guys."

Watson sighed. "Not what I wanted to hear, Mr. Frederick."

He gulped audibly. Tyson reached out and put her hand on his arm as if to reassure him. "With all due respect, this isn't their fight. So instead, let's figure out what Williams and Callahan are doing in Japan."

Percy raised his hand on the video screen. "Uh, if I may, I think I might have uncovered a clue to that."

Stevenson swiveled to face the screen. "Go ahead, Mr. Lewis."

Percy looked down. "Once I received word of what happened, I started digging into Mr. Williams' financials. They're quite convoluted. He's created shell companies in the Cayman Islands to hide much of his assets. It turns out he's worth somewhere in the neighborhood of $22 million dollars."

Steve whistled. "That's a really nice neighborhood." He looked at Stevenson. "I didn't realize you paid so well."

Stevenson growled, "I don't." He looked at Percy on the screen. "Mr. Lewis, can you trace where those funds came from?"

"It will take some digging. But the majority has been deposited in the last 6 months."

Stevenson muttered under his breath. "That murdering scoundrel. He sold us out."

Lucy nodded. "Dale's preliminary report seems to bear that out. About ten months ago, Williams set up a separate hidden encrypted server in your data center. It coincides with the time he became security chief."

Watson looked uncomfortable. "We... when his field partnership ended, we thought his expertise would best serve us there."

Lucy shook her head. "No, almost from that moment, it seems he had another agenda. When Dale attempted to access that server, it deleted the data. Dale was only able to capture a small portion of it, and it's heavily encrypted. But what he's been able to find...it isn't good."

Stevenson pinched the bridge of his nose. "How bad?"

"False Mirror may not be the only project compromised. Additionally, Mitchell's been communicating with Callahan for at least four months. And as Percy noted, someone paid him really well for this."

Amy looked at Lucy. "Would Williams have been sophisticated enough to fake the videos of Mr. Stevenson?"

Watson nodded. "Yes. It's called digital puppetry, and it's relatively easy to do. We developed it years ago. Sold it to Disney, in fact — you can see a version of it at their theme parks."

Percy interrupted. "Sir, there is one other thing. Mr. Williams is using a broker out of Zurich and has moved a significant amount of his assets in the last twelve hours. He's placed several orders to be executed when the markets open."

Amy and Steve glanced at each other. "Which markets?"

Percy looked again at his data. "All the major markets. But they all do the same thing — he's shorting every major market index across the globe by an average of 15–20 percent. It's a foolish bet...unless he knows something."

Stevenson started to consider this, but Steve had flashed into his Talent and was already running the scenarios in his head. The answer hit him like a thunderbolt. He flashed back and exclaimed, "He's going to crash the Tokyo Stock Exchange!"

Everyone in the room looked at him in shock. Watson glanced around the room. "Can he do that?"

Tyson looked at Frederick for a moment. "False Mirror just re-routed two international flights in mid-air, crashing one into Tokyo Bay. There's no reason to believe he couldn't have crashed those planes into almost anywhere on purpose if he'd wanted to. Yeah, I'd say he could do this."

Stevenson considered this. "But, how? There could be a dozen scenarios that he could use."

Amy tapped Steve on the shoulder. He looked at her and whispered, "What?"

"You're the smartest guy in the room here. You already know how he's probably going to do it. Tell them."

Steve looked at her for a moment, and saw, for the first time, that she was looking at him with a mixture of warmth and pride. "Okay." He cleared his throat. "Excuse me, but I have an educated guess."

Watson and Stevenson glanced at each other for a moment. Stevenson turned back to him. "Well, Mr. Tate, by all means, educate the rest of us."

Steve glanced back at Amy who nodded in encouragement. Steve walked over to the data table and looked at Ethan. "Can you bring up a map of Tokyo and throw it on the board?"

Ethan nodded. "Sure."

As Ethan went to work, Steve turned to the others. "I'm working off two assumptions. One, they want a big score. But two, based on what he said on Treasure Island, I think Williams wants to humiliate Triangle, and more specifically you, Mr. Stevenson."

Ethan completed his task. "Map's coming up." He slid the image sideways, and it moved from the data table onto the wall. Steve expanded it until it took up most the wall screen, and then made the window active. He modified the scale, zooming it out until it showed the city in sectors.

"I think he's planning to use False Mirror to spoof all the Tokyo Exchange's electronic data displays so that they will report false data everywhere. He'll make it appear that the market is taking a dive. Investors will react, forcing the market into an actual downturn. If he drives the downward pressure hard enough, he could collapse the stock exchange in a day. But I don't think he wants that much damage — I believe he's just betting on a huge correction."

Tyson piped up from across the room. "But why the orders in Hong Kong? Or Berlin? Or New York?"

"Markets are interconnected. There's a saying — if one market sneezes, all of them catch a cold."

Watson shook her head. "But for this to work, he'd have to spoof every data stream coming out of the TSE, going everywhere in the world. They stole Dr. Naziri's prototype, not the full-scale device. It couldn't handle that many individual streams at once."

"As it's built, no. But put it at a nexus where that data funnels through and give it enough power to boost its output, and it can do the job."

Frederick blurted out excitedly, "Oh, that's brilliant!"

Everyone in the room turned and stared at him. He tamped down his enthusiasm as he continued. "Err, heh, or at least it would be, if it wasn't going to like, you know, destroy the world's economy and all."

Stevenson closed his eyes and pinched the bridge of his nose again. "Pray tell, Mr. Tate, where could he do this?"

Steve scrolled the map one more time, centered it on a point, and expanded it. "There."

Watson looked at the screen and read the caption aloud. "Tokyo SkyTree?"

Ethan worked the data table for a moment and pulled up another image, which he threw onto the main screen. "The world's tallest free-standing tower, currently the second tallest structure in the world. It went online one year ago, and serves as the central national hub for all digital communications in Japan." A schematic appeared next to the picture. "Six hundred and thirty-four meters tall, with observation platforms at 450 and 350 meters. The base covers the entire neighborhood between Nahihirabashi and Oshiage stations." Ethan paused for a second. "And it appears—"

Stevenson interrupted him. "That's quite enough, Mr. Nowitzki." He turned to Steve. "How sure are you about this?"

"Oh, about 80 percent. But I can up the odds." Steve looked at Rob. "Can your... ah, 'friends' let us know where in Tokyo they're headed?"

Rob nodded. "I think I can get you that much from them. Where are you thinking?"

Steve did his thing again, then looked at Rob. "My first guess is Sumida, but also include Taito."

Rob nodded. "If you'll excuse me." He headed out the door.

Stevenson and Watson had walked over to study the schematic. "So where would he put the device?"

Percy piped up. "Logically, the closer to the broadcast array, the better. I would assume he's going to be at or above the upper observation platform."

Steve nodded. "The data is fed from the control center at the base of the tower, on the top floor of the arcade they built. For this to work, we'll need someone up high—"

Amy stepped forward. "And someone down below."

Watson nodded. "It makes sense. It's a psychologically significant target."

Tyson looked puzzled. "I understand how he'll go for the money, but how does he get revenge against Triangle?"

"Two ways," Steve replied. "First, when the chaos has finished echoing around the financial markets, I'll bet he's going to release some sort of manifesto, and in it, he's going to reveal Red Labs to the world. I mean, think about it. He tells folks that Triangle develops doomsday weapons that can destroy the world, and it'll be torch and pitchfork time."

Amy looked at him. "You said first. There's more?"

"Yeah, A.J., there is. Mr. Stevenson cut Ethan off before he could reveal it. You see, he helped build Tokyo SkyTree. So he loses twice, when it's revealed his own security failed, and it was his own device that endangered the world." Steve looked at him. "Sir, I don't know what happened, but this man is very angry with you. That makes him very motivated, and exceptionally dangerous."

Amy looked at Steve. "Uh, duh again, Captain Obvious. When is Williams going to do this?"

Steve pulled up two clock displays on the data table and shifted them over. One showed local time, the other, Japan Standard Time. "Well, given the markets open at nine a.m. in Tokyo on Monday, and they are thirteen hours ahead of us, I figure we have a little less than twenty-eight hours left."

Ethan shook his head. "No, Steve, less than that. He'll have everything in place before the morning broadcast shift arrives on Monday. Figure that between five and six a.m., Japan Standard Time. Realistically, we've got just over twenty-four hours to do something."

Watson looked at Stevenson and nodded. "Mr. Tate, this is your mission. What do you need?"

My mission? Steve looked around the room. *Yeah, I can do this.*

He looked over at Amy. "A.J., are you in?"

Amy bit her lip. "I'm not so good with heights, Steve. But I can handle the control center."

D. G. Speirs

"Good, that's where I wanted you anyway. Ethan, do you think you can manage the ICC for two agents?"

He glanced at Watson for a second, then looked at Steve and nodded. "Piece of cake, sport."

Steve started to turn away, but then he did a double-take. *Sport? Where'd that come from?* "I'll need someone who can pilot—"

Tyson stepped forward. "Oh, you're not going to have all the fun, Tate. Count Rob and me in. I can pilot, and Rob can handle logistical support on the ground."

"Fair enough. Lastly, do you have any HALO gear?"

Watson nodded. "Certainly. Wait, you plan to jump? That seems an awful risky approach."

Steve shrugged. "Only one I can take. Williams will be looking for it, too. I'm going to have to slingshot my landing as well."

"Slingshot the landing? I'm not familiar with that term."

Tyson whistled. "I am. Wow, and I thought I could do anything." She walked over to Steve. "You realize you get one shot. If you miss, you're either a smear on the ground or the observation deck windows."

Steve smiled at her. "So, I better not miss."

Amy looked at Steve as if he was crazy. Which, come to think of it, he probably was. "But, Williams is sure to be expecting a plane."

Steve smirked. "And that's why I need to one-up him." He turned, the smile breaking into a full-out grin. "So, tell me, Reggie — has anyone ever jumped out of Firebird?"

Chapter 24

They'd gone over the plan a dozen times, making sure everyone knew their parts. Before Amy and Rob Frederick left the Triangle base, Steve took Amy aside.

"Look, A.J., be careful. You're playing a vital role in disabling False Mirror, but you're also my decoy. Williams and Callahan need to focus on you and Frederick, at least while I'm in the air. They're going to throw something nasty at you to be sure."

Amy smiled at him. "Don't worry, Sport, I'll have your back. Just don't miss, please?"

Steve looked surprised. "Sport, huh? I guess I deserve that."

"And remember, you need to be out of range when we destroy the prototype. Otherwise, you'll be unarmed if you run into Williams."

"Don't you worry about me, Amy. I'll be fine." He checked his SAVANT's watch function. "We'll rendezvous at the base of the tower once False Mirror is disabled. Now get going. You have a plane to catch."

He held out his hand to her for a handshake. She looked at it for a moment, then rushed in and gave him a hug. She whispered in his ear, "Please be safe, Steve. I can't lose you, too." She gave him a quick peck on the cheek, then turned and ran around the corner out of sight.

A short time later, Frederick and Amy departed from Dulles in the Songbird.

June 16, 11:41 a.m. JST

Rob and Amy's flight had taken just over three hours. Unlike Steve, they were working to get Williams' attention, so they were deliberately sloppy in their spycraft. Songbird lingered a bit too long on the tarmac at Narita airport. They made their way to the Taito district in the open, dressed in black suits, using obviously false cover IDs as U.S. Marshals in pursuit of a suspect. They flashed Williams' picture with the local authorities. They spoke to known criminals. They lingered in the Taito and Sumida districts for the better part of the day, asking at hotels and restaurants. They saw no sign of Williams or Callahan but made sure the two would know they were there, pursuing them.

4:40 p.m. JST

It was mid-afternoon when they arrived at Tokyo SkyTree. The plan was to scout it in the daylight so they could make any last-minute changes to the plan, if needed. As they got out of the taxi, Amy stared skyward at the structure looming over her. *Steve is going to land on that?* From here, the top looked about as large as a bottle cap.

Rob walked up beside her. "Sort of takes your breath away, doesn't it?"

"I'm not all that great with heights."

"Yeah, I wasn't at first, but, Lucy — she has a way of convincing you that you can do almost anything."

"Oh? How's that?"

Rob grinned. "By going and doing it. Usually without thinking about it first. Sort of like your partner. Come on, let's look around."

They went inside and paid the admission to head up in the elevator. Three minutes later, they stepped out onto the lower level platform.

As they stood on the 350-meter observation deck, the city spread out before them in all directions, Amy couldn't help but fidget. She worried that at any moment Williams (or worse, Callahan) would leap out and attack her and Frederick. When Rob walked up behind her and offered her a cup of tea, she nearly jumped out of her skin.

"Whoa, step back, it's just me."

"How can you be so calm?"

"Honestly? Years of practice. I've had a lot of experience being—how do I put this — Lucy's distraction. She always had the knack for this work. Me? I just had a really cool friend I wanted to help out, at first."

Amy nodded. "I can see that. But don't us distractions end up getting, well..."

"Beaten down pretty badly? It happens, although Lucy doesn't always win, either. Nature of the game. You don't always win the battle, but in the end, you got to win the war. Otherwise... well, I'd hate to experience the otherwise, with some of the folks the two of us have dealt with."

He looked down at the city. "But it all comes back to those people down there. Most of them have no idea what we do. That's the way it should be. If we do our jobs right, we fix things before they become a problem. If not..."

Amy's voice was brittle. "People get hurt. Or worse."

She closed her eyes for a moment and saw the faces of Jason and Rose in front of her. Frederick moved over and put his hand on her shoulder. "Hey, I'm sorry for your loss. No one should lose someone that way." He got a look of determination on his face. "But it's payback time now. Let's go over again how this is going to work."

Frederick used the view like an intel photo briefing, pointing out travel routes, rendezvous points, and, of particular interest to Amy, her primary target and access route to it. "They didn't make it particularly easy for you, but if you've paid attention and know how to use your gear, it should be a piece of cake."

"Don't worry, I can handle the job. Now what?"

"One more place to look." He pointed to the elevator to the upper level and then held out an arm for her. "Care to join me, Ms. Rogers?"

"Why, I would be honored, Mr. Frederick." Amy grinned at his goofball approach — *a little like Steve, but with less of an edge.* She took the proffered arm, and the two walked with great dignity to the line.

The elevator chimed, and the doors opened. A few moments later, they were whisked upward rapidly — so quickly that Amy's ears popped. It hurt Frederick, too.

"Ow, ow! You'd think they'd warn people about that!"

"Uh, Rob, they do." She pointed at a sign on the elevator wall in Japanese that included a cartoon bear holding its head.

He looked at the message and shook his head. "Man, that's the problem with foreign countries. They're always so foreign."

Amy stared at Frederick, trying to figure out if he was serious or joking.

The elevator slowed and came to a stop. There was a soft chime, then the doors opened, and Amy walked out of the elevator car and onto the upper observation platform. She immediately was drawn to the diagram on the wall next to the elevator. *This is amazing. It's more like a six-story building than just a walkway around some windows.*

Frederick stepped out beside her and grabbed her arm to steer her to one side. "Why don't you scout around a bit and meet me here in five minutes. Just make yourself obvious — you know, accidentally knock over something in the gift shop, or get in a confusing discussion with one of the SkyTree guides."

Amy wrinkled her nose. "Oh, so now *I'm* the distraction?"

Frederick nodded. "Pretty much. I have to, ah, check something out, but I'll be right back, I promise."

Amy turned to her left. A gift shop hugged the curve of the central column. She studied it for a second and shrugged. "So, any suggestions as to how..."

She turned back to talk to Frederick, but he was nowhere to be seen. She hadn't heard him leave. *Wow, that was weird. I only turned away for two seconds. You don't think?* She shook her head. *No, there's no way. Time for that mystery later. Better get to my new job. Distraction, huh?*

She headed for the gift shop, which was filled with lots of expected items — pictures of the tower on shirts, glassware and more. Amy examined a rack of postcards. *Does anyone actually mail postcards these days?* Then she found her target.

On a shelf near the register was a six-inch tall cylinder holding ornamental lacquered chopsticks decorated with images of the tower. There were four different designs, so Amy started to root around as if trying to make a full set. She picked up the cylinder and turned it. All the chopsticks slid out and clattered onto the hard floor.

The store clerk hurried over to where she was, huffed once, and bent down to pick up the merchandise. Amy smiled and started talking to her, pouring an extra-large helping of southern honey into her voice.

"Oh my, I am so sorry. Oh, wait, what was the word I was supposed to use? *Sue-mee-may-son.* Clumsy little ol' me." She bent down to help the clerk, a middle-aged female. "Well, lookie here! This was an accident, but it does remind me of a game I played as a little girl back in Georgia. Did you ever play pick-up sticks? Well, this would be pick-up chopsticks, I guess. Now let me see... my turn and I pick this one."

Amy grabbed a chopstick from the bottom of the pile. Other chopsticks dislodged and rolled in all directions.

"Oh, fiddle-dee-dee! That never happens to me back home. I usually win the game there," Amy pouted.

The store clerk stopped, looked at her for a second and muttered something under her breath about *gaijin.* She went back to her task picking up the chopsticks.

Amy reached for another stick. "Here, I can help—"

The clerk reached out and quickly grabbed her hand. The two made eye contact, and the clerk said carefully. "*Te kudasai.* You no help."

Amy took back her hand and acted shocked. "Well! The rudeness of some people."

"I don't know, Princess. She did say please."

Amy froze where she was. She'd only heard that voice once before in her life, but it was indelibly etched into her memory. Amy took a deep breath, then poured back into the southern belle she was creating. "Why, Hannah Callahan! As I live and breathe, it's simply been ages since we saw each other!"

Amy stood up and turned. Leaning against the curving wall, her arms folded, was Callahan, in the flesh. "Now, Princess, you know when I heard you were in town, I just had to look you up."

Amy walked over to Callahan as if to hug her. Callahan put her hand up. "Now sugar, we didn't part on the best of terms last time, so don't go all lovey-dovey Scarlett O'Hara on me now. Your friends who are listening probably don't want a big scene. Especially one which involves a big hole in your chest and lots of blood." Callahan's eyes flicked downward. Her other hand was in a pocket, where there was a distinct gun-shaped bulge to it.

Amy smiled slightly. "Oh, come on, Hannah. I have to warn you that those things don't work on me quite the way you think they do."

Hannah smiled as her eyes narrowed. Suddenly, her pocket emitted a single puff of smoke, and Amy felt a sharp pain in her right shoulder. Shocked, she looked over and saw half of a two-inch-long steel dart embedded there. She looked back at Callahan.

"You see, Princess, I know more about the way you're built than you do. Like how you're not comfortable with sharp, pointy things. Call them your own personal kryptonite, if you will. Oh, don't worry, that one was just a test round. The next chamber has lots of them. Enough to turn you, and anyone around you, into hamburger quite effectively."

Amy swallowed once, fighting against the wave of pain and nausea she felt. She nodded and put on a false smile. "In that case, shall we take a stroll by the windows?"

"What an original idea — look out the windows of an observation deck. And here I thought Tate was the brains of the outfit." Callahan tilted her head toward the window. "After you, Princess."

Amy nodded slightly, inwardly seething. Here was her target, a mere two feet away, taunting her, and she couldn't do anything about it. *Where is Frederick?* She started to walk toward the windows, then turned to the left and continued counterclockwise along the window line. After a few moments, she began to talk. "So, Ms. Callahan. That is your name, right?"

"It'll do for now."

"Why are you doing this?"

Behind her, Callahan chuckled. "My, aren't you the curious one? Well, for one thing, the money's good. After tomorrow, really good."

Amy nodded. "That's what I hear. But what you're doing... a lot of people are going to get hurt."

"And your point is?"

"Doesn't it bother you? All the people who will be devastated by what you're planning to do?"

"Listen, Princess. In life, anyone who stands between where you are and where you want to be is nothing more than an obstacle to either go around or mow down." Callahan chuckled again. "I just prefer the more direct approach."

Amy stopped. "You killed my boyfriend."

Callahan closed the distance and stood directly behind Amy. "If it's any consolation, it wasn't personal. He was simply another obstacle to eliminate." The gun barrel poked into Amy's back. Callahan whispered in her right ear. "You, on the other hand... killing you is going to be a pleasure." She grabbed the dart and yanked it out of Amy's shoulder, causing her to double over in pain.

Amy clenched her fists, the stood up slowly, waiting for the attack as Callahan stepped backward. *How could I have been so stupid? I've failed everyone.*

The moment turned to two, and then another, and then a dozen, as the seconds ticked by. Amy decided to risk turning and facing her. *Maybe Callahan just wants to see my face before she kills me.* She turned quickly.

Callahan wasn't directly behind her anymore. Amy quickly scanned the room and saw her at the far edge of the curve at the central column, still with her right hand in her pocket. She waggled one finger on her left hand toward Amy. "Next time, Princess." Then she turned and started to walk away.

Amy's face clouded with anger.

Oh no, you don't. Not this time.

She bent down into a sprinters crouch and started to slam her hand down when she felt a hand on her left shoulder. She quickly wheeled up and to her left, her right fist coming around with her to strike at whoever had grabbed her.

Frederick met her fist with a cupped hand and absorbed the blow with no effect. "It's okay, you're safe now."

Amy looked at him, the adrenaline built up inside, anger just below the surface. "Okay? Callahan was here! I might have been able to catch her."

Frederick shook his head. "I just caught the tail end, but it looked like she had the drop on you. Unless, of course, you can outrun a bullet." He looked at her sideways. "Can you outrun a bullet? Never mind. Besides, you're hurt. Here, sit down, let me look at that."

He led Amy over to a bench and sat her down. "That doesn't look too bad. She didn't nick an artery or break any bones. How does it feel?

"The truth? Stings like hell."

"Yeah, let me see what I can do about that."

Frederic took off his jacket and unzipped the lining. Inset in it was a set of Velcro pockets. He found the one he wanted, opened it, and extracted a small biogel patch.

"Technically, I'm not supposed to have this outside of a field med kit, but having been Lucy's distraction for a while, I find it's better to be safe than sorry." He pulled off the activation lining and slapped the patch over her wound.

She felt the familiar tingle as it went to work numbing and healing her.

"How do you feel?"

"Better."

"Good. By the way, great job being the distraction."

Amy looked surprised. "You're kidding, right?"

"Nope. I got done what I needed to. My contact confirmed what I suspected — Williams has already been here and hidden the device. Smart man, too — he's disguised it as a broadcast power boost relay — one of sixteen of them on that level. That's an extra wrinkle Tate needs to know about."

She stared at the exit Callahan had taken. She bit her lower lip. "Callahan knows we're coming. She'll be waiting for us."

Frederick nodded. "We figured that from the start." He put an arm around Amy. "Look, Amy. You've let her get inside your head. She's playing you like a cat would with a wounded mouse. What did she say to you?"

She stood up and walked back to the observation windows. "That anyone who stood between her and her goal was just an obstacle to be avoided or obliterated." She glanced over at Frederick. "She prefers the more direct approach."

He walked over and stood next to her. "You know, a friend of mine once told me, 'Learn much from the humble bamboo, for in the face of the wind it may bend, but never break.'"

Amy waited for a few seconds to see if Rob would continue, but he just stood there, looking out at the skyline. "Rob?"

"Yes?"

"Please tell me there's more to that little lesson."

Frederick grinned a little sheepishly. "Sorry, that's all I got. My friend, he can be a little obscure at times."

"Ya think? Fine. What do we do now?"

"We get back to Sunbird and get you cleaned up. That patch should have you mission ready in time." Then he turned to her and in mock seriousness, saluted her with a fist against a flattened hand, and bowed. "Then, young warrior, we shall return and prepare for tonight."

She suppressed a giggle as she returned his salute and headed for the elevator.

Chapter 25

June 16, 10:25 a.m. EDT

In the Triangle hangar complex at Dulles airport, Steve finished getting into his HALO gear. Time was already racing away from him. In Tokyo, it was thirteen hours ahead, approaching midnight. He'd have to complete his mission before the sun rose there again or Williams and Callahan would have won, and the world would become a much more dangerous place.

No pressure, right, Steven?

As he grabbed his helmet and headed for the door, he at least felt the satisfaction of knowing his prediction had been correct. Williams was spotted visiting the SkyTree complex just as the sun set over Mt. Fuji. Amy had confronted Callahan there herself. Steve thought back to their video call just two hours earlier.

"They know we're coming, Steve."

"Never thought they didn't. But Williams and Callahan don't know what I'm doing. In fact, they may believe that it's just you and Rob on this. And I need you to keep them thinking that way."

Amy looked doubtful. "Are you sure? Williams has been a step ahead of us every time—"

Steve looked at her carefully. "Amy, what aren't you telling me?"

She paused for a moment, biting her lower lip. "Steve, the only person I've ever told about my Talent until now was Rose. I've... I've never told anyone about how I'm afraid of blades and stuff. I always have been, and never understood why. And I didn't even know I was bulletproof until just a few days ago. So how did Callahan know to use a dart on me?" Amy looked at him directly. "Steve, these two know a lot more about us... about what we are, than we do. And I think they're not afraid to use that knowledge to destroy us."

He nodded. "We just have to be more ruthless than them."

Amy's eyes widened. "I don't know if I—"

Steve cut her off. "We don't have time to argue. You just said it. These folks are out to kill us. So, as much as it would be nice to have answers, we're going to have to find them elsewhere. So — we stop the device, we stop Williams and Callahan, and then we find out what's actually going on. Deal?"

Amy nodded. "Fair enough. And, Steve?"

"Yeah?"

"I've been up there. It's windier than all get out. Be safe, okay?"

"Always, A.J. See you soon."

Of course, it wasn't all bad news. Rose had woken up an hour ago. From Ethan's reports she seemed alert. He sent word to her that as soon as he returned, she'd be the first person he saw.

And now, it was time for his entrance.

Steve walked out of the locker room and headed for the hangar. In the background, he could hear and feel the hum of the engines, the massive power plant ready to launch Firebird skyward. As he rounded the corner, Lucy Tyson waited for him, wearing a high-altitude flight suit. It felt weird working with someone other than Amy, but it was necessary.

She looked over his HALO gear, double-checking all the seals and connectors. "You ready for this?"

He grinned. "Who doesn't love stepping out of a perfectly good spaceplane?"

They started walking together toward the hangar again, Lucy matching him stride for stride. She began to brief him. "Total flight time to the jump point will be about three hours and twelve minutes. For the last hour before the jump, we'll pressurize the cabin with pure oxygen, to reduce the nitrogen levels in your blood. Then, you'll go on the oxygen generator just before you head into the airlock."

He looked down at the small square box on the left front of his chest plate. It had three LED indicators on it, indicating power, operation, and an alarm if it failed. "This get-up has got to make me look a little like Darth Vader. How long is it good for?"

"In theory, fifteen minutes. But it's never been used at that altitude. The number of jumps from this height can be counted on one hand, but no one's done a HALO from a moving platform at that altitude — ever."

"Well, first time for everything, right? Besides, I have an emergency oxygen cylinder as a backup."

"Yes, but that's standard military issue — it only has three minutes' worth, tops. Less if you're stressed. When it expires, you need to be below 10,000 feet, or you'll experience hypoxia. And if that happens..."

"I know; game over."

Tyson's expression was grim. "Right. So, you step into the airlock five minutes before the jump site and depressurize to atmospheric pressure. When the outer door opens, move on my mark. Deploy the drogue chute, curl up in a ball and hang on — you're going to be decelerating like crazy."

Steve nodded. "I've read up on HALO jumps from that height. It's like stepping out into a vacuum. Wind resistance doesn't really start up until you reach around 60,000 feet." Something around his back suddenly felt like it was catching. He reached up and touched the connectors on his harness again.

Tyson stopped and helped him adjust the suit. "That's the other concern. You've heard of intrinsic velocity?"

"Sure, that's what I have initially when I separate from another body in motion. Like, for example, exiting a perfectly good spaceplane going Mach 3."

Tyson nodded. "Well, if you're going too fast when you dive into the thicker parts of the atmosphere, you'll generate friction. A lot of friction. Let's just say we'd prefer not to have you toasted like a marshmallow. So, deploy the drogue chute right away. It will interact with any atmosphere there is, even as thin and wispy as what you'll get up there, and bleed off some of that speed. We need to get you subsonic on this jump as quickly as possible."

Satisfied his suit was back in place, Lucy slapped him on both shoulders and started walking again. "We've pre-programmed your SAVANT to provide airspeed and altimeter data to you audibly, as well as via a small heads-up display inside your helmet. The heads-up will also give you GPS targeting data, so you'll see you're aiming at the right spot. It wouldn't do for you to end up at the Imperial Palace — either in Tokyo or Las Vegas."

Steve chuckled. "Even if they comp my drinks?"

"Cute. SkyTree is illuminated with its purple lighting scheme tonight. That's good because it's designed to only light one side of the tower. The north side is in shadows, so if you can approach from that side, that might give you an additional element of surprise."

They reached the office outside the main hangar and stepped inside. A maintenance technician was waiting for them with a data tablet. He handed it to Lucy. She nodded in acknowledgment and checked it. "The calculations say you're going to be dropping at 107 meters per second at terminal velocity. We're deploying you at 90,000 feet — 27.5 kilometers. So, you have approximately four minutes to locate and align with the tower. If you deploy your chute at 800 meters, you'll reduce your speed just enough to hit that platform. But you must release your chute as well, or the wind will pull you right off the platform roof as soon as you land."

"Good to know."

"When your jump concludes successfully," she turned and poked a finger into his chest, "—and it will be successful — you'll have approximately sixty minutes to disable the False Mirror before the first workers show up at the broadcast complex."

"The Tokyo police have no idea what's going on. Ethan will work from the ICC to deflect them as long as he can, and Rob is going to be the distraction. Trust me, it's his thing. He's good at it. But even so, you must finish and get out of there in that sixty-minute window. Otherwise, your presence is going to compromise Triangle. You'll end up accomplishing what Williams wants anyway."

Steve nodded. "No pressure then."

Tyson cleared the data tablet and looked at him. "You're not quite what I expected, Tate."

"You know, I've heard that a lot lately."

They entered the hangar and walked across the floor to Firebird as it completed its final stages of preparation. Stevenson and Watson were waiting at the bottom of the boarding ramp. "You have two copies of the upload. Don't lose them, Mr. Tate. We're counting on you." Stevenson reached out his hand, and Steve shook it. "Good luck."

"Thanks. I'll say hi to Williams for you."

Stevenson nodded. "You do that."

Lucy nodded to Watson and Stevenson as she boarded Firebird. The hatch was dogged behind her, and the leaders of Triangle retreated into the hangar office to watch the spaceplane taxi out into the sunshine.

11:02 a.m. EDT

Watson spoke up. "How do you rate his chances?"

Stevenson watched on the monitor as the plane approached the end of the runway to line up for its takeoff. "Fifty-fifty. Maybe a little less."

"That's a bit harsh."

"He's dealing with perhaps the best operative ever to work here. He's doing so after a death-defying jump that could go wrong in any of six hundred different ways. He's carrying the emotional baggage of the attack on Johannsen, Williams' attempt to kill him, the attack in Nassau, and the discovery that Callahan was the murderer of his family. And he's doing it within weeks of arriving at

Triangle. Sorry, Doctor, if I fail to sound optimistic about our chances."

Watson looked over at Stevenson. Something wasn't adding up. "For someone who thinks the plan will fail, you seem awfully sanguine."

"That's because I already have Plan B in place, in case they fail."

Watson arched an eyebrow. "Oh? Care to elaborate, Reggie?"

"No, Rhonda, I don't. Not unless it becomes absolutely necessary."

They watched silently as Firebird powered down the runway and roared into the sky.

June 17, 2:03 a.m. JST

Ninety minutes before Steve was scheduled to jump, Frederick dropped Amy off on the opposite side of the shipping canal from SkyTree. She moved quickly through the shadows along the ground to the apartment building they'd identified as her staging point and climbed to the roof. From this vantage point, Amy could scan both the SkyTree complex and the skies above. She waited quietly, hoping.

An hour later, Ethan's voice came over the commlink, tight with tension. "They're approaching the drop zone. Any sign of Williams and Callahan?"

"None yet, but they'll be here."

Frederick joined the conversation. "Amy, I have some news. My friends just informed me that their vehicle is already in the SkyTree parking structure. Sorry, they didn't see which entrance they used, but they're already here."

"Great."

"Are you ready, Amy?"

"Yeah, ready as I'll ever be," she replied.

She could have sworn she heard Frederick smile. "Then it's time for Rob-san to do what he does best. See you on the other side."

A minute later, there was a large, loud explosion by the river a mile and a half away that startled Amy. She could see a column of smoke, and inside it, other, more colorful explosions. She activated her commlink.

"Ethan, what just happened?"

"That would be Agent Frederick and his distraction."

"Let me guess. Fireworks factory?"

Ethan sighed. "Agent Tyson says that he apparently has a knack for this sort of thing. That will definitely keep people from looking at SkyTree for a while."

"I'm moving in to deliver the second package."

Ethan acknowledged. "Tracking. Proceed 120 meters east of the southwest corner of the building."

"Acknowledged. SAVANT, Mode 3."

Amy reached into her pack and took out a black motorcycle helmet and a ten-inch long metal tube. She put on the helmet, which immediately interfaced with her SAVANT, giving her targeting data. Amy took the tube, reached high over her head, and slammed one end of it against the concrete wall next to the door. Holding it in place, she depressed a switch with her thumb. There was a brief flare of light as the tube bonded to the surface.

"SAVANT, seek target."

Amy turned around and looked at the SkyTree Arcade building. The SAVANT presented her with a targeting reticule on the interior of the faceplate. She used it to locate the target location Ethan had specified.

"SAVANT, paint target and fire line."

Above the faceplate of her helmet, a small port opened and a green laser beam lanced out and lit a spot on the wall of the SkyTree Arcade. The second it struck the arcade wall, the tube she'd attached to the apartment wall fired a projectile that hit the target. The same actinic light flared at the far end. When it faded, a thin monofilament zip line stretched tautly between the two anchor points.

Amy reached up and twisted the tube, releasing it from the anchor. She pulled down to test the slack on the monofilament, then grabbed the tube and slid down the instant zip line, dropping to the grass five yards from the wall. She ran over and pressed a stud on the bottom anchor. There was another brief flash of actinic blue light. The zip line and components crumpled to dust.

She rubbed her right shoulder where her earlier wound was bandaged. It was sore, but it hadn't felt like it was pulling or tearing. The biogel patch was helping, speeding the healing process. She needed to be at full strength for the rest of this.

She took a blue grapple gun out of her left thigh pocket — a gift from Frederick, who for some reason warned her to keep an eye on her pants when she used it. She stepped back, took aim, and fired. The dart arched skyward fifteen stories, extruded three claws, and landed inside a ventilation grill with a clatter.

Amy winced, glancing about to see if anyone heard and reacted to the sound. Seeing no one, she clipped her backpack harness to the gun and pressed the retract stud. A surprisingly strong motor retracted the cable, pulling her quickly up the side of the building. When she reached the ninth floor, she stopped and peeked inside the window. The office looked clear, and a quick sweep with her SAVANT indicated no alarm on the window.

From a belt pouch, she took out a pair of devices the size of tennis balls. Amy pressed a control on one and eight legs popped out, like a spider. She set if firmly on one edge of the window. She swung over and repeated this on the opposite side. When she returned to center, she said, "SAVANT, activate spiders."

The two devices popped up a rotating head, searching for each other. When they did, they started to walk around the edge of the window in unison, staying exactly opposite each other. The window seals they passed over began to smoke as lasers from the spiders melted it. The spiders methodically made a full circuit. When completed, the robots planted themselves on the building and lifted out the glass with a 'pop.' Holding it six inches away from the building, they slowly slid the window pane upward until a two-foot wide gap existed between the bottom of the glass and the frame.

Amy smiled in appreciation. "Ethan, remind me to get Quincey a very nice Christmas present this year."

"Will do. You're in?"

"Just getting there. Stand by."

She slid through the gap and onto a credenza under the window. She pressed a retrieval stud on the grapple gun, and a few seconds later, it reeled in the cable and dart. She said, "SAVANT, reverse spiders." Behind her, the spiders reversed their actions, resealing the window in place. When completed, the spiders scurried up the side of the building and awaited further orders.

Amy was already long gone.

Chapter 26

Amy rounded a corner in the broadcast complex and skidded to a halt. She'd taken a wrong turn and now faced a glass wall and a six-story fall outside it. Behind her, she heard the pump action on a shotgun ratchet a shell into place and turned to face her pursuer. Callahan came around the corner, her shark's grin growing wider. "Goodbye, Princess."

Amy tried to raise her SAVANT to fire at Callahan, but her arm was like lead, and she couldn't raise it in time. Callahan fired once, and then again. Amy felt the twin blasts hit her full in the chest, throwing her through the window. As she fell backward, she looked up and saw the tower and a parachute approaching it.

"Steve!"

Everything went black.

Steve bolted awake from the dream with a cry, disoriented for a second. Slowly, his eyes focused, and he recalled where he was.

Slow down, Tate. Breathe. Amy's all right. It was just a dream. We're onboard Firebird. Wearing a HALO suit and a face mask. You're on pure oxygen now, purging the nitrogen out of our system. You just fell asleep. He took another deep breath and focused on the data display on the wall screen, which showed he was only minutes away from his jump.

The wall monitor lit up, and Lucy Tyson's face appeared. She brushed the red hair away from it. "Tate, is everything all right? Do you need assistance?"

"No, I'm all right, Tyson. I must have dozed off. Had a nightmare, that's all. Nerves."

She nodded. Steve noticed she was seated at the engineer's station and that the two pilot chairs were empty. "Who's flying the plane?"

"Otto."

Steve looked puzzled. "Otto, who?"

Tyson grinned. "Otto pilot, of course." She started laughing. "Man, I haven't gotten anyone with that joke since my brothers fell for it years ago. Of course, I hadn't learned to fly then."

Steve grinned back. "I guess I deserved that. So, Tyson, how long have you worked for Triangle?"

"Please, call me Lucy. And I don't work for them as much as with them. I'm more of a troubleshooter, you could say. But I've been on their radar for almost five years."

"Five years?" He had trouble believing that. This woman couldn't be much older than he was. In fact, he'd be willing to bet she might even be younger. "If you say so."

Lucy chuckled. "I'll make you a deal. Get through this safely, and we'll swap stories. After all, yours has to be fascinating."

"What do you mean?"

"I saw you in the briefing room. Not sure how you did it, but you were thinking circles around everyone there, including myself. That's not easy to do."

He shrugged. "You're right; it's sort of 'my thing.'"

"And you have the guts to try a jump that maybe a handful of people in the world could accomplish. Ergo, interesting story."

"I don't know what to say."

"Well, think of it on the way down. We reach the jump coordinates in ten minutes. Get yourself buttoned up and in the airlock, Mr. Tate."

"Aye, aye, Captain Lucy." He grinned as he stood and tossed a mock salute to her image on the screen.

She looked at him and nodded. "Seriously, be careful. I want you back in one piece — and I suspect someone else does, as well." The camera turned off, and the screen changed to a map showing their flight path and a countdown to the jump point.

Steve reached over and grabbed his helmet. Next to it was a small metal case. Curious, he opened it. Inside was what appeared to be an oversized high caliber red pistol, but without an ammo clip. He looked carefully down the barrel and saw a barbed point. There was a note in the box.

Steve,

I thought I'd give you a little extra insurance. It's a grapple gun, based on a design my team started with. This is my personal one. I'd appreciate it if you'd return it after the mission.

Good luck,

Lucy

He looked at the gun for a moment, made sure the safety was on and secured it in his outside right thigh pocket. He slipped on the helmet and secured the manual seals. There was a quick hiss as the pressure seals engaged, and then the heads-up display came to life.

"Times Square to Mirror Flight, comm check."

Steve swore he could hear Tyson's eyebrow go up as she responded over the commlink. "Times Square?"

"Well, sure. After all, if you're dropping a False Mirror Ball, where else but Times Square?" He heard Lucy chuckle.

"All right, I'm crossing to the airlock. SAVANT, altitude check?"

The SAVANT's warm contralto responded. "It is 90,127 feet. Distance to target, 153 miles."

"SAVANT, set altitude to metric."

"Altitude is 27.470 kilometers."

"Control, comm check. Ethan, have your ears on?"

Ethan's voice came through, clear and strong. "Roger, Steve. Are you ready?"

"Wait, are you talking to Roger or Steve?"

"I'll take that as a yes."

"Any word from my earthbound friends?"

"They're about to enter the facility. Mr. Frederick is going to, how did he put it, 'get down' with being the distraction."

Tyson chuckled over the commlink. "Yeah, that sounds like Rob. Okay, Steve, if you're ready, I'm depressurizing the airlock."

"Fair enough. Going off cabin oxygen and on internal O2 generator effective... now." He reached down and pressed a control on the oxygen generator. The middle LED switched from yellow to green, and Steve could taste a slight difference in the air — a sort of metallic tang. *Ozone*, he thought. SAVANT, give me a countdown on the remaining generator capacity, please, lower right." A new small data window appeared, counting down from fourteen minutes.

He looked around, checked his gear one last time, and closed his eyes as Amy taught him. *Breathe. Center. Focus.* He opened them and calmly said, "Ready."

The airlock door slid into place and sealed shut. Steve could hear the seals engage. There was a slight whistling sound, as valves opened slowly to bleed down the pressure. They had to be careful — even with the suit and breathing system, too rapid a change in atmosphere would be the equivalent of an explosive decompression. He wouldn't have a chance to adjust to breathing instantaneously in the near vacuum.

Tyson's voice was steady. "Airlock passing 30,000 feet. Hang in there, Steve."

As the air in the room grew thinner, he noticed it was getting harder to take a breath. He had to concentrate and push to exhale. The difference in pressure wanted to keep his lungs full of air. *Read about this, but never experienced it before. This could be a problem.* He touched a control on the HALO suit to compensate.

"Passing 60,000 feet. Two minutes to drop point."

Ethan's voice came online. "Steve, your heart rate is elevated. Are you all right?"

Steve fought for breath as the pain on his right side started to grow. "Yeah, well, I forgot to include something in my calculations."

Ethan sounded concerned when he asked, "What was that?"

"A pair of cracked ribs that hadn't fully healed."

Steve groaned for a second and closed his eyes to focus his mind. *Pain is a construct. I already know the ribs are damaged. I don't need the alarm. Turn off the alarm.* He concentrated, envisioning pain messages shunted into a side container, to be dealt with later. The container filled, so Steve added a second and a third. The pain subsided. His breathing and heart rate slowed.

Tyson's voice came across the commlink. "Passing 80,000 feet. Drop point in forty-five seconds."

Steve held a thumbs-up toward the video pickup, and stood up, facing the rear hatch. A thought occurred to him. "Hey, Tyson, what would've happened if I couldn't make the jump?"

She chuckled. "Well, then they'd have had to find someone else crazy enough to volunteer for something this risky and made sure they were in place to take over."

"Too bad I don't know anyone that reckless."

"Yeah, too bad." She became serious. "Pressure's equalized; I'm opening the hatch. Drop point in fifteen seconds." She looked at him in the video pickup. "Good luck, Tate."

He watched the door start to slide open in front of him. Suddenly, Steve Tate was on the edge of space looking back over the Pacific Ocean, the curve of the Earth and thin bubble of atmosphere below him. He glanced up at her image in his helmet. "Thanks. And, Lucy?"

"Yes?"

"Don't worry. You'll get it back. Trust me."

She smiled again. "I better. Drop in three, two, one, now!"

Steve grabbed the upper D-ring on his harness and pulled it as he performed a forward roll out of the spaceplane's hatch. His drogue chute deployed, streaming out behind him and yanking him suddenly backward, reducing his forward velocity. Behind him, Lucy was throttling back the engines as she pushed Firebird into a steep dive to the right, reducing the wake turbulence Steve would pass through.

At that moment, at the height of 90,000 feet over Tokyo Bay, Steve Tate became a rock falling from the sky.

3:34 a.m. JST

The initial shock of leaving the spaceplane had Steve tumbling behind it. He fought for a moment to gain control. His biggest concern was being tangled in the drogue chute. It was supposed to slow him to a manageable speed, but if it encumbered him, he'd have to cut it loose. Otherwise, it would make it impossible to deploy his main chute and complete the jump safely.

He ran through his options rapidly, his brain in overdrive, and then he selected the correct maneuver — a half twist to his left, then a downward lean like a diver, in what skydivers call the delta position.

Steve looked down at the ground. His faceplate displayed an augmented reality overlay — coordinates for SkyTree. It was below and to his right. He used his arms and legs to rotate himself until he was lined up with the landmark, facing it directly.

He maintained this posture for what felt like a minute and then checked the heads-up display again. His rate of descent was 105 meters per second. He'd shed almost half his altitude in the first ninety seconds.

Ninety seconds? That can't be right. I guess time does fly when you're having fun.

He hit the release for his drogue chute, put his arms against his side, and dove head down again toward the tower.

The heads-up display showed his descent. He passed 10 kilometers as his speed slowly ticked upward. "SAVANT, display time to target." At this speed, he'd be there in just over two minutes.

"Warning. Oxygen generator approaching depletion. Time to depletion forty-five seconds."

He glanced at the heads-up and quickly figured he'd be at 6,000 meters at that point. *I'll need to use the bottle. Okay, it's why it's there.*

The ground was still coming up rapidly as he slid through the night sky. As he passed through 10 kilometers, he glanced to his right and realized they'd forgotten something.

"Uh, Ethan?"

"Yes, Steve?"

"Can you monitor Japanese Air Traffic Control and make sure I'm not passing in front of any of the friendly skies folks? I'd hate for you to try to explain me off as a really big bird strike."

June 16, 2:38 p.m. EDT

Back at the ICC, Ethan held his breath as he quickly pulled up a screen showing the Tokyo sector Air Traffic Control feed in real time. He overlaid it on the monitor displaying Steve's progress. After a moment, he relaxed. "It's all right. What you're see is a JAL 737 two miles north of you, but he's heading away, and anyways, you're passing through his flight level... now."

June 17, 3:39 a.m. JST

"Whew. One less worry."

An alarm sounded. "Warning. Oxygen generator depleted. Oxygen level dropping, 22 percent."

"Secure alarm." The ringing stopped. Calmly, Steve reached behind him, found the valve for the reserve oxygen cylinder on his waistband, and turned it.

Or at least he tried to. The valve was stuck.

He tried again. Nothing.

"Oxygen level 19 percent."

He reviewed his options. He was already passing 5,500 meters. Could he hold his breath for thirty seconds? Under these circumstances, probably not the best idea. Not much time left, and he was already starting to feel foggy.

His voice was urgent. "SAVANT, auto command. At 3,500 meters, switch to atmosphere rebreather and make enough noise to wake me up."

"Acknowledged."

Already, he saw black spots in front of his eyes as the oxygen level dropped below 17 percent. Steve's eyelids drooped, and then closed. He started tumbling out of control.

June 16, 2:42 p.m. EDT

In the ICC, Ethan was working his console frantically as alarms blared. "Something's gone wrong!"

Watson was at Ethan's side in an instant. "What's happening?"

Ethan silenced alarms as he checked the indicators. "His pulse is thready; oxygen level is 16 percent — no, 15 percent and dropping. The SAVANT indicates he's tumbling." He looked up at her. "He's lost consciousness."

"Can you do anything?"

Ethan just shook his head and watched helplessly as Steve tumbled through 4,000 meters at close to 130 meters per second.

June 17, 3:42 a.m. JST

Five seconds later, at the designated height, the rebreather valves on the pressure suit snapped open. Fresh outside air poured in, scrubbing the built-up carbon dioxide from the suit. The SAVANT started playing the sound of an alarm clock ringing at 100 decibels inside the helmet.

Steve jolted awake, still groggy, to find himself tumbling out of control. Disoriented for a second, he focused on the world around him and recognized the heads-up display. He yelled, "Cancel alarm!" Then he extended his arms and legs out to try to slow his descent. He concentrated for a moment, and the world started to slow.

Except that his Talent wasn't working quite right. The world hadn't stopped, just slowed down, so he was continuing to tumble, albeit very slowly. It had taken him too far north of the tower. He saw the maneuvers he would need to do to stop his tumble and return to the tower. Steve slipped back into real time and executed the maneuver, turning his body to try to slide back toward his target.

Time was against him — he had maybe twenty seconds left. In desperation, he decided to deploy his parachute early at 1,000 meters. As the black canopy billowed and filled above him, dramatically slowing his descent, he reached and grabbed the steering handles, trying to work his way south, closer to the tower.

At 850 meters, another gust of wind blew him out to the north again, farther away from the tower. The broadcast antenna started to slide by him to his left as he circled. He saw the original landing target, the top of the building's grid structure, pass out of reach. The observation platform below was sliding away to his right.

Reaching quickly into his right thigh pocket, Steve he pulled out the grapple gun and flipped off the safety. He aimed at the central broadcast antenna and fired. The barbed dart left the gun, trailing a thin monofilament line in an arc behind it. The dart extended three hooks from its length and struck the central antenna. It bounced off, wrapping under one of the structural grid supports and the line pulled taut.

He was immediately yanked sideways and turned, holding the pistol with both hands. The breeze filling his parachute was pulling him away from the tower and the brake on the grappler's cable reel started to slip as nature engaged in a tug of war with him.

He jerked once and slipped three feet farther from the tower. Then came a second jerk; this time he almost lost the gun.

Desperately, Steve gripped the grapple gun tightly with his right hand and with his left, desperately slapped at the quick release on the parachute harness in the center of his chest. All four straps released and he dropped in free fall while the chute billowed away to the north.

The monofilament line went rigid, and he swung like a wrecking ball straight for the tower. He angled his body and brought his legs around in front of him, ready to take any impact. He felt as if he were swinging on a vine. But he'd managed to change the arc of the swing, so he started to spiral around the tower to the west until he reached the end of the line.

Still, the tower was hard. It hurt when Steve hit it. But he hung on. After he was sure he wasn't going to fall, he let himself breathe. *I did it. I actually did it*, Steve thought. *How cool is that?*

He slowly climbed around the antenna grid back to the north side and then used the grapple gun to lower himself to the platform roof some 15 meters below. When Steve touched down, he put some slack on the line and pressed the retract stud on the side of the gun. The three hooks retracted into the side of the dart, and the monofilament rewound onto the internal spool. He slid the dart back into the pistol with a click, and for a moment, admired the device. "Oh, yeah, I definitely have to get me one of these."

He looked at his chute billowing downward, raised his SAVANT and fired. The plasma bolt hit the chute, and the nylon flashed into flames. Within seconds, his parachute and harness were consumed, leaving only ash floating downward.

Steve removed his helmet and took a deep breath. "Control, Tate here. I'm safely on the roof of the upper platform. Let's get this over with."

Chapter 27

Amy opened the hall door a crack and peered out, then checked the building floor plan again. By design, she'd come in two floors above the arcade level in the office building. The idea was that Callahan would more likely expect her from below than from above. Now she needed to descend, then cross over through the arcade to the broadcast center. But which would be better — stairs or elevator? She decided the elevator shaft was her fastest means.

She opened the door to the hallway a little wider and did a quick scan with her SAVANT. "Ethan, security analysis?"

"Motion sensors 20 meters behind you and 30 meters in front. Passive infrared and a pressure mesh grid on the floor of the elevator lobby. There's a guard making rounds two corridors over. No time to wait for him; if you can't avoid him take him down. Gently, please."

"Gotcha. Deploying spiders."

She'd taken her helmet off and stored it in her again in her backpack. Now she reached around it and pulled a small pouch out of the pack. Opening it carefully, she poured five black spheres the size of walnuts from the pouch. She touched a switch on each one and tossed it into the hall. It landed and one by one, five metallic spiders emerged, eagerly awaiting her commands.

She switched her SAVANT to Mode 2 and used it to issues orders to each one: two to disable the motion sensors, one to disable the infrared sensors, and the fourth to turn off the floor pressure grid. The last one, assigned a unique mission, climbed the wall and disappeared into shadows overhead.

The first three spiders quickly found their sensors and disabled them. As soon as their indicators went green on the SAVANT display, she was on the move down the hall.

The fourth spider was sawing into the carpet as Amy came around the corner. She stopped and looked at it, putting her hands on her hips.

"Really?"

The spider looked up at her, tilted its head for a moment and then dove back into the corner of the carpet. A second later, there was a shower of sparks as it found and chewed through the pressure grid's power supply.

Amy grinned and moved to the elevator.

She pulled a black box from her left vest pocket and put it over the elevator call button. "The car is six floors above you," Ethan's voice informed her as he read the interface. "I'll hold it there and open the doors for you."

Amy smiled. "And they say there are no gentlemen left in the world."

There was a rumble and a small chime as the doors slid open. The air pressure changed as Amy looked down the darkened shaft for a moment and gulped. "You know, Steve's a lot better at hanging in mid-air on ropes."

"You're doing fine so far, Amy... Uh-oh."

"Uh-oh? I hate uh-oh."

"The guard! Behind you on your right!"

Amy wheeled and tossed a blue beanbag from her vest pocket at the guard. It flashed brilliant white, blinding him, and then released a quick knockout gas.

"Think he saw you?" Ethan asked.

"I doubt it, but let's not stick around to find out." She looked down the shaft, then grabbed the grapple gun and fired up. The dart struck and held to the underside of the elevator car. She grabbed the black box, clipped the gun to her vest harness and swung out into space. After a second hanging there, she used the gun to play out another

20 feet of line, until she was suspended outside the 7th-floor elevator doors.

"Amy."

"A little busy here, Ethan."

"Thought you'd want to know; Steve completed his jump. He's on the tower safely."

She let out a breath. "Thank God. Now, may I have a scan outside these elevator doors?"

"Yes. I'm not reading any security outside them."

"Nothing?" Amy's face grew determined. "Callahan's already here, waiting for me. SAVANT, Mode 3." Her right hand and forearm were quickly encased in the living metal gauntlet. "Right, wish me luck."

She swung over and put the black box on the inner door circuit. "Ethan, on my mark, please?"

"Ready, Amy."

She readied herself, and then pushed off hard with both feet. As she swung back, she said, "Now!"

The elevator doors opened Amy jumped through the gap, rolling as she hit the floor. She came up in a crouch, right arm out in a firing position, and swept the elevator lobby for a hostile target.

Nothing. The room was dark and empty, silent except for the sounds of Amy scrambling to her feet on the black marble floor. Quickly, she retrieved the grapple gun again, stowed it in her left thigh pocket and had Ethan use the SAVANT to scan again for life signs.

Empty. Amy looked around. *Where the hell are you, you bitch?* She raised her SAVANT again and cautiously started down a side corridor. "Ethan, give me some directions here."

"Scanning. Still no alarms. Take the right corridor. It's a long hallway. Go to the fourth doorway down, then a left." Amy did, sweeping each space and cubicle for any sign of another human being, or anything else that might be a danger.

"Now take the second right, and then go to the end of the hall. The data broadcast control center is through the double glass doors there."

Amy took the right turn and started down the long corridor. "Ethan, you are sure you're not reading anything?"

"Positive, Amy. Still nobody here but you."

Amy pursed her lips. "No. This isn't right. We know for sure both Williams and Callahan are in the complex. They must be hacking the SAVANTs again. You'd better warn Steve."

Ethan sounded grim. "Very well. And Am—"

Her commlink burst briefly with static, then went dead. "Ethan?"

No response. Amy gulped, then took a deep breath and opened the doors to the broadcast center.

The room again reminded her of mission control from a high school field trip to NASA in Houston. One wall was a floor to ceiling array of video screens, each showing a different commercial data stream. There were four stacked tiers of consoles, each monitoring and controlling one part of the broadcast array. In the center on a raised dais, was a large white desk and swivel chair, where the master producer for the broadcast center would sit and supervise the operation.

"Hello again, Princess."

The white chair swiveled around. In it, wearing a black jumpsuit and holding a very large pistol in her right hand, was Hannah Callahan.

"My, aren't you the clever one?"

3:52 a.m. JST

It was relatively easy to find the access door atop the tower. Steve used his SAVANT to override the digital keypad and in seconds was inside and out of the wind.

He took a few moments to ditch the cumbersome pressure suit. He was used to running parkour, with its ethos of being one with your environment, and the suit, while necessary at the edge of space, made him feel like a microwave burrito here on the surface. He knew it wasted a few minutes, but he considered the flexibility it afforded him worth the trade-off.

He stuffed the suit in a corner and pressed a control on the SAVANT. Specialized nanites emerged from a sealed container on the suit and started to consume it. Within seconds, it would be gone, and the nanites would deactivate themselves, becoming dust.

He quickly located the present Frederick has stashed for him the previous afternoon and put it on. Once it was secure, he activated his commlink.

"Ethan, I'm here. What now?"

A projection from his SAVANT appeared on the wall. "Proceed down two levels. The broadcast antenna controller array is located there. Intel says the False Mirror prototype is plugged in there, but..." The controller paused.

Steve grimaced as he started down the stairs. "Not my favorite word, Ethan."

"Our intel is that it's been concealed inside another component — a power boost relay. There are sixteen of them on that floor, all identical. We have no way of knowing which one is the right one."

"So it's a logic puzzle for me to figure out."

"Looks that way."

Steve grumbled. "Great. How's Amy doing?"

"She's inside and on her way."

"Tell her I said hello."

"Will do. And Steve, remember, once you've loaded the command codes, get out of there. When Amy activates them, if you're in range, the EMP will destroy not only the prototype but your SAVANT as well."

"Leaving me defenseless against Williams and Callahan. Yeah, don't think it hasn't crossed my mind, Ethan."

Steve quickly made his way down the two flights of stairs and to the array controller floor. The door was locked, but after a few seconds with a lock pick, it was no obstacle. *Sometimes old school is still best,* he thought, as he surveyed the room.

He switched his SAVANT into Mode 2 and used it to bring up pictures of the False Mirror prototype from Naziri's lab and a generic power relay from the manufacturer. The relays were evenly spaced along the outside wall, in groups of four. To get a feel for the device, he examined the closest one first.

Power boost relay. Bigger than a carry-on bag hinged on top, outer casing swivels upward. That means evidence of use is going to be on the bottom. Right. The electrician's seals. He quickly surveyed the room and found four that had newer seals on them. "Gotcha. First ones to try."

Using the multitool from his web belt, he snipped the first seal and undid the latch. The casing slid out and up, showing a confusing, jumbled array of wiring. He held up the SAVANT and scanned the interior — nothing.

He repeated the process three more times, each with the same result — no device. By the time he'd finished closing and resealing the last relays, he'd wasted twenty minutes.

Steve grimaced. Williams had known what he'd ping on and duplicated it. He was spending too much time up here. There wouldn't be enough minutes to check them all.

"Ethan, this isn't going to work. He's got this thing too well camouflaged. I need some other kind of clue. Can you patch me through to Amy?"

Ethan's voice was reluctant. "That's may be a bit problematic. Amy's off-line."

Steve's head came up sharply. "What?"

"On her last transmission, she identified that Williams and Callahan were probably using the False Mirror to spoof the SAVANTs again. Right after that, we lost contact with her."

"How long ago was that?"

"Five minutes ago."

"Listen. Your priority is to regain contact with Amy. She needs to know as soon as possible when I've entered the software update. Find a way to get word to her. Call in Frederick if you need to."

"What about you?"

"I'll be okay. Now get to work."

Steve walked around the floor in a circle, again, and again, slowly, carefully, his eyes observing everything. He closed his eyes, stood in the center of the room, and willed his Talent into action. Time slowed to a crawl. He let his mind sift through all the data of everything he perceived in the room.

Don't think about Amy. Forget about Mom, Marie, or Rose. All that matters is the mission. Just the mission. He's hidden it in plain sight, Steven. Look things over carefully. Look how everything fits together, how everything follows in order from beginning to end, from first to last, from master—

Suddenly, he snapped back into real time, and his eyes flew open.

"How could I have been so stupid!"

4:02 a.m. JST

Callahan pulled the trigger, but Amy already anticipated her. She went into overdrive and pushed off to her left, diving over a desk there. At the same time, out of the overhead, the black metallic spider that had been shadowing her dropped down onto Callahan's gun in front of the barrel.

The darts struck the spider, shredding it in a shower of sparks. Shards flew up at Callahan's face as she screamed and dropped the weapon. Amy stood up, took aim and fired once with her SAVANT. The blue-white plasma bolt hit Callahan on the side and spun her around out of the chair. She hit the ground like a wet sack of cement, out cold.

Amy walked to the unconscious woman and rolled her onto her back. Her face was bloody from where pieces of the shredded spider robot had sliced into her. Amy stood there, the rage building inside her over everything that had happened to her, to her friends, to her lover.

She raised her gauntleted right fist and aimed it right between Callahan's eyes.

"SAVANT, increase power to plasma bolt, 100 percent."

"Acknowledged."

Amy's right hand shook as she stood there, fist pointed at her enemy.

Callahan groaned once, then opened her eyes and looked up at her. "Don't think you've won, Princess. This game's just getting started."

"Just shut up."

Callahan coughed once and grinned. "Go ahead, Princess. You've switched it to high power, right? It's what I would have done. Come on, you know it's what you've been waiting for. Just squeeze your dainty little fist, and I'm toast. You get what you wanted — revenge. Along with the knowledge that you're just like me."

"I'm nothing like you!"

"Oh, but that's where you're so very wrong, Princess. You were built to be exactly like me — able to kill in cold blood."

Amy's hand wavered slightly but stayed aimed at Callahan. She steadied it with her left hand. "I said, shut up!"

Something's not right here, Amy thought. *I'm missing something. She is way too relaxed for someone who's at the wrong end of a weapon.*

"What's the matter, Princess? Conscience getting in your way?" Callahan smirked. "Maybe you aren't the working model. Maybe I need to go find your sis—"

Callahan went back to dreamland when Amy kicked her in the head. "You know what? You talk too much."

Amy quickly searched Callahan and found a control device in her pocket. She examined it, trying to figure out the off switch. "Well, when all else fails..." She put it on a desk, aimed at it and fired a plasma bolt. The device exploded in a shower of sparks, along with most of the desk.

Oops. Forgot to dial back the setting. "SAVANT, decrease plasma bolt to 30 percent."

"Acknowledged."

Ethan's voice was suddenly yelling inside her head.

"–got to figure out some way to get word to her—"

"Ethan, calm down. I'm here."

"You're... Amy? You're online?"

"You were expecting someone else?"

Ethan's voice was filled with relief. "When we lost contact with you, we weren't sure what it meant."

"What are you talking about?"

"You went completely dark, including vital signs. That only happens if an agent is, well..."

"Dead. Yeah, I get it. Well, I'm not. And neither is Callahan. But I fried her remote control for the device. Any word on Steve?"

"Last word was he made it to the room where they'd hidden the prototype, disguised as one of sixteen identical components. He has to find the right one and remove the case to access the prototype."

"Any luck?"

"Unfortunately, he's 0-for-4 and getting frustrated. And we're running out of time. He only has twenty-two minutes left."

Amy glanced at her SAVANT and frowned. "Ethan, my mission clock says forty minutes. What aren't you telling me?"

She heard an argument off-microphone. "Ethan? I asked you a question. What's going on?"

"Amy, this is Dr. Watson. There's a... complication. Mr. Stevenson had a backup plan in place, and he's activated it."

Amy looked around the broadcast center. "Ethan, can we rig a two-way visual using a monitor here via my SAVANT? I want to talk face-to-face."

"Yes. Switch to Mode 2." Amy did so as she hurried to one of the broadcast control stations.

Ethan continued. "Now take the universal cable from your SAVANT and plug it into the side of the display." She did as instructed. The monitor flared to life, and the picture quickly resolved to show Ethan in the ICC, following multiple video screens, his eyes darting back and forth. Watson was just behind him, pointing at something.

"I can see you. What's this plan by Stevenson?"

Watson looked into the camera. "Amy, we're running out of time. You must wait for Steve to load his command codes first before you do run your search algorithm. Otherwise, the plan fails."

"Uh, yeah. That was the plan. So tell Steve to get moving."

"He's aware. However, here's the wrinkle. You know Triangle helped build the Tokyo SkyTree complex."

"Steve figured that out earlier. Stevenson wasn't too thrilled he twigged on that right away."

"What none of us knew was that particular major structural supports in the tower are rigged with explosives."

"What!?"

"Mr. Stevenson has activated the timer for these and only he has the disarm code. He refuses to use it until he knows you've succeeded. If you fail, he's going to bring down Tokyo SkyTree to prevent False Mirror from being activated."

Amy's knees went weak. She sat down, her face a pale white. "But that would collapse it on top of a sleeping neighborhood with no warning. It... that'll kill... thousands."

Ethan swallowed hard. "Our last estimate is over 100,000 people."

"My God." She could see Stevenson in the background and yelled, "Are you out of your mind?"

Stevenson walked in the range of the camera. "No. Just willing to do what's necessary to stop this, once and for all."

Amy thought. "Ethan, is there any way I can disarm the explosives?"

He shook his head. "No. There's not enough time. Just... just be ready to implement the search algorithm the second we get word from Steve."

"But if he's not clear..."

"We don't have a choice. As soon as you've received word you can run the command, do so."

Amy paused, then nodded. "Understood. Anything else?"

Ethan shook his head. "No, wait a second." He looked at his screen, then back at the pickup again. "Did you say you'd subdued Callahan?"

"Yeah, I'm looking at her. She's out cold."

"Your SAVANT indicates someone else in the room with—"

The screen dissolved into static.

All the screens in the room dissolved into static.

Amy's blood went cold. "Ethan, say again? Someone else is in here with—"

The lights went out, plunging the room into darkness. From behind her, Amy heard two words.

"Hello, Princess."

Amy froze. Disbelieving, she turned slowly and stared.

Silhouetted in the light streaming through the street side windows, wearing a white jumpsuit, was Hannah Callahan.

4:17 a.m. JST

Steve quickly exited the room and climbed the metal stairs up one level. As he entered the control technician's room, he called out. "Ethan, I've located the False Mirror device. Tell Amy to stand by."

Silence.

"Ethan, come in."

"We've jammed your communications. He won't be talking to you again, Tate. Neither will your partner."

Steve turned around and found the speaker behind him, on a clean, uncluttered desk by the door. To the right of the desk was another power boost relay station. On it was stenciled the numeral '1'. He walked over to it, looking around, as Williams' voice continued. "I must admit, I'm impressed. How'd you figure it out?"

Steve undid the seal at the base and opened it up. "Two things. The markings on the sixteen relays in the room downstairs were numbered 2 through 17."

"Clever. Anything else?"

Inside the casing, he found the False Mirror prototype, nestled among the wires. "Yes. The four I examined were configured as slaves. So, there had to be a master somewhere."

"And why did you choose up?"

He quickly checked it for traps and found none. He took out the USB drive and slid it into the device. "Lucky guess." The three LED indicators on the drive lit up, indicating it had finished downloading. He pulled the drive out and lowered the lid.

Williams chuckled. "Excellent work. You'll go far in our organization if you choose to."

"What organization is that?"

"Oh, that's strictly on a need-to-know basis. Of course, you do realize finding the prototype doesn't mean you've won. My associate down below has Miss Rogers all tied up right now, so to speak. She'll never implement her half of the fix. Chaos will still erupt today."

"You'd let that happen?"

"Of course not. I'm not a monster. I just used to work for one."

Steve stopped short. "What do you mean?"

"What I mean, Mr. Tate, is that you're wasting your time. False Mirror was never going to be activated today."

"But the Stock Exchange—"

"False Mirror would never be able to hurt it. This version is too small. The next one won't be. But you had to *think* it might work so that you would try to stop it. Try... and fail."

Steve hesitated. "What?"

"What did you think would happen if you failed, Mr. Tate? Did you really think a man like Reggie Stevenson would allow False Mirror to wreak havoc on society? He's always had a backup plan in place."

"A backup plan?"

"Look at the monitor on the desk." It flared to life, showing several camera angles. "Here's video of SkyTree two hours ago, and here's now. You're the observant one. Let's play I Spy. You tell me what's different."

Steve looked at the two sets of video images. *Come on, Steven, think.*

Wait.

"The aircraft warning lights. They aren't blinking. And the color's changed."

"Very good. Now whatever might that mean?" Up on the screen popped a confidential Triangle Construction memo. Steve scanned through it and stopped. His blood ran cold.

"Yes, Mr. Tate. Eight critical structural supports hollowed out and filled with explosives, rigged to detonate on a remote signal by the builder from anywhere in the world. The aircraft warning lights are a signal to informed Triangle personnel in the region to evacuate the area surrounding the tower." Williams chuckled. "I ask you again. Who's the monster?"

Steve growled. "Williams—"

"Oh, but wait — there's more. After all, dropping a building this size on top of one of the biggest cities in the world won't go unnoticed. Someone has to take the blame." The screen image shifted to a copy of the New York Times website. As Steve read it, the chill in his blood turned to pure ice.

On the screen was a story, datelined tomorrow, talking about the criminal masterminds behind the terrorist attack on Tokyo SkyTree, including pictures of the two suspected terrorists.

Steven Tate and Amelia Jane Rogers.

Inside Steve's head, he heard a rush of words, but foremost was his father's warning — *they see everyone as assets to be discarded when their usefulness has ended.* He closed his eyes for a second.

"It's a lie. Watson would never let Stevenson hang Amy and me out to dry like that."

"You really think she has a choice in the matter, Tate? Even if she does, you're here. And I didn't make that story up, any more than I built this place ready to be destroyed if need be."

"But you made trades based on the market crashing."

"For someone so smart, you really are thick. What happened after 9/11? The Dow dropped fourteen percent in a week. Dropping this tower will make 9/11 look like a garden party."

Steve looked at the speaker. "You're a real piece of work, Williams. How did you get to be this evil?"

Williams' voice grew harsh. "Grow up, Tate. You think this is just a simple black and white game? There are many shades of gray involved. Triangle may claim to be noble, but in the end, they're only defending their own interests. And as you said, how good of a job are they really doing?"

"So what's my alternative, Williams? You?"

"Not just me. The people I'm working with now."

Steve looked at the speaker. "Who are they?"

"They've got a view of the long game, and they know more about you and your Talent than you do."

"What?" Steve's mind reeled.

"Let me put it this way: they built us well. Although I must say, if you and Rogers are any indication, the newer models still need a lot of work. Well, you know what they say. It is so tough to update a classic."

Steve's mind was racing. "I don't have time for this. Williams, how do I stop the bombs?"

"That's the beauty of it, Tate. You can't. Only Stevenson can, and he needs to know you've succeeded. But you need Ms. Rogers to do that, and she's never going to know you've already loaded the command file."

Steve kept his voice neutral. "I don't know what you're talking about."

"Spare me, Tate. I've had you on the monitor the whole time. I could have stopped you at any time. But the only thing I have to do to succeed is to make sure one of you fails. And I told you weeks ago — Rogers is the weak link." Williams paused. "Or rather, she was, by now."

"If you've done anything to her—"

"You'll what? Kill me?"

"Yes."

Williams sighed. "They said killing you would be a waste of resources, but I told them you'd never listen. Tell you what, Tate. I'll give you a chance. Come take your best shot. I'm in the Glass Lounge, on the bottom deck of this observation platform. But you'd better hurry. You're almost out of time." Williams started to laugh.

Steve picked up the speaker, and yanked the cable from it, giving him a moment's silence. He looked at his SAVANT and checked its charge, then started down the stairs. When Steve reached the bottom level, he pushed open the door and entered the lounge. He ducked in a crouch behind the bar and scanned the room but registered nothing.

"I'm here, Williams. Come out and show yourself."

"This way, Tate. Just follow my voice," Williams mocked him. But at least now Steve had a direction. *Discotheque.*

As he stepped out from behind the bar and onto the dance floor, all the decorative lighting switched on. Between the myriad of mirrored balls, pin spots, programmable LEDS and more, there had to be at least a hundred different light sources.

In all the visual confusion, Steve barely saw the red sighting dot in time. He didn't think or calculate; he just dropped and fired along the line the laser came from. The bolt from his SAVANT caught the bullet in mid-air and with a sizzle, vaporized it.

Williams was seated in a circular booth against a window. He clapped his hands. "Very entertaining. But that was a mere parlor trick, Tate." He snapped his fingers.

Suddenly, Steve felt like a tiny speck in an immense universe.

The decorative lights winked out. Where there had been one laser sight before, now there were dozens, coming from all directions — in front, behind, above, below. He'd seen this strategy in a movie once — they'd called it 'englobement.'

Steve decided right then and there he hated that movie.

He looked over at Williams. "This is a bit much, even for you."

"Tate, if I've learned anything from watching you these past few weeks, it's that when it comes to your Talent, there's no such thing as overkill."

"But you said I'd have a chance!"

"I did? Fair enough. There is one sure way to survive this. Join us."

Steve considered it briefly, then shook his head. "No. If you and Callahan are any indication, your organization is even worse than Triangle."

Williams smiled. "I told them you'd never join. You'd already said no once, and how could I ever trust you again?" He shook his head. "In that case, Tate, you're about to learn a new lesson."

"What's that?"

"How you deal with a no-win scenario. See if you can figure that out by the count of three. One."

Steve looked determined and tried to activate his Talent, but for the first time he could ever remember, it didn't work. Steve looked around, frantic, seeking the way out of the trap. He couldn't see any.

"Two."

He closed his eyes, defeated.

He realized he was going to fail.

Stevenson was going to blow up the tower. Thousands of innocent people were going to be killed. Williams was going to win. Because he failed.

Because he wasn't good enough.

Amy was going to die.

Because he wasn't good enough.

Again.

Something inside him roared to life — an anger white-hot, a fury he'd never known.

Not this time.

"Three."

Steve channeled that power and activated his Talent. It snapped into place with an audible ferocity, practically humming around him. As the microseconds slowed to a barely perceptible crawl, he looked at his body and smiled. Everything was bathed in a cold azure light, crystal clear and in sharp detail. It was as if his Talent had gone from full power to supercharged. For the first time, he felt free to interact with his surroundings, not to just observe them, but to *affect* them.

He now fully understood what was happening. He'd barely touched this subconsciously before when he'd bent the path of bullets or stopped them cold in mid-air. Now, it was his choice what to do. He stepped *aside* from himself in slow-time and started to work.

The first bullets crept toward him from all sides, imperceptibly slow, their paths appearing to him in three dimensions, data about them updating slowly about caliber, rifling, rotation, velocity hanging in the air by each one. The data now appeared in layers that Steve could walk around in and interact with. Steve reached up to touch the closest bullet. *I wonder.* He located it's velocity value and changed it to zero.

The bullet dropped out of the air into his hand.

Steve looked over at Williams, and an angry smile grew on his face as he reached a decision. Instead of the bullets stopping in midair, this time they were just going to disappear. *Not today, Mitch,* he thought, as he manipulated and picked the projectiles out of the air, one after another, like acorns in the field. *Not ever again.*

The longer Steve did this, the more he felt a pressure building up behind him — he was damming up time like a river, and it would release when he returned to normal. He wondered what the effect would be like.

After hours and hours of subjective day of slow-time, the bullets stopped. Ten seconds had passed in real-time.

In the club there was a crack of thunder as on the center of the shattered discotheque floor Steve Tate knelt on one knee, eyes closed. He rose and turned toward Williams. His eyes snapped open, blazing with anger.

Williams stared in shock. "That's not possible."

Steve opened his hands. A cascade of hundreds of spent bullets rained down from them, clattering onto the dance floor and bouncing away. As the last bullet hit the ground, Steve began to walk deliberately toward Williams.

The traitor stood up, and in a blindingly fast motion, pulled out both his pistols and fired.

The only sounds he heard were clicks as the hammers of each gun fell on an empty chamber.

Williams looked at his weapons, and then at Steve, who stood in front of him, holding up a pair of ammo magazines.

"Lose something?"

Then Steve punched him in the face.

Williams swung back to retaliate, but suddenly Steve wasn't there. Instead, he was behind him, pushing him forward, over the table, and onto the glass dance floor overlooking the city.

Williams stood and rushed at Steve, launching arm sweeps, kicks, punches — no matter the move, Steve blocked them all easily. Seeing an opening, he connected a snap kick to the side of Williams' right knee. It buckled, sending the older man tumbling to the far edge of the floor.

Williams looked down at the drop below and started laughing. "You've improved, Rookie. But you even if you beat me, you still can't win."

Steve raised his SAVANT and aimed it at Williams, but hesitated. Instead of firing, he stepped onto the floor himself, his expression grim. "You know what, Mitch? Someone once taught me that sometimes winning just means changing the game that's being played. So, I'll tell you what. I'll race you!"

Williams looked confused as Steve stopped five paces away from him. "Race me where?"

"To hell."

Steve dropped his left arm to his side and fired his SAVANT straight into the glass floor. The plasma bolt shattered it instantly, and the two men plummeted through the shards like a pair of stones.

Steve reached behind him and pulled a D-ring on the bottom of his backpack. It immediately deployed a small BASE jump parachute.

The last thing Mitchell Williams saw was Steve floating away out of his grasp. He hit the 350-meter platform and pinwheeled off it, landing seven seconds later the street below.

Steve grabbed the steering controls for the chute and angled himself northwest toward a landing on the roof of the arcade building below.

Now to find Amy and end this.

Chapter 28

Amy turned back and looked at the ground. There was Hannah Callahan, unconscious, bleeding.

She turned again and looked. Standing there was Hannah Callahan, right down to that damned white scar, cold gray eyes and sharks' grin.

Amy's insides turned to ice. "But... that's impossible."

Callahan laughed and kept her gun trained on Amy. "Impossible? Honey, you work for Triangle. You know... they invent doomsday, six impossible things before breakfast every day, et cetera, et cetera, blah blah blah?"

"But, how?"

"Hmmm. How, indeed. All sorts of possibilities. Identical twins, genetic cloning, parallel dimensions. Ask your boss. She's going to hate trying to explain this one to you — if you live long enough to tell her. Of course, if you look closely, maybe you'll figure out that seeing is believing."

Amy closed her eyes for a moment. *Steve, you promised if I ever needed you, you'd be here. Now would be a really good time...*

No. Got to stall. Got to keep her talking.

Quietly, she said "SAVANT, Mode 3, Weapon, full power." Then she opened her eyes and stared again at Callahan.

"You know, this is really starting to get old, you always holding a gun on me. It's almost like—"

Amy whipped her right arm and SAVANT up into a firing position, but before she could get off a shot, Callahan grinned and fired. The dart came out of the gun much faster this time and buried itself in Amy's left arm, just above the elbow. She screamed in pain and crumpled to her knees.

"Cute, Princess. But I was built for this. You aren't. You don't know how your Talent works. A weakness for sharp, pointy things, remember?"

Amy sat up and looked at her arm. The shaft of the dart went straight through it, the jagged head sticking out the back and glistening with her own blood. She bit her lip as she reached over with her left hand, grabbed the head and tried to pull the dart out. The pain grew so bad she almost passed out. As it was, the world swam unsteadily for a few moments and when it came back in focus, here was Callahan, standing over her, the weapon aimed at her forehead.

She met Callahan's gaze. "Twins. Two people sharing the same identity."

Callahan nodded. "Very good, Princess. Identical, down to the scar. Sucked when we had to do that, too. No choice, though, had to keep up the illusion."

"Which one are you?"

"I'm the original recipe, kiddo. Hannah Callahan. My little sister there, the one who normally hides backstage, that's Karen. And she is going to be pissed at you. Too bad I'm going to ruin her fun by killing you first."

Amy looked over at the unconscious woman, then back at her tormentor. "Can you at least explain something to me?"

"Sure, why not. Last meal for the condemned. Because you're going to die this morning, Princess. Either I'll kill you, or your boss will."

"So I've heard. Fine. But what I don't get is... if you don't need to kill me, why do it anyway? If you're so good at what you do, why do you have to kill outside your contracts, too?"

"Karen keeps asking me the same thing. The fact is, it's a kick. It thrills me. Watching that last moment of life trickle away, it's like the highest high I know. Especially with special ones."

Amy's eyes got wide. "You're a psychopath."

"*Moi?* No, I'm just enlightened. After all, who cares about normals. They're too easy. No sport. But the others, hiding in plain sight, Talents like you or me? Now they make for a magnificent hunt. Like your new boyfriend upstairs, or that boy toy of yours back on the island."

Amy froze. "My what?"

"I have to admit, he was a surprise. I wasn't expecting someone who could—"

"Wait. What are you saying about my boyfriend?"

"Tate? I'm afraid he's walking into a trap that's going to kill him—"

"Tate's not my boyfriend! Jason Avant was."

Callahan looked at her and raised a scarred eyebrow. "He's not? Pity. He is kind of cute."

Eww. "My boyfriend?" Amy insisted.

"Oh, right. Jason." Hannah smirked. "He really was a surprise. Caught me off guard. I wasn't ready, you know, so I couldn't take full advantage of it. No chase, no pursuit. No thrills in that kill. But he was special."

"Wait. You're implying Jason was some sort of Talent?"

"Not just anyone could break through a glamor I threw on, or make them permanently invulnerable to it either. That made him dangerous. You as well."

"But he never said anything—"

Callahan looked at her with pity. "You really never knew? Oh, this is rich. Princess, of course he was. Otherwise, you and he would never have connected. Talents and Norms, we're just not compatible. It can happen, but it has to be something really, really special." Callahan chuckled. "And even then, something happens. Usually me."

Amy felt deflated. Her voice became quiet, shaky, and unsure of itself. "I never knew. He never told me."

Callahan smiled cruelly. "Poor child. You really don't know who and what you are. Here, let me lay it out for you, Amelia Jane."

Amy looked up sharply at her. "How do you know my name?"

"Oh, my little baby girl, I know so much more than that. I know that you're a product. You were designed. You and your twin sister. Steve Tate and his twin. Jason and his twin. We all were. That's how we can do what we can. Only some of us..." Callahan patted Amy on the shoulder as she stepped backward. "Some of us are much better than others. A truth that, unfortunately, is about to be the end of you. Say goodbye, Amelia Jane."

She brought up the weapon to fire, and Amy winced, closing her eyes as she anticipated the impact. But her end was interrupted by a bright flash that made the insides or her eyelids glow red and a loud crash accompanied by a strangled cry that cry that cut off abruptly.

Cautiously, Amy opened her eyes. On the floor in front of her, Hannah Callahan lay face down, a smoldering charred streak covering most of her back.

Fifteen feet away, Steve lowered his gauntleted left fist. "Sorry I'm late. Did I miss something?"

Amy knelt next to Hannah and rolled her over. She lay there, gray eyes staring lifelessly at the ceiling. Amy checked and confirmed. No pulse.

Steve moved over to her. Amy grabbed him with her good arm, drew him close and kissed him, hard. After a moment, Steve broke the embrace. "Nice to see you, too. But can we put a pin in that? We're still in the middle of saving the world."

Amy blushed. "Yeah."

"You're hurt."

"No duh—"

"Captain Obvious. Yeah, I know. Hold on, this is going to hurt." With a quick yank, he grabbed and pulled the dart through her arm, then tossed it aside. He grabbed a pair of biogel dressings from his field medkit and slapped it on the entry and exit wounds. "How's that?"

She grimaced. "Hurts like hell. I sincerely hope I'm done getting holes poked in me. Are you offline?" Steve nodded. "I am, too. I wonder..." She bent down and checked through Hannah's pockets, but came up empty. "Not here."

Steve knelt next to her. "What are you looking for?"

"A remote for the False Mirror. Turns on and off the jamming function."

"You mean there are more than one of these things?"

She shrugged. "Two Callahans, two remotes."

"Makes sense."

"Thanks. But how would we find it if there was one?"

Steve stepped over to where Hannah had been standing when he shot her and closed his eyes. Amy assumed he was doing 'his thing' again. His right arm flew up. He turned and moved past a half dozen consoles, then crouched down and looked under a desk.

"Found it!"

He carried back the control device. Amy just shook her head. "Do you ever lose your car keys?"

"Only once. Long story." He put the device on a desktop, aimed his SAVANT and fired. As it blew up in a shower of sparks, Ethan's voice roared in their heads. They both winced.

"—the report is someone fell from the tower. Have Frederick stand by to verify—"

Steve replied quickly. "Relax, Ethan, it wasn't me. It's Williams. He's dead."

There was a cheer in the ICC. Ethan yelled for everyone to quiet down. "Is Amy all right?"

"She appears to be. I was about to have her run the second protocol—"

"You mean she hasn't yet? My God, man, do it now!"

Amy nodded and sat at the nearest working computer. She reached into a belt pouch and pulled out the USB drive, plugging it in. The drive immediately captured the system and sought out the False Mirror.

4:26 a.m. JST

In the control technician's workroom at the top of the Tokyo SkyTree, the False Mirror prototype received the search command through the network. As it processed the command, the faint blue glow from the nanites suddenly shifted to red, then flared a brilliant white. There was a high-pitched hum that lasted for three seconds, and then the device went dark.

Everything was still for a moment. Then, like a sand castle collapsing beneath a wave, the prototype crumpled into dust.

4:27 a.m. JST

"Ethan, did it work?"

"Monitoring... Wait, this can't be right. It says it was accepted by the first, and rejected...by the second?"

Watson's voice came over the commlink. "The second?"

Amy and Steve looked at each other. Amy turned white. "Oh, my God—"

Steve finished her sentence. "—two remotes. They built a duplicate prototype. Ethan, is there a way to find the energy signature?"

"This one is close. Within 50 feet of you."

Amy had an idea. "Can we use the SAVANTs in tandem to pinpoint it? You know, triangulate the energy signature?"

Ethan was typing furiously. "Yeah, if there's enough time and you two are far enough apart—"

Steven yelled. "Make enough time!" He ran to one corner of the room.

Amy sprinted in the opposite direction. "I'm with Steve on that one. And in position!"

Ethan's voice rang out. "Sending a ping!"

Amy and Steve thrust their gauntleted arms in the air as the SAVANTSs let out a sweeping pair of tones. The sounds circled their arms twice, and then both aligned toward a single point in the far corner. Steve started toward it, but Amy was faster. It was a locked metal cabinet. Without thinking, she unleashed a furious roundhouse kick. When she made contact, there was a bright flash and the door sheared off.

Steve backed off. "That's it. You. Terminal. Now!" Steve reached into his pocket for the backup USB drive and plugged it into the machine. The indicator flashed three green lights, and then went dark.

"Now, Amy!"

"But our SAVANTS—"

"Screw 'em! We'll get new ones later! Go!"

She unplugged her own USB drive, then jammed it back into the port. The command set took over the machine the moment it connected.

Steve ran to Amy and the two of the dove behind a desk as the second False Mirror device glowed red, then brilliant white and let out an ear-screeching whine.

June 16, 3:30 p.m. EDT

In the ICC, Ethan watched as a second False Mirror icon blinked, then faded to black. "All Clear!" he yelled and turned to Stevenson.

Stevenson leaned over his tablet and spoke in a four-word code sequence. The eight aircraft warning indicators seen on the SkyTree cameras switched in order from red to white to green as the charges were disarmed.

"At his workstation, the SAVANT interface signals cut off and his screens dissolved into static. Silence filled the ICC for a few seconds. Then Steve's voice emerged from the speaker.

"Ethan?"

"It's over, Steve. We're secure."

"Whew. For a minute, I thought maybe Mr. Stevenson was going to blow us all up or something anyway."

Stevenson blanched. "Now, Mr. Tate—"

"Just shut up. You and I will talk when I get back. Doc Watson, are you online?"

Stevenson turned stiffly and exited the ICC as Watson stepped forward to Ethan's console. Her voice was calm and measured. "I'm here, Steven."

3:31 p.m. EDT

Watson stood next to Ethan's control station. I don't think they know just how close that was, she thought, looking at the digital timer on the wall display. It was frozen with 44 seconds remaining.

Steve's voice came over the commlink. "Look, we've got a situation here. Amy and I are now unarmed."

"That's all right. We'll reequip you when you return to base."

"Yeah, well, it's the least of our worries. You're not going to believe this, but we've got two Callahans here."

"Two of them?"

Amy took over. "Yeah. They both look alike, down to the scar over the eyebrow. But the second one referred to the first as her twin sister, Karen. Does that make any sense?"

Watson's mind raced. *Mitch was working with two Callahans? And managed to keep them both hidden from us? That would explain a lot. But still, how did they even cross paths with him—*

Her thoughts were interrupted by Steve's voice. "Look, we don't have the time to analyze this now. And Amy and I didn't plan on transporting any prisoners on this mission. But we need her — especially what she knows."

"Do you have a suggestion?"

"Have the Tokyo police take her into custody. I'm sure Triangle has the resources to get to her after that."

Watson paused and looked at Ethan, an eyebrow raised. "Mr. Tate, I'm surprised. I'd have thought you'd have wanted both Callahans... well, disposed of."

There was a pregnant pause over the comm channel. Watson could imagine Steve and Amy looking at each other, trying to decide how to answer the question.

It was Steve who replied. "Hannah Callahan is dead. She was the assassin you've been tracking. She was also the one who killed Jason Avant."

There was another pause. "Mr. Tate, what aren't you telling me?"

"I'm not sure which Callahan was involved in my family's murder. Even if Karen Callahan wasn't, she'll know who was. More importantly, she'll know why. I need those answers, Dr. Watson."

Amy added. "I'm with Steve on this. As much as I want revenge, Karen said some things I need answers to, as well."

"What was that, Ms. Rogers?"

Amy hesitated a moment. "That I don't really know who or what I am. What either of us is."

Rhonda Watson *closed her eyes and pinched the bridge of her nose. Not yet. You weren't supposed to find out yet.* She took a deep breath and slowly exhaled. "I understand. But you need to leave the premises immediately. Get out of there and leave the Callahans behind for the Tokyo police. We'll arrange for the body to be disposed of and Karen Callahan to be taken into custody."

Steve's voice sounded grim. "Good. Now, get us a ride home. We'll talk later."

June 17, 4:35 a.m. JST

Steve reached up and touched the control disconnecting his commlink.

Amy looked at him. "Are you okay?"

He walked over and stared down at Hannah Callahan's body. His expression shifted between grief, anger and anguish. "I don't know if I'm ever going to be okay again, A.J." He clenched his left fist and the remains of his SAVANT exploded into dust and drifted over the body.

She walked over and stood next to him. "How did you manage that 'show up in the nick of time' trick?"

"Ever hear of BASE jumping?" She shook her head. "You'll love it. This way, you don't have to wait for that perfectly good airplane to fly by." He grinned slightly and kissed her on the forehead.

She grinned back. "Forget I asked."

"Is Frederick still around? He could come get us."

Amy giggled. "Rob's running around being a distraction right now."

Steve raised an eyebrow. "How much of a distraction?"

"Fireworks factory on the river."

Steve winced. "I hope he's safe."

"He will be. He's got a good partner looking out for him."

Steve smiled at her. "I do, too."

Amy sighed. "Steve, we won."

He looked down at her for a moment. "Maybe. But just what did we win, A.J.?"

Chapter 29

4:41 a.m. JST

Rob Frederick was driving his car, a red Acura sports coupe, down an alley in the Akihabara district when he received the call. Well, technically, it wasn't his car. He'd borrowed it from his 'friends.' But, hey, it felt like his.

His controller, Dale Johnston, appeared on the dashboard screen.

"Dale, my man! What's the good news?"

"They've successfully completed the mission. You need to loop back and pick them up."

Frederick looked in his rearview mirror, where seven Tokyo police cruisers were following him. "Sure, no sweat. Give me five minutes."

Three more cruisers and two motorcycle cops joined the chase.

"Uh, better make it ten, just to be safe."

"I'll have them meet you, south side, near where Amy made her ingress."

"Her what?"

Dale sighed. "Where she entered the building. Just be there in ten."

Dale cut the connection and Rob looked for his exit strategy from the chase. He quickly found it — a tunnel under the river. He gunned the engine, heading for it, passing a truck and slipping into the lane in front of it.

As they reached the tunnel mouth, Rob toggled a switch on his steering wheel. From the rear of the vehicle, a thick cloud of white smoke billowed out. A second later, high-intensity lamps on the rear of the Acura lit up, creating a brilliant flash that momentarily blinded the following vehicles. Frederick used the distraction to pull the Acura to the left shoulder and stop. He pressed a switch on the center console labeled 'KAGAMI.'

Skirting lowered and covered the base and wheel wells of the car. On the surface of the Acura, sensors noted the surroundings and transmitted the images from around the car onto LED panels on its surface. The custom software handling this was sophisticated — it even color-corrected for shadows, eliminating those caused by the car itself. The one issue it wouldn't handle was parallax, but careful positioning would prevent that from being an issue, at least in the short term.

Unless you knew what to look for, you'd never see it. Particularly in a dark tunnel at high speeds.

The ultimate ninja car. Just like Rob's friends.

The police cruisers sped out of the smoke cloud and around the truck. All they saw was an empty tunnel. They assumed the red Acura had sped away and accelerated in pursuit. Frederick smiled as the police disappeared into the distance. He deactivated the mirror cloak, pulled back into traffic and exited at the next off-ramp.

5:10 a.m. JST

The ride from SkyTree to Narita Airport was quiet and subdued. Amy and Steve sat exhausted in the back, while Frederick just played chauffeur.

I've seen that look before on Lucy. Heck, I'm sure I've looked like that once or twice myself.

He cleared his throat. "They should have Songbird fueled up and ready to leave in about an hour. Do you guys want, you know, anything? Food or a shower? Or maybe just some quiet time alone?"

Steve just looked out the window, his face grim.

Amy turned to him and reached out to touch his hand. "Steve..."

He pulled his hand away. "Not now, Amy."

Looking surprised and slightly hurt, she turned and looked out her own window. Frederick, feeling suddenly awkward, decided to conspicuously concentrate on his driving.

5:15 a.m. JST

Tokyo police had shown up shortly after reports that a man had fallen from the upper observation platform of SkyTree. Eyewitness accounts were confusing, with some people talking about a giant eagle that had followed the man down and then veered away to the north and disappeared into the dawn.

When they entered the tower, they found signs of a struggle throughout the complex, but surveillance cameras had been disabled by the intruders and showed nothing. There was damage to the broadcasting facilities and the nightclub on the upper platform and in the broadcast control center. Police suspected the possibility of a dispute between two rival *yakuza* syndicates that had turned deadly. However, as usual, the *yakuza* were efficient and had removed all traces of the bodies.

The security team took pictures of the damage, and then called in the building support team, who were respectful and efficient. On their sleeves were embroidered patches for Tokyo SkyTree as well as the facilities' owner and builder — Triangle Tokyo Properties, Ltd.

The foreman for the building support team bowed to the police commander, then headed for his office. Closing and locking the door behind him, he brought up a program on his computer that sent a priority secure communication to his contact at Triangle Ops, advising them that no body had been found and incredibly, despite one of them being reported dead, the Callahans had somehow escaped again.

6:10 a.m. JST

Steve and Amy sat in the office in the Triangle hangar on the northern edge of Narita airport, waiting as

Sunbird was prepped. Steve was off to one side, pensive, while Amy and Frederick watched him with concern.

Amy walked over to him. "Steve, I'm sorry to interrupt. Ethan's on the commlink. He says he needs to talk to you. It's important."

Steve nodded and reached behind his ear to switch his commlink back on. "I'm here, Ethan."

Amy's voice chimed in. "Same for me. Do we need to loop in Rob Frederick as well?"

"Actually, Dr. Watson is going to video conference with you in a few moments. There's been a... development." The way he said the final word made Steve uneasy.

The wall screen came alive, and Watson appeared. They walked over to it.

"Good morning, you two. First, congratulations. You saved a lot of lives today—"

"Did we?" Steve's reply was harsh. "Seems to me, we saved a Triangle-owned facility and a financial market from meltdown and collapse."

Amy turned to him "Steve—" She placed a hand on his arm, but he shook it off.

"No, Amy, I'm serious. How exactly, did we save any lives? Oh, wait, I remember. By keeping Triangle from *blowing up and collapsing the tower on top of a sleeping neighborhood in Tokyo!*"

Watson stared at Steve. "Go on."

Steve's voice took on a harsh edge. "Just what gives you the right to play God with the lives of innocent people? You say you're part of the solution, but that sure looked like the cure was worse than the disease."

Watson folded her arms and sat on the edge of her desk. "Look, Agent Tate, don't for a second believe there aren't disagreements within Triangle about these things. There occur all the time. But our intentions have always been noble. If the stock markets around the world had collapsed, and global panic ensued, how many people would have died? How long before that chaos would have led to war, or worse? We used you and Agent Rogers make a surgical strike. We were prepared to make a larger one if needed. In either case, we would have stopped False Mirror, and ended the threat to society."

"We're an organization made up of people, Agent Tate, so by nature, we will be imperfect. But we strive for the greater good, which is as noble a calling as anyone can have. If I didn't believe that, I'd have left a long time ago."

"But I didn't call to get into a debate with you. We've had a development."

Watson grabbed her tablet and pulled it up. The window split into three screens. The other two now showed videos of SkyTree — specifically, the data control center. "Tokyo police arrived ten minutes after you departed the site. This is what they found."

Amy walked up to the screen. "Wait. Where are the Callahans?"

"The Tokyo police found neither bodies nor prisoners tied up at the broadcast facility. Somehow, after you left, they exited the facility."

"But how?"

"Unknown. Security camera footage from the facility shows that the Callahans' vehicle remained behind, and she was not spotted using any exit before the police's arrival. Also, no one arrived to assist the two of them."

"What about the cameras in the data center?"

"They were already off-line due to the False Mirror tampering. But we managed to grab the only video they had before the police thought to look for it. When the system rebooted, it showed you and Agent Tate exiting the facility. Then, two minutes later, the image dissolved into static for four minutes. When it resolved, the Callahans were gone."

"But it doesn't make sense. Nobody just disappears—"

Steve's voice was flat. "What does it matter? She got away." He walked away to the far side of the room, then kicked over a chair in frustration. "Son of a bitch! I let her get away again!"

Watson shook her head. "No, Agent Tate. We'd all agreed that Callahan would be left for the civilian authorities. After all, one of them was dead. No one recovers from a full plasma bolt — period."

Amy looked at the Ops Director. "So, where did they go? That woman had answers we needed to know."

Watson paused. "I don't know. We need to figure that out. But this raises both questions and opportunities."

"We promised you both the chance to pursue and defeat Mr. Avant's killer. But now, considering this news, we'd like to make you a different offer. You have skills that our organization finds useful. We'd like to bring you on permanently, and give you another shot at finding Callahan."

Amy glanced over at Steve. "We'd be Triangle Ops agents?"

She nodded. "Yes, Amy. Remember what our mission is at Triangle Ops. We find the problems and solve them before they can hurt people. You'd be the tip of our spear, so to speak."

Steve walked to Amy. "A.J., you can't seriously be considering this."

"Why not? I don't have anyone to go back to. My parents are dead, my grandmother's in a nursing home with Alzheimer's — she doesn't even know me anymore. My best friend's in a coma. Even though we stopped Callahan, we haven't found the truth yet. And if her sister managed to escape, you can bet she's going to hurt more people. She needs to be stopped."

Steve was shaking his head. "A.J., do you realize how crazy this sounds? Do you know the kinds of things they're going to ask you to do?"

Amy looked at him. "I don't have the luxury you have, Steve. All my Talent does is make me the muscle, the blunt instrument. Yours makes you the smartest guy in the room."

He shook his head. "Don't sell yourself short, Amy." He looked at Watson on the screen. "Even I don't have to work out all the possibilities to know how bad this is going to be, huh, Doc? After all, you just had me kill someone for you. Correction. You just had me kill your ex-partner."

Amy looked at Steve, shocked. "What?"

"That was his beef, wasn't it? You got the job, the promotion, and he got stuck training wannabes like us."

Amy looked at Watson on the screen. Her face had become a mask of stone, as she fought to control her emotions. "Williams and Watson were partners?"

"Yeah. Partners. I'm even willing to bet that wasn't all. Or am I wrong, Rhonda?"

Watson's voice was barely above a whisper. "You weren't wrong. Mitch and I were...close."

Steve's laugh was sharp. "Close. Right. Well, from what I saw, you and your organization chewed up what had probably been at one time a very good man, Doc, and spit him out. And then you didn't have the decency to finish him off yourself. You sent me to do it." He leaned in close to the screen. "So you tell me, Rhonda. Is that what you're going to do to A.J. when it's her turn?"

Watson cleared her throat. Her voice cracked when she started to talk. "Agent Tate, rest assured that as difficult as that choice was personally for me, it was still for the greater good—"

Steve backed up three steps, hands in front of him. "Please, stop. Look, if you want to claim that's all that's going on, if you want to keep lying to me, then I'm done. I'm out of here. I won't fight your fights without the full story next time." He turned and looked at Frederick in the corner.

"Hey, Rob?"

Frederick had been watching this exchange quietly, not wanting to interfere. He spoke up from his perch in the back of the room. "Yeah, Steve?"

"Can Tiger Team arrange to get me home to Seattle?"

Frederick appeared to think for a second before responding. "Sure, I can handle that. It's just—"

"Fine. We're leaving."

Frederick opened his mouth to say something but then hesitated as he saw the look on Steve's face. "Right. I...I'll just wait outside for you." He walked out of the room.

Watson spoke up from the video screen. "Agent Tate...Steven, you're not thinking rationally. Come back to Virginia and give us a few days. I'm sure we can find a way—"

"No." Steve shook his head. "When you're ready to be honest with me, Doc, then we can talk. Until then, I'm done. I'm going home to Seattle, back to my friends, back to my life." He turned and walked out of the room.

6:23 a.m. JST

Amy caught up with Steve outside the hangar. "Steve, wait! Please, talk to me!"

He stopped and stood there in the parking lot, eyes closed, his back to her. As she approached, he started talking. "Look, A.J., I'm done. Triangle wants to pretend to be noble, but look what I had to do today..."

Amy stared at him defiantly. "Yeah, what did you do? You kept a madman from killing you. Then you saved my life, and the lives of, what, over 100,000 people? To me, that sounds like a pretty awesome thing."

Steve shook his head and turned around to face her. "Amy, they were willing to throw us away. They didn't see you, or me, or any of those 100,000 as people. We're just pawns on a gigantic chessboard to them." He looked away. "Do you remember when we left the Bahamas? You blamed me for Jason's death. You called me a coward for not going after Callahan."

She walked closer to him. "Steve, I was hurting at the time—"

"Let me finish, damn it! Yes, you were hurting at the time and you didn't know my story. But I'll be honest, A.J. One of the reasons I came along for this ride was because I knew if you went after Callahan by yourself, there was a good chance you'd be hurt, or maybe even killed. I couldn't let that happen. Not again. Not to someone I cared about."

He turned and looked at her. They made eye contact, and he took her right hand in his.

Amy's breath caught when he touched her hand. It felt right. Then unbidden, Hannah Callahan's words rushed back into her mind.

Of course, he was a Talent. That's why the two of you were attracted to each other. The implication hit Amy full force.

No, no, this can't be happening. Not now. Not with him. It's too soon. I'm not ready. She fought back a rising sense of panic as she tried to put some space between them.

"Steve, I appreciate you wanted that for me. But there is something a lot bigger at work here. And I believe Triangle works to make the world better for mankind, both by improving our lives and by keeping the wolves at bay." She smiled wryly. "I just happen to have attracted a bigger, badder wolf — but I think that you and I both know why."

Steve let go of her hand and looked up at the distant hills surrounding the airport. He rubbed both hands through his hair and covered his face for a second, then looked at her. His eyes looked almost haunted. "Amy, you really have no idea what Triangle is capable of. Do you know what they had planned if we failed? They weren't just going to kill 100,000 people, Amy. They were going to blame us for it."

Amy stared at him, her mouth agape. "What?"

"It's true. Williams showed me. He didn't just show me the plans Stevenson had to destroy the tower. He also had the news stories that Triangle was going to plant if we failed—"

Amy turned on him, angrily. "Mitch Williams showed you this? And you believed him?"

"He was right about the explosives! Stevenson and Watson never denied it when I accused them of..." He stared at Amy, more items clicking into place in his brain. "You knew."

"Steve—"

He looked up at the sky and swore softly to himself. "You knew they were going to blow up the building."

She stepped over to him, putting a hand on his shoulder. "I found out during the fight. I understood it for what it was — a desperation play to cut off Williams and Callahan if we failed. But I also knew we'd succeed. I believed in you."

He shook off her touch and stepped away. "Right. And you're okay that Stevenson was going to blame us—"

"You have no idea if that was the truth or just something Williams created to screw with your head. Besides, it doesn't matter. We won."

Steve looked at her again. "Did we? Amy, Triangle is going to change us and not for the better. They already have. Do you hear yourself? 'It doesn't matter, we won.' The Amy Rogers I met that morning before we docked in Nassau would never have believed that the ends justified the means like this."

Her gaze was defiant. "Steve, you're sweet. But, you're wrong. And you're naïve."

"Oh, really? How so?"

She walked up to him until their faces were inches apart. "Because the truth is, neither of us knows exactly what we are. But someone inside Triangle does."

Steve opened his mouth to say something and then stopped. His mind started racing again. "Twelve months."

Amy smiled. "Yes. Twelve months."

"Williams had been working with Callahan for only four to five months. But back at that initial briefing, they said they were monitoring me six months ago—"

"—and me twelve months ago. You finally saw it." Amy nodded.

"So..." Steve trailed off for a moment, his eyes getting a faraway look. Then he turned and looked at Amy. "Why would they be monitoring us, exactly?"

She smiled. "Come on, Steve. This is a Captain Obvious moment. They knew of our Talents. And we're not alone. There are more out there. Other Talents."

"Yeah, I've been trying to parse out what Williams said to me before he died. But if he knew..."

She looked back toward Tokyo, where SkyTree was barely visible on the horizon. "Someone else was behind Callahan. Behind all of them. So, who else out there knows about us? And about the others?" She shook her head. "Besides, Callahan told me something in Tokyo before she died. If it's true..."

He walked over and put a hand on her shoulder. "What is it, Amy?"

She looked up at the redhead and saw the concern in his eyes. "Steve, Callahan said that Talents are twins. And think about it. You are, and Callahan was."

He considered the implication of that statement. His eyes got wider. "Amy, that means you might have—"

"Yeah, I know. A twin sister to be exact, if Callahan wasn't lying. And she's out there somewhere — and if these guys were after me for my Talent, you know they'll be after her." She looked up at him. "That's why I need Triangle. I need their resources to pursue my own agenda. I need to find my sister and protect her." She looked up at him again and reached out for his hand. "And that's why I need you there with me."

"Me?"

Amy brought Steve's hand up and held it in both of hers. "Yes, you, Steven Tate. Because, as annoying as you are at times, I trust you with my life. And right now, I don't know if we can trust anyone else."

He closed his eyes for a moment. Amy wondered if perhaps he was activating his Talent again, but he took a deep breath, then opened his eyes and looked at her. "Fine. I'm in. But we're still going to have to deal with things. Rose, for example."

"Rose is out of any equation."

"You didn't hear? She came out of her coma just before I departed—"

"She did? That's great news. We'll go see her together when we get back. Hopefully, she'll be able to help us soon."

"So, what should we tell her?"

Amy looked at him. "The truth. We'll need an inside person, and I think Rose may be the only other person both of us can trust."

He looked at her as if examining something carefully. "Are you sure you're the same Amy Rogers? I thought I was the strategist, but you seem to have this all mapped out."

She giggled a bit. "Oh, don't worry, Sport. You'll be through playing catch-up soon enough, and I figure once you're up to speed, you'll have us looking into things I could only dream of."

He smiled. "Fair enough." He looked around. "I don't see Rob. I better find him and tell him I won't need that ride." He started to walk away.

Impulsively, she ran up to him and gave him a hug. Steve looked surprised for a moment and then returned the gesture. As she broke away, Steve smiled at her. "Thanks, A.J." He headed west and rounded the corner, looking for Frederick.

Amy activated her commlink. "Ethan, are you there?"

His voice came online instantly. "Standing by."

"Tell Watson to get the nest ready. We're both coming back in."

Chapter 30

Grey Tate was doing paperwork in his office when the secure phone chimed. He double-checked his office was signals secure, then opened his desk drawer and placed his hand upon the black wood box inscribed with the white Möbius strip symbol. It responded to his biometric signature and opened. He grabbed the gray phone, and the connection was made.

"We may have a situation."

Grey was surprised. The voice on the other end sounded breathless, almost strained. "Calm yourself and tell me what's happened."

"Tokyo."

"My boy performed well there, didn't he?"

"Yes, and his partner as well."

"So?"

"The problem wasn't them. It's a Gen One sitch."

Grey leaned back and looked out the window. He took a deep breath and blew it out slowly. "Well, that's unfortunate. But you knew in this case that eventually paths would cross, and questions were going to be asked. We've managed to keep the curtains closed for a very long time."

"Grey, it's too early. It's not the right time yet for them to find out. We don't know which way they'll turn."

He stood up and walked over to the window, frowning. "You're making a mistake trying to keep this hidden. It's going to blow back on you. And in the end, we may all lose because of your paranoia. Tell them, Ro. When

---

they get back to Virginia, pull them into a briefing, and tell them."

"I'll take it under advisement."

"You'd better. Because if he comes to me and asks, I will tell him the truth. All of it."

There was a pause. "Grey, that would be...unwise."

"Don't threaten me, old friend."

Another long pause. "You should also know. Steve killed Hannah Callahan."

"You're sure?"

"Yes. Rogers confirmed it in her report."

Grey closed his eyes and pinched the bridge of his nose for a moment. "I hear a vast 'but' attached to that statement."

"Karen is in the wind."

"Any idea how she got away."

"Our net closed pretty fast on that site. Considering the way they left her... I have an idea. And if it's true, our lives are about to get a lot more complicated."

"Why?"

"Because if it's what I think it is, it's worse than anything Red Labs has ever imagined."

Grey considered that for a moment. "I understand. Keep me posted."

"I will, old friend."

The connection ended. Grey dropped the phone back in its cradle and resealed the box. He closed that drawer and opened the one on the opposite side. From it, he took out a bottle of Glenlivet and a rocks' glass. Grey poured himself two fingers worth and carried the drink with him as he looked at the different pictures around his office.

These were moments of triumph in his life — various planes he'd flown, trophies he'd won in his life through determination and luck, being in the right place at the right time.

He stopped in front of the moment he considered his greatest achievement. Back at the picture on his son's desk, taken on a June afternoon at a football stadium in

Issaquah, where he and his wife had celebrated the twins' graduation.

A family portrait. The four of them. Grey, Rose, Marie and Steven. Smiling. Beaming, in fact.

The last picture the four of them would ever have together.

Grey took a sip of the Glenlivit, felt the familiar, comforting burn, and then reached out and touched the glass over his daughter's face. He stroked his thumb along the curve of the edge of his wife's face.

We got her, Rose, honey. We caught the bitch.

A tear rolled down his cheek.

Jun 16, 6:35 p.m. PDT

David Archer had just closed shop for the day. The Sunday afternoon foot traffic in Pioneer Square had been fair, with the baseball game today, but it was all lookie-loos — no sales for the gallery today. Still, hope springs eternal, he thought. We have the new digital installation next week, and the Seattle Art Walk at the end of the month. I'm sure we'll make a sale. And we only need one to make the rent.

He went out the back entrance into the alley to dispose of the finger foods they'd had out all day for visitors. It was a shame, but hummus really doesn't keep well. As he approached the recycling station, he noticed a black pant leg sitting out on one side from it.

Ah, probably Leroy again. Although, it is a little early in the evening to have gone and pickled himself again. David dumped the containers in the proper bins — foodstuffs in the compost, containers in the recycling — then walked around the corner.

"Come on, Leroy, let me give you a ride to the shelter—"

It was most definitely not Leroy. It was a woman in her early 40s, wearing a black jumpsuit, who looked like she'd been in a fight or attack of some sort. She was injured, bleeding from her face, and had a boot print of some sort stomped onto her chest. Her hands and feet were bound with electrical cables, with her hands behind her back.

David grabbed his cell phone and dialed 911, as he went to undo the woman's hands. "Look, I need an ambulance here in the alley behind the Archer's Glen Gallery on First Avenue. There's a woman here who's badly injured. It looks like she's been beaten up and tossed from a car. Hurry!"

7:03 p.m. PDT

The police arrived quickly, followed by a Seattle One rescue aid unit. The woman was unresponsive, there was no wallet or ID on her, and her fingerprint ID scan came back unregistered. So, while the police canvassed the neighborhood, Jane Doe was loaded into the ambulance and sped on her way toward Harborview Medical Center.

Inside the ambulance, the EMTs quickly went to work, taking vital signs. As the vehicle made the turn onto James Street, she went into cardiac arrest. The senior EMT quickly yelled out the situation to the driver, then grabbed the paddles of the ambulance's defibrillator. When it reached a full charge, he yelled "Clear!" and applied the paddles to the patient's chest.

More specifically, to Karen Callahan's chest.

The electricity coursed through her body and jump-started her heart. Her eyes flew wide open, and she sat up, gasping for breath.

"What the... hell... was that!"

Karen had never felt like this. It was as if her entire body was tingling and crackling, buzzing with power. She felt more alive than ever before. She turned to the EMT tech, who was trying to push her back down onto the gurney.

"I don't think so, buddy!"

She had just intended to reach up and push him back with her left hand. However, before she made contact, there was a brilliant white flash and a massive crash of sound. The ambulance swerved right and coasted to a halt, its engine dead.

Karen sat back up, her ears ringing and saw the EMT. He'd been thrown against the back door of the ambulance hard enough to dent the door. His eyes stared lifelessly at her. On his chest was a hand-shaped scorch mark.

Karen grinned. "Oh, now this is an unexpected development! I wonder..." She undid the restraints holding her to the gurney, and stood up cautiously. The driver opened the side door. He saw Karen staring at him.

"Hiya, fella."

She raised her right hand, palm out, at the driver, and concentrated. A white ball of arcing electrical energy formed, small at first, but inflating like a soap bubble to the size of a grapefruit. The ambulance driver backed up, his eyes wide with fear, then turned and started running. Karen pushed her right arm forward and an electric bolt arced out, hitting the driver square in the back. He exploded in a shower of orange sparks and collapsed to the ground. Whether he was unconscious or dead, she didn't care.

She looked at her hands and unclenched her fists. She quickly checked over the dead EMT and took his jacket, hat, and wallet. Then she walked out of the ambulance, down James Street and cut over on 2nd Avenue to the Metro Station.

As she entered the Metro, she caught sight of her reflection in the window. The cuts on her face were healing rapidly, disappearing from her face. The white scar above her left eyebrow was glowing slightly in the shadow of the ball cap. And her eyes... somehow, they both glowed and looked empty at the same time, like a film negative. She liked the new look.

She smiled, a cold shark's grin below those glowing gray eyes.

Get ready for a rematch, Princess.

ACKNOWLEDGMENTS

They say it takes a village to raise a child. This book has very much been my baby, from its initial conception, through a very long gestation, and even a few labor pains getting it born and into your hands. I'd like to acknowledge my village.

- The folks at the Office of Letters and Light, who gave me the push to get this party started.

- Courtney Berkley, who was a great first friend to a lonely writer in this strange land called Flor-ee-dah.

- Dominique Marlow, the first person to hear about the adventures of Steve and Amy and say, "Tell me more."

- Tammy Gross, who told me to keep writing it so it "reads like a movie."

- Dana and the overnight staff at the Starbucks at South Florida and Beacon in Lakeland, who always knew the perfect recipe for a second wind during many an all-night writing session (a venti extra shot no-whip Cinnamon Dolce Latte and a Cranberry Orange scone).

- My father, who was wildly enthusiastic (if inaccurate) in believing that I was ready for publication on day one. (Thanks, Dad!)

- Nicole Dubuc, Tom Hart, Brian Swenlin, Mark Palmer, Andrew Robinson, Chris Bailey and Kurt Weldon, who have what I consider to be the best jobs in the world, and whose work entertaining others inspires me constantly.

- Bob Schooley and Mark McCorkle. No, we've never met, but they had a moment of inspiration in an elevator that turned into a decade of inspiration for my daughters and me and led me to so many wonderful things in my life, including this novel.

- Jess Winfield, who at the last moments became a source of inspiration and showed me a link to a creative heritage that I'd always dreamed of and hoped for.

- My ex-wife and best friend, Debbie - sounding board for ideas, tester of jokes (mostly the ones that didn't make it in here), and shoulder to cry on at appropriate moments.

- And finally, Lea Ellen Borg, the best editor a newbie author could ever hope for.

Thank you, everyone, for sailing with me on this first voyage.

- Lakeland, FL
September 2012

Addendum

It's not often as an author you have the chance to revisit your work. One's it's done, it's done and you have to live with it, mistakes and all. However, with the publication of my latest novel, I've no longer including the preview chapter in this book (that preview chapter, it turns out, didn't make it – killed, oddly enough in a draft stage by a lightning strike in late 2013 – it's a long story). This update affords me the chance to do a bit of housecleaning – specifically, fix some grammatical errors and tighten up a couple of spots. I hope it will make for a more enjoyable read for you in the future.

Steve and Amy's adventures aren't finished, but I am no longer foolish enough to set a fixed date - the Universe has laughed at my plans once too often. Just know I am already hard at work on the next chapter, TRIANGLE ZODIAC. Until then, friends and readers, stay well on your journeys.

- Lakeland, FL
December 2016

Other publications by
D. G. Speirs

Triangle: Wildcard

Amy Rogers and Steve Tate are Talents, enhanced humans with special abilities born of personal tragedy. They use these skills as agents of TRIANGLE, a shadowy organization that works on the edges of society to keep humanity safe from dangerous technology and the people who would abuse it. But now, instead of rogue scientists and despots seeking a new way to terrorize a populace, they face a new threat. The message is hidden inside a devastating terrorist attack, but the signs are there. Someone is striking at the very heart of TRIANGLE itself. Someone from its past.

Now Steve must partner with an old colleague as he and Amy search for the mastermind even as they face their attackers - one Steve is very familiar with...

...and one Amy never dreamed she'd meet.

Triangle: Rescue

Steve Tate is a one of the lead draws on the World FreeRunning Tour. Fast, handsome, agile in ways that seem almost supernatural, his abilities have made the sport a success and him a superstar. But when one of his fellow racers has his entire family kidnapped and held for ransom by the Somali warlord faction known as Scorpio, his choice is clear – even if the boss is going to be upset. Of course, he could always use a little backup...

Books available at Amazon.com

About the Author

Born in New York and raised in California, D. G. Speirs has been a traveler all his life. He graduated top of his class from the Naval Nuclear Power School and served in the US Navy for over a decade. He traveled the world, coaching American Rules Football in Australia, modeling for Issey Miyake in Japan, playing Santa Claus for a stadium full of NFL fans, and making t-shirts for fans of a certain animated television show in Germany (yes, she can still do anything).

He's owned his own marketing firm and been on a national consulting board that assisted other entrepreneurs. He's been a public speaker, board member of a local Chamber of Commerce, Rotarian of the Year, a retiree, a family man, and a performer of some sort for over four decades. In other words, a pretty average guy with an IQ of 154.

He's written blogs about Walt Disney World, about life in general, and for the last three years a daily inspirational one that draws wisdom from the intersection of lessons in Eastern philosophy with those taught on a show about candy-colored ponies and unicorn.

He's a connoisseur of fedoras, bow ties, and black cherry soda, and believes there's always a better story out there, even if you just have to make it up yourself.

D.G.'s currently resides in Florida at Storyteller's Crib with his cats, Houdini and Sissy.

www.ingramcontent.com/pod-product-compliance
Lightning Source LLC
Chambersburg PA
CBHW070732180626
46818CB00007B/2816